SF   BAZ.

PINS   07/21.

"Pinsker has one of the strongest voices for character in fiction today; everything her characters do is compelling. When I put the book down, I actually suffered from FOMO because I felt like the characters were continuing on their stories without me."

Mur Lafferty, author of *Six Wakes*

"Sarah Pinsker plays genre like a favorite guitar, and I am in awe of her talents. How can a writer so new be so central, so necessary?"

Andy Duncan, author of *An Agent of Utopia*

"*A Song for a New Day* is a compulsively readable story about music, freedom, taking chances, and living with your past. I meant to read it slowly, savoring Pinsker's near-future world-building and her perfect descriptions of performance, but I ended up gulping it down, so eager to see what happens."

Kij Johnson, author of *The Dream-Quest of Vellitt Boe*

"A full-throated call to arms in the service of music, creation, and shared experience, *A Song for a New Day* resists both extremes and easy tropes, offering hope in the face of catastrophe through the engrossing stories of characters you'll want to spend more time with. Pinsker gives us a future rooted in fully-drawn, believable characters and sensory, unflinching descriptions."

Malka Older, author of *Infomocracy*

WE ARE SATELLITES

SARAH PINSKER

An Ad Astra Book

For Amira & Ellie,
best of sisters,
and for everyone who has
ever been disbelieved about
their own health.

PART ONE

CHAPTER ONE

VAL

There was a blue light in the balcony. Val lingered in the stage wing, looking out on a darkened auditorium and one illicit pin-prick, electric blue. The girls squirmed and tapped their feet and whispered to one another by the glow of the ancient anti-drunk-driving smash-'em-up film. A mournful pop song that had been old long before she herself hit high school gave their boredom a soundtrack.

The school had a strict policy on electronics: no checking phones except between classes, tablets in school mode to allow work and emergency contact, but no social media. She slipped away from the stage. The light probably wasn't worth chasing, but this assembly always felt interminable, and the hunt gave her something to do.

Around the back and up the stairs and then she was there, scanning the darkness for the steady light she had noticed from below. Only seniors were allowed to sit in the balcony, and most had skipped the assembly. There was supposed to be a teacher up here, but she couldn't remember who had been assigned; if they were here, maybe they weren't at the right angle to notice whatever she had seen. She spotted it again, still the same tiny light though now she was closer. It twinned itself as she made her way down the aisle.

"Phones off, girls," she whispered, though she didn't see any devices out.

Nobody moved. One student had a binder open on her lap, but Val wasn't policing that. She settled in a vacant seat, waiting for her eyes to adjust to the dimness. She saw blue again, a flash in the dark as a girl across the aisle regathered her microbraids in a ponytail. Val thought at first it was a ring on a finger, but no, it hadn't been on the girl's hand. An LED earring, maybe? She descended to the railing, on the pretext of looking over the edge, then turned. As she looked up again, the fiery car crash on the screen below illuminated the girls in the balcony.

"And when I turned again, I realized they weren't earrings. Two girls had lights embedded in their temples! Tell me this isn't some new fad, please."

An hour after the assembly, Val recounted the experience to Angela Lin, soccer coach and history teacher, in the cafeteria. Both had brought their own food to lunch duty.

"I can tell you, but I'd be lying." Angie motioned with her celery stick at a nearby table, where several girls had the tiny blue lights at the edge of their hairlines.

Val groaned. "What is it? Head studs instead of ear studs?"

"Some new study gadget, I think."

"A study fad? Is that an oxymoron?" She was glad to hear they were new; disconcerting to think she'd missed something like this for long.

"Maybe. I only started noticing them a few weeks ago. Haven't gotten to looking into them beyond what one of my players told me."

Val eyed the students. She couldn't tell from this distance whether it was adhesive or a piercing or what. She didn't know anyone in the group, which meant they didn't run track, and none were freshmen; she taught freshman gym and geography in addition to coaching. As she watched, one girl without the light reached out and touched the light on another's head; she looked thoughtful.

"Is it something we're going to get a memo about?" she asked.

"I'm pretty sure it's legal, for now at least, and I'm not sure it's a bad thing. Attention boosting has to help us, right?"

"I guess so. What if your goalkeeper comes in with one? Or Grover High's goalkeeper faces off against your girl with one when yours doesn't have one?"

Angela bit her lip. "Good question."

"Is it pricey?"

"I really don't know. I'd guess so, given who has them. That's a corporate lawyer's daughter and a pro football player's daughter sitting next to each other. I don't know the other girls, but they have expensive-looking hair. Next week we'll probably be seeing fakes or knockoffs or other colors. You know how it goes."

Val did.

She watched for the lights in her classes after lunch, but didn't see any on her freshmen. A couple more students with them passed her in the hallway. They didn't act any different from the other girls.

Val wasn't much for boosters in general. She'd seen a fair number, legal and illegal, and thought they were better left out of the equation. She tried to teach her runners, rich and scholarship alike, that it all came down to their feet and their heads, the physical and the mental.

The same went for the new technologies that appeared in the school, outpacing her own glacial change. Inevitably she came around to one conclusion: people want what they want. She dragged her heels at every step, but never stopped anyone, ever, an anchor without enough weight behind it, slowing the ship without the ability to keep it from running aground. Metaphors weren't really her thing, but she tried. She tried. Whatever this fad was, she'd deal with it as she had all the previous ones.

CHAPTER TWO

VAL

B y the time David started flat-out begging, he really was one of only a few boys left at his school who didn't have a Pilot. Val had watched it happen at the school where she taught, the sister school to his. If half her students had them by the time class had let out for summer, three quarters had them when they returned in the fall. She had no doubt his school was equally awash.

"You're a scholarship kid among rich kids," she pointed out over dinner. "You know better than to get hung up on not having something they have."

She piled brown rice onto her plate before passing the rest along and helping herself to the next bowl's contents, steamed broccoli. Her health kick put the whole family on a health kick, so as far as she could tell they were busy resenting her for that, too. David sat opposite her, his gangly body rigid with annoyance. The food hadn't reached him yet, and he clenched his empty plate in two white-knuckled fists, like a steering wheel.

"Next you say, 'I grew up with nothing, and that's how I learned I didn't need anything to be happy.'" As David said the words, Sophie mouthed them along with him, and Julie stifled a laugh. Was she that predictable?

"But you went to public school, Ma. I'm different already.

Why make me even more different? It's not like the surgery is expensive." He must have seen Val cringe at the word "surgery," because he changed his approach. "Who ever heard of parents refusing their kid something that helps him study better?"

"I go to public school, right?" Sophie asked.

"Yes," said Julie, spooning rice onto her own plate, then their daughter's. "Until you're old enough to go where Ma teaches."

Julie passed the rice back to Val, and the rest of the serving dishes made their way around the table to each of them in turn. David relaxed his death grip on the dinnerware to heap rice, then broccoli, then half a chicken onto his plate. They always served him last these days, a forced measure after the night an entire French bread disappeared before his mothers and sister had gotten any. Making more didn't help; his teenage stomach expanded to greet whatever food arrived in front of him. Val had called him BC for a while, for "boa constrictor," after she dreamed he'd unhinged his jaw to swallow the whole Thanksgiving turkey.

There was silence while they all chewed; Val hadn't been patient enough with the rice and felt mildly guilty about it. She was a decent cook, as long as she didn't rush things, but on school nights her poor family ate everything al dente.

A moment later, David raised his fork in triumph, a spear of broccoli impaled on the tines. "Think of the health benefits, Ma! I'd have more time. I could join the track team . . ."

Val exchanged a look with Julie. They'd been trying to get him into some kind of physical activity for two years. He had steadfastly refused to join any clubs or teams. They hadn't pressed, as long as he kept up his schoolwork and spent dinner and the hour afterward with the family.

"Let us talk it over," Julie said.

"Is that 'I want to say no but I don't feel like fighting over dinner' or will you really talk it over?" he asked. Sophie giggled.

"Both," Val said. "Time for a new topic. Sophie, how's fourth grade treating you today?"

"My teacher farted during math."

Julie's shoulders started shaking. Val tried to hold it together. "That's it? Did you learn anything?"

David grinned. "Maybe Sophie didn't, but I guess the teacher learned not to eat beans for lunch."

"How do you know what my teacher ate for lunch?"

"I know everything," David said, waggling spooky fingers at his sister.

She looked impressed. Val glanced at Julie, knowing she, too, was savoring the moment of normalcy.

CHAPTER THREE

JULIE

David had a point. Julie had seen it instantly. She remembered being the last kid in school without a phone or tablet. She'd been raised in a dying western Pennsylvania town, and even there you could be the last, the only. There was never such thing as equally poor; someone always had less of one thing or more of another.

That was why she had dedicated herself to climbing out of that situation. In college, she'd taken every business class available, from statistics to microeconomics, determined never to fall into her parents' cycle of poor financial decisions. At the time, she hadn't been thinking about a future family; she'd been thinking she wanted to buy the things she wanted without weighing the cost. If she didn't end up in exactly the place she'd hoped for, it wasn't for lack of trying. Her internship in Congressman Griffith's office had led to a job there, and then Val had encouraged her to concentrate on upward mobility in a place where she had traction rather than risk starting someplace new.

She tried to balance her desire to make sure her kids had everything they wanted and needed with practicality. They had more than either she or Val had growing up, but had never arrived at a point where they couldn't be derailed by an emergency. A point where the argument revolved solely around whether it was a good idea to get the implant, not whether they could afford it.

The lights had already been off for several minutes when Julie called Val back from the edge of sleep.

"I understand why this is a big deal for you," she said.

"Which?" Val grasped for the subject. Julie realized there had been several big deals over the course of the day, starting with the discussion of whether to replace Val's tires or repair the sagging gutter and continuing after dinner with Sophie's first seizure in four months, breaking through yet another medication, the giggly ten-year-old from dinner replaced by her own zombie doppelgänger. They should have known control was an illusion too good to last. Still, that was a big deal for everyone, not only Val.

"The Pilot?" Val asked, sounding more awake. "How could it not be a big deal?"

"Maybe it would help him in school. He's having a rough time—it sucks to feel different."

"And the answer to a rough time is this? How could a kid whose sister has epilepsy ask his mothers for voluntary brain surgery?"

"It's just an outpatient procedure. I've read the risks. No more dangerous than a piercing or a tattoo, and a lot more benefits." She wasn't ready to admit how much research she'd done on the subject already.

"Piercings and tattoos get infected, and they aren't in your brain when it happens." Val rolled over to look at her in the dark. "Are you serious? You're on board?"

"I'm open to it. The people in my office who have it say it's safe. Almost nobody gets infections from piercings or tattoos anymore. It wouldn't break the bank; we'll just have to wait a little longer on your tires."

"And the gutter?"

"And the gutter," Julie said, wrapping herself around Val. "Small price to buy our kid's happiness."

"Voluntary brain surgery. I'd be crazy to agree to this, and you're crazy to ask."

"Mmhmmm." She lay awake listening to Val's breathing, waiting for her to fall asleep, for the sign that she wasn't following the branching worst-case scenarios through her head. Maybe Val was right that it should bother her more, but it simply didn't. There was a difference between what David needed and what Sophie needed. Comparing them did no good.

She'd been waiting for this, really. Val had been complaining about Pilots for a few weeks when Julie spotted her first one at work, on Representative Griffith himself. He'd stopped into the district office to introduce his new chief of staff, Evan Manfredi, and "put our goals into alignment," in his words.

The meeting had been tense. Manfredi had come from a position as a senator's press secretary and appeared to have no clue what Julie's office actually did; he just wanted it to look prettier for the cameras. Julie knew from research—online creeping, really—that he was at least ten years younger than her, even though his hairline made him look ten years older. Yes, they were supposed to work together, but his every "we" and "our" came across as an attack on how she ran things. His predecessor had understood that it was okay if her district services and his DC concerns didn't always align.

She'd worked for Representative Griffith for twenty-one years now, almost the entire time he'd been in Congress. Every time he hired a new chief of staff she wondered why it wasn't her, his long-time district office director. Then she remembered it was because she had a family who didn't want to relocate to Washington or to lose her for seasons at a time. Leroy Griffith had always supported her and championed her; she was the one who held herself back, not the rep, and not the new guy, even if she didn't think much of the latter.

She was so busy hating Manfredi, she didn't clock to the blue light on Griffith's head until he was packing his briefcase to leave. The second she saw it, she knew it was the implant Val had been talking about.

"That's one of those Pilots, right? 'Step into the light?'" If she got out ahead of it, maybe she'd get points for being observant.

He did sound impressed. "It is! Have you been thinking of getting one?"

"Yeah," she lied, though it hadn't crossed her mind until that moment. It had been a kid thing, something for Val's students. What did adults gain from it? She'd have to look. She didn't know the right question to ask. "What's it like?"

He smiled. "So far, so good! It's got my brain racing, but I think I'll find a balance soon. If it's as handy as I think it'll be, I'm going to look into grants to give them to all the staffers who want one."

"Are there grants like that?"

"I wouldn't hold my breath, but you never know. Maybe it'll wind up covered by our insurance. It would benefit everyone in the end. And they're in district, you know, so their success means jobs, jobs, jobs for us."

She gave up feigning knowledge. "In district? Ours?"

"Yeah—the manufacturer is a company called Balkenhol Neural Labs. Pharmaceuticals and devices. They built their headquarters inside our northern border."

"I guess you don't get out there much," said Manfredi, intruding on the conversation.

His dig wasn't fair. Either she hadn't driven past or she hadn't noticed, but that didn't mean she didn't get out there to town hall meetings and the like.

"People first, then businesses," Representative Griffith said. "Right, Jules?"

"Right." She could have hugged him for his support. "Or at least, not until businesses start talking about moving their jobs elsewhere, in which case I start hearing from people."

"So in other words, we'll all work on keeping this lovely new company in our backyard." He walked out whistling, Manfredi trailing in his wake.

Not long after, the twentysomethings in the office had started getting Pilots. Both summer interns, too, and the campaign volunteers. It figured that after the Pilot spread among rich teenagers whose parents wanted to give them a leg up, offices like Julie's would be the next demographic. Twentysomethings in high-pressure, detail-oriented jobs. Twentysomethings making too little for any hope of living without roommates, but too much not to be tempted by exciting new things. Sure, she had a house, but their clothes were nicer than hers, and they bought their lunches every day while she boxed and bagged leftovers from whatever dinner Val had made the night before.

In truth, Julie had been just like her younger colleagues what seemed like a minute ago. There had never been a point in her adult life when she hadn't wanted the latest everything. The newest phone, reader, tablet. If it was a choice between clothes or restaurants or vacations or a new gadget, she picked the gadget every time. These kids didn't know that about her; they probably assumed she was just another middle-aged mom. Which she was, but that didn't mean she didn't have her own wants and desires. She tried not to feel left behind, but when David had asked tonight, she had to admit she knew how he felt.

CHAPTER FOUR

VAL

Val tried to sort it out for herself with a run the morning after David finally asked what she'd been waiting for him to ask. Running had always helped her think; her legs and her mind felt intimately connected. The rhythm of footfalls, the rise of the road. On the days she needed clarity she left her music behind and ran alone with her own thoughts.

She'd marked all the family milestones, good and bad, with actual miles. The decision to have children, Julie's terrifyingly difficult pregnancy, Sophie's adoption, Sophie's first seizure, the endless treatment discussions. Most of those were things she and Julie went through together, and still there were conversations Val had alone with herself on the road; conversations regarding which concerns to share aloud and which to swallow. She was sure Julie did the same, though she couldn't say when or where or how.

That was why she'd encouraged David to run, though he had never taken her up on it. Despite her lack of biological contribution, he was built like her, tall and lanky. Moreover, he thought like her, or so it seemed. He got concerned and retreated into his head and holed up there, unable to see his way around the obstacles presented. In her opinion, his video games just added to his stress. They implied there was always an external solution if you looked hard enough. She'd often thought if he tried running in addition to gaming he'd discover that sometimes the solution existed in making peace with your own mind.

She broke into a jog, then an easy run. As her muscles warmed up, she pushed herself a little, trying to reach the place where each step generated the next, and it was easier to keep going than to stop. She thought about her serious children and then ran away from that concern. She thought about brains and their intricacies and vulnerabilities and how one person might perfectly harness body and mind, for sport or science or craft, while others couldn't even walk across a room without pain or exertion. And then she was just running, and all was quiet in her head, and in the quiet she found her own answers. And then she was just running.

When she got back to the house, drenched in sweat, she found her family eating breakfast around the kitchen table. She gave each of them a kiss on the head, met with various degrees of acceptance and revulsion and a general agreement that she should shower.

On David's parent-teacher night, Julie stayed home with Sophie. The doctors had upped her dosage again, hoping this time it would do what it was supposed to do. Otherwise they'd be starting over again with another medication, another round of trial and error. How could David want his brain messed with when the best neurologists in the country still played trial-and-error games? How could recreational surgery be so precise when there was still no surgery to help Sophie? There was no logic to any of it.

Val hadn't expected to fight his teachers over it as well, but they spouted the same lines as David and Julie.

"He really is getting left behind without a Pilot," said his math teacher, Ms. Sloan. She was young, closer to David's age than Val's, with a fading sunburn on her nose and cheeks. At one point Val had known all the teachers at both schools, but she hadn't kept up with the new hires, and Ms. Sloan was a stranger to her.

"Getting left behind how?" Val had spoken with other teachers who had observed as much, but she wanted to hear specifically how it pertained to her kid.

"His peers with Pilots are using their time more efficiently. It gives them more time to study, and it lets them keep working things out while they're doing other tasks."

"It's a fad." That was what she hoped, though it looked less and less like that was the case.

Ms. Sloan walked around the front of her desk and sat on it. It came across like a move she rehearsed in her spare time. "It's not a fad. It's an *optimizer*. They get more out of their brains. Multitasking. The kids with Pilots have more time to study and more time for extracurriculars and fun—like gaming—because it lets them do it all at once. With upside-down learning I'm recording lectures for them to watch at home anyway, so we can focus on problem sets in class. This way they can do something fun while they listen, and I can help where they're having trouble. They're using their brains and time better."

She swept her brown hair into a knot and cocked her head. A blue light gleamed above her right ear. She smiled like a zealot, Val thought, even as she knew it wasn't fair. At least now she had an idea how Ms. Sloan found the time to practice dramatic desk-sitting.

The teacher reached for a tablet and swiped through a few pages with only a glance down. "Right now I'm talking to you and I'm thinking about my lesson plan for tomorrow and I'm reviewing David's quiz grades. I could be doing three or four more things as well—listening to music, messaging my boyfriend, reading an article."

Val pictured a cartoon octopus messaging and reading and grading and rocking out all at once, then tried to refocus. What Ms. Sloan said was true; Val would have sworn she had the teacher's full attention. "How do you, um, access it all? How do you know you're paying enough attention to each thing?"

"Practice, for starters. I've trained my brain, the same as you've trained yours. It helps me use my time better. I know David got seventy-two percent on our last quiz, for example."

Val sighed. She was willing to be the parent who didn't let her kid get the latest toy, but she didn't want to disadvantage him in school. Maybe Julie was right and she was being overcautious; that was her default state. She'd try to consider it with an open mind, even if she didn't like it.

CHAPTER FIVE

JULIE

Julie kept thinking about David's request, long after he'd let it drop, more because she wanted a Pilot than because he did. How cool would it be to divide her attention and yet still be fully present? That was what the literature said it did: "Boost your brain and approximate functional multitasking!"

She thought of a million uses. She could get work done for the congressman while still spending time with her family, so she didn't have to choose one or the other. She could get work done while getting other work done; she was never sure if she was doing enough. Did she have time to take on one more constituent request? What would suffer? Would she lose her job if she refused to take on more?

Best of all, she could concentrate while keeping an eye on Sophie. As it was, whenever Sophie was in the house, Julie couldn't help being distracted. Was she playing quietly or seizing? Were her medications' side effects altering her personality again? Julie tried her best not to hover, but it was hard not to. With a Pilot, she could pretend she wasn't watching constantly, but still fulfill her need to watch constantly.

Those were all justifications; beneath those reasons, that blue light exuded cool. There was a strange sexiness to it; an embrace of something corporate but beyond corporate, with no commercial use, no add-ons, no in-app purchases. She watched her Piloted officemates with actual jealousy.

She knew how much it would bother Val if she got one. Val worried in infinite permutations; the little insecurities would grow. Val would wonder if Julie was thinking about other things when they were together. She would resent the split attention on family nights, even if Julie did it to help the family. It wouldn't be worth the stress on their relationship.

But did you wait until everyone had one? Until you were left hopelessly behind? She wouldn't have signed up for the first year of a product like this, the same as she never bought a car from a model's first year of manufacture. Val's mechanic father, even more careful than his daughter, had taught Julie that one before he died.

This wasn't the first year, though. According to the pamphlets David had left around the house, the company had done years of trials on rats and adolescent chimps. This was the fifth year for the earliest human adopters, and the third for teenagers, though Val had seen it for the first time in her school only the previous spring.

Julie went so far as to call some of those early adopters' parents. She asked David for names from his own school, rather than rely on referrals provided by the company. Nobody spoke badly of it. One parent said her son had gone from Cs and Ds to As and Bs. Julie was glad the B grades were mentioned; she would have been less likely to believe a mother who said her child's mediocre grades had been replaced by perfection. The B implied the Pilot was a booster, not a panacea. It couldn't entirely replace natural ability and study skills and applying oneself. It couldn't replace her child.

Julie and Val decided Julie would take David to the consultation appointment without Val. Balkenhol Neural Labs' Pilot Installation Center was a sleek and modern stand-alone building in an upscale mall's parking lot. If they put the same money and thought into the devices as the architecture, Julie thought, David would be in good hands.

They were met at the door by an efficient-looking redheaded white woman whose entire job appeared to be tech store–style triage. She found their appointment on her tablet and led them down a spotless hallway, gray walled, lights echoing the one on the redhead's temple. They were brought to a cozy room with four chairs around a glass table and a window onto a central greenhouse, lush and bright.

"Impressions, kiddo?"

David stroked his single chin whisker reverently, a move that had been amusing both his parents since they'd noticed it. "It doesn't feel like a doctor's office. It's more comfortable."

There was a knock on the door. "Hi, I'm Dr. Jordaan. You're David and Julie?"

The doctor shook hands with them and indicated the chairs she wanted them to sit in. She had tight, springy curls on top of her head, the sides shaved to let her Pilot stand out against her dark skin. Her white coat was tailored and immaculate, and she exuded confidence. Julie appreciated that she'd greeted David, the potential patient, first; they'd met so many doctors who talked past little Sophie as if she weren't in the room.

"So, David, I hear you're interested in a Pilot." Dr. Jordaan had a slight accent Julie couldn't place. "I've looked over the health records your doctor sent over, and I think you're a good candidate, but first I want to tell you what the Pilot can and can't do for you."

David nodded, as serious as Julie had ever seen him.

"Your friends may have told you it lets you concentrate on multiple things at once, but that isn't quite true. What it does is it lets you approximate functional multitasking."

"How?" Julie pressed. That phrase was verbatim out of the brochure.

Dr. Jordaan pointed to her Pilot. "Stimulation of the right temporoparietal junction, behind here. The rTPJ is associated with reorienting attention in response to unexpected stimuli. What we've discovered is that rTPJ stimulation results in the ability to get as close to actual multitasking as a person can currently get."

"So it's not actual multitasking?"

"Functionally so. As close as a person can get. Closer than anything you can imagine until you have this in your head. I would have killed to have this in med school, let me tell you. You don't even know how distracted you are until you feel the difference. Speaking for myself, it's a powerful, competent feeling."

David had told Julie his questions in the car on the way over, but now he just looked at the doctor's Pilot with open longing. Julie had to admit the description sounded glorious, but she tried to ask the questions that careful Val would ask. Will it change his personality? Not his personality, only his mood, and only for the better; people with Pilots reported they were happier, less stressed, less tired. What's the youngest age you recommend it for? It doesn't affect brain development; it's been successfully installed in children as young as thirteen. Julie probed for flaws, to make it more real and less miraculous. In the end she settled on the one boy's B grades: no perfection, only improvement.

What was so wrong with perfection, anyway? She thought of David sitting at the dining room table, running his hand through his hair as he worked on math problems until it all stood on end, the hair and the math. She wanted all the good things for him, the happiness and the wakefulness and the stress reduction. She wanted him to succeed, though she'd never say it out loud; she didn't want to put it on either kid that they had to be world-changers, even if she believed they had the potential to do special things. If it had to start with David getting a Pilot to keep up, she didn't have a problem with that.

Dr. Jordaan ran through the procedure details, the science, the finances. "So what do you think? Do you need to talk with the rest of your family, or do you want to go ahead and schedule this?"

David looked at Julie, all hope. She sighed. "We still have to talk it over at home."

She made the decision and waited for Val to come around. Her own parents had been so paralyzed over choice she'd ended up making decisions for them, too. Things she had to justify in her head, so later she could justify for them when they asked why the power was off ("because it was a choice between the rent and the electricity") or the cat was gone ("he was sixteen and in pain—I took him to the vet") or whatever other big thing they'd forced her to take on when she shouldn't even have had a say.

It wasn't fair to make that comparison. Val was careful, not indecisive; a brake on Julie's own tendency to keep issues from dragging out. Julie gathered her own information to complement David's brochures, read clinical reports, wrote a position paper and bullet points to counter her wife's fears, like it was another issue for Representative Griffith to consider. She'd prefer Val's support, but she'd settle for a grudging endorsement until Val came to understand that Julie had David's interests at heart.

CHAPTER SIX

VAL

V al drew the line at attending the procedure, then erased it, then drew it again, then erased it again. In the end they all went, a Saturday-morning outing for the modern family. From the passenger seat, she counted how many pedestrians they passed without Pilots before they passed somebody with the implant, about seven to one. The blue lights were eye-catching advertisements, if nothing else.

David drummed his fingers on the window as Julie drove, a massive sound in an otherwise silent electric car. Val would normally have told him to knock it off, but she was perversely happy that at least he had the sense to be nervous. Sophie slept in the seat next to him, though she had just woken an hour before. Another side effect to weigh against benefits: no seizures yet today, but a comatose ten-year-old.

Julie had been the one to meet with the doctor and make the arrangements, so this was Val's first visit to the Pilot Installation Center. She'd expected something more hospital-like outside, and the inside didn't match her expectations, either. Private waiting rooms, warm and inviting, full of comfortable-looking armchairs and couches rather than the metal and plastic torture devices where they'd spent so many hours waiting for Sophie's doctors. It didn't even smell like the hospital; it smelled like fresh-baked cookies.

"That can't be hygienic," Val muttered under her breath. "And what's with 'Installation Center'? Is it a clinic? It sounds like someplace you get your computer set up."

Either nobody heard her, or they ignored her. Sophie broke away to investigate a shelf overflowing with children's books. Val kept an eye on the kid as the nurse explained everything they'd already read and heard, trying to nod when she thought she was supposed to. Maybe she needed an implant herself, so she could watch Sophie and listen and process without losing anything. She had definitely missed something, because David looked crestfallen.

"It's okay," Julie said to him, putting her arm around his shoulder. "It'll be ready by the time you have to study for exams."

Val remembered something from the brochure, though she couldn't recall having pointed it out to David. They would do the installation that day, but the device wouldn't be activated for another month.

"Your head has to get used to having something else in there," Val said, pleased to have something to contribute to the conversation. "Plus you have to attend a couple of orientation sessions to learn how to use it. If that's a sticking point, it's not too late to change your mind, you know. Ha."

She knew she shouldn't have added those last bits, and David responded with a vicious shake of his head, punishment for both the pun and the implication he might not be fully committed. "I want this, Ma. Mom understands." He looked to Julie for support.

"Your ma knows," she said. "She's here, isn't she? You're allowed to change your mind, but we're committed if you are." She shot Val a glance that Val read as *back off*.

"Mom is right," Val said. "We're here. Ready when you are."

The nurse had apparently finished her checklist, because she beckoned to David and pivoted on her heel.

Val watched their boy disappear through a mahogany door. "That's it? Off he goes?"

"Looks like," Julie said. "Feels odd we aren't supposed to follow, but I guess they'd tell us if we were."

"I can't believe it's an outpatient procedure. Since when is brain surgery so easy?"

They settled near the corner where Sophie sat reading in a beanbag chair. Val picked up a celebrity gossip magazine and was amazed to discover it was the current month's issue; another difference between the hospitals and this pay-to-play "Installation Center."

Julie pulled out her tablet and started typing. Her fingers moved quickly and surely. As always, Val was impressed by her wife's ability to put aside the things she couldn't affect and concentrate on something else. Val flipped the magazine open to a random article.

She was still on the same page ninety minutes later when a nurse emerged to invite them into a recovery room where David dozed under mild anesthesia, his boyish face looking younger in slack-jawed dopiness. They'd shaved a patch of honey brown curls from the right side of his head. He looked lopsided. A bandage above his ear was the only evidence of the surgeon's trespass. Beneath that bandage was a hole, raw and neat, and in that hole, a tiny bio-LED.

Behind the light, a gross intrusion on his perfect brain. How could the positives have outweighed the risk? How could they do so much so easily? When the neurologists had considered surgery for Sophie they'd removed the top of her skull. They mapped her mind, gridded it with electrodes in a silk-based substrate that settled into the curves of her brain like it belonged there, all to discover her seizures were not the kinds that could be safely ablated or removed.

David's new implant, threaded in through one small hole, would settle into his head, relax, get comfortable, put its feet on the coffee table. In an hour they'd be on their way home.

Val ran dozens of extra miles over the ensuing weeks in a futile effort to assuage her fears, though most of them had proved unfounded. No infection, no seizures, no noticeable change. David, whom she had started calling "Ze Brain" in her best Hervé

Villechaize, did not act any different, except for an endearing tic where he raised his hand halfway to his head, realized he shouldn't poke at it, and raised it in a fake stretch and yawn instead.

He did a lot of stretch and yawning. He dutifully attended the online follow-up classes, learning to access something that was still only theoretical. As his access date grew nearer, he began drumming his fingers on all available surfaces.

One night, while they all watched a movie together, the finger tapping got to be too much for Val and she tossed a pillow at him; he surprised her by bursting into tears. Sophie leaned over to wrap her arms around him. He hugged her back.

"What's up, Brainy?" Julie asked him, lowering her tablet. She'd made it only a few minutes into the movie before pulling it out to see what she'd missed in the dinner-sized connectivity gap.

"What if it doesn't work?" He lifted his hand to his head and then forced his arm down, clutching his sister to him. "What if I don't like it?"

Val wanted to say, *It's not too late!* Instead, she told him what she thought he needed to hear. "It's what you wanted, kiddo. You'll be able to keep up with your classes and spend more time doing stuff you like."

"It's natural to be scared, Davey," Julie said. For all Val's creative nicknames, Julie was the only one he allowed to call him Davey.

"I swear I want this. I really do."

Sophie sat back. "You know what I do when I'm scared? I pretend I'm somebody who wouldn't be scared. Like a superhero, or Mom."

Val glanced over at Julie, who caught her eye.

"This is going to be great, David," Val said. "You'll see. Hey, I'm not into the movie. Who wants to play a game?"

"Ooh. Me! Spoons!" Sophie jumped up from the couch and returned with three soup spoons and a deck of cards. She had been obsessed with the game since Julie had taught her a few months before.

A game was a good solution. With the activation looming, David would do anything either mother wanted, and even Julie would have to put work aside to play.

"Those aren't in the center," David said, reaching for the spoons Sophie had spread on the table.

Sophie pulled them back in her direction. "My arms are shorter than yours."

Val leaned over and positioned the spoons so two were in the center, and one angled slightly closer to Sophie. She was all for fairness in sport, but Sophie's argument was valid.

"Jules, put it away." Her wife tossed her tablet on the couch and joined them.

Val dealt first. She memorized her own hand, then started passing cards off the deck to the left, trying to keep an eye out for the remaining two jacks. To her right, David focused on his cards; she'd positioned herself on this side so she wouldn't have to look at the strange little spot on his other temple. Julie tilted her head, one eye on the cards, one on the spoons. On Val's left, Sophie passed cards along at a surprising speed.

A seven went by, then another, and Val wished she hadn't hitched her chances entirely to jacks. Too late, unless they came around again. David grabbed a card, then she palmed the third jack. The fourth jack showed his face. Val darted a hand out and quietly pulled a spoon into her lap, even as she kept passing cards with her other hand. Sophie dived for the spoon nearest her, not bothering with subtlety. Julie grabbed the third.

David looked up and frowned. "But I just got my last ten."

"You snooze, you lose," said Sophie. "You don't win with just cards. You watch the spoons."

"But if everyone does that, nobody will ever win. Somebody has to get four of a kind, or we'll go round forever."

Sophie shrugged. "Grabbing a spoon is more important. Where did your cards get you? You've got the s in s-p-o-o-n-s."

David sighed.

They played a few more times. Each won a round or two, and

each got left without a spoon at least once, except Sophie, who took the second spoon every time and declared herself victorious.

At breakfast the morning of David's Pilot activation, Sophie had a tonic-clonic seizure. Heartbreak city after a seizure-free month; another failed medication. David, closest, lowered her from her chair to the kitchen floor before she could hurt herself. Val wasn't sure when he'd gotten big enough to do that so easily. He pulled his sweatshirt off and placed it under her head, then turned her on her side. Another piece of Val broke off and caught fire and burned out under its own fuel; she wished his actions hadn't looked so routine.

Julie took David to the activation. Val stayed with Sophie while she dozed, updating her online seizure log, checking in with her doctor to say the seizures had broken through again, reading through various epilepsy parent groups to learn whether anyone had anything new or different to say. Those were her only social media interactions, on those private groups, and even there she lurked; she hated the idea of companies monetizing and tracking her.

She browsed BNL's website for the millionth time, looking for information on postactivation life, and this time stumbled upon a section she hadn't noticed before: a Pilot parent forum. There were only a few dozen posts, all of them positive, which made her all the more suspicious. Everything got at least some negative reviews, from peanut butter to puppies. If she posted something negative, would it be deleted? She was tempted to try, just to test that paranoid theory.

Julie and David were gone for three hours, returning with a clatter of groceries.

"Celebration!" Julie announced, sliding an ice cream cake box onto the table. Val wished she had thought of it. "Where's the young 'un?"

"Still sleeping." Val turned to David. He didn't look any different. "So, Extra Brainy? Are you solving world hunger yet? How does your new improved brain feel?"

He grinned. "Enormous. Electric."

"Are you doing the exercises now?" Val caught his chin with her hand and gently turned his head to see the light marring his perfect skin. He grunted and nodded.

"So you're talking—well, grunting—and unpacking the groceries and doing what?"

"The exercises, Ma. I'm doing times tables, like they told me to. They said it's like rubbing your head and patting your stomach."

"Rubbing your stomach and patting your head. Keep practicing." Val pointed him toward the groceries and turned to Julie. "Cake now, or cake later?"

Julie glanced at the clock. "Lunch cake, in an hour, if Sophie's awake. Otherwise, after dinner. Maybe by then the boychild will be doing quantum physics."

"I'm not deaf, you know. Soon I'll be paying better attention than ever, and you'll have to be extra careful what you say when you think I'm not listening."

"What have we doooone?" wailed Julie, mock horrified. "Back to the doctor, quick!"

He finished unloading the groceries, tossing a head of purple cabbage like a basketball between his hands. "Do we really have to wait an hour for lunch? I could eat a horse."

Definitely still the same kid.

CHAPTER SEVEN

DAVID

David knew what it meant that his parents had agreed to get him a Pilot. Money when they had none to spare; elective brain surgery when his little sister had seizures. As long as he could remember, he'd always felt the responsibility of being the one who didn't need anything from them, who could do what was expected of him without being asked. He'd really, truly waited until he was the only one left in his class without a Pilot before asking, and they'd seen that, too, and even then he'd felt guilty.

Which was why, whenever anybody asked, he said he loved it. Those words came easily enough. There were parts of it he did love. The feeling of doing two things at once, three things, of attention smoothly shifting, carried a euphoric energy that didn't fade. Nobody had told him it felt good, but it did. Powerful. Electric. Capable, or more than capable—competent. Studying was less of a chore when you could do other stuff at the same time, and it turned out studying actually made school a little easier. Those were the good parts.

All of which made the weird sensation harder to express. David didn't know how to phrase the thing he needed to ask, or who to ask even if he did. He didn't want to bother his mothers, not when he couldn't say for sure something was wrong. Not when he'd sworn he needed this; that it was safe, tested, something to give them fewer worries, not more.

His best friend, Milo, was the most obvious choice of confidant. They were supposed to be studying for their bio exam, which meant they were alternating five minutes quizzing each other with twenty-five minutes of *Forger Heist*. *Forger Heist* had been designed to teach people getting used to new Pilots how to maximize the implant's potential. You were supposed to play it while a certain podcast droned in the background and afterward answer questions about the podcast and the game's details. It wasn't a great game, but on the plus side it counted as studying.

Except it was part of the problem, too, or at least it contributed to his feeling that a problem existed. David used part of his new attention to watch Milo. The game had him tense, of course, leaning forward from the waist, both feet on the ground. His left foot tapped an awful nonrhythm, no beat David could count, different from the music on the screen. Now that he'd noticed it, it joined the long list of things he couldn't unnotice.

Even with that foot going, Milo exuded control. Focused on the game, not on David or their surroundings. He didn't look like he knew there was a fly in the room with them, or that David was watching him; if he knew, he didn't care.

"What are you seeing?" David asked. They were in this clichéd laser-alarmed room, the same level they'd lost a few times already. You had to track all the laser beams, and there were mirrors throwing everything off, and a steady stream of changing access codes and a guard, and speed metal that you couldn't turn down blasted from the guard's earphones, and even though the guard was an NPC and there was no real person to think about, you couldn't help wondering how he wasn't completely deaf with his music playing that loud into the room.

All of which was the point, overstimulation to get you to focus on the things that mattered: the guard's patterns of alertness, the lasers, the jewel case at the room's center, your own steady progress. Except. Except David couldn't shake the nagging feeling he was doing it wrong.

This was the first time he'd had the guts to ask Milo.

"Ssh," said Milo. "I'm almost to the jewels. Get to the access panel."

"I'm at the access panel. Waiting on you. We have two minutes before the guard's wife calls and wakes him." It had happened like clockwork the four previous times they'd been caught here.

"I can't go any faster."

"I know, but go faster."

"Fuck you. Argh! Dammit." Milo must have miscounted. He hit a laser with his trailing foot. An alarm sounded, the guard woke and jammed a button, and shutters caged the room, trapping them. TRY AGAIN appeared in block letters.

Last time, David had been the one to wake the guard, so he was happy Milo had screwed up this go-round. "We were close."

"We weren't even as close as last time. Back to pig organs?"

"Yeah, but my question . . . What were you seeing in that room?"

"The same thing I'm going to see when I fall asleep tonight: laser beams coming from every angle, making me do controller gymnastics I don't know how to do."

"And what are you hearing? What else is going on?"

"There are the codes, but I'm trusting you to deal with those, unless you want to switch. And, um, the dude's music, I guess? Why?"

He could say it now, or shut up. If he couldn't explain it to his best friend, though, whom could he tell? "When I'm in there, the whole room is shouting. Every one of those beams hums at a different frequency. Between that and the music and the podcast and the video, it's like torture."

"The video?"

"Yeah, the guard watches some warrior race thing on his phone, and even if I don't look at the screen, I hear the announcer shouting in Spanish like it's a soccer match, and the volume is almost as high as the music."

"Are you saying you think it means something? A clue we've missed for how to get through the room?"

"No! I think it's the opposite. I think it's noise we're supposed to tune out, only it sounds like you have and I can't." He didn't add the other things: the faint sounds of the museum crowd beyond the guarded room, the whisper of air in ducts, the rattle of the one loose screw still attached to the panel they'd removed to enter, the guard's soft snore. Beyond that, David's actual bedroom: the gurgling radiator, the fly trapped between the blinds and the window, the scent of whatever his ma was cooking, chili maybe, news television chatterboxes keeping her company.

"Huh."

Now was the time. "It's always like this. Is yours?"

"Like what?"

"Loud. Noisy. Like everything needs your attention at once, but not like a wash—like every single thing is individually and specifically trying to get your attention?"

"Huh," Milo repeated, and he didn't need to say more for David to know he didn't understand. "Have you told anybody? That doesn't sound right. I pay attention to the things I need to pay attention to. I haven't noticed all that other stuff."

"I'm telling you. I thought maybe this is how it's supposed to be, and I'm just bad at it."

"I dunno. Either mine is defective or yours is, I guess, or you're getting used to it slower. Are you doing your exercises like they told us to?"

"Yes! But I don't feel like exercises make the difference. Maybe you're right that I'm getting used to it slower."

"I dunno. You wanna try that room again or quiz each other on pig parts?"

"Once more, then back to the pig?"

"Deal."

David surrendered. He'd tried, but the thing felt indescribable. Like, how did you know if you were seeing colors the same as someone else? How would you ever know if your blue sky was someone else's pink? Maybe he was oversensitive to a thing everyone else had dealt with. He'd do the exercises and learn how to tune it out, the same as they had. The important thing was that he had a Pilot, and nobody could tease him anymore, and he could catch up again. The rest was just noise.

CHAPTER EIGHT

VAL

December exams rolled around, and David got respectable B grades across the board. They celebrated with another ice cream cake, season be damned. Val cut Sophie the smallest slice she could get away with without protest. The ketogenic diet hadn't worked for her, but Val was still convinced they might be able to control the seizures better if they controlled her sugar intake. And her stress. And her sleep. And her temperature. Poor kid; wait until she hit her teens and they broke the news about alcohol and caffeine.

And what if Sophie's class was soon full of Pilots, too? Surely it was a matter of time. They had managed to keep her just a year behind her age level and working well despite the brain-addling medications, but her head could never host that enhancement. She'd fall further behind. Maybe there would be special classes for all the kids who couldn't get Pilots for one reason or another. Val let that train of thought chug into the logical future before recalling it to the present. They would deal with it when the time came.

In January, David asked Val if he could start running with her before school, so he could be in better shape to try cross-country when the season started. She agreed casually, though she was secretly overjoyed. She took him to buy new running shoes, since he'd grown out of his last pair over winter break. His feet were like snowshoes; she teased him that he could walk barefoot after a storm and someone would think a yeti had passed.

For their first run, she allowed him to set their pace, slightly slower than her usual; she didn't think he was pushing himself as they set out through the neighborhood. Val debated whether to talk or run in silence. She didn't want running with her to become connected with invasive conversations, but it seemed like a good opportunity.

She settled on the topic at hand. "So, you're going to try out for cross-country?"

"It's not a tryout. Anybody can join and run with the practices. They only have to make decisions when there's a race with limited entries, and I'm not really into racing."

"No?"

"Nah. I just want to run with my friends. And"—he paused to navigate some roots pushing through the sidewalk, then stayed quiet a little longer than she expected—"you know how you used to tell me you wanted me to run because it helped you think? I was hoping it would work for me, too. You said it helped you think, and it helped you stop overthinking. That's what I want."

"Is the Pilot bothering you? Is something wrong?"

"No! I mean, I know I need it, and I'm doing way better in school, and it can be fun. It's just . . . loud."

"Is there a way to adjust the volume?"

He looked at her weirdly. She shut up again. "No, not volume loud . . . how can I say this? Busy. My head is always busy."

"Mine is like that, too, sometimes, so I can't imagine what yours must be like." She stole a glance at him. He ran with his head neutral and his shoulders back, easily, naturally perfect. She wondered what else he was doing in his head while they ran. Math problems? Spanish conjugations?

"Yeah . . . I thought maybe if I ran I'd shut it up for a minute."

"I hope so, too." She increased the pace, and he matched her stride for stride.

CHAPTER NINE

DAVID

David had never felt more adult than when he called the Installation Center on his own. The brochures had said that follow-up appointments were free. He was proud of himself for having read that, and for remembering it all these months later, and for finding his patient number in the user app, and for making the appointment to talk with a doctor, all without asking for help or telling anyone he'd done it.

It wasn't that he wouldn't have accepted his parents' assistance; he was just ashamed to ask. Asking meant admitting something was wrong, admitting it beyond what he'd said to Val while running, or what he'd asked Milo about. And which mom to ask? Val worked hard not to judge and hadn't pressed him when he'd mentioned it to her, but she'd been opposed to the whole Pilot thing to begin with. She'd tell him to get it removed and call it a failed experiment. Julie had clearly been more into the idea, had pressed him more than once about what it felt like and how effective it actually was. She also loved talking about how BNL had brought jobs to her boss's district and boosted his popularity. Admitting a problem to her felt like a betrayal.

Or more than a betrayal; a personal failure. Failure to adapt, failure to thrive, failure to use a device that was supposed to be too straightforward for user error, so that he felt like a fool. Failure to do easily what everyone else did easily. Story of high school so far: run twice as fast to keep up. Now he had to face that if nothing was wrong with his implant, something must be wrong with him.

All of which was why he took a bus to the Installation Center rather than tell anyone he was going. He only had to skip last period and track practice to make his four p.m. appointment. The schools shared their athletic facilities and Val would be there coaching her girls, but his own coach liked to send them out to run in the neighborhood; she would assume she'd missed him, not that he wasn't there.

He'd researched the route and how to pay, but the bus presented a challenge beyond the fact that he'd never taken city transit on his own. The challenge was part of why he needed his implant checked out. He sat at the back, and the engine rattled the seat, and there was a window open even though it was still pretty chilly outside, and it was midafternoon, so students hadn't started filling the bus, but there were enough people to make him dizzy.

Dizzy because his Pilot thought every detail deserved attention, like a photo where everything is in focus, so you don't know where the photographer meant for you to look. The mother singing to a crying baby, the man muttering to himself, the person with a protesting cat hidden in their bag, the skinny-necked man with the greasy mustache wearing an enormous trench coat stuffed with grocery bags in every pocket and who smelled like the worst body odor David had ever smelled, and the kid with music spilling out of his enormous headphones, and the stop-start of the bus, and the traffic streaming by outside, and the litany of upcoming stops through the unintelligible PA. Nobody else on the bus seemed bothered, and he didn't notice any other Pilots; sometimes he forgot his rich-kid school wasn't like the rest of the city.

The noise was a good reminder of why he'd made the appointment; when the bus finally reached his destination, he was relieved to escape onto the hilltop above the fancy mall. He had to dodge a few cars that cut across parking lot rows at angles, the drivers glaring at him like it was his fault they almost hit him just because he was on foot. All the stores had names that sounded too expensive for his family; the wealth was in the ampersands. Or in the syllables, like Balkenhol, spelled across the stand-alone building in tastefully futuristic–brand font.

It felt strange to walk into the place alone. Adult. He'd have to learn to do all this stuff on his own sooner or later, so he might as well start. If he took over booking his real doctor appointments, too, maybe he could show his moms a new level of responsibility, to reward their investment in the Pilot, to show them he was doing okay. One less thing for them to worry about.

He expected the greeter to give him a hard time, but she took his name and device registration and led him straight back without asking for his insurance or his age or where his parents were or anything. This room didn't look like a doctor's office any more than the consult room had. No sharps containers, no posters of kittens telling him to hang in there, no diplomas. Instead, framed fine art prints on soothing beige walls, two leather armchairs, a wheeled office chair, and a reclining exam chair with paper over it. He sat in an armchair, since he didn't know yet whether they wanted to poke at his head or ask him questions.

There was a courtesy knock on the door and a doctor entered with no pause. The doctor was in the range of older than him but not as old as David's moms. He was white and fit-looking, with a white coat hanging open over khakis and a green plaid button-down shirt and a navy tie. His tie was tucked into his shirt, but David didn't know if that was accidental or on purpose. His left shoe squeaked with every step.

"David, right? I'm Dr. Cohen. What brings you in?" His expression looked as carefully curated as the walls, welcoming but neutral.

Most doctors were preceded by nurses who weighed you and checked your height and asked you questions, so this straight-to-the-point question made David stumble for the explanation he'd crafted in planning the visit.

"I'm—uh—I can't tell if maybe something's wrong with my Pilot."

The doctor didn't change his expression. "Oh, I hope that's not the case. Let's get to the bottom of this. What's going on?"

"Well, it's . . . the best way I can describe it is *noise*. It's, like, everything from outside is coming inside at once, but then it's all fuzzy around the edges, too, like I'm supposed to be paying attention to certain things, but each of those things has sub-things that want attention. Like petting a dog and becoming aware you're petting every single individual hair, and every flea. And also it's snowing, so there's snow on the dog, and every single snowflake is different and wants to show me how different it is."

"Whoa."

" 'Whoa' isn't a thing you want a doctor to say."

"Yeah, sorry, David. That sounds like a lot, and you described it well. Let me check the diagnostics on your implant." He pulled a small tablet from his coat pocket.

It was cool they could read his Pilot without poking him. David peered over at the screen. "You're getting that from my head?"

"The data's encrypted, of course. We're the only ones who can see it other than you."

That hadn't been David's question. "It looks different from my app, is all."

"Oh! Yeah, the user interface has a different purpose. I'm looking at your implant's readouts, but it looks like everything falls inside the accepted parameters. No error codes, no misfirings, nothing out of the ordinary. Tell me, have you ever been diagnosed with a sensory processing disorder?"

"What? No. Are you saying it might be me, not the Pilot?" That was what David had feared most in coming here: that they would say something was wrong with him.

The doctor raised placating hands. "Sorry—processing disorders aren't my area, so I don't want to imply I'm making a diagnosis. Obviously, you know what you're describing is not the typical

Pilot experience, or you wouldn't have come in today. That leaves me thinking either you should ask your parents to help you get tested for a processing disorder, or maybe you haven't done the exercises enough. Did you practice the things we told you to? And play the game?"

David had made this appointment on his own, so a doctor telling him to ask his parents to make another appointment somewhere else implied the doctor was treating him like a kid. He tried not to let his annoyance reach his voice. "I've done all my exercises and played the game. I never had any problem processing my senses before this. Could the Pilot have broken them?"

"It doesn't work like that." Dr. Cohen laughed, and just like that, David was done with him. His question had been serious, even if it came out silly. A doctor shouldn't laugh.

He must have noticed he'd offended David, because his tone changed again. "Look, David, I'm glad you came here with your concerns and gave me the opportunity to check that everything was okay with your Pilot so I could reassure you it's working fine. Sometimes it takes a while to get the hang of it."

"How long a while?"

"As long as a year, in some cases." The doctor shrugged, further dismissal. *A year!* He'd be impossibly behind by then. "—Otherwise, if it's working the same as everyone else's, maybe your noise is everyone else's normal and you just need to get used to it. I'd suggest starting the exercises over and maybe doing them once or twice more per day, to get you where you should be. Did you have anything else you needed to ask while I'm here?"

"Yeah," said David. "Why don't you have a Pilot yourself? Isn't it kind of weird to be telling me what normal feels like when you don't know yourself?"

The doctor smiled. "I'm Orthodox Jewish, so it's against my religion to get one myself, but trust me when I say I've talked with enough people with Pilots to have a sense of normal. I was involved with the research from the beginning. Very observant, David.

Anyway, I've got to get to my next patient, and I'm sure you've got places to go. Come back if none of those solutions gets you feeling your Pilot is doing what it's supposed to do."

David nodded and thanked him, knowing he wasn't ever coming back.

CHAPTER TEN

VAL

In April, Sophie started seizing more often, though at least they weren't the convulsive kind. Focal seizures, impaired consciousness, knocking out her awareness but not bringing her body down. She disappeared on an almost daily basis, disappeared for seconds or minutes to a place she couldn't find words to describe.

"It doesn't matter where," she said at dinner one night. "It's not here. I miss here when I'm there."

"So long as you don't miss there while you're here," Julie said, doling out the black bean spaghetti Val had made. Research pointed to high-protein diets as a path to seizure freedom.

"No, I like here, Mom. I just don't know how to stay."

Another piece of Val broke off, and she watched it beat its wings against the walls. That night, after Sophie went to bed and David had locked himself in his room to do homework and play video games, Val bent her own rule about not running after dark. Julie watched her change into shorts and nodded in understanding.

Dinner felt heavy in her stomach. Cool spring air usually energized her, but her limbs felt like lead. Still, she ran. She ran until her thoughts no longer lingered on their daughter who didn't know how to stay, or their boy becoming an adult in a world that demanded so much more from him than she would ever have imagined. There was always a part of her that wanted to keep running, to run so far the problems disappeared behind her. The darkness amplified it.

When she got back to the house, it was quiet, except the sound of David's game spilling under his closed door. She tiptoed past Sophie's door.

"Mom?"

"No, Soph. It's me." She walked into the room, aware she was dripping sweat.

"Ma. You smell like you went running. You never run at night."

"I needed some exercise. I promise I was safe."

"And the moon is full."

Val couldn't see it from her angle near the door. She crossed the room and sat on the floor next to the bed, her head against the hated bedrail. From there, she saw the moon. Had she even noticed it when she was running? She had been so in her head, though surely she'd noticed the brightness. Or not.

"Is that a shooting star?" Sophie pointed at an object moving quickly through the sky. She let her hand fall gently onto Val's head.

"No, it's a satellite." Val kept still so Sophie wouldn't withdraw her hand. "See how steadily it moves? It's circling the Earth, not falling."

"Oh. Are there a lot of them?"

"Satellites? Yeah, I think so. Some relay phone calls and communication, and some are for navigation, like when the car's GPS tells us where to drive, and"—she ran out of types, though she knew there were more—"others. The moon! The moon is a satellite orbiting Earth, too, in a way."

"Do any of them run into each other?"

If Sophie was into this, Val would learn it all, but at that moment all she could do was try to remember. "I think it's kind of like when people are running at the same speed in the same direction, so they never catch each other." There were different orbits involved, she knew she was being reductive, but this would do for now.

"One of them should take a shortcut so they can meet and run together, instead." Sophie hadn't been asking if they would crash; she'd been asking if they were lonely.

They both fell silent. The moon was huge and reflected the sun's brightness back at them in a way that made it seem like its own white glow. Sophie's breathing changed, and her hand dropped away from Val's head, the trailing end of a benediction she hadn't known she was giving.

The next day, Val collected Sophie from school and took her to do some grocery shopping. The route home passed close to David's school, and as she pumped her squealing brakes, waiting to take her left turn, she caught movement in the side mirror.

"I see David!" said Sophie, face pressed to her window in the back.

David's cross-country team. Val searched for him and found him in the pack, his face serene. They all looked serene, their bodies straining and sweating but their faces showing no sign of exertion. A few joked with one another, sharing relaxed smiles. She hoped their multiple attentions included remembering to look both ways as they crossed the busy streets back to the school.

They were a strange collection of animals: a herd of boys, scrawny bare chests thrust forth and heaving, legs churning as they vied with one another for position. They would achieve great things, these boys. Their parents had given them everything they could. They would spend another year or two or three at their excellent school, with their excellent brains doing more than any brains had done before. How could they not succeed?

And yet, as she watched them navigate a perfect spring day, Val worried. What kind of society were they creating where kids voluntarily changed their brains to keep pace with all the input coming at them? She couldn't help imagining the noise in all those Piloted heads, not as David described it.

A boy near David stumbled. Val watched her son reach out an arm to steady the other without breaking stride, but another kid behind him tripped and fell. Two more jumped over him before someone at the back of the pack stopped to help him stand. He brushed his bloody knees with his hands, then took off after his friends.

The traffic light changed and they left the runners behind. Back at the house a few minutes later, Val turned off the car but lingered, key still in the ignition.

She turned to face Sophie. "I have a secret to tell you."

Sophie unbuckled herself and climbed between the seats and into the passenger seat to hear what Val had to say. She was all about secrets.

"I can see the future," Val said in a conspiratorial voice. "Not all of it, but a little. In a few years, almost everyone is going to have a Pilot, except you and me."

Sophie's eyes grew wide. "Even Mom?"

Val considered, and realized she knew the answer. Not a prediction; an inevitability. "Yes. Mom will have one. People with Pilots are going to do some good things, but you and I and a few other people will be the only people without them. The others are going to make it seem like we need them, but it'll be okay."

"Because it's okay to be different?" She looked skeptical; she'd heard that line before.

"Because we're going to be different together. As long as you don't have one, I won't have one. We'll both do fine." She almost added, "I promise," but stopped short. She didn't believe in making promises about things outside of her own control.

Sophie nodded like she understood. Val kissed her daughter's forehead and counted the hours until she could run all this out of her mind.

PART TWO

CHAPTER ELEVEN

JULIE

Julie stared at David through the vines. February rain on the aquarium rainforest pavilion's glass ceiling enhanced the illusion they were someplace tropical. They went to the aquarium once a year, always on the dreariest, slushiest, most miserable February day. Some guesswork was involved in the decision. Was this the day? Or might there be a worse one?

She felt like they'd chosen right this time. Icy rain spattered the glass high overhead, but the rainforest humidity had already stripped their winter layers; her coat was heavy in her arms. Bright-plumed birds swooped through the upper reaches, unperturbed by the masses of running, screaming children. Her mind wasn't on the children, or the birds, or the rain.

"You're doing what?" she repeated. She didn't know how many times she had asked already.

"Mom, you don't need to raise your voice." All David's attention seemed to be on her and her reaction, and whether she was going to make a scene. She was.

"What do you mean, you're not going to college? Your applications are in. We visited fourteen campuses. Do you know how long those stupid financial aid forms took?"

"Mom, maybe we should talk about this at home."

"You're the one who brought it up here."

"I, uh, think that might have been a mistake."

"That's the mistake?" She raised her voice a notch. He winced, and she dialed it back again. "The mistake is that you're telling me in a goddamn rainforest, not that you've changed your mind about college?"

"I've thought about this. I just wasn't sure when to tell you. It's not a big deal."

"Oh, I'm pretty sure it's a big deal."

David sighed and studied some moss. Julie took the moment to glance around. No sign of Val and Sophie, who had left to find a bathroom ages ago. David looked on the verge of tears. He cried only when he was really frustrated.

She took a deep breath. "Okay, I'll tone it down, but you better start explaining. What's going on, Davey?"

"This guy came to school to talk to us. He said they'd teach us how to use our Pilots better. He said it was a good match of skills, not making us fit into the old ideas of what we should do next."

"What guy, Davey? Who is 'they'? And why didn't he talk to you before we paid the application fees?"

David stared at the moss, then scratched at his Pilot light and met her eyes. "The Army."

"The *what*?" This time, it didn't take a Pilot for Julie to notice people staring. She didn't care.

"I thought you'd understand better than Ma," he said. "I'm taking control of my future."

Val and Sophie appeared beside them as if on cue.

"Did we miss something?" Sophie asked, looking from Julie to David and back.

"Your son," Julie said, as if Val had spoken rather than Sophie, "has decided to get killed in some foreign country instead of go to college."

"What's she talking about?" Val posed her question to David.

This time he put some force behind his answer, a cannonball instead of a toe in the water. "I'm joining the Army." He looked at

Val's face, then Julie's, clearly trying to triangulate where the sympathy and understanding would come from. Julie set her expression.

Sophie furrowed her brow, trying to follow. "You're not really going to get killed, are you?"

"No, I'm not." David threw an arm around her. "I'm going to get trained. They said they have a special track for people who pass a fitness test and an academic test and have had a Pilot for more than two years. We did the tests in school. I made ninety-ninth percentile in both. That's the best score I've gotten on any test ever." The last bit was clearly for their benefit, not Sophie's.

"Parents pay how much to that school and they let in recruiters?" Val muttered to Julie. Julie squeezed her hand.

"I'm serious about this. You know I wouldn't have said it if I hadn't thought about it." That was true. He was not a boy who ever came to them with notions; by the time he verbalized anything, it was a plan.

"Is it me, or is it two hundred degrees in here?" Sophie asked.

"It's definitely hot," Val said. "And I don't know about the rest of you, but I'm ready to move on. Come on, the best part is still ahead."

Sophie followed her toward the exit and the long ramp through the shark tank. Julie watched to make sure Sophie made it through the airlock vestibule designed to keep the birds in. Anytime Sophie noticed the temperature it was worth a change in situation; heat triggered her seizures as surely as anything did.

Julie put a hand on David's arm to hold him back. "I get that you're serious, but this one is going to take me a while to wrap my head around. Can we table it until some colleges respond? Maybe some school will offer you a scholarship for that ninety-ninth-percentile brain."

Don't do it! she wanted to say. He put his giant hand over hers, then removed hers from his arm. He did it with such tenderness she almost wouldn't have realized it was a brush-off. Almost.

"I'm sorry, Mom. I'll wait until more colleges respond, if you need me to, but I won't change my mind. We can talk about it until you're comfortable with it, or until you realize I'm doing it whether or not you get comfortable."

Julie tried to summon pride in his decision, but settled for mild respect for his resolve. She wished, not for the first time, that Pilots helped with executive function as well as attention and multitasking. There was still no way to rush good choices. He left the rainforest ahead of her, tall and strong and smart and young and dumb.

She attacked everything for the next several days. She attacked the drive back from the aquarium, attacked it so hard Val insisted she pull over and switch seats. She made Sophie cry when they got home, insisting she hadn't promised to take the kid to a friend's house when she knew she probably had. She wished it weren't the ugliest day of the ugliest month, wished she could weed, or mow, or build something or hit something. No wonder David wanted to go to war. It must be genetic, this desire to do violence. Her desire was limited to plant life, but she understood how it might combine with testosterone in a more dangerous mix.

The recruiter agreed to see her more easily than she expected. She had wanted to show up at his office armed for battle. Instead, he suggested meeting at a coffee shop, maybe under the same theory that had inspired David to make his announcement in public.

She arrived exactly on time and scanned the room for uniforms. Shouldn't a military officer be punctual? Maybe he wasn't going to come and had arranged this to demonstrate what little power she had in the situation. He'd gone to David's school and derailed eighteen years of hope and planning and he didn't even have the decency to say it to her face.

"Mrs. Geller?"

She scanned the room until she found the speaker. The man at the corner table had risen from his chair, a welcoming smile on his face. He had a deep tan over an already-tan skin tone and white, white teeth. He looked like a movie star. Maybe that was how he sold children on war: you too can be a movie star if you sign on the dotted line.

"You aren't wearing a uniform." *Good start, Julie. Play your hand early so he knows you're hostile.*

"I don't like to wear it when I'm meeting with parents. It can be intimidating. Plus, this saves me on dry-cleaning bills." He brushed a hand down his body with a self-deprecating air. His polo shirt and pressed khakis were as much a uniform as anything else he might wear, she realized; no creases in sight.

"I'm sorry, that was rude," she said, then wondered why she was apologizing to the enemy. She grasped for level ground. "But you haven't introduced yourself."

"Sergeant First Class Fuentes, US Army. I thought you knew since you were the one who called me. And you're one of David's mothers?"

How much had he and David talked already? She nodded. He came to her side of the table and pulled out the chair for her.

"Do you want something to drink? On me."

She stood again. "I can order for myself, thanks."

No way would she let him buy her anything; she didn't want to owe him. She walked over to the counter and ordered a large black coffee. She preferred cream and sugar, but she felt like the black coffee lent her extra mojo in a situation she was still trying to get a handle on. She didn't order a pastry, to spare herself the indignity of eating in front of him.

She warmed her hands on the mug while she waited for Fuentes to return. He slipped back into his seat a few minutes later, dropping a plate with a bagel and cream cheese on the table and scattering poppy seeds. In his other hand, he held a mug of hot chocolate topped with a whipped-cream mountain, chocolate sprinkles, and cinnamon. Apparently he hadn't gotten the memo that his order might have significance in their encounter. There was a bowl of packaged creamers and sugars on the table beside theirs, and she reached over to steal one of each. Not a defeat if he didn't know they were playing.

She waited until he'd taken a bite of bagel. "So, what do you want with my son?"

He chewed for a moment, then smiled. "That was direct."

The poppy seed stuck to one of his perfect teeth gave her courage. "I don't think we have anything else to discuss, so there's no point to small talk."

"Fair enough. I'll be direct as well, then. We want your son because he's exactly the sort of man we're looking for."

"He's a boy."

"He's eighteen. He'll be a man soon whether you want him to be or not."

"He has plenty of time to be a man," she said. "I wanted him to go to college, have a few more years to figure out who he wants to be."

Fuentes smiled again. The poppy seed had vanished. "Is that what he wants? Maybe he knows who he wants to be already."

She shook her head. "I don't buy it. None of us know who we are at eighteen. We're just full of ourselves enough to think so."

He smiled again, but the wattage had dimmed. It seemed more genuine. "Fair enough. How about this? Maybe he doesn't know what he wants, but he's actively looking for it, and he doesn't think he can find it in college or we wouldn't be sitting here having this discussion. He didn't check off the 'send me more information' box; he signed up."

Julie was dumbfounded; she tried to hide it by sipping her coffee. It burnt her tongue, but she held the mug there anyway, buying a minute. David had already enlisted? He'd said "I'm joining," not "I've joined," which she'd assumed meant he'd made the decision but hadn't done the thing yet. She didn't know whether to act like she had known that, or to drop her facade.

"Why did you bother meeting with me if he's already yours?" She tried to keep her voice from wavering.

"He's eighteen, so he has the right to decide for himself, but obviously we'd rather you were on board with his decision. We want you to understand why we're interested in him."

"David said you were interested in smart, athletic kids with Pilots." She couldn't bring herself to say "men." David still couldn't do a load of laundry without dying all his underwear pink. No way was he an adult.

"That's what we want, but not why. Do you know what a difference it would make to have young people like him in control rooms? People with stamina and brains who can pay attention to multiple stimuli, who can think on their feet?"

She took another sip of coffee. "You say 'control rooms,' but you mean battlefields. You mean storming through deserts and towns and compounds. You mean people who can aim a gun while figuring out if three guns are aiming at them."

"Yes, that, too." He dropped the smile entirely, at last. "That's true, in the long run, but these are still the first people with Pilots to enter the service, and we still need to figure out how best to use them. This is a special program.

"My assignment is to look for smart, athletic young people with Pilots, to be trained for Pilot-specific maneuvers. I can't say where he will or won't be sent, but I can promise this program's intent isn't to train these soldiers and then lose them. There's going to be a lot of money invested in them. We want them to stick around."

The practicality of the money argument calmed her more than anything else had. She thanked Fuentes for meeting with her and left the café. She still couldn't believe David had signed up—he had lied when he said the decision could wait until the acceptance letters came in—but at least Fuentes's last lines had seemed honest enough.

"There's going to be a lot of money invested in them," he'd said. That was numbers, and numbers were her thing. David was an asset to the Army, not a pawn. She'd have to hang her hat on hope.

CHAPTER TWELVE

VAL

After David's announcement, the world took on a different color. Army drab, maybe. Val drove him to school, as she did every day, letting him off outside the gate so he wouldn't be seen with his mother. She tried not to take it personally.

Her day's first class, her homeroom, was the eleventh-grade girls. Since the weather outside was still too foul to consider an outside activity, she readied the gym for volleyball, tensing the net and rolling out the ball cart.

"Have any of you gotten a visit from a military recruiter?" she asked the first few girls to straggle in. Joshlyn, one of her varsity runners, bobbed her head.

"Yeah, Ms. B. A few weeks ago? In civics?" She had an amazing capacity to turn statements into questions. Of course. In civics. Civic duty. Civic pride.

"What did they tell you?"

"She said it was a good opportunity? That we were exactly what the services were looking for, and they'd pay for college after if we wanted, right? And that she knew we were still weighing our options since we're only juniors, but they'd be happy to cover senior year tuition for anyone whose parents agreed to sign a commitment for them 'til they're eighteen. Ms. B? Are you okay? I didn't say yes, Ms. B, just maybe. I don't need their scholarship since I have a track scholarship already? Ms. B?"

Val realized she was staring at Joshlyn. The others had gathered on the bleachers. Morning announcements started, and the girls heaved themselves to their feet for the national anthem. Val put her hand over her heart, but didn't mouth the words as she usually did. Commitments from parents to sell their kids into the service? Her mind was officially boggled. The morning announcements talked about a charity bake sale and a new bank of parking spots converted to charge electric cars. Nothing about recruiters.

After announcements, she had Tamara Habana lead some quick dance-style warm-ups, and then sent them off to make ten circuits of the gym. Blue lights bobbed, ponytails swished; everything was different, nothing was different.

Her second period was a spare. She picked a fight with poor Mr. Alvarez in the break room, accusing him of having used her mug, then accidentally used aspartame in her coffee instead of stevia. When an assistant principal walked into the lounge, she redirected her rage at him.

"Nick, what the hell are you thinking? Recruiters? Incentivizing?" She realized she sounded like Joshlyn, all question marks, and tried to locate her inner calm. She found it in her gut, punching her organs from the inside out, and tried to push away the hated temper that hulked inside her.

"We can talk about this. I'm sorry you're upset." He looked genuinely surprised at her reaction. He sat on the couch and motioned her to join him.

She perched on the arm. "Of course I'm upset. There are soldiers in my school, trying to convince my kids to fight their war when half these girls can't even drive yet."

"It's part of the program, Val. I thought you knew, since David has one and all. The money for those new scholarships had to come from someplace. Anyway, they're hardly recruiting. They're laying out options."

"Bull. Joshlyn Trent says they're offering to pay for senior year for girls whose parents sign a commitment form."

"It's nonbinding." He opened his palms. "They can change their minds, as long as . . ."

". . . As long as what? As long as they pay out the loan? Do you know how bad that sounds?"

He let his hands fall to his lap. "I think it sounds pretty good to the girls whose parents are already going into debt to keep them in this school, and the ones who don't know how they're going to pay college tuition. I'm sure you understand. You'd be in the same position if you didn't work here."

He had her on that point; they would never have been able to afford to send David to the boys' school without the faculty waiver. That was the main reason she worked here.

"But, Nick, aren't we just sending the poor kids off to be cannon fodder again? Isn't that what keeps happening, over and over again these last few wars?"

"I see what you're saying, but I don't think so. They're offering the senior-year deal to the scholarship kids, sure, but they're offering the college-tuition deal to everyone, and there's more than a few nonscholarship kids who need to consider that. They've said there's a training program for kids with Pilots, that they're going to be specialists. They'll learn to use the Pilots better than they do now. I don't think it's a bad option to present."

Val rubbed her shoulder, where she felt a knot forming; that was where her stress usually settled. There was no winning this argument, in any case. It was too late. The recruiters had come, and she hadn't even known about it. She hadn't known the military was helping to subsidize Pilots. She hadn't known, and she hadn't prepared, and they had stolen her son.

David hadn't even used the money argument. She wondered if that had come into it for him, if he thought he was being pragmatic, if he thought this was a way to help the family; that sounded like David. Or was he just looking for a way to silence what he called the noise in his head? None of her students had ever mentioned noise.

She could pretend her upset was on behalf of her students, good students like Joshlyn, who deserved a full array of options, but all she could think of was David, who had been given a full array of options and made his own terrifying choice.

CHAPTER THIRTEEN

JULIE

It wasn't so much a decision as an inevitability; Julie just had to find a way to tell Val. She predicted the conversations: Could they afford it? Yes. She balanced the family finances; with David not heading to college after all, with the GI Bill as an option if he eventually did, they had some money to spare. She was still furious with the recruiters, furious with David, but the irony didn't escape her that her anger directed itself at his unilateral decision while she longed to make a unilateral decision of her own.

It was an investment in their future. She could do her job twice as well with a Pilot. She'd be faster, more efficient, listening to messages and performing constituent-issue triage and updating the budget and listening to the congressman's podcast and sending him talking points on the constituent issues she'd heard and answering her staff's questions without the hopeless whirl of *what was I doing ten minutes ago before the phone rang?* She could get stuff done while simultaneously calming a caller, instead of watching minutes tick by that she'd intended for something else. It all made perfect sense.

Part of her wanted to go ahead and schedule the procedure, telling Val only after the installation. She wasn't that kind of person. Was she? Val's concerns were getting old. They'd seen how well David's Pilot worked: so well he'd been recruited by an elite military unit, like something in a bad action movie. If he complained sometimes, it wasn't enough to worry about, and the good points far outnumbered the bad. She liked living on the cutting edge, or at least somewhere on the blade.

Better to be the blade than the chopping block. If you fell behind, you fell behind forever. Like her father, solid on e-mail but uncomfortable with social media and video calls, still insisting on a landline and physical albums as if records weren't grooves in wax, and CDs didn't convert music to ones and zeroes. She found the ones and zeroes reassuring. They were proof that it was important for her to adapt and stay ahead.

Before she'd brought it up with Val, before she could tell the congressman her plan to get one, Evan Manfredi called her from the DC office.

"We're not allowed to require that people get Pilots," he said. He leaned toward his computer's camera and rubbed a hand over his close-cropped hair, bringing her attention to his own Pilot, consciously or not.

"But?" He was always so obvious.

"But we've found a way to subsidize the procedure for any employee of more than three years. I know you may be nervous about it. A lot of people your age are, but I can promise you . . ." She let him drone on about the painless procedure, how easy it was to get used to the enhancement, how much more productive she would be once she had it. Better to let him think she needed convincing than to tell him she'd already decided to do it. He'd probably find a way to renege on covering the cost if she admitted she'd been prepared to pay for it herself.

If she acted put upon, he would owe her one for taking the chance. "Let me talk it over at home and get back to you later this week, Evan. I'll consider it, but I want to make sure my family is on board."

He nodded, though she knew those words were foreign to him. She sensed his skepticism whenever she came back from family medical leave. He had no place in his world for external distractions. At least he was so transparent she knew exactly where she stood.

CHAPTER FOURTEEN

VAL

Another night together, apart. Apart together. David was in his room killing monsters with his friend Milo. Julie sat at the dining room table, intent on some project spread in front of her. Sophie occupied the table's remaining corner, doing one of those obnoxious 3-D puzzles, which she'd insisted on tackling alone. The box showed a medieval castle, but not that all four castle walls were nearly identical, and the foam pieces never quite aligned right; or more precisely, they never quite aligned wrong, so you could build an entire wall without realizing a piece was out of place. Val pointed that out every time Sophie found one at a garage sale, which was probably why Sophie refused her help, leaving her flipping channels.

Sophie looked over her shoulder. "Why is Mrs. Moritz on TV?"

Val backed up a couple of channels, to the local news broadcast she'd gone past. Sophie was right: her principal sat in a row of people on a dais behind the superintendent of schools, Quentin Marshall. The camera angle was such that Val was able to count six Pilots among the ten seated, not including Marshall's.

"That man is a giant," said Sophie.

"A giant jerk," muttered Julie under her breath. Val knew there had been some political issue he'd gotten himself involved in that had not endeared him to her wife.

A news anchor's voice spoke over the scene. "In another controversial move, Mr. Marshall has announced the city school system is partnering with Balkenhol Neural Labs to bring their Pilot implants to underprivileged youth."

Cut to Mr. Marshall. "Our city has an obligation to its students. We need to give them every opportunity to succeed. Right now they are being left behind more and more every day. If we are going to close this gap, we need new advantages."

The voiceover returned. "BNL's CEO, Sylvia Keating, was also on hand to discuss this momentous decision."

A fiftyish white woman in an impeccable blue pantsuit stepped to the microphone. Her perfect hair swept back from the right side of her head in a way that showed off her Pilot's light, which matched her suit. "This partnership is an opportunity to bring our children into a future in which they are competitive, in which they are current, in which they . . ."

The piece cut to reactions from others who had been in the room. A west side mother told the reporter, "My daughter has been asking for a Pilot since they first came out, but we haven't been able to afford one. This is a blessing, a real blessing. I'd like to hug Mr. Marshall."

"I want my kids to have opportunities I didn't have, but that's always felt out of reach," said a father from a southern neighborhood. "I thank the people responsible for this."

One of the principals, an older woman, spoke next. "Our school is one hundred ninetieth out of two hundred in the city, which is consistently last in the state. We teach to the tests, and we set high standards, but they are continually unreachable. We are blessed to have the opportunity to try this."

Back to the studio, and Val muted the newscasters, who both had Pilots of their own. She turned to face the dining room.

"Fair and balanced reporting, huh? They couldn't find anybody skeptical of the idea?"

Julie shrugged. "I think it's the best thing Marshall has done since he took over the district."

"Really?"

"He's right. The schools are underwater. The buildings are falling apart, they're hemorrhaging teachers. Private schools have a thousand advantages. Why shouldn't they try to reduce that number?"

"My school is falling apart?" Sophie looked alarmed.

Val glared at Julie. "No, Soph. Your school is in okay shape, but a lot of schools need repairs. I don't see how this will help get repairs or teachers."

Julie brandished her tablet, some random spreadsheet on display. "Money. Students with Pilots get better grades, better test scores. Better test scores, more grants, more cash flow. Super long view: more students graduate, more students go on to college, more students get better jobs, make more money, more students look back fondly on the advantages their school gave them, more students donate back to their alma maters, more students return to the city with ideas that create jobs and improve the local economy. Schools finally have money to put where it's needed. Where's the downside?"

"They should have interviewed you. The school system should hire you to do their spin."

"Hey!" Julie frowned.

"Counterargument. We know Pilots don't make anybody smarter. They don't teach good study skills. They aren't a replacement for teachers or books. If a kid is in tenth grade and reading on a third-grade level, he's not going to magically start comprehending quantum physics or *To the Lighthouse* just because he has a Pilot. It's a superficial fix. A bandage for a paper cut on a finger when there's a sucking chest wound, too."

"Eeew," said Sophie.

"Exactly. Gross and pointless and super sketchy in my book."

"Your paranoid book." Julie came over to sit beside Val, leaning into her. Val recognized the move as appeasement, not apology. She sighed. "I guess we'll find out one way or another, but what about all the Sophies?"

Sophie turned around from her puzzle again. "How many Sophies are there?"

"One is plenty, I'm sure," said Julie, nudging Val in the ribs.

Val ignored the hint. "You know what I mean. What about the kids who can't get Pilots? What about the Orthodox Jews and the Seventh-day Adventists, for that matter?"

"I don't think there are many Orthodox Jews in this school system."

"Fine. The Adventists?"

". . . but if there were, I guess they'd opt out. I'm sure there's an opt-out. For Sophie's class, too."

Val let it go. She didn't ask her last question, because she didn't want it answered in front of Sophie. What happens to those who opt out? There would always be somebody left behind. She wished it weren't the little girl at the table, still determinedly matching indistinguishable puzzle pieces, still refusing help.

CHAPTER FIFTEEN

SOPHIE

Sophie continued writing until the moment Mr. Kenworth came past to take her test, slamming her pencil down with a flourish to make sure he knew she was done. Technically she was allowed as much time as she needed to finish, but she hated playing that card if she didn't have to. English was her best subject.

"Wait!" she called to Kevin Boatman. He swung around, his wide shoulders filling the doorway.

"How'd you do?" he asked as she caught up with him.

"Good enough, I think," she said. "How 'bout you?"

The cadence of his speech was slow and measured, as always, like every word tested itself in his chest's cavern before finding its way out into the world. "Okay. I haven't started the book, so I guessed some answers. How did Johnny hurt his hand? I said he got bitten by a zombie."

"Um, yeah, I think you might not get full marks for that one."

Somebody shoved Sophie into Kevin. Hard. "Tugboat and Slow Boat! A perfect match!"

"You can't even tell them apart!" said someone else.

Sophie whirled to face her attackers, who were already halfway down the hall. Their Pilots looked like they were twinkling, but that was just the effect of their bouncing hair as they laughed. She didn't remember the name of the tall girl who had shoved her. She thought maybe they shared gym class, the only class she took with the Piloted kids; she was never good with names and faces of people who weren't her friends. Whoever this girl was, they were definitely not friends.

She dropped her bag at Kevin's feet, hoping he would keep an eye on it. She caught up with the other girls before the end of the hall. They weren't looking in her direction anymore, so when she stuck out a foot to trip the taller one, she managed to catch them by surprise. Tall Girl sprawled across the floor, spilling books in front of her.

The friend shrieked and didn't stop shrieking. *Like a banshee,* Sophie's ma would say. Sophie tried to slip back down the hall unnoticed, but the screeching girl pointed at her. "Teacher! Teacher!"

Mr. Kenworth poked his head out into the hallway, then ducked back into his classroom. The Code Orange alarm went off, telling the students to get themselves to the nearest classroom and close the door. Code Orange? Attacker-at-large? Sophie reached for the nearest classroom door, but Mr. Kenworth had appeared in the hall again.

"Don't move, Sophie." He looked like he wanted to grab her by the scruff of the neck like the police in some old movie about juvenile delinquents. She didn't move. The hall was empty now except for Mr. Kenworth and the two girls, the one screaming and the other silent. Kevin must have gone into a room like they were supposed to in a Code Orange. Her backpack sat abandoned by the English classroom; hopefully that wasn't enough to merit a Code Green suspicious-package alarm.

The bully sat where she had landed, a felled tree, clutching her right wrist in her left hand. Sophie knew she should ask the girl if she was okay, make some effort at reconciliation. Instead, she went for her backpack. She knew what came next: the office, her mothers, trouble, trouble, trouble.

Sophie wasn't sure which mother she hoped would come until she saw Julie pull into the parking lot. Mom would be quicker to defend Sophie instead of considering the teacher perspective. Maybe.

"Seriously? She did what?" she asked, after hearing Mr. Kenworth's take on what had happened. She turned to Sophie. "Did you push this Tonya girl?"

"Sort of," Sophie said, shrugging. "I tripped her, but she pushed me first."

"I didn't see that," said Mr. Kenworth.

Sophie crossed her arms. "You didn't see me trip her, either. You saw her on the floor and assumed I pushed her 'cause that other girl pointed at me."

"But you did push her?" asked Mrs. Moritz. She sat behind her desk like a presiding judge, with everyone else in chairs facing her. Sophie thought it made them all look equally guilty.

"No. I tripped her. I told you, she pushed me first, into Kevin. She called me Slow Boat."

Mrs. Moritz smiled a concerned smile. "Did you have to react, Sophie? Could you have told a teacher?"

Sophie shook her head and mustered patience. Adults were so dense about what went on. "There were no teachers. If I let her push me, she'd push me again harder next time."

"How is the other girl?" asked Julie. "You said on the phone she was taken to the hospital?"

"Yes, for X-rays of her wrist," said Mr. Kenworth. "It looked broken to me."

Julie's smile was thin-lipped and insincere. "Well, hopefully it's not broken. I assume you asked Sophie if she was okay, too?"

"I'm fine, Mom. I just don't like getting shoved when I didn't do anything."

"So, are we done here?" Julie sank back into the chair.

Mrs. Moritz spread her hands. She looked like she had all the time in the world. "I'm afraid I can't let it go that easily. A student was assaulted. That's grounds for automatic suspension."

"Suspension? You've got to be kidding!" Julie gripped her chair's arms and sat straighter. "She defended herself. It wouldn't have happened if you had teachers in the hall monitoring the class transition, I'll bet."

"Nevertheless, a student is in the hospital. I have a duty to protect everyone."

"Sophie is half the size of most kids in her class. You know she doesn't have a behavior plan, and you know kids in her class get bullied for not having Pilots. Are you sure you don't have this backward? Shouldn't the other girl's parents be called as well?"

Mrs. Moritz put a hand to her Pilot without seeming to notice she was doing it. Kids with Pilots never did that, but all the adults who had them always touched the light when somebody mentioned it. "When I talk with her father, I'll tell him I don't think he needs to press charges."

"Press charges?" Julie was out of her chair now. "Don't you dare put those words in his head. Do you really think Sophie is a threat?"

"Cool," said Sophie under her breath. Mom threw her a look and she shut her mouth again.

"Sophie is not generally aggressive or a problem student. We'll certainly take that into consideration. In the meantime, a two-day suspension should give her time to think about what she's done and tell the other students this is not acceptable behavior."

"This is ridiculous," said Julie, pulling Sophie to her feet.

Sophie didn't think two days' suspension sounded bad, but she figured she shouldn't say so. She followed her mother from the office and out to the car. She was supposed to be in math, so as far as she was concerned, this was nothing but a victory. She knew better than to say that out loud, too.

They drove away from the school in silence. At a red light a few blocks later, her mom turned to her. "If you ever get caught fighting in school again, you are grounded for life."

"But—"

"If you ever get *caught* fighting in school again, you are grounded for life." Julie stared at her, and Sophie got the picture. "I understand it's hard not to react when somebody hurts you and calls you names, but next time, think about if it's worth it, and if you're going to get caught. And if you're going to get us sued. We can't afford to go around paying hospital bills for other people. Understood?"

"Understood," said Sophie. "Stay cool, don't get caught."

Julie sighed. "Close enough. Ice cream?"

"Yes, please."

They might be embarrassing sometimes, but Sophie's moms were pretty cool when it came to it.

CHAPTER SIXTEEN

VAL

The mall's food court was crowded for a Monday night. Val beat a pack of teenagers to the lone empty table, dropping her gym bag in what turned out to be a lake of cola, which probably explained why the table had been unoccupied. She had to wait for Julie and Sophie to arrive before she could grab napkins to sop up the soda, lest she lose the table or the bag.

"Hi, love," Julie said, kissing Val on the cheek and tossing her jacket onto an empty chair. "How was your day?"

"Uneventful. Yours? Hang on a sec." She crossed the dining area to grab a stack of napkins.

"Ask the kid," said Julie when Val returned.

Val turned to Sophie as she wiped the table. "Soph?"

Sophie grinned. "I got suspended."

"What?" Val looked from Sophie to Julie and back. "What are you talking about? And why are you smiling?"

"Oh yeah," said Sophie, reaching up to physically turn the corners of her lips down. "I know I'm not supposed to smile about it. I got suspended for fighting, but I wasn't fighting. I was protecting myself. Can I have a Shamburger?"

"No," said Val. "You know your seizures get triggered by some ingredient they use."

"She's right," said Julie as their daughter's mouth opened in protest. "And no dessert. You already had ice cream."

Val wondered how ice cream had followed suspension. "In that case, how about brown rice and steamed veggies?"

Sophie shot them a look so forlorn Val almost laughed out loud.

"Sandwich or pizza. No pepperoni. And bring me back an Italian sub." Julie reached into her purse and fished out a twenty. "What do you want, Val?"

"Just water, thanks." Her eyes followed Sophie across the food court. "What was that child saying about a fight?"

"She tripped a girl who had shoved her. The school over-reacted."

"Suspended for tripping? That's a hell of an overreaction."

"The girl broke her wrist."

"Shit."

"Shit," Julie agreed.

"Did the girl have a Pilot?" Val asked, shredding a wet napkin.

"What does that have to do with anything? How would I know?"

"Why'd she get shoved?"

"Just a bully, I think."

Sophie stood in line at the sandwich shop. Val frowned. "There's no such thing as 'just a bully.'"

"I know, I know. I didn't mean it like that. Sophie made her point, though. I don't think it'll happen again."

"I guess we should be grateful we didn't raise a pushover."

"She's no pushover," agreed Julie.

Sophie returned to the table, balancing a tray with two sandwiches, a soda, and a water. Val reached across and snagged the cola, even though she didn't like the stuff.

"Hey!" said Sophie. "You wanted water."

"And you know you can't have soda after ice cream."

"You didn't say that. You said no burger and no pepperoni."

"And yet you could probably infer that for the same reasons you can't have sulfites, you also can't have caffeine."

"Seizures?"

"Bingo."

"But I haven't had a seizure in months."

"You haven't had a *bad* seizure in months," Val said. "We'd like to keep it that way, right?"

Sophie sighed. "Right." She lifted the water glass and eyed it with such a look of disgust that Val couldn't help but laugh.

"Why are we here again?" Val asked after they'd finished eating.

"Sophie needs new shoes."

"And a new jacket," Sophie added.

"We couldn't have gotten that someplace less chaotic?"

"This way we get it all over with at once."

Malls had always made Val claustrophobic. Nobody had any concept of personal space, and everything was too loud and too bright and too commercial. She wondered, not for the first time, if this was anything like the noise David talked about when he talked about his Pilot. Oversaturation, overstimulation, a thousand things demanding her attention, none of which were of any actual importance except the two people beside her, whom she would rather be spending time with anywhere else.

A gaggle of teenage girls pushed past, splitting her and Julie from Sophie, who was walking closer to the shop windows. "Watch it!" she said, though they were already past, giggling and absorbed, their Pilots glowing.

"Sorry, Ms. B!" someone called after her.

She glanced back to see who it was, though they were already too far past for her to tell. In the next moment, she realized Sophie was no longer beside them.

"Where's Sophie?" Julie asked at the same time. Guilt flooded Val. Distraction had taken her eyes off the girl.

"Hey!" somebody shouted from behind them. Val whirled to

follow the voice, which was followed by a crash. Sophie stood in front of a jewelry kiosk. Beaded necklaces had spilled from a tray onto the floor.

"Kid, what are you doing?" asked the woman running the cart, shaking Sophie's arm. "Security!"

Sophie trailed her fingers through the tray, knocking more necklaces onto the ground.

"She's having a seizure," Julie said. "Leave her alone a second, okay? Take your hand off her."

The vendor looked confused, but let go of Sophie, allowing Julie to put her body between the two of them. Forty slow seconds passed, according to Val's watch, though it felt like an hour, as always, before Sophie returned to herself and let Julie guide her to a bench.

Val knelt to gather the necklaces. One had broken, and she collected individual beads as she found them, dodging feet and stroller wheels. All they needed was for someone to slip on a bead and sue them. That would be the fitting end to this day.

"We'll pay for anything broken," she said, holding up the pieces. The woman nodded.

A security guard walked over. "Is there a problem?"

The vendor looked at Val, who had pulled out her wallet, and shook her head. "No problem. Sorry. False alarm."

Val winced at the price named for the overpriced beads, which the vendor presented in a gift bag. She carried it over to the bench where Julie and Sophie sat.

"New necklace for you." Val held out the bag.

Sophie opened it and frowned. "That's just loose beads."

"It can be a necklace again. We'll string it back together."

"That was the one I liked, actually." Sophie sighed. "I guess I fished my wish."

Julie rubbed Sophie's shoulders. "Next time, just ask, okay?"

Sophie stuck out her tongue.

"Do you still want to look for shoes and a jacket?" Val asked.

Sophie considered, then shook her head. "I think this day needs to be over. Another time?"

"We have to come back here again?"

"Maybe you don't have to come next time, Val. No reason this has to be a family field trip."

"We can decide later." As always, Val felt torn between wanting to do what the family was doing, and not wanting to be in the mall even a little bit.

That night, after Sophie was in bed, Val settled onto the couch to read. Julie appeared a minute later with her tablet and a cup of coffee. Her ability to drink caffeine at all hours was a constant source of amazement for Val.

"Nice relaxing family evening, huh?" Julie asked.

"Nothing like it," Val responded with a wry smile.

"There is nothing I hate more than that moment of wondering where she is."

"You spotted her before I did, though. I feel like I'm always a second behind you."

Julie lowered her cup and turned so her whole body faced Val. "Speaking of . . . I had something I've been wanting to ask you, but I wasn't sure how to do it."

"What's that?"

"What would you say if I said I wanted to get a Pilot?"

Val saw concern in her wife's eyes. Concern and . . . anticipation? Dread? Julie had no idea how long Val had been expecting this moment. "I would say do it if you need to do it. You know I don't like the things, and I can't understand why anyone would want one, but . . . I guess I can understand, kind of."

"I could watch Sophie better."

"That's today's reason. There are other reasons, too, right?"

Julie sighed. "Yeah. I'd like to be able to get more done. I see how effective Piloted people are and I want to be like that. The new kids at work can do twice what I can. I'm afraid of being left behind."

"You won't get left behind. You love your work, and Griffith loves you."

"Yeah, but he won't keep me if I'm not performing, and we can't live on one salary."

"Would you want one if you weren't worried about work?"

"Yeah, I would. I've wanted one since before we got David his. I've tried to be practical, but now I think I *am* being practical."

"Yeah. I understand," said Val, though she didn't, not really.

CHAPTER SEVENTEEN

SOPHIE

Sophie couldn't get away with anything. She used to be able to sneak into David's room when he had the door open. He'd be playing games and she'd curl up in his corner chair and wait for him to notice her. When he saw she was there he would be genuinely surprised, or at least he'd pretend to be. Sometimes he'd smile and let her play for a few minutes, or he'd pretend to be mad and toss her under his arm and drag her out, which was fun, too. She knew it was pretend because if he really didn't want her in there, he'd have closed the door. She respected closed doors, mostly.

Take today, for example. She'd been perfectly sneaky. She had dropped to her belly in the hallway outside his room, where he and Milo were playing some zombie-killing game. She made sure the moms weren't watching so they didn't assume she was having a seizure just because she was hanging out at floor level. That was the worst drag, beyond not being allowed to climb trees anymore: having people assume anything you did that was the least bit out of the ordinary must be a seizure. If she couldn't climb, you'd think they wouldn't have a problem with her crawling. That way she'd be on the ground already if the Big One hit. The Big One was a monster living in her head. It liked to sneak up on her the way she liked to sneak up on David.

She rounded the corner in silence, a snake in the grass, but she'd barely slithered an inch into his room when he said, "Out, Soph."

"Busted," said Milo.

Neither David nor Milo bothered to turn in her direction or pause their game. The lights glowed steady blue above their right ears. She didn't hate Pilots like her ma did, but it did make it impossible to surprise David. The snake slithered forward into the room.

"I mean it, Softserve. We don't need any distractions."

She sat, a cobra. "But I'm not a distraction. You aren't even pausing to talk to me."

"Just because I can play without pausing doesn't mean you're not a di—on your left, bro—distraction. Left! Left! You know which is your left hand, right? The weaker one?"

Milo took his left hand off the controller for a second to punch David in the arm. "Maybe if you didn't let so many get past you I wouldn't be back here cleaning up your mess."

The snake slithered from the room. His Pilot wouldn't let her distract him, but David and Milo kept talking in that weird aggressive zombie-hunter-speak. She didn't like when David's friends were around; he was different with them than he was with family.

Julie rounded the corner. "Sophie! Are you okay? What are you doing on the floor?"

She sighed. "I'm fine, Mom. Just playing."

Mom gave her a weird look but seemed to take her word for it.

"Are you bothering your brother? Why don't you go read a book?"

The snake formed legs. Evolved. Rolled its eyes in its most obvious fashion. She would be the most well-read kid in the history of fifth grade. That was all they ever wanted her to do, read books. She couldn't get hurt reading a book. Actually, she probably could, if the Big One came out to play. It could make her gash her head on the spine of a hardcover, or fall while she reached for a high shelf. If the Big One had its way, she would sit in the middle of a room full of pillows for the rest of her life. Her mothers would probably breathe relieved sighs, too. Maybe she was the only one who cared if she ever got to do anything.

She went to her room, trailing her hand along the smooth coolness of the wall as she walked. She wouldn't read; she had better things to do. David chased fake monsters in his video games, but she had a real one to kill.

She pulled her sketch pad and colored pencils from her desk. The Big One, as always, needed to be drawn in gray, graphite, 4B soft pencil. It took different shapeless shapes each time. When she figured out what it looked like, it changed again; that was how it kept ahead of her. She drew herself standing on top of it, stabbing it with a sword.

She rummaged in her desk, this time for her geometry compass. She used the sharp point, the one that was supposed to be the circle's center, to prick her pointer finger. One dot of blood welled up.

She couldn't remember ever having been squeamish about blood, though she didn't know which came first, the acceptance that she was a human pincushion or the fact of being a human pincushion. She'd heard other kids screaming and wailing, but it didn't do any good. They still got poked and prodded; might as well cooperate and earn a reputation as a good trouper.

She stared at the beading blood, trying to see where it ended and medication began. The doctors and nurses and moms always talked about titers and blood levels. They had done it for so long she'd begun to understand some of it. The medication she took every day by mouth somehow found its way into her blood. The right amount of the right medication would banish all her seizures forever, the Big One and the Small Ones and the Ones That Shall Not Be Named, but they hadn't found the right medication yet, or the right amount, or something.

She smeared blood into the graphite on the page, the skin and the fur and the sword wound, until the Big One was reddish-gray. Someday her blood would kill it dead, just like this. She tore the drawing out of her sketchbook and hid it in her secret box under her bed.

Back to the sketchbook, this time to draw a boy sniffing a rose with a bee in it. She tried to make the boy look like David, and the drawing look like a normal drawing her parents would laugh about if they went snooping. Nothing like the monsters under her bed.

"Dinner!"

First call meant the food was almost ready, but the first kid to appear got stuck setting the table. Normally Sophie would hang back and hope David beat her to the kitchen. She preferred cleaning afterward, so if she had a seizure and dropped something, she wasn't wasting any food or making people cranky. Today, because she'd been home all day, she decided it wouldn't hurt to look conscientious.

She considered slithering all the way downstairs, but she was starting to feel less snakelike, and any points she got for prompt arrival would cancel out if she acted weird. They'd decide she shouldn't help, and then David would get annoyed with her when he had to do it all. She missed their old chore chart, but David skipped so many dinners these days they'd abandoned the system. She also missed the old David who didn't get irritated, but her parents said he was just being a teenager.

"Dinner!" Val made the second call.

Sophie bounded into the kitchen before she lost the advantage of volunteering instead of being drafted. "I'm here! Four or five?"

"Four." Val was transferring pasta from the colander to a serving bowl and didn't look up. "Milo went home, I'm pretty sure."

Sophie took advantage of her ma's inattention and stepped on a chair to reach the plates. For days after a seizure, even a minor one like at the mall the day before, they always got extra protective. No standing on chairs. No reaching for heavy things. If her ma hadn't been concentrating on the food, she might not have even let Sophie carry plates or glasses to the table.

She did those first, plates and glasses, before anyone said she couldn't. Then the water pitcher from the fridge, then napkins. She did full silverware, in the proper order, just to show off, even though it was silly to put knives on the table when they were eating penne and salad.

"The table looks lovely, Soph. Thanks for helping." Ma carried the serving bowl to the dining room herself, before shouting "Dinner!" for the third time.

"For real!" Sophie added, to be helpful.

Julie came in from the living room. Sophie wasn't allowed to bring a tablet into the dining room, but Mom put hers on the floor in the corner before Sophie had a chance to point it out. David still hadn't come down.

"I thought the Pilot was supposed to make him able to pay attention to more things at once," Sophie said.

Ma sighed. "He's eighteen. Just because he can hear us doesn't mean he thinks it applies to him. Sophie, I'd love it if you skip past the whole teenager attitude phase."

"I'll try," Sophie said. She was serious, but both her parents laughed. "I'll go get him."

"Be careful on the stairs," Ma said.

Sophie knew how to show teenage attitude. She could have said, *Thanks for the concern. I was going to climb the stairs on stilts, but now I'll walk.* Instead, she pretended she hadn't heard. She took the stairs two at a time, since nobody was looking, holding the railing as a small concession. Attitude or no attitude, she tried to remember they were looking out for her. If the Big One came for her when she was on the stairs, she really would get hurt, but she didn't feel it lurking.

Before she even knocked on his door, David said, "Come in."

She peeked her head in. He was playing a different game. No zombies, but warrior angel things.

"How did you know I was here? I was quiet."

"There's a creaky floorboard."

Maybe that was how he'd caught her sneaking earlier; she'd have to figure out which one it was for future reference. "Dinnertime. It looks pretty edible."

He punched a couple of angels, then paused the game and smiled at her. "Okay, let's go, Softserve."

The smile made up for his use of her least favorite nickname. She never realized how much she missed him being nice to her until he was nice to her.

They ate dinner and chatted about everyone's day. Nobody mentioned Sophie's suspension. She said she had read more of *Johnny Tremain* for school and part of *Powers* for fun. They were encouraging. *Way to read your life away, Soph.*

When everyone had gotten a turn to talk, Julie said, "I have something else to discuss."

They all looked at her and waited.

"I'm getting a Pilot."

Sophie wished for one second she had a Pilot herself in order to take in everybody's reaction at once. She was watching Mom because Mom was talking, so she missed David and Ma. When she turned to them, David looked curious but not surprised, and Ma's face was guarded, with no surprise showing, either. Mom said it was a discussion, but she also said "I'm getting," not "I'm thinking of getting," so they probably had talked about it already, and this was the formal Telling the Kids.

She remembered something her ma had said to her once, that someday she and Sophie would be among the only ones without Pilots. She didn't think Ma had meant this soon, but it was already pretty true. Most classes at school were divided between Pilots and non-Pilots, with the non-Pilots being mostly kids like her, with seizures or intellectual disabilities or autism or other things that made them "unlikely candidates," and one or two with religious objections. There wasn't even a rich-poor divide since the company covered them for kids unable to afford the procedure; the divide was between approved brains and unapproved brains and degrees of acceptable neurodiversity.

Nobody had said anything yet, so Sophie asked the only question that came to her head. "Why?" She understood the reason for kids, but didn't get what was in it for a grown-up.

Her mom looked grateful that somebody had said something.

"It'll be useful for work. There are a lot of people in my office who have them now and I'd like to keep up."

Val looked at her, and she added, "Not that I couldn't do the work without a Pilot."

Sophie knew that last part was for her benefit.

David looked up from his pasta. "It sounds like you're telling us, not asking us. I'm okay with it either way. Just remember what a hard time you both gave me when I wanted mine."

Julie nodded. "Noted."

David cleared the table after dinner. Both parents had gone to the living room, but Sophie lingered. "Do you want me to dry?"

"Sure," he said, smiling as he turned on the tap. She grabbed a towel and stood on one leg while she waited, like a flamingo.

David eyed her. "That's not some weird new seizure, is it?"

She shook her head, trying to keep her balance.

"Y'know, Soph, if Mom is getting a Pilot it's going to mean some changes for both of us."

"What do you mean?"

He handed her the colander to dry and lowered his voice. "You know how I can play a game but know where you are in the room? Imagine if Mom can do that. No sneaking. It'll be harder to get away with anything."

"What do we get away with?"

"That's the thing. You don't know how much you get away with until suddenly somebody is watching and listening all the time. If she had a Pilot she'd look like she was reading but she'd be listening to us at the same time."

"If she had super hearing. She's two rooms away."

He splashed her. "True. I'm just saying things might get stricter, even if that's not her plan. I know they're already strict with you."

Sophie swatted David with the towel to make up for the splash, then nodded. What he said made sense, but more important, for the first time in ages it felt like he was taking her seriously.

CHAPTER EIGHTEEN

SOPHIE

Kevin Boatman caught Sophie after English on the day she went back to school. "What was it like?"

Sophie shrugged. "My mom worked from home and made me sit on the couch and read. Not that different."

"Why would they think suspension is punishment? I'd rather be anywhere than school."

Sophie didn't mind school, but she didn't disagree. It hadn't felt like a punishment, especially since her parents weren't mad at her.

She glanced down the hallway and saw the girls from Monday at a distance. She fought the urge to run back into the classroom, but the tall girl—Tonya—had a cast on her arm, and that gave Sophie courage. Not that she would hurt anybody on purpose, but she felt proud she hadn't let herself be pushed around.

"Hey, Slow Boat!" Tonya had spotted her. She and her friends strode toward Sophie and Kevin.

"That's not my name," said Sophie. Her heart beat faster. Hadn't everyone said she wouldn't have to deal with that anymore? Wasn't Tonya supposed to respect her or be scared of her or something?

"You broke my wrist, bitch."

Sophie had heard the word before, but nobody had ever called her one. It stung like a slap, but the slap reminded her of something. "I didn't mean to hurt you. You guys started it."

Tonya stepped toe to toe with Sophie. Sophie wondered if the other girl was going to club her with her cast. She looked for a teacher, but didn't see one. Figured.

"Slow Boat, I don't care what you meant to do. You're not even a person as far as I'm concerned. You and your friends in your slow class are so sad, trying to keep up with the rest of us. Why don't you drop out? You'll never get through school without help. We're the new humans and you are unevolved."

The word "unevolved" reminded her of her sneaking snake from two days before, and Tonya reminded her of the Big One. Not the seizure itself, which she never remembered, but the sensation of something looming, waiting, ready to bring her down. At least Tonya was here in front of her, a monster she could defeat.

Sophie wanted to take a step away, but she knew she'd better stand her ground. She swung her backpack off her shoulder and fished in the front pocket for her geometry compass without lowering her eyes. When she found it she dropped her bag to the floor.

She lifted her compass. Tonya stepped back, and Sophie smiled. "Who hasn't evolved? You have a device in your head, that's all. My brother has one. One of my moms is getting one. No big deal. You know what's a big deal?"

She paused for effect, then jabbed the compass point into her left thumb. Blood welled. She didn't flinch. She stabbed the next finger, and the next.

Sophie smiled. "I can't feel pain. You said I'm not even a person. So ask yourself: Am I someone you want to pick a fight with?"

She dropped the compass back into her bag in case a teacher appeared and accused her of using it as a weapon. Blood trickled between her fingers. A little, but enough. She kept her hand in front of her.

Tonya turned to her friends. "Come on. She's crazy." She

walked away without saying another word to Sophie; the others followed in her wake.

Sophie watched them leave. She smiled when they turned the corner, and dug in her bag for a tissue to wipe the blood off her hand. Would her mothers have approved? She hadn't hurt anybody, and she hadn't gotten in any trouble. She wondered what those girls were saying about her. *Crazy? Freak?* She preferred "warrior." She might not be able to beat the Big One yet, but at least she had used it to her own benefit for once. She had to admit she liked the feeling.

CHAPTER NINETEEN

SOPHIE

Sophie waved at the driver as the school bus drove away. It had taken her ages to convince her mothers to let her take the bus. She was supposed to go straight inside, but instead she walked to the end of the block and sat on the low stone wall that curved around the corner. A pair of mourning doves landed across the street and began pecking at the fallen chokeberries that stained the sidewalk. They were pretty birds, elegant and soft-looking. Her mom said they were basically pigeons, but she liked them anyway.

A car sped by and honked at her. The doves flew off making sounds like squeaky wheels. She waved, though she hadn't seen the driver. Her family had lived in the neighborhood for her whole life; even if she didn't recognize the person in the car, they probably recognized her, which meant she should get home before she got in trouble. She didn't want to get in trouble; she just liked carving out a few minutes where she wasn't watched. A few minutes where a stranger might think she was a regular kid allowed to play on her street alone.

She dug in her pocket and found a button she'd pulled off her shirt during a seizure, thirty-five cents, and her house keys. When she let herself in, she found her mom asleep on the couch by the front window. There was a shaved patch and a bandage on the side of her head.

Sophie hadn't expected this to happen so quickly. She took the moment to look more carefully than she usually could. Even parents found it odd when you stared at them too closely.

Julie looked tired and peaceful. She wore a checkered skirt that reached just below her knees, leggings, and a rumpled white blouse. Around-the-house clothes, not work clothes. Two dots of blood marred her shirt's right shoulder, one small and the other smaller. A sun and a planet, or a planet and a moon.

Sophie found the two dots comforting, proof that a Pilot was not as easy as everyone pretended. It was an operation, even if a minor one. An operation involving drills and bone and blood and brain. People with Pilots weren't so different from her; she wished they could see that.

"Hey, Soph. I didn't hear you come in." Her ma came around the kitchen corner. She spoke in a quiet voice. "How was your day?"

"Okay."

Sometimes answering "okay" meant she had to answer follow-up questions, but Ma just kissed her on the head. That meant she was free to go upstairs. She surprised herself by lingering.

"She did it, huh?" Sophie looked over at the sleeping figure on the couch. Ma looked over, too, and nodded.

"Just like you said she would," Sophie said.

Ma turned up one corner of her mouth. "I didn't know you remembered that."

"I remember it exactly. You said everyone was going to have a Pilot except you and me, and we would be okay without them, even when everyone else has them."

Ma pulled the elastic from her hair, then smoothed it back and redid her ponytail. "That's exactly what I said. Did you believe me?"

Sophie shrugged. "I didn't understand what you meant when you said it."

"But now you do." It wasn't a question.

"Yeah."

"I still believe it, Soph. It'll be okay."

"I know."

"You and me, right?"

"Right." Sophie hugged her ma, then headed upstairs. At the top she turned and looked back. Ma still stood in the same place, looking at Mom. Maybe she saw the blood spots, too.

CHAPTER TWENTY

VAL

Julie didn't suffer the same foreboding that had plagued David in the month between Pilot installation and activation. If anything, Val thought she looked impatient. Val, meanwhile, found herself trying to savor the days. She tried not to think of them as leading to some cliff, some unscalable before and after. David's personality hadn't changed; she had no reason to think Julie wouldn't still be her Julie.

And yet she still found herself running extra miles in the morning, trying to excavate some new pit in her stomach. She climbed back into bed after showering, taking extra time to wrap herself in her wife's familiar body. When they reached for each other that night, she tried not to acknowledge her fear that she'd never have Julie's undivided attention again.

"You're somewhere else," Julie said, running her fingertips over the curve of Val's hip. Irony of ironies. Then, because Julie always knew what she was thinking: "You know, the Pilot will make me more able to focus, not less."

"I know—sorry. I'm here, I promise. Let me show you."

She didn't want anything to change.

She took an afternoon off to drive Julie to her activation. She had been there for David's installation but not his activation, so she didn't know what to expect. The same waiting room, the same current magazines, the same strange fresh-baked-cookie smell.

"Do you want me to go in with you?" she asked, eyeing the same mahogany door.

Julie shook her head. "I don't think so. You'll make me nervous. Remember our first date?"

Val laughed despite herself. The thing they called their first date had started out as a trip to a county fair with a group of mutual friends. They'd been flirting all night, with Julie daring Val to go on rides Val thought looked too rickety to be safe, and to try the deep-fried beer, which she hated and drowned in regular beer. It had taken Val the entire night to find something Julie didn't want to do: the House of Horror.

"I don't like being scared," she'd said. "I get jumpy when I'm nervous."

"Chicken!" Finally, Val had a way to turn the cute girl's taunting around. A Tilt-A-Whirl with a loose bolt could kill you, and what if it had been damaged on the ride from one fair to the next, but haunted houses were a place to let go of your worries, to erase and replace them with a delicious mindless terror divorced from real life.

Except Val was standing too close behind Julie when some carny in a Leatherface costume stepped from the shadows, and Julie, as promised, jumped. Her head collided with Val's lip, which collided with Val's front tooth. Blood everywhere, real blood, which made Leatherface faint, and the House of Horror had to be closed temporarily to hose off the real blood. Lips and scalps both bleed an awful lot.

Julie drove them to the emergency room—they told their friends not to waste their evening going with them—and they each got seven stitches, which they both thought was a lucky number despite the circumstances. They'd since been in hospitals together far more than they'd expected, far more than they'd have preferred, but the family joke was not to make Julie nervous.

Julie looked at the door, and Val turned her face to hide the tears. This was the last time Val could hope Julie didn't notice her tears. She already had trouble hiding her feelings; now she wouldn't be more obvious, but Julie would be more observant. Either way. Before and after. Val leaned over and kissed her, trying not to think this was the last Before kiss.

She couldn't point to anything different on the way home. Julie looked out the window, backseat driving from the passenger seat. That was usual. Julie chatted with her, her hand occasionally drifting up to touch the spot above her ear. That was usual for this past month, though it always reminded Val of when David had first gotten his Pilot. If anything was different, it was that Julie was a little extra talkative, overanimated.

"Do you feel different?" Val asked.

"Yes. More awake? Alert. Like some people describe too much coffee, but not in a bad way." Caffeine never affected Julie.

"Is it like David says? Noisy?"

Julie closed her eyes like she was consulting something inside her own head. "No. I wouldn't use that word."

Val took a deep breath. "Do you still love me?" She meant this to sound lighthearted, but as it came out of her mouth it sounded scared to her own ears.

She glanced over at Julie, who frowned. "Of course I still love you. You know this could never change that."

"Sorry. I know I'm being silly."

Julie took her hand and held it until Val needed it to make the turn onto their street. She felt foolish for it, but the fear didn't dissipate. There was no before, she told herself. There was no after. She'd get used to the blue light. She couldn't even see it from the driver's seat. They were fine.

She found it bizarre to watch her wife do the same exercises David had done. Times tables while doing crossword puzzles, head patting and stomach rubbing, repeating phrases Val supplied while she read about something else entirely. That weird heist game, when Julie had never gone for video games.

Val hated it. "How is this better than when we used to complain about people checking their phones while holding a conversation?"

"It's better because I'm able to pay attention completely to what you're saying, even though I don't look like it." Julie didn't look away from her tablet.

"Can we try it the other way around, then?" She knew she sounded petulant. "Can you look at me while we talk, and make the tablet think you're ignoring it?"

Julie frowned. "These are exercises. I won't do this to you once I've got the hang of it, but I'm still learning."

Val sighed. "I know. Sorry. Back to the script. 'Sally sells seashells by the seashore.'"

"Sally sells seashells by the seashore. I wonder how that's going in this economy?"

"Not much market for seashells these days?"

"If there ever was."

If she weren't so opposed to getting a Pilot herself, she could draft her student progress reports while reciting these stupid tongue twisters. She supposed that was her own fault, or her own decision at least.

"Spoons?" Julie asked, surprising Val. She had never been the first one to suggest family games, either; she usually preferred movies.

"If you can convince the kids."

"Oh, they'll play. I can be persuasive."

Whatever she said worked. First Sophie, then David, came down from their rooms, quicker than Val would have expected.

"To what do we owe this pleasure?" Sophie walked past them into the kitchen, returning with three spoons for the bare table.

"I was just thinking it's been a while," said Julie, watching David. "And it may be a while before we get to do something all together again."

David winced. "I'm going back upstairs if you're going to guilt me."

"Stay. No guilt." Val kissed the non-Piloted side of his head.

"I'll deal first." Julie held her own cards in her left hand, dealing from the deck with her right. Val, in the fourth position, had a chance to watch. Julie had an expression on her face that Val didn't recognize, a half smile that suggested amusement. The cards passed from her to Sophie, who passed them along without looking, her eyes on the spoons, as usual. Then to David, on the edge of his seat, all concentration.

David was the first to reach for a spoon, but Julie's hand darted out almost simultaneously, and came away faster. Sophie and Val both grabbed at the third spoon, but Val got there first.

"Wait," said Sophie. "Who had it?"

David fanned out four sixes.

Sophie frowned. "But Mom took a spoon before you. Mom, what did you have?"

"Nothing yet. I saw David reaching, so I took a spoon, too."

"But you took before him. You can't take the first spoon if you don't have the cards."

"Fine. I'll take the s, kid. I didn't mean to cheat." Julie threw her spoon back on the table.

"I didn't think so." Sophie accepted the win with magnanimity, scooping the cards toward her to shuffle. Julie won the next round, and David the one after, but each time, Val could swear Julie's hand reached out quicker. There was a hitch in the movement: she reached, then pulled back, slightly, to not get there first.

That was why she'd chosen this game, Val realized: to test her new implant. Julie holding back didn't take away from the game. Sophie still grabbed for the spoons every time, David still tried to find the winning hand, and Val still took more pleasure in watching everyone interacting with one another than in the game, which, truth be told, she found more stressful than fun.

CHAPTER TWENTY-ONE

JULIE

And just like that, David was gone. Julie blinked and the last few months with him evaporated. She had tried to savor them, to follow Val's lead and not complain when he wanted to hang out with his friends instead of them. She played it casual, while on the inside she was screaming and clinging to him. She didn't care what Fuentes said: David was still a boy; her boy.

She might have gone overboard. She forced him to write polite letters to the schools that had accepted him, then kept them in her purse until the last possible day to mail them, still hoping he'd change his mind.

He didn't. If anything, he got more into the idea. He ran every day, sometimes with Val and sometimes farther and faster than her. He lifted weights in his room, EarPods blasting at obscene levels that he paradoxically said chased away some of what he called noise, while studying for final exams. Fuentes had made it clear to him he couldn't blow off his classes, at least.

Graduation was a surreal experience. The sight of the auditorium full of boys in black caps and gowns, all with a pearl of blue above one ear, nearly bowled her over. She wondered how many of them had enlisted.

Then he was gone, leaving a David-shaped hole in their lives. They all compensated by spending more time with one another.

Sophie, who had become fairly independent, asked for a night-light and refused to go to epilepsy camp that summer. It was only in August that she told them she hadn't gone to camp because she didn't think they were ready to be alone. They had laughed, and Sophie had been offended, and in the end Julie had to admit Sophie was right. They weren't ready to be alone.

It was good she had the Pilot, since otherwise she would have found herself spending all of her time—time meant for work—trying to figure out anything she could about David's unit. She was upset and glad at the same time that she couldn't find much. It meant the program really was being kept low-key, which meant it really must have some importance.

They talked with David on the rare occasions he was allowed to talk. He always looked happy to see them, but distracted, like they'd caught him at a bad time, when he'd been the one to call.

"Are you eating well?" she asked him, sounding like her own grandmother.

"Are you getting enough sleep?" Val asked, sounding like her father.

"When you come home will you take me to the Renaissance Faire without the moms?" Sophie asked, then added for their bene-fit, "No offense."

What felt like seconds later, he'd apologize and go, leaving them staring at a blank screen, their questions mostly unanswered, even more unasked.

CHAPTER TWENTY-TWO

VAL

The David they met at the airport looked like the expanded director's cut of the David who had left.

"You're taller!" Sophie threw herself into his arms.

He caught her like she weighed nothing and hugged her back.
"You, too, Softserve."

"Only an inch. I'm still short for my age."

Sophie was right. He'd grown a lot. Not just taller, but broader,
with wider shoulders and better posture and a more angular adult
face superimposing itself on the boy face. In the calls he always sat
close, leaning into the screen so they saw him from the shoulders
up; the differences in person were striking. When Val took her
turn for a hug, she had to stretch. He had been her height, five feet
ten, when he left.

"You're solid muscle," she said, squeezing an arm.

Julie didn't stretch. "C'mere, boy." She reached up and pulled
him to her level, kissing the top of his head. "I'm so happy you're
home."

He looked around. "Not home yet. Unless we've moved to the
airport?"

"Surprise!" said Julie. "Do you want a gate for a bedroom, or
the chapel?"

"How about baggage claim? I could sleep on the belt, round and round." He circled his finger in the air.

Julie pointed to the conveyor, crowded with luggage. "You'd have to dodge bags."

"And people would watch you while you slept," said Val.

"And people aren't allowed on the belt. It says so." Sophie got the final word.

David grinned at her. "Good point. Wouldn't want to get in trouble. I guess I'd rather go back to the house, if I can't live on the baggage claim. Where's the car?" He shouldered his duffel and stood at loose attention.

"E6," said Julie. "We've got some walking to do."

"Yes, ma'am." He fell into line behind her, grabbing Sophie's shoulders and making her shriek. Val followed, enjoying the sight of the two kids together.

"Isn't it past your bedtime?" David asked his sister as they walked toward the skyway.

"I'm allowed to stay up 'til nine thirty these days."

"Nine thirty? That's pretty late. But it's past eleven now."

"I wanted to see you."

"You could have seen me in the morning."

"Yeah, but that would be different. I didn't want to wait."

Sophie fell asleep in the car on the way home, her head against the window. Val watched her in the vanity mirror, then shifted it again and caught David's face instead. He smiled.

She smiled back. "Just checking that you're really here."

"I'm here," he said. "For a couple of weeks, anyway."

"We'll take what we can get," said Julie from the driver's seat. "I imagine some of your friends are off partying somewhere instead of going home."

"Yeah. Milo's in New Orleans, but I needed a break from the South. I can't believe I complained summers here were hot and sticky."

"Summers here are hot and sticky," said Julie. "But there are definitely hotter and stickier places."

"Yeah, I know that now. And it's good practice, I guess."

"Good practice?"

"Yeah, for deployment."

Val's heart dropped into her stomach.

It didn't take a Pilot to catch that Julie had stiffened and swerved slightly before tightening her hands on the wheel. "I thought you weren't supposed to be deployed."

"Everybody gets deployed, Mom. It's a matter of when."

"That Fuentes guy said control rooms, not battlefields." Julie's voice carried a knife edge.

"They have control rooms over there, too, Mom, but everyone takes a turn."

"Where is over there?" Val asked, watching Julie watch the road. "And when?"

"When I get back. I can't tell you where. Look, I—"

"For how long?"

"A year."

Val's breath left her. Could she hold her breath for a year? She'd find out.

David leaned forward between them. He'd outgrown this car's back seat; his knees bumped Val's seat and his head brushed the roof. "I didn't want to tell you until later. I wanted a nice visit home, no worry or fuss. Can we still do that?"

"Yeah." Julie wiped a hand across her eyes. Val didn't say anything.

"Do you want me to tell the squirt? Or do you want to tell her?"

Julie said, "We can do it together, Davey, but maybe you were right about waiting 'til the end of the visit. Don't ruin it for her."

Val shifted the mirror to look at Sophie again, but she was sound asleep. For a moment, she envied the kid; she would have liked to miss this conversation, too. David was right. The whole visit was going to be tarnished, even more than it had been already. She envisioned a countdown clock, then blinked it away.

She could lock him in the basement, keep him from leaving.

They could move to Canada. She could say those things alone to Julie, who would recognize them for what they were. David would misinterpret them, think she wasn't proud of him, or wanted to keep him a child forever, though that wasn't it. She didn't wish him to stay a child, and she knew she couldn't keep him safe. She just wanted to protect him.

"I know what you mean," Julie said when Val voiced it later that night. They spoke with low voices, in case David was still awake. "It's like, we don't need to keep him bubble-wrapped, but did he have to pick such a dangerous career?"

"Maybe he's making up for having been such a trouble-less kid."

"And in fairness, I don't think he picked it."

Val frowned. "He picked the Army. Though I'm not sure he did it because he wanted to do something dangerous, so much as because he thought it was his only good option?"

"Why should that have been his only option?"

"The thing he talks about—the noise . . ."

Julie waved it away. "I've never figured out what that was about. He looks happier than he's looked in a long time."

"I guess. It's just maybe we should have tried harder to help him with that, or to help him figure out what came next, so he didn't go off and make this decision on his own."

"We did try. You ran with him. We had a million conversations about what he might want to study, and visited a million schools, and helped him with a million essays. What more were we supposed to do?"

"Maybe we should have asked."

"Maybe, but I'm not sure he would have answered."

Val wished she thought that were true.

CHAPTER TWENTY-THREE

SOPHIE

Sophie heard all kinds of things if she pretended to sleep. That was how she'd found out she wasn't a candidate for brain surgery, and how she'd learned the phrase "intractable seizures." Sometimes she understood the things she overheard. Sometimes someone explained later or she looked up words, and the mysteries sorted into neat boxes.

All in all, her parents were pretty good about telling the truth, but often it took a while. They talked it out between themselves before telling her, even when it was something that concerned her. The "brain surgery" conversation took place in her hospital room. "Intractable" in the car. The two best places to learn things were on the couch when they were talking in the dining room, or pretending to sleep in the back seat.

When she was little she would add in the occasional fake snore, but she had since taken a theater class and learned that the trick to acting was not overacting. "Most people playing drunk exaggerate," the teacher had said. "Real drunk people try hard to come across sober." Sophie thought that was an odd thing to explain to middle schoolers, but she filed that information away, too.

The hardest part was when she overheard something major and knew they were never going to tell her. Money stuff. Money stuff because of her. Seizure stuff they thought she wasn't ready for. It was about her; why wouldn't she want to hear it? She deserved to know.

Now the thing David said—that he was being deployed. She already knew the word; they used it in school when discussing current events. How long did they plan to keep this from her? David had said he wanted to wait until the end of the visit, and Julie had supported that, and Val hadn't said anything. David had called her "squirt," too, like she was a baby. It was one thing to have your parents lie to you; another when it was your brother.

What else had he not told her? Sometimes she hated being so much younger than David. It had always been cool having an older brother; she had counted on him to look out for her, even if he'd pretended she bugged him when his friends were around. Now he'd come back acting like a grown-up, and she was stuck as the only kid. If that was how it was going to be, she was going to make sure it was hard for them.

"I'm glad you're here," she whispered to David when he nudged her awake to go into the house. "I missed you."

The truth, exaggerated for maximum effect.

The next morning, Saturday, Sophie was all smiles. Some of her mood was legit and some was an act. Once she started smiling, it was hard to figure out where one ended and the other began, but she was both happy and mad, and she would let only the happy show.

It didn't help that David was already downstairs making French toast. French toast was her favorite, and she never got to have it. Ma would make it too healthy, hiding vegetables in the batter. Mom would research a dozen recipes online, maybe buy the ingredients, then abandon the project before she ever got around to cooking. David had started the coffee machine, too. She loved how coffee smelled and hated the taste.

"I missed you," she said again to David, still calculating truth to sting. She sat at the end of the table where she could watch him at the counter.

David mixed batter. He smiled without turning. "You missed me, or you missed French toast?"

"Both." Truthful again.

"I'm going to have to use that gross sprouted bread. It's the only one in the house."

Sophie made a face. "Will that work? Peanut butter bounces off it."

"I'll make it work."

"I could go to the store and get real bread. Fake bread. Whichever is which. The other one."

He turned, a surprised look on his face. "Are you allowed to go to the store on your own now?"

"No, but I could do it." Sophie shrugged.

"Somehow I thought they'd go easier on you if I wasn't here. I don't know why I thought that."

"Me, neither. It's the same. I can't go anywhere on my own. I think they would have me sleep on their bedroom floor like a dog if I was willing."

"Why aren't you?" David pulled a slice of bread from the bag and dunked it in the batter. He poked at it, pushing it deeper.

"Why aren't I what?"

"Willing to sleep on their floor? Woof woof?" He scratched an imaginary flea from behind his ear with his hand.

Sophie looked for something to throw at his head, but didn't spot anything and settled for a "Jerk."

Julie stumbled into the kitchen. She grabbed a mug from the cabinet, filled it with coffee. Fingers wrapped around the warm mug, she slid into the seat opposite Sophie but turned the chair to see both kids. "Who's a jerk? Not the boy who made me coffee?"

"Nobody," said Sophie, remembering at the last second her plan to smile through the morning. "David's making French toast."

"Trying to," he said with a frown. "Are we sure this is bread and not shingles left over from redoing the roof?"

Julie made air quotes. "I call it 'breadish.' Make do, or go buy something else, but if you buy, you have to explain to your ma why you're bringing processed flour products into the house."

"Because they make better French toast? Nah, I think this'll work. I'll just soak it longer. And it's going to need a lot of syrup."

"Nooooo," said Sophie in mock despair. "Not lots of syrup. Anything but that."

She crossed to the fridge, grabbed the jug of syrup, and returned to the table with it. The handle was sticky, and she put her knuckle in her mouth where it had touched. It was hard staying angry when she had real things to smile about. *They're lying*, she reminded herself. *Treating you like a kid like they always do.*

She spotted a rubber band on the table and shot it at David's back. "Ow!" he said, though it couldn't have hurt at that distance. "What was that for?"

"Before," she said sweetly.

The kitchen started to smell like cinnamon and nutmeg and something else she couldn't name that she had smelled before, like déjà vu perfume.

"No," Sophie said. "No, no, no."

Mom and David both turned to look at her.

"I'm fine," she said. Unless she didn't say it.

She ⎯⎯ⵊⵊⵊⵊⵊⵊ⎯⎯

Mom's face was too close to hers and David stood behind Mom and something sizzled somewhere (on the stove) (French toast) (David was making French toast) (David had left the French toast to sizzle because he was over here because why because she must have had another stupid seizure) (What kind of seizure? Not the Big One because they were near her but not on top of her and she wasn't on the floor and they looked like they were waiting for her to say something and why? Because she must have had a seizure). (Say something.)

Mom bit her lip and smiled. "Hang on, honey. You had a seizure."

Gather the words. "I'm okay. I'm okay."

She stood and walked into the living room. Not with any thought behind it. Following her feet. Something was burning.

"Shit!" said David.

The scrape of a chair told her Mom was following her. She wished they'd get that she needed a few minutes alone. They couldn't help it, though. Bad Things Could Happen, they always said, at the same time as saying *There's no reason you can't live a perfectly normal life.* Contradiction, she thought, pleased her brain had picked such a large round word and that she knew what it was and it was the right word. If she pushed for other words they would come in a minute. She sat on the couch and waited for her head to clear.

"Deployed," she said, trying another word a minute later. It didn't have the same balance as "contradiction." The *p* and the *y* facing each other in the middle of the word were ugly. An ugly word. A word with a "ploy" in the middle. She knew what a ploy was; it was a plan, but a tricky one. She didn't feel like pretending anymore. All of a sudden it was like a bad taste in her mouth, all the fake smiles. Game over.

"What, honey?" Mom riffled through the mail on the front table, but Sophie knew she was there to keep an eye on her.

"Deployed," she said again. "David's going away and you were all going to lie to me about it."

Sophie watched her mom squirm. Lie about lying? Tell the truth about lying? Even if her own head weren't jumbled, that would jumble it again.

"We were going to tell you, but why ruin your enjoyment of the time together with counting the days?"

"I'd be counting the days in any case. He was going to leave either way. The difference is where he's leaving to and that nobody thought I deserved to be told."

Her mom didn't respond, which meant she was right.

"Breakfast?" The note of question in David's voice didn't speak well for its edibility. It didn't matter. Sophie was hungry or maybe not hungry. She headed back into the kitchen. At least David's idea had been to hold out on all of them; equal-opportunity lies were better than lies that excluded only her.

"Sorry, Soph. We shouldn't keep things from you." Her mom's voice called her back.

"You don't have to baby me."

"I'll try to remember, sweetie. I'm sorry."

Sophie nodded, but she knew it would happen again. That was how it went when you were the youngest.

CHAPTER TWENTY-FOUR

VAL

David vanished into the terminal.

"You can just drop me at the airport. No need to stay," he'd said. "That way you won't get stuck in morning rush hour."

No need, but what if they had wanted to? An airport good-bye is for everyone, the leaver and the left. Val would gladly have followed him in, all the way to security, but instead she hugged him curbside at his insistence and watched the automatic doors swallow him. He turned once to wave at her, grinning. It was too broad a smile, and she was pretty sure he'd put it on for both their benefit; he was telling himself everything was fine, too.

She had trouble reconciling the soldier with the careful, thoughtful boy who had looked out for his sister and run with Val and worked out his math homework at the table with Julie. Nobody gained that much confidence in a few months. It had to be a facade. A car horn honked and she turned to see if she was blocking anyone; when she turned back, he was gone.

For all Val's appreciation of running in silence, this was not a silence she could tolerate. She wished Sophie were there to break through the quiet with something funny or random. Kid excitement, that was what she wanted, but the kid had refused to come.

"I don't like good-byes," she had said. "And anyway, he'll be back to visit as soon as he can."

Val frowned. "But what if he feels bad that you're not there?"

"Don't guilt her." Julie looked up. "I'll stay with her. You take Davey."

"You don't want to go to the airport?"

"Of course I do, but Sophie doesn't, and we can't leave her home."

"You can leave me alone. I don't mind. I can get ready for school on my own."

"No way, buster."

"Maybe she can go to a friend's house? Lisa West?"

Julie shook her head, and Val remembered that Lisa's parents had taken the girls ice-skating the previous winter, and Sophie had gone down on the ice. They didn't get the full details of what type of seizure it had been, but she'd fallen without protecting her hands or her head from the other skaters who didn't have time to avoid her, and returned with a bruised chin and cuts that went clear through her gloves. The Wests had assured them they understood what to do if Sophie had a seizure, but knowing in theory wasn't the same as seeing one for the first time.

"Lisa doesn't invite me over anymore." Sophie echoed Val's memory.

So Julie and Sophie had gotten up in the dark to say their good-byes at the house, and Val had driven David, and now there was too much silence in the car, threatening to leave her alone with her thoughts. She jabbed at the radio until she found a talk radio host so reprehensible she could focus on hating him instead of the people who had taken her son away. Except nobody had taken him; he'd gone willingly. He had chosen, but who lets an eighteen-year-old make a choice like that? They aren't ready. They don't have the sense.

She pressed buttons again until she found a song she'd heard her students play. She turned it up and sang along at the top of her lungs, inventing the words she didn't know, which was all of them.

Singing made her feel a little better, not anywhere near right, but better. When she got to school, she remembered it was a charity fundraiser day, and those were always entertaining, too, as the different homerooms derived new and interesting ways to earn donations off their fellow students.

Her homeroom girls' fundraiser involved a narwhal costume they'd found in the theater closet. "It'll only work if you do it, Ms. B," someone had said. She had promised that if they raised enough money, she would spend one lunch hour—just one—standing in the lobby in the costume. She hadn't considered it was a Friday, and she would be sharing the lobby not only with the other fundraiser tables—the bake sales and the various o-grams—but also with the recruiters.

If that wasn't enough, the recruiters had set up their table directly beside hers, forcing her to stand next to the handsome young man in his Air Force dress uniform. He was stunning, really; no wonder they sent him to the girls' school. By the time four juniors had stammered their way through conversations with him in which he gallantly held up the other end, seemingly oblivious to their awkward flirtation, she'd had enough.

"So," she said in a lull between students, "Do you get a cash bonus for bringing in a certain number? A car?"

"I'm sorry?" He looked confused.

Maybe it was her costume; she lacked gravitas. "Bonuses? Quotas? You must have target numbers."

"My priority is to give our best and brightest an opportunity to serve their country." He threw a look at the Army recruiter to his right, a prim young woman who couldn't have been much older than the students.

Val felt as if somebody else were speaking through her. They were all words she wanted to say, but she couldn't believe she was saying them out loud. She raised her voice, as her parents had done, as she'd promised herself never to do. "What are you here to do? Lie to my students? Tell them they'll be safe and then send them halfway around the world to get shot at?"

Students watched, whispering to one another. She saw someone raise a phone: they were being recorded. She knew she should stop.

The Air Force guy clearly realized they were being recorded, too. Had probably realized it long before she had, thanks to his Pilot. She was shouting and he was calm, though his perfect smile had faded. "Ma'am, we aren't lying to anybody. We offer opportunities. Financial opportunities, career opportunities. I'm not sure what you're upset about, but I've never done anything to you."

A single tear rolled down Val's face as she struggled to keep her temper under control. She hated confrontation; hated even more that she cried when she was angry. Better to run it off than turn and face someone, yet here she was. "You people rolled into my son's school and told him you were his best chance to succeed. He believed you. You said he'd be safe and far from the action and now he's being deployed."

"Ma'am, we don't lie to the students." Air Force had a new look on his face. Sympathy, maybe, or else pity. "I promise. You can ask anyone I've spoken with. We make sure they understand the risks. They decide if it's worth it."

Army joined him. "Are you sure he was lied to? What if your son was just trying to make you feel better about his decision?"

"Now you're calling David a liar?"

"No, ma'am," the girl said with sincerity. She lifted her hands in a placating gesture. "I'm only saying, um, you think he's smart, right?"

"Of course. He wasn't great in school, but he's a good kid."

"I'm sure he is. You raised him to be a good person."

Val nodded.

"So maybe you need to trust that he enlisted because he's smart and a good person and this was what he wanted for himself."

"He's a kid!"

Air Force crossed his arms. "He's old enough to try to make something of himself. That's up to him, not to you. At the risk of stepping out of line, maybe you should try telling him you're proud of him instead of telling him he's made a mistake. Ma'am."

Val buried her face in her hands. The horn/tooth on top of her costume's head flopped forward. She was sure the video was being uploaded even now. She knew she shouldn't have baited them, but could she at least have waited for a day when she wouldn't look like a total fool? Maybe she could blame the costume, say she'd over-heated and gotten testy. Maybe someone would buy that.

Lunch period ended and the lobby emptied. The recruiters packed their materials and left without saying another word to her. The bell rang. Val knew she had a class waiting for her in the gym, but she didn't move.

"Val?"

She looked up. Nick Horton stood at her table. "What are you doing, Val?"

The fishbowl of dollars she'd raised before her outburst sat be-tween them on the table. She pointed at it. "Fundraising."

He didn't look amused. "I had two students tell me you were having a breakdown, and I think you're late for class."

"I should get moving, then." She turned and walked toward the gym with as much dignity as she could muster in her narwhal costume with the floppy horn and tail-shoes. When she'd turned the corner, she stopped to remove the costume. If she was lucky, that was the end of the matter.

It wasn't. A note flashed on her whiteboard halfway through the last period, asking her to stop in the principal's office. Her stomach dropped. Now she knew what her students felt like when they got busted for skipping. She changed into street clothes as slowly as she could get away with and walked with dragging feet toward the of-fices.

There was a crowd. Not only Nick, but the principal, Ann Kim, and Val's own department head, Thomas Healy. Nobody smiled when she entered and took the empty seat.

"What the hell, Val?" Tom was the first to speak.

"I'm sorry. I—I had a bad day."

"A bad day is forgetting your gym shoes. You had a meltdown in front of students."

Nick jerked his thumb at Mrs. Kim's computer. "On video."

Val sank in her chair. "How bad is it?"

"You should know." Tom cocked his head. "You were there."

"I was there, but I'm not sure what I said. I know I probably didn't represent very well."

Mrs. Kim's tight-lipped smile didn't reach her eyes. "It sounds like you're under a lot of stress at home."

"My son . . ." Val said, stating the obvious. They all nodded in varying degrees of sympathy.

"I told you the recruiters were off-limits," Nick reminded her. "I told you to let them do their job."

"I know, but David is getting deployed, and I guess I got angry."

Tom frowned. "You can't get angry." He should know, Val thought. He of the purple-faced lectures.

"We have a situation, Val," said Mrs. Kim. "If any parents see the video, we're not going to be able to protect you."

"Protect me?"

"Keep you. Anyway, maybe it'll blow over. In the meantime, it's the weekend. Why don't you take two weeks off and we'll bring in a substitute? Get yourself together. You can give your lesson plans to the sub."

"What about coaching? We have meets coming up."

"You have an assistant coach, right?"

Foolish to think she was necessary, or that she'd done enough for the school that they'd protect her in a moment of weakness. Or maybe that was unfair, and this was the best protection they could give to keep from firing her. Val nodded, numb.

CHAPTER TWENTY-FIVE

SOPHIE

"Okay, y'all, Listen up! We have a new student with us today."

Sophie's class never got new students. If anything, their numbers dwindled month by month, as kids got Pilots and left the non-Pilot classes. She lowered her pen and paid attention. Everybody did the same; only natural to size up the new person. They were tall, which Sophie definitely wasn't, and Black, like most of her school, with short, intricate braids that pulled their hair back tightly from their face.

Competition? Friend? Foe? It came to those options in most classrooms Sophie had been in, at least in the school-at-large. In this classroom, there was a little bit more camaraderie than in most. That was how it felt to Sophie, anyway.

Ms. Colcetti glanced down at a piece of paper. "This is—"

"—I'm going to interrupt you, ma'am, because there's a chance whatever it says on that paper is wrong. My name is Gabe Clary. Pronouns he/him."

Ms. Colcetti nodded and crossed something out on her paper. "Got it. Gabe."

Gabe surveyed the class in a way that suggested he was used to attention and bored with it, then chose an empty chair toward the middle and sat without checking if that wrecked the seating plan.

What kind of kid interrupted the teacher, and didn't wait for her to tell him where to sit, then pulled out a notebook and started drawing without acknowledging anybody? Even Ms. Colcetti was at a loss, staring at Gabe as if she was still trying to figure out what had just happened. Sophie was going to have to meet this person.

She got her chance later that afternoon, when they were paired in science lab.

Gabe groaned when he saw what they were doing. "The *how to drop an egg from a height without breaking it* experiment? I did that years ago."

Sophie felt a need to defend Mrs. Rodriguez. Mrs. Rodriguez was definitely her favorite teacher, and science was probably her favorite class, even if she did better in English. Science affected her every day: David and Julie's Pilots, her own medications. "She wouldn't be teaching it if it wasn't on the test for our grade. It must be important."

"If they're only teaching it because it's on a test, how do we know it's going to apply to anything else we ever do in our lives? We learn math so we can pay our bills and figure out which box of cereal is the better deal. We learn computers and robotics because that's the future. Why do we learn how to drop an egg without breaking it? It wouldn't even make sense if we were all studying to be farmers."

"I think, um, you need math for computers and robots, too, and this teaches us how to problem solve and maybe engineer things. There must be a reason if Mrs. Rodriguez says we should." Sophie crossed her arms and then looked more closely at Gabe. "Are you messing with me?"

Gabe's bored expression twisted into a smile. "Maybe. I think I like you. You've got spunk, kid."

The expression sounded archaic, like something in one of the old movies Sophie's moms watched sometimes, so she tried not to take it as an insult. "I'm not a kid. We're in the same grade."

"Ah, but I've been in this grade before."

"Me, too. Well, not this one, but I had to stay back a year when I was little. When I couldn't remember anything."

"We should both be revered as elder statesmen, then. Statespeople. Why isn't this whole class overwhelmed by our cool?"

Sophie looked around. "Because this whole class is full of people who don't care about cliques or age or anything. We're here trying not to get left behind any farther than we already are."

"You don't seem very behind."

"Yeah, well, I don't have a Pilot, so I can't keep up in the regular class where they're doing six things at once."

"Maybe it shouldn't be your responsibility to be keeping up with those freaks."

"Those freaks are ninety percent of the school. How come you don't have a Pilot?"

Gabe shrugged. "I didn't want one. I'm smart enough already."

The only other person Sophie had ever met who didn't want one was her mother Val. Everyone else who didn't have one had something else going on in their brain to prevent it. "It doesn't make you smarter. It makes you use your brain better."

"Are you arguing for it? I don't see a pretty blue light by your ear."

"I can't have one. Seizures. But I'm okay with not having a Pilot."

"Good. We don't need 'em." Gabe contemplated the egg like Hamlet eyeing Yorick's skull. "So how do we keep this from breaking?"

Gabe caught Sophie as she stepped onto the school bus.

"I'm going home with Sophie," he said to the bus monitor.

The bus monitor, Mr. Knight, looked skeptical. "I've never seen you before."

"I have a note." Gabe waved a piece of crumpled paper in Mr. Knight's face. He read it and looked at Gabe for a second, then typed something onto his list and waved them both on.

"These are not the droids you're looking for," said Sophie, twitching her fingers.

"Huh?"

"Never mind. How did you do that?"

Gabe smiled. "Like I said. I had a note."

"You only met me today."

"And I wrote the note after I met you. I started here today; how would they know my dad's handwriting? The secret to adult handwriting is that it's messy. The harder it is to read, the more they believe you."

Sophie couldn't do her sit-on-the-corner ritual, but that was okay. She didn't need it today; bringing a new friend home was way cooler than hanging around outside.

Mom sat at the dining room table and glanced up when they came in. As usual when she worked from home, she had an array of tablets and phones and papers in front of her. Her expression brightened. "Hey, Soph! Who's your friend?"

"This is Gabe. He/him pronouns. Gabe, this is my mom."

Mom smiled. "Call me Julie. Or Mrs. Geller. Whichever you're more comfortable with. She/her."

"Nice to meet you." Gabe returned the smile.

"We love meeting Sophie's friends," Mom said. Sophie sent mental commands at her mother not to say something like *We meet so few of them* or *We didn't know she had any* or *Sophie never brings anyone home.*

"Do you kids want a snack?"

Sophie did, but she waited for Gabe to say.

"That would be great, thank you, ma'am."

Sophie let out her breath; she knew better than to let someone else make that decision. She needed to eat when she got hungry. It kept the monsters at bay.

The next concern was whether Mom would attempt to make something and accidentally poison them both, but she just jerked her thumb at the kitchen. "Have at it, kids."

Sophie scanned the shelves. A box of cookies everyone in the family knew was stale, but nobody bothered to throw out. A Tupperware of Val's home-dried kale chips, too risky.

"Apples and peanut butter, or cereal?"

"Apples and peanut butter," Gabe said.

Sophie celebrated inwardly that her options hadn't been mocked or dismissed, and celebrated again that even though Julie had probably heard Gabe's selection, she didn't come in to oversee Sophie with the knife in case she had a seizure while cutting. They ate in the kitchen.

"Your mom has a Pilot, huh?" Gabe whispered around an apple slice.

Sophie thought that was obvious, so she shrugged.

"Do both of your parents have them?"

"Nah," said Sophie. "My other mom doesn't believe in them."

"Oh, weird. Do they fight about it?"

Sophie considered. "No. Maybe right at the beginning? No point in fighting about it now. What about your parents?"

"It's only my dad. He doesn't believe in them, either. He hates them."

"Yeah, my ma, too."

"No, I mean *really* hates them."

Sophie couldn't see the distinction between "hates" and "really hates," so she took another bite of apple.

"Have you ever been to a protest?" Gabe asked.

Sophie shook her head, and Gabe sat straighter like it was a teachable moment. Every time he did that it made Sophie feel like a kid. Protest what?

Gabe answered as if she'd asked aloud. "You'll love it! I've been to a million with my dad. We have to take you! You'll fit in perfectly."

Sophie knew better than to say she'd never fit in anywhere. She was afraid to say anything in this brave new world of friends, cool friends, friends at her house, friend who hadn't yet been scared away. She reached for another piece of apple.

CHAPTER TWENTY-SIX

VAL

"Why haven't you been running?" Julie asked.

A reasonable question, but Val chose not to treat it as such. She shrugged and returned to her lesson plan. If she was taking a forced vacation, the school would at least get the best lesson plans they had ever seen. Perfect lesson plans. The kind that made a substitute compliment you to the principal. The kind that made it harder to get rid of such a team player.

Julie persisted. "Seriously. I can't remember the last time you ran."

"I don't feel like it."

"Love, when you don't run you get cranky. As demonstrated."

Val should have answered. Instead, she went into the kitchen and rummaged in the fridge for something to chop. Chopping was better than running. She needed something that took concentration without thinking. She closed the fridge and reached for the sweet potatoes. Perfect.

She dropped the potatoes in the sink and turned on the water, then grabbed the vegetable brush and began scrubbing dirt away. Behind her, Julie came into the room and pulled out a chair, scraping it on the floor to announce her presence. Val started hacking bad spots from the first potato. A slice down one side gave it a flat surface to rest on. Chop. Fluid strokes with a sharp knife, the point never leaving the cutting board as she fed potato to blade.

Julie sighed loudly, and when no response came from Val, she spoke. "What is going on with you? I don't think I did anything to deserve the silent treatment."

"I'm not giving you the silent treatment. I'm cutting potatoes. Maybe if I had a Pilot I would've heard you come in."

"Bull. You heard me."

"Okay, I did, but I don't want to talk. Is that allowed?"

"Nope. Not if you're not running and you're turning your back on me. Not allowed. You can tell me why you're upset, or you can prove you're not upset, but you can't hang out in between."

Val glared at her, then lowered the knife. How had she gotten so much dirt under her fingernails when she'd used a scrub brush? She picked at them. Anything could become a mindful task if you concentrated hard enough. She turned on the tap and mindfully washed her hands, like a surgeon. Julie was gone when she finished; if she'd had a Pilot she would have known how long ago her wife had left the room.

It was wrong to take it out on Julie. She should explain. This was too important to hide, but she was embarrassed. She thought she knew what Julie would say, and Julie would be right, and she didn't want to hear it.

The next day, Val woke at her usual time, as she had every day during her suspension. She made lunches for all three of them, like usual. She dropped Sophie off at school, and as usual, watched until the doors had closed behind the girl. That was as far as she could protect her. After that, Sophie was in the school's hands; in the hands of people she trusted, to some extent, to recognize if there was a problem.

Those same people also missed the problems they were creating by dividing Piloted and un-Piloted students, so how could she expect them to recognize and respond well to Sophie's seizures? No, she was being stupid. Piloted teachers probably had a better chance of noticing; they could keep tabs on all the students at once.

Maybe she was obsolete. Maybe teaching had moved on, and she was behind the times. At least they still needed her to coach, if nothing else. A Pilot couldn't help someone run faster or fix bad body mechanics; that was her job. Except right now it wasn't.

Right now she wasn't supposed to go to school. Instead, she drove on past storefronts and houses and then to the place where the spaces between storefronts and houses widened. She pulled into the dirt lot at the entrance to the state park. Julie was right that she needed to run, wrong about when. She was running because she didn't know what else to do with the time.

She walked down the hill into the park. When she reached the riverside trail she stretched against a tree, and then she ran. This time, everything followed her, as it had for every run during her suspension. No escape when you brought your problem on yourself.

CHAPTER TWENTY-SEVEN

JULIE

When Julie was twelve years old, she realized an important thing about her family: everyone was lying. It was only the three of them, her parents and her. She thought it had always been that way, until the day she found the shoebox. The one filled with photos of an infant boy so small he was held in one gloved hand, wires and tubes snaking everywhere around his tiny body. There were no labels, no names, no dates. It could easily have been someone else's child, but then there would have been no reason for the photos to be in a shoebox in her mother's closet, and there wouldn't have been a tiny knit blanket in the box, and she wouldn't have recognized her father's favorite plaid shirt in one photo's background.

She put the pictures back, replaced the blanket, closed the box, and never mentioned it again. She waited her entire life for her parents to mention she'd briefly had a brother, to take her to a cemetery, to tell her whether he'd been older or younger than her, to let her in on their secret. Nobody ever mentioned him. Sometimes she wondered if she'd imagined finding it, if she'd conjured the whole thing.

She resolved to pay attention, to notice details. She resolved that when and if she had children, they would have siblings. She resolved never to keep anything big from her own family, when she had one of her own, and to make it clear they didn't need to keep anything from her, either.

Julie waited for Val to tell her what had happened, though she'd already figured part of it out. The video was everywhere online: teacher in narwhal costume loses her cool at a recruiter. The student who had posted the video hadn't been Val's, Julie guessed, since they hadn't named her in the video description. One tried in the comments section, but spelled her name wrong. It probably helped, too, that Val was practically the only person left in the world with no social media presence, so nobody could find her to tag her.

It was possible Val didn't know the video had been uploaded, but the fact she hadn't mentioned the incident to Julie meant either it hadn't been as big a commotion as the clip implied, or it had shaken her so much she couldn't find a way to talk about it yet. If that were the case, she would be running. Before school, after school. She'd be running to cope, to give herself a release valve. And yet her shoes stood by the door every morning, and she was spending twice as much time as usual on her geography lesson plans.

Val usually left for work an hour before Julie. She was more of a morning person in any case, but it always worked out well to have one spouse showered and ready while the other dragged herself out of bed. It also meant that on the occasions when Julie opened the fridge and discovered Val's lunch still standing beside hers, she dropped it off at the school.

There was a whole procedure for dropping off stray lunches, for teachers and students alike, implemented when the school was evacuated and a bomb squad called in over a bag lunch a parent had innocently left for his son. Now you had to be rung into the building, then into the office, where the lunch recipient would be called to meet you for a person-to-person exchange.

Julie's name was permanently on the entry list, so she only had to flash her ID and smile for the camera in order to be let in. She went straight to the office, per protocol; the easier thing would be to go directly to the gym, but the last thing she wanted was to instigate a lockdown.

"Hi, Julie," said Dinah Magness, the receptionist. "What can I do for you?"

"Val forgot her lunch. I'm dropping it off." She waved the purple lunch bag.

Dinah frowned. She looked uncomfortable. "You know Val's not here this week, right?"

Julie didn't know what was going on, but she didn't like looking foolish. She slapped her forehead. "How could I forget? Everything's so hectic these days. Sorry to bother you!"

One of the great things about a Pilot: you could pay attention to the person with whom you were conversing and also catch the reactions of anyone else in your line of sight. There were two others in the room, the principal's assistant and a vice principal, both of whom she caught staring. She kept herself from glancing back as she left the office; she didn't want to see them snickering or talking about her.

She made it all the way back to the car before she let herself think about what she'd been told. "Val's not here this week" could mean any number of things, and she'd pretended she knew, saved face, which meant she'd failed to get any real information. Maybe there was a training or a meet off campus that she'd forgotten about? Unlikely. More likely that she'd been put on some kind of probation: benched, or penalty-boxed, or whatever sports metaphor worked for this situation.

The next question—where Val actually was if she wasn't at school—Julie suspected she knew the answer to. If she wasn't running before or after school, she must be running during. Val was lacing her shoes in some park or neighborhood and running the whole day away. It was as good a reaction as any, except that she'd flat-out denied it. That was the likely truth Julie was left holding, alongside a purple lunch bag full of—she checked—two packets of that disgusting runner's gel, two protein bars, and a peanut-butter-and-banana sandwich. Her wife had chosen to pretend to go to her job every day rather than admit what had happened. It was a lie, or a lie of omission, and they weren't supposed to do that to each other, at least not on things that mattered.

And now she had to get to work, too. Staff meeting this morning, all hands on deck, which would provide ample time to think about how to broach the subject with Val while Evan talked at them for an hour.

Julie left work early with some files she could work on remotely; she wanted to beat Val to the house. Sophie had asked if she could have dinner at her friend Gabe's, which Julie had maybe said yes to a little too readily, but it made what Julie wanted to do easier.

She set the table with their good plates, on each of which she carefully arranged one protein bar, half a peanut-butter-and-banana sandwich, and an artful drizzle of chartreuse energy gel. It was the most elegantly composed plate she'd ever created, even if it lacked some important food groups. She lit candles and ironed the napkins. What wine paired with peanut butter? The Internet said Lambrusco, which she'd never heard of, so she went for a cabernet they'd had in the cupboard for a while.

Val returned at exactly the time she usually came home from coaching.

"Hi!" she called. It wasn't unusual for Julie to bring work home in the afternoon in order to be there when Sophie got in. Julie heard a bag drop to the ground, then shoes being tossed toward the shoe pile.

"How was your—crap." Val's response to the table was everything Julie had hoped for, so she didn't respond. The white-tablecloth, bag-lunch spread said that Julie knew what Val had done, and exactly how Julie had found out.

"I'm sorry, Jules. I should have told you right away."

"That's for sure. Wine? I was told to pair a sparkling red, but we didn't have any of those, so I had to fire Jeeves."

Val sat in the chair opposite Julie and eyed her glass. "I'm so sorry. I shouldn't have tried to hide it."

"Agreed."

"I was embarrassed, and I thought it would fix itself without you ever finding out."

"Do you still have your job? What are the terms of this leave?" Julie didn't need to say they couldn't afford for either of them to be unemployed.

"They said I had two weeks of vacation banked, and I should use those and then they should be able to bring me back."

"Should?"

"Yeah. I mean, I caused a scene, but I didn't hurt anyone or use any language I shouldn't have. It's 'conduct unbecoming,' not a fireable offense, I'm pretty sure. I just got loud."

"You got really loud."

Val frowned. "What did they say?"

"Only that you were out this week."

"So how do you know how loud I got?"

Julie pulled her phone out of her pocket. "You do remember these things exist, right?"

"Ugh. So you saw?"

"Where did you get that costume? Your narwhal tusk needed starch or something."

Val's shoulders relaxed at the joke and she risked a sip of wine. "So . . . how mad are you?"

"Still pretty mad about the lie. I don't begrudge you reaming out the recruiters."

"And this is dinner?"

"This is dinner."

No point in holding a grudge. She could be furious and stay furious, or she could invent a situation so absurd that Val recognized the absurdity of her own choices. Val would feel guilty over it, as she should, and Julie could let it go. Win-win.

Julie bit into her sandwich, dry after a day in the fridge, and washed it down with wine. The pairing worked surprisingly well.

CHAPTER TWENTY-EIGHT

SOPHIE

The first surprise on the drive to Balkenhol headquarters came long before they reached the building: a highway billboard advertising Pilots, with a dirty-faced soldier in a tan helmet staring intensely into the camera. David was the soldier. The words above his helmet said PILOTS KEEP US SAFE and below his head, THE FACES PROJECT.

Sophie stared back at him, locking eyes with the poster. "That's my brother!"

"Where?" Gabe asked, looking in the wrong direction.

"On the billboard we just passed. Weird." She made a mental note to tell her parents later.

Balkenhol Neural Labs' national headquarters were practically in the country. The ride went houses, houses, horses, houses, Balkenhol. Sophie had been out this way only once, for a corn maze with her family. She kept slipping away between the stalks, hoping they wouldn't notice; she wanted to reach out and grab their legs and scare them. Every time she started to sneak, somebody would put a hand on her shoulder and draw her back, like a puppy that needed reminding she was on a leash.

Mr. Clary left the highway and drove past a suburb with identical houses and no sidewalks. Then a field with white fences and horses grazing, then suddenly an enormous parking lot. Beyond

the parking lot stood a high fence with razor wire, and a guard-
house. Inside the fence, it looked like more parking, and then a
giant building.

"How come some parking is inside the gate and some is outside?" she asked as Mr. Clary pulled into a spot along the fence. She
didn't want to sound stupid, but that seemed like an innocuous
question.

"This is visitor parking," Gabe explained. "Inside is where the
employees park. They don't call the cops so long as we don't block
the gate."

"So Balkenhol lets the protests happen?"

"As long as we don't block the gate," Gabe repeated.

Sophie wanted to ask more, but decided against it. The first
question she didn't ask was *Are we the only ones here?* It was a nice
day outside, so they lowered their windows and sat in the car.
Waiting for something. Sophie checked the time on her phone: one
thirty. Normally on a Saturday afternoon she'd be at home reading. She was glad for the opportunity to do something else, but
wished she'd brought a book.

Ten minutes passed before a minivan pulled up beside them.
Someone in the passenger seat lowered their window to talk with
Mr. Clary.

"Want to play war?" Gabe asked, pulling a deck of cards from
the seat-back pocket.

The next time Sophie looked, five minutes and half a deck
later—she was winning, she thought—the lot was almost full.
More cars jockeyed for position, dodging people who had begun to
assemble near the gate.

"Come on, guys," Mr. Clary said. Gabe scooped up the cards
as if it didn't matter who won.

The crowd pressed around Sophie as she followed Gabe toward
the front, letting him push people out of the way for both of them.
Sophie's palms began to sweat. It wasn't that she was afraid of
crowds; she was afraid of herself. Her fear in a group like this was
that she would have a seizure and nobody would recognize it; that

she would fall, or be trampled, or wander off and be separated. Really, it was her mom's fear, not hers, but it had lately started to rub off on her.

"Come on, Sophie," Gabe said. He offered his hand; Sophie wiped her palm on her jeans, then took it.

Gabe pulled her to a spot near the fence. Mr. Clary had beaten them there. The crowd formed a half circle around him, but didn't press against the wire. Sophie couldn't tell how many people were here from this perspective—fifty, maybe? Fewer than it had seemed from inside the crowd, but still a good number.

She realized she'd been expecting a protest like she'd seen in movies or in her history textbooks, with cops in riot gear and flaming torches. These people seemed pretty tame in comparison to what she'd imagined. Some carried homemade signs. Most looked old enough to be parents or grandparents, dressed in what she considered normal clothes: jeans or leggings and light jackets. Black and white and brown people. No riot cops. She let go of other expectations.

Her nervousness faded as Mr. Clary began to speak. He had acted like an ordinary parent in the car, but he sounded different now. Commanding. Inspiring. It dawned on her for the first time where she was. Forget the ages and the crowd size and who was here and who wasn't: nobody here had a Pilot. When was the last time she had been anywhere like that? Even in her special classroom the teachers had them. Even in her family, her mom and brother.

These people were old enough that they'd gotten to grow up without Pilots being the only option. They had a right to be nervous about the future, afraid for their kids or whatever else. For the first time, Sophie didn't just feel resigned about it; she was angry. She glanced at Gabe, and Gabe grinned. His father must have given this speech before. Like a mind reader, he mouthed, in concert with Mr. Clary, "So what are we going to do about it?"

Sophie grinned back, and the smile turned her anger into power. For a second, she wished her ma were here to see this. She would appreciate it, too; all these people with the same fears she had. All these people who faced the same problems at work and at school, whose kids faced the same prejudices she faced.

Sophie worked hard to not let anyone bully her. Usually she felt like it was a losing battle, which maybe it was, but the rebel army had more allies than she had realized. Maybe they had a chance to do something on a bigger scale, against bigger bullies.

She realized Gabe was staring at her. Mr. Clary beckoned her to join him. She took a few steps forward. "This brave young woman is here for the first time."

"Welcome!" people shouted, along with a scattering of applause.

He held out his megaphone. "Do you want to say anything?"

"Go on," whispered Gabe. "Say whatever you want. It's better if it isn't a speech. Say something quick, from the heart."

"You do it first."

Gabe shook his head. "I hate public speaking. Not my thing. Besides, I'm not new."

Sophie had never spoken in front of anybody, so she didn't know if she hated it or not. David used to complain about it in high school, but nobody ever asked kids in her class to do stuff like that; they didn't even bother to invite them to run for student council. She hesitated, took a deep breath, then took Mr. Clary's megaphone. One way to find out.

"Um, hi." Her voice shook. She expected someone to laugh, but nobody did. They all looked friendly, expectant. It gave her courage.

"Hi, this is my first time here, but, um, you knew that 'cause Mr. Clary just said it." They laughed this time, but not at her. "One of my moms has a Pilot, and my brother, but I can't get one. And I don't want to! Is it smart for everybody to go changing their brains without knowing everything about it? Brains are complicated, and um, we only get one. Maybe we shouldn't mess with them."

That felt like a good place to stop. She walked back to Gabe without looking at the crowd. She didn't need to look to hear them cheering for her. It was a pretty awesome feeling, like a reward mixed with invitation.

CHAPTER TWENTY-NINE

VAL

From the scant television coverage of anti-Pilot rallies, Val had expected a handful of ragged old hippies. She should have known the same stations that had sold the idea of Pilots in schools would also have a stake in making the protests look feeble and pointless. Not that this didn't feel pointless; despite the crowd outside their gates, nobody from Balkenhol looked in the least bit concerned, if they were even there on a Saturday.

If the protesters were tilting at windmills, at least there were a lot of Don Quixotes: the aforementioned ragged old hippies, but also businesspeople in suits, professor types and punks, parents and grandparents. She counted at least sixty from where she stood at the back. The group tightened toward the center, but it wasn't a mob. Nobody mentioned plans to storm the gate or do anything other than peacefully demonstrate. That made Val relax a bit. She and Julie had argued over this one.

"Why should she protest Balkenhol?" Julie had asked. "Nobody's making her get a Pilot."

"Maybe she thinks it's the right thing to do."

Julie shook her head. "She doesn't care about a cause. She's going because she has a cool new friend she wants to impress."

"Is that true? And even if it is, maybe she should have the experience? Just because we've never been the marching type doesn't mean she isn't."

"What about David? Is it right for her to be protesting the company that makes a device that's keeping him safe?"

"False argument, Jules. This protest won't put him in any more danger than he's already in. Don't you dare use that on her."

"Sorry." Julie sighed. "I thought we'd agree on this one. I don't get why you want her to go to an event with that much excitement. I don't even like it when she does that weird thing where she sits on the street corner on her own before coming into the house."

"She wants a little freedom." If that was how Sophie tested her limits, Val was all for it.

"Okay, fine. I just don't think picketing Balkenhol for some silly movement is the freedom she's looking for."

"Silly movement?"

"You know what I mean. Ineffectual."

"Just because it's ineffectual doesn't mean it's silly. They're fighting for something they believe in."

"No. They're fighting against something they don't believe in. There's a difference. It's a perfectly good technology."

"And kids like Sophie are getting left behind."

"Should they stop making them, then? Hold everyone back?"

"Not hold back—anyway, I'll tell you what: What if I go, too? I can stay out of sight. She won't know I'm there."

Julie looked skeptical. "A disguise?"

"Not like a mustache and a trench coat. Something subtle."

Val settled for trading ball caps with a rival coach at the Thursday-night track meet. With a new sweatshirt and her ponytail tucked under a cap in Grover High purple, she didn't think Sophie would spot her.

She stood on the fringe, trying to blend in. At least there was one way she fit in here better than she had anywhere else of late: this was the first place she'd been in two years where no blue Pilots glowed on the heads around her. She had started searching crowds for the others without. Only last week she'd noticed a teenager eyeing her as she ran. It looked to her like the guy was trying to figure out her damage.

"Personal choice!" she'd shouted, and then increased her pace, immediately ashamed. Personal choice couldn't be a mark of pride. It kicked Sophie into the gutter of "other," something she never meant to do.

She should be one of these people. They believed the same thing she believed, that Pilots were a slippery slope to a quarry whose depths had not yet been plumbed, where anything could be lurking. Everything seemed so rushed, fast-tracked for a future she wanted time to get used to, at the very least. *Slow down*, she wanted to say to the schools and the Army and the news outlets. What's the end result of all this? Maybe these things would usher in a new age of humanity; until they did, it looked premature to her eyes.

"Our young people are being used as guinea pigs!" shouted an orator with the cadence of an experienced preacher. "We are letting them cut open our children, and put machinery in their heads, and sew them up again as if they are the same, but they are not the same."

"No!" shouted someone in the crowd.

"They are *not* the *same*, nor are they better. Nor should it matter. Who are we to mess with these beautiful creations, these beautiful children? Who are we to corrupt? To 'improve' in the name of 'progress'? Why do we trust this company with our children's perfect brains?" He gestured at the building behind him, and the crowd erupted in boos.

"This experiment is being conducted in our schools, on children whose parents think they have no choice. They do have a choice. My son is in public school. He's a bright boy, but they put him in special classes now. He understands. He understands he's better off in a classroom of struggling children, learning at their own pace, than being mocked by teachers who have already forgotten they are there to teach, not to enable."

Val craned to see, and confirmed what she'd just realized. The boy he gestured to, standing near the front and off to the side of his father, was Gabe. Sophie was at his side. Val couldn't read her daughter's expression from so far away, but judging from her posture, the studious tilt of her head, Sophie was entranced.

The speaker motioned with both hands for the crowd to settle. "We won't change their minds today, but we'll come back, again and again. We'll speak out, and we'll reach people one at a time."

Gabe's father stepped aside, and a beatboxer began to perform. Val knew she should leave, but she lingered, thinking about what she'd heard. It could have come from inside her own head. She wished she had said it sooner, much sooner, before David had ever convinced them he needed to fit in with his class. They should have said *no*, should have said *wait*.

She started to run. Away from the Balkenhol compound, away from the preacher speaking her own truths, away from the sudden realization that she had failed David. A parent protects a child. A parent doesn't give in just because the child wants something, just because everyone else has one. A parent doesn't take a teacher's word above her own common sense. They had failed him.

She sprinted until her lungs burned and the sweatshirt disguise was soaked in sweat. Head bowed, hands on knees, she heaved. When she had her breath again, she headed back to her car.

She saw the three figures by her car from a long way off, and groaned. Of course if Gabe's father was a speaker he probably stayed until the end. Of course Sophie would notice her mother's car in the nearly empty parking lot. She steeled herself for confrontation, but Sophie didn't look upset.

"Were you here for the rally?" she asked when Val neared.

"I was running."

"I see that. In those clothes?" Sophie waved a finger at Val's attire. "And a Grover cap?"

Val shifted from one foot to the other. How strange for the roles to reverse like this, with Sophie playing interrogator and her playing the child caught out.

It didn't need to be that way. Not if she told the truth. "I checked out the rally first."

"What did you think?"

Truth. "I only heard part, but I thought it raised some good points. I thought you raised some good points." She directed the second sentence to Gabe's father, who looked amused at the whole conversation.

She held out her hand. "I'm Val Bradley, one of Sophie's mothers."

"Tony Clary. Gabe's father." His handshake was firm.

"You're an excellent speaker, Tony. I hope your group here appreciates that they have such a good leader."

He shook his head. "I'm not the leader, but they know I can deliver a good speech when they need it."

"It's a people's movement," said Gabe. Sophie nodded in agreement with her friend, leaving Val to wonder when her daughter had learned what a people's movement was.

"I should get going. I told Julie I'd be back ages ago. Do you want a ride home, Soph?"

"Can I go with Gabe? We were going to stop for dinner." Sophie's eyes were full of pleading, though she tried to keep her tone casual. Full of something else, too, something Val couldn't recognize.

Val shrugged. "Sure. You have money?"

"Yes."

"You know the rules?"

"No cola, no sulfites, no fun. Check." Sophie finished with an eye roll that Val knew she'd been working on for some time, but Val was satisfied.

She looked to Mr. Clary, who nodded. "Your wife gave me the rundown the first time Sophie came over."

Sophie slumped at that news, and Val's heart went out to her. She wished her daughter could visit friends without parental intervention. Someday soon they'd have to let go and trust her; not yet.

"See you later, Soph."

She watched Sophie's body language in her rearview mirror, the way she straightened up again as her mother drove away. No matter how much she wanted to be the good guy in the scenario, it looked like she was cast in the role of suffocating parent.

Or maybe it wasn't about her. Maybe that something else she'd seen in Sophie's eyes wasn't about her mother. The more she thought about it, the more she realized it was likely that Sophie wasn't just excited about a meal away from prying parental eyes: she wanted to talk about what she had just taken part in. Val had just watched her daughter transform into an activist, and she was still concerned about French fries.

CHAPTER THIRTY

SOPHIE

Sophie attended three more Saturday rallies with Gabe and his father before the school year ended. They all went more or less the same. Mr. Clary spoke, sometimes followed by others, mostly people who had decided not to get Pilots or not to let their kids; a few claimed to have seen Pilots go wrong. The second group made her think of David and Julie: her mom had never complained, but she'd heard David mention noise. One of these people said his kid had committed suicide, but he didn't know why.

Some speakers were even scientists or doctors. "Look at all the mental health diagnoses that begin in puberty and young adulthood," one said. "Should we be putting this additional stress on underdeveloped brains?"

That one scared her, too. She understood. She wasn't allowed to have a Pilot—even if she wanted one, which she didn't—because the company didn't recommend them for people with certain disorders. What happened to people who got Pilots and then got diagnosed?

She and Gabe watched from near the fence. She learned a lot watching Mr. Clary and the way he organized things. She would never have realized that something so chaotic-looking was actually carefully orchestrated, with every speaker chosen for maximum impact. Nobody got the mic until he vetted them.

"He learned that one the hard way," Gabe confided. "At the end of the first rally he did an open-mic thing to let anyone who wanted have a chance to speak. One lady stood to talk about her son's Pilot, but started talking about his drug problem instead, and then we kinda realized she had a drug problem, too. She went on for twenty minutes before Dad got the megaphone away from her."

Sophie considered. "How come he let me speak my first time?"

"I told him you'd be great; I had a good feeling about you."

Mr. Clary seemed to like her. He'd trusted her to speak, even if it was only a few words, and he'd given her the mic a few more times since then. Sometimes, when he spoke, he pointed at her and Gabe and called them "The Future of the Movement." She liked that part. He followed it with: "But I hope this movement doesn't need a future. I hope Pilots are a fad, and the fad ends, and these young people get to go on to the adult lives they deserve, adult lives where they are not second-class citizens." She practiced his timing and phrasing in her mirror at home, booming some words and stretching others out.

One night, eating baked chicken with the Clarys, she worked up the nerve to ask the question that had been bothering her. Mr. Clary was talking about upcoming rallies, about speakers and schedules. Gabe argued with him about whether a guy who had spoken the week before was worth having back.

Sophie loved to listen to them argue, loved the way Mr. Clary treated Gabe like an adult with an opinion worth considering. It reminded her of her own family, back when David was around and their dinners were loud and boisterous, though she knew that memory probably wore rose-colored glasses. If she thought about it too hard, she started remembering people laughing at her, not with her. She was always the youngest, always left out of conversations.

"Is anybody listening?" She surprised herself with the question. Both Clarys paused in their conversation, a rare lull.

"To you?" Gabe asked. "We are now."

"No. To the protests. I mean, I think everything that's being said is really important, but isn't it being said to the wrong people? The ones who come are the ones who believe you already. It's the same faces every time. It's a good crowd, and I love being around people who don't have Pilots, but . . . what if everybody else just thinks we're crazy? How is anything ever going to change?"

Mr. Clary gave her a long, thoughtful look. Sophie felt her face flush. Ice clunked in the freezer, but she willed herself not to look away or get distracted.

"You're not wrong, Sophie," he said at last. "We're preaching to the choir, and maybe we're protesting too often, and maybe nobody's listening anymore. How do you propose we fix the situation?"

Nobody had ever asked her that question before. She loved her parents, but she couldn't think of one time when they'd ever asked her to solve a problem outside of homework.

She bit her lip, thinking. "We need to show them we're worth listening to, but I don't know how we show that. Maybe we're in the wrong place. We're not going to get them to stop making Pilots, so why are we protesting at the headquarters?"

"Where would we go?" Gabe asked.

"Everywhere. Places on public transit, so people who can't drive out to a factory in the suburbs can come to the protests, too. I don't know. Places people can see us. Schools? Government buildings? Balkenhol makes the Pilot, but they're making it because schools buy into it and the military buys into it and the government encourages it and bosses pressure their staff to get it. They all need to hear us, too."

Gabe and his father both stared at Sophie.

"What?" Sophie asked after a second. "Never mind. I don't know what I'm talking about."

Mr. Clary frowned. "Have you been saving all that up to say?"

"Yeah, I guess so."

"Why?"

Sophie lowered her eyes. "Sorry. I thought it might help."

"No, silly!" Gabe grinned. "Why save it up when you could have been helping this whole time?"

"You don't think it's stupid?"

Mr. Clary tilted his water glass in her direction. "Stupid? Those were great observations. Your opinions are welcome any-time."

Sophie felt herself flush again, but this time it was pride. She could get used to this.

PART THREE

CHAPTER THIRTY-ONE

SOPHIE

The key to storming out, in Sophie's opinion, was to put all the information into the closing door. Nineteen years of life had taught her that entire wars had been lost and won in this precise and undiplomatic language. How much time passed between the final exchange and the walkout? How long did the door linger open? Did it swing shut or was it pulled? Did the walker pause on the stoop or stride off with purpose?

She slammed the door behind herself, making sure her mothers knew she was leaving and they had caused it. She'd grabbed her boots without putting them on, and she took each step faster than the last, to put as much space as possible between herself and the house.

Once around the corner, she paused to pull her boots over now-muddy socks and peek back. It didn't look like either mom had followed; her slam had done its job. They didn't have the power to ground her at this point, but they could still make her life miserable. Nineteen was a crap age. Old enough to make decisions for yourself, but not old enough to be trusted or taken seriously.

The neighborhood smelled like fresh laundry. There were still more leaves on the trees than on the ground, but here and there a maple or an oak leaf had left its shadow on the pavement. She didn't know how they did that. David would know, she thought, as she always did when a question came to mind. He was due home soon, at last, maybe.

She refused to let anyone tell her exactly when he was expected. Counting led to bad things. She had seen war movies: the tearful wife, the confused children. *He only had two more weeks. I can't believe he's gone.* Call her superstitious; she didn't care. She'd arrive for dinner one night to find him sitting at the table and she'd be surprised and overjoyed. She'd believe it when she saw him.

Her bus idled at the red light, giving her time to get down the hill. A couple of late-shift commuters stood at the corner and she lined up behind them, balancing her pack with one hand as she dug in her pocket. She could ride for half price if she swiped her disability ID card, but when the bus pulled over she deposited the full fare in change. That much harder to track her. That much harder, also, for the people staring at her to vindicate their stares.

She knew she made them uncomfortable. First there was her clothing: the torn jeans, one of David's old Army jackets restitched to say Y ARM? Bright blue hair, shaved close on the sides to make sure nobody missed that she wasn't Piloted. Their eyes always strayed to her hair, then her jacket, and only then did they notice she didn't have a Pilot. They inched away. Who didn't have a Pilot? Nobody normal.

Javon drove the four forty-five bus, as usual. He gave Sophie a long-suffering look as the coins jammed his fare box then sorted themselves. She saluted him with the crisp gesture she'd learned from David. It always surprised people more than if she gave them the finger. She liked to confound expectations.

The bus lurched and Sophie shuffled toward the back. She was heading downtown at the end of the day, the opposite of most people, so there were more than enough seats. She shrugged her bag off and rested it on her feet, one arm looped through the strap to keep it steady, then glanced at the other passengers, most of whom studiously ignored her. One little boy, on his mother's lap, stared. She smiled at him and waved. His eyes widened and he ducked his head into his mother's armpit.

A few more seats filled at the next stops. Not enough to crowd the bus, but the riders no longer enjoyed the luxury of sitting in every other seat. Sophie scooted over to accommodate two elderly women who were clearly traveling together. The one closer to her thanked her. She didn't even shift toward her companion, the way so many people did when they saw Sophie. Score one for cool grannies.

"My goodness, it's hot in here," one of the old women said. Sophie hadn't noticed, but now that it had been pointed out, she realized the woman was right. Even her seat felt heated. Others fanned themselves and tried to force the windows open. The cool autumn air would be welcome, but only one window actually slid the way it was supposed to.

"Driver, you got the heat on or something?" somebody called from behind Sophie.

"It's September, you can turn off the seat warmers!" shouted the mother with the little boy.

A block later, Javon pulled to the curb.

"Ladies and gentlemen," the PA crackled. "The engine is over-heating. I've called my supervisor and we'll get on our way again as soon as we can."

"Just once I'd like to get to work on time," a man in scrubs muttered.

"Just once I'd like to get anywhere on time," another person agreed, "but that ain't going to happen on a city bus." Everybody laughed.

Sophie wasn't in any hurry, but she didn't like the heat. She fanned herself with her hand, feeling her face flush. A familiar anxiety crept over her. *Not now, please,* she willed herself. *Not now, not now not*

~~~\/\/\/\/\~~~

A woman beside her was holding Sophie's arm, and Sophie shoved her hand away, inching the other way in her seat.

"Whoa!" said somebody on that side.

Three people were picking something up off the floor.

"You dropped these," said a man in scrubs, placing some coins in her hand. "Threw them, actually."

She shoved them into her empty pocket, where her own change should have been. The other two people handed her more coins.

She tried to gather her mind back. First check: Bladder okay? She shifted in her seat to check. Yes, thank goodness. That had happened only once, but once had been enough. Wallet? Yes. ID bracelet? Yes. Keys? Yes. Change? All over the floor. Where was she? Bus. Heading to the meeting space. Heading away from home. Engine problem. Brain present and accounted for? Mostly. A few casualties, Sergeant.

"Are you okay?" whispered the old woman on her left.

"I'm okay. I'm okay." What was the proper response to that question. "I'm okay. Are you?"

"Yes, but I didn't just fling money across the bus and then stare into space while everybody else picked it up." The woman took on a reproving tone. "If you're okay, that's a strange thing to do. If you're not okay, it's more understandable."

"I'm okay." Sophie stood and swung her bag onto her back. She didn't want to be on this bus anymore. She pushed the rear door, but it didn't open, and when she tried the stop-request cord, it didn't ring.

"Can I get off?" she called to Javon.

"Sit tight," he said over the intercom, to her and everyone. "I promise we'll be on our way shortly. They're sending another bus."

"I've got to get off."

"Then come to the front door."

Sophie walked the aisle with all the dignity she could muster. She felt every eye on her. Where before she had relished the attention, demanded it, now she wished herself invisible. Why couldn't they ignore her?

"Thanks a lot," she said to Javon in her most sarcastic tone as she stepped off.

"No transfer if you leave now," the driver said. "Are you sure you want to get off in this neighborhood?"

"This is my stop. I was heading here."

She walked in the direction the bus had been heading. Where had they stopped? She recognized the neighborhood. Javon was right: it wasn't a great one. Nothing but liquor stores and check-cashing joints. She didn't want to be here on her own if she had another seizure, however unlikely that was. She could always call her moms from one of the liquor stores and sit tight. Val would arrive no questions asked, the guilt trip unspoken, or else Julie would ream her out and then it would be over and done with. She couldn't do it.

She walked until the bus was out of sight, then stuck out a hand to gesture for a ride. Hack cabs, private drivers picking up passengers for cash, were the only ones that traveled this stretch of road, but that worked for Sophie. Hacks were cheaper, and besides, a hack would take her money and not give her grief. A ride-share app would trade her information privacy for convenience; not to mention she'd left without her phone.

Three minutes passed, then five. The new bus roared by. As it passed, Javon saluted her, but didn't stop to let her on again. This night had to get better.

CHAPTER THIRTY-TWO

JULIE

Sophie displaced a lot of air these days, with her stomping feet and her slamming exits. By now, Julie had practice in non-response. She didn't rush to the window, or worse yet, the door, as Val did. She didn't shout after her departing daughter.

Instead, she started a bath. She poured herself a generous glass of cheap Malbec, cranked her *let it out, sister* curated station loud enough for Blondie to make sure she couldn't hear herself think, cycled down her Pilot to its lowest setting, and dumped enough lavender bath salts into the tub to saturate herself in relaxation. She picked the cheesiest-looking audio romance novel in the library app, pressed play, and closed her eyes.

She chose not to think about the dangers that lurked beyond their front door. Not that the house had ever kept Sophie safe. There was no safe place for Sophie in this world. A room full of pillows, maybe.

Val was so much better than Julie at hiding her protective instincts from Sophie. Sophie had developed into the kind of teen who would do the opposite of anything you wanted her to do. She homed in on anything you held back, like a boxer recognizing an opponent's weak point. Maybe someday she would recognize that her mothers had her best interests at heart. For now she chafed, she seethed, she slammed the door on them hard enough to blur the literal and the figurative; and Julie bathed, and bathed again, and smelled of lavender.

She had only offered to drive Sophie to her FreerMind Association meeting space; she shouldn't have. Moreover, she definitely shouldn't have said she'd prefer Sophie get home by midnight, and definitely definitely shouldn't have said Sophie should get a hobby outside of protest-planning meetings. She hadn't meant FreerMind was a hobby; it was amazing they'd hired Sophie and Gabe to run the local field office. Even if it paid a pittance, it was the only job around that truly valued non-Piloted staff over Piloted. She'd meant she'd love to see Sophie doing art or puzzles or something again, maybe going to community college, but Sophie had taken it as an attack.

Val handled her better than Julie did these days. It was a funny turn from their early years, when they both would have admitted Julie was by far the more instinctual mother, Val afraid she might break them. Of course, Val had one major advantage in the Sophie-parenting department these days: she had no Pilot.

As far as Sophie was concerned, a Pilot was a deal-breaker. No trust for anyone Piloted except for David. David was allowed; he hadn't known better. Julie, from Sophie's perspective, had been in possession of all the information she needed to say no, but she went through with it nonetheless. Julie knew they would see eye to eye again at some point in the future. Sophie's opinions would shift as she grew up. She would miss her mothers, maybe come to understand them. Julie would bathe, and wait, and hope never to get the phone call she dreaded.

When the water had cooled and the fizz had fizzled and her fingers and toes had pruned, Julie climbed out and dried herself. She put on a thick sweatshirt and leggings, wrapped her hair in her towel, and decided that making dinner could be her next distraction.

She opened the fridge in search of inspiration. A few assorted vegetables languished in the drawer, all on the far side of crisp and waiting to be diced or discarded. Soup. They'd be good enough for soup.

A key turned in the front door and her heart leapt in joy. Down, she quashed it. Sophie would never come back that quickly after a fight, even if she realized she had overreacted. She would never give her parents the satisfaction.

Val walked into the kitchen, her shirt and hair drenched with sweat and sticking to her. She filled a water glass and drank deeply. Repeated the action, then put the glass in the dishwasher. Only then did she notice Julie, still standing beside the open fridge. The hazards of the unPiloted: perpetual surprise.

"What are you doing in here?" Her tone was amused.

"Is it that much of a surprise? I'm going to cook dinner."

"Really?"

"It's been known to happen." It hadn't been. Not for a while, at least. They mostly ate dinner salads when Sophie wasn't around, but Val put those together, too. Julie found herself trying to justify the whim. "I felt like soup."

"Fair enough. Do you need help?"

"Not while you're sweating like that. How is it possible to sweat that much on a day this cool?"

Val stepped forward, mock-wringing her shirt in her wife's direction. Julie raised her hands in defense. "Go! Take a shower. You can help me when you come back if I'm not done already."

Val blew her a kiss. Minutes later, water rushed through the pipes. All these things had happened before, except for the soup.

The soup wasn't bad. Cauliflower and cheddar and lentil. Not great, either, but not awful. Julie watched Val take a hesitant sip, then relax.

"Nice job, Jules," she said.

She ate three more spoonfuls before reaching for the salt. Julie loved her for the three extra spoonfuls, which said, *I would eat this exactly as it is, if you needed me to do so.* Twenty-five years ago, she probably would have eaten the whole bowl bland rather than risk hurting Julie's feelings. That was their level of comfort now, measured in spoonfuls.

If it were the other way around, if Julie were eating a soup Val had made, she wouldn't add more than one courtesy spoonful. Val's ego didn't need the stroking. She cooked swiftly and efficiently, for the delivery of maximum nutrition, if not maximum taste, and she liked her time in the kitchen. Like running, cooking was for Val a solitary pursuit. A conversation with herself, a personal contemplation.

For Julie, food preparation brought adventure. Knives bit, stoves burnt, everything cooked at different rates. A pinch of thyme: Whose pinch? Season to taste: Whose taste? The Pilot had improved her results—not as many distracted cuts or forgotten burnt offerings these days—but still she preferred tasks she could control and measure.

They ate in silence. Every meal without the kids at the table felt wrong. Once when both David and Sophie were out, they'd tried eating in front of the television. "The table is for the family," Julie had suggested. They had watched and balanced their plates on their knees, until Val said, "This feels way too much like the way I ate dinner with my parents." They finished that first and only meal back at the table. The table was for family, absent or present.

For Julie, the absences altered everything. She couldn't help but hear David begging for seconds before everyone else had finished serving themselves a first portion. She saw every Sophie sitting at the table, from picky infant to quiet child to impossibly volatile teen. She only ever saw one David, sixteen and serious. David had somehow been sixteen and serious his entire life, even when it didn't suit him yet. She ate her mediocre soup with her wife and her absent son, and her thousand tortured absent daughters.

Julie knew that Val also felt the wrongness of their two-person table. Any night without Sophie was a fraught night, but these were the worst: the ones where she stormed out without her phone and without telling them when she would be back.

"Have you heard from her?" Val asked.

Julie shook her head. "No. You know if she'd call either of us tonight, it would be you."

She didn't say it resentfully. At this point in Sophie's life, any connection with either parent was something to cherish and protect: a fire reduced to ember could still be coaxed to life again. If Sophie thought Val was more sympathetic to her cause, Julie wouldn't step between them. One was better than none.

Val took the dishes to the kitchen. She joined Julie in front of the television a few minutes later, handing her a mug of Earl Grey with milk and sugar, the scent of which clashed with whatever herbal concoction Val had made herself. They watched the local news and then the national news. Julie had her tablet out, scanning for the two names she didn't want associated with the news: Sophie's and David's. They would be in different places, if she ever came across them, likely on different sites. She searched all the common aggregators, then the one for military families.

She lingered for a while in the place she didn't mind finding Sophie's name, or rather her username; Sophie didn't know Julie was a card-carrying member of her FreerMind movement's action chat. A Judas? More of a Trojan horse.

Julie's user name was Godnotmod, and she posted frequently. The character she'd invented was an elderly Canadian Christian who believed—and frequently posted—that humans were made in God's image and should not be altered. Julie got a kick out of playing an exasperated shut-in, connected to the world via her computer. The others had shortened her handle to God at first, and she had thrown a very in-character fit until they called her GNM instead. The ones who liked her sometimes called her Grandma. That included Sophie, who was far more patient with GNM/Grandma than with her mother.

Julie routed her little deception through an e-mail she'd created for the purpose, on a VPN she'd set up to give her a Canadian IP address, since Sophie had once said that FreerMind occasionally investigated new online members. GNM had been there long enough now to move beyond their skepticism; a valued member of the anti-Pilot community.

Sophie hadn't posted anything yet tonight, which in itself was enough to ratchet up Julie's anxiety. Shouldn't she be at her meeting already? Shouldn't they be planning actions and broadcasting to their waiting public? The possibilities began to swim through her head: Sophie had seized on the way to the meeting. She'd been robbed, taken to the hospital. Seized and robbed and injured, no ID, unable to provide their phone numbers as emergency contacts.

"Turn it off, Jules," said Val. Julie looked up. "Turn it all off. You're getting that frantic look. Put down the tablet. Read a book, or watch a movie with me."

"A movie," Julie agreed, drawing out the movement of turning off her tablet to glance at one more headline. Val scrolled through movie options and picked something they'd both seen before, an old comedy, the compromise between her own preference for horror and Julie's preference for romcom.

Julie leaned into her wife's shoulder, taking comfort in contact. If something had happened, the universe couldn't be cruel enough to let it happen while they were watching *Young Frankenstein*. Julie's Pilot awareness agitated for stimulation for a few minutes before fully latching on to the movie. She let it focus on hyperdetail, let herself watch, let herself feel Val's arm and Val's shoulder and Val's steady heartbeat. Their kids had been in this room watching this movie with them a thousand times. They still were. She focused her gaze on the screen, so the phantom Davids and Sophies could fill the rest of the room.

CHAPTER THIRTY-THREE

SOPHIE

Given the bus ride from hell and the walk, Sophie was pleased to arrive only fifteen minutes late at the decrepit former Moose Lodge they called headquarters. They were co-leaders, and Gabe wouldn't normally start without her on one of her nights to run the meeting, but since she'd left home without her phone, she'd had no way of conveying she was still en route; she understood why the group had already gathered in a circle at the far end. Gabe had the floor and was gesturing, fist to palm, his short locs bouncing as he spoke.

Whatever he was saying had to be interesting; nobody turned when she opened the door. Gabe's back was to her, a breach of protocol; the meeting host always picked the far side, the twelve o'clock seat, to acknowledge any new members coming through the door, and be alert for potential attacks. It was a responsibility they both took seriously.

She touched his shoulder as she walked past him, and he smiled and gestured to the empty chair at twelve o'clock. He had left the host's chair for her; her ruffled feathers smoothed themselves back into place. She dropped her backpack and sat. There were about twenty attendees tonight, not their best or their worst turnout. A few regulars were currently in lockup, awaiting arraignment after that morning's civil disobedience. The turnaround time at Central Booking these days was obscene.

She scanned the group for new faces, finding a few interspersed around the circle: a middle-aged Black couple; a fortyish white woman in a wheelchair; a wiry, nervous-looking white teenager, maybe fourteen or fifteen. She knew his type: he was at the age when the pressure to get a Pilot started to build, but he was too smart or too idealistic or too scared to fall for it.

"Have you done names already, Gabe?" she asked.

He nodded. "Names and not much else. We waited for you. I was just telling them about this morning."

"Damn zombies," someone said, then made a spitting sound Sophie hoped didn't contain actual saliva. Officers didn't want their soldiers losing discipline, either.

"Agreed on the sentiment, but no spitting in our meeting space," she said. "I don't want to have to wash the floor before I sleep on it."

"Can we sleep here?" asked the new boy.

Sophie gestured toward the mountain range of yoga mats and spare sleeping bags along the back wall. "Any of you that don't feel safe elsewhere, you're welcome to crash here as long as Gabe or I are here, which is most nights."

She realized she should take back control, now that Gabe had ceded it to her. "Anyway, I haven't had a chance to introduce myself yet. I'm Sophie. She/her. Feel free to introduce yourselves later if I haven't met you yet. When you speak, start whatever you're saying with your name and pronouns, so others can start to get to know you. Now, then, Gabe, where were you?"

She sat, satisfied that the group understood they were both equally in charge. She was glad he'd started the meeting without her. Too much reliance on a single leader wasn't a good thing in this movement; that was part of why they'd insisted on co-running this field office. The whole point was that people should be able to think and act for themselves. She sat back to listen to what Gabe had to say.

As always, he took a moment to get started, like an old car that needed to be coaxed to life. He hated his voice, she knew. Those first moments of public speaking were always agony for him, until he got over the self-consciousness and into the stuff that impassioned him. Tonight there was no shortage of topics to get worked up about.

"Okay, I'm going to start with them, then come round to us. 'Them' for tonight is Balkenhol Neural Labs as usual, but also Congress. The House of Representatives yesterday voted to subsidize Pilots for all ninth graders living under the poverty level, under the assumption that the parents of all the others will pay for theirs. This was the first state with subsidies, since Balkenhol is in our backyard, and that has spread to about twenty other states, but it's bad news if this goes federal."

One of the regulars, with a geometric haircut and full-sleeve tattoos on both arms, raised her hand. Gabe looked her way. "Daya?"

"So all students are required to get them under this law?"

"No. The government will pay for them for those who can't afford them. They're not mandatory, but it's easy to see how we'd get there from here. Yes?"

"Dominic, he/him," said the new boy, identifying himself as Sophie had said to do. "It's not a law yet, though, right? You said 'passed the House,' but it still has to pass the Senate, too, right?"

"Right. That's where the next mobilization is going to come in," said Gabe. "Sophie, do you want to talk about that?"

She stood. "Okay, as always, we'll do it their way and our way. Before we leave tonight, everyone willing is going to write a letter to our senators. On paper, old-fashioned style, so they can see we exist and we have good penmanship. I'll mail them tomorrow. I'll also encourage you to post your letter online, send it to all your friends, and tell them to reach out to their own senators. Bonus if you can tell them those two names, in case your friends aren't as smart as you.

"You're welcome to try to make appointments with the senators personally as well, but don't be surprised if they won't see you. They're pretty locked down right now, and they consider us a fringe group. And yes, John"—she raised a hand to silence an older white man who had opened his mouth—"I know some of you are fully anti-tech and will not be sending e-mails or any of that. We respect your perspective and your beliefs." They'd long ago learned to control the various factions within their group, including both the anti-tech and the techies who thought Pilots were a step too far.

"There should be new protest flyers to distribute shortly. Again, tell your friends, get people involved. Last, FreerMind has lawyers already working on a challenge to the law if it passes the Senate. Any questions?"

As expected, they all wanted to know when the protests would be. That was what these folks were best at: showing up. She had to force them to write letters and do the other small-seeming stuff. Those things mattered at least as much as marching to the school board or the state house and getting arrested again. Still, the trick with a group like this was to play to their strengths, to encourage them and let them feel their burgeoning strength.

The power movers at the national office didn't come to local meetings, making Gabe and Sophie their sergeants, carrying out the orders of generals. As far as the foot soldiers were concerned, the two of them were giving the orders. This was Sophie and Gabe's group to command as they saw fit. She loved the authority; it was still new to her, but she knew she wore it well. She wished her parents understood how she thrived when given some trust and control.

That had been the fight this afternoon. How could Julie still tell her to be home by midnight? She was nineteen. Her friends spanned decades older than her, some were older than her parents, and every one of them assumed her more capable than her parents did. She and Gabe were the only two people with keys to this building, for starters.

She knew the moms' fears, the old bogeymen they trotted out

of seizures around people who might take advantage of her. Add in that a FreerMind chapter in California had been bombed three days before and they were ready to lock her in the house and close all her connections. They said they loved her political involvement, and that she had found something she believed in and excelled at, but couldn't she work on it from home, where she would be safe?

She knew Val understood, at least on some level, why she did this. Val had even come to one protest, years before, and maybe gotten into it, even if she wasn't going to take action while Julie and David had Pilots.

Gabe was talking about the arrests, giving the rundown of who had been taken in and why. Most protests didn't end in arrests, he stressed. Some people liked to go further than FreerMind encouraged. "I beg you to talk to me or Sophie before taking extreme action. One, so we don't sound like an incompetent body that doesn't know what our left arms are doing if the media comes calling for quotes. Two, so we have money and lawyers arranged in advance. Three, so we can talk you out of it if we think it will be harmful to the cause."

The meeting wrapped, and Sophie pulled out her supplies: paper, pens, envelopes. She was always prepared. In a million years, she doubted if anyone in her family would have guessed she could be this good at something. David had never done anything like this. He'd gone off to be a different kind of leader, in a different kind of war, but he'd always been expected to do great things.

Oh, her parents had told her she could be anything she wanted to be, do anything she wanted, but reality hadn't been as kind. High school had been agony. She had been teased and bullied by students, berated by teachers. Even if she'd finished high school instead of dropping out and getting her GED, she wasn't sure she would've gotten into college, or gone. She wasn't stupid, but she'd had enough of being left behind when she couldn't learn what they wanted her to learn at the speed they wanted her to learn it.

It hadn't been until Gabe introduced her to the movement that she felt truly at home. A growing community of the Pilot-less, people who thought for themselves and acted for themselves and looked you fully in the eye when they talked to you. She had jumped in and they had embraced her.

They didn't even care about her seizures. Some of them had seizures too, or autism, or other neurodiversities that rendered them somehow unfit for society's new standard. Others had simply rejected the concept, either out of political or personal or religious belief. They didn't judge.

She wished her mothers understood how much it meant to her. They said they did, but they didn't. Julie especially, now that she was one of the zombies. She still couldn't believe her own mother had betrayed her like that. At least Val would never get one, even if she didn't speak out against them, either.

Maybe if they saw the way Sophie was treated here, the deference she was given, the responsibility; maybe then Sophie's family would treat her like an adult. She could handle herself. She had handled herself on the bus today, she'd gotten through the seizure and the daze afterward without doing anything too regrettable. They had to trust her sooner or later, so they might as well get used to it now.

CHAPTER THIRTY-FOUR

JULIE

Three days passed before Sophie came home, during which time Julie cleaned the house and completed four work projects early. She puttered on the military mom site and the Pilot action site and was relieved to find her daughter hard at work on several new calls to arms, proof she was alive and safe. GNM chatted up a storm with her fearless leader.

I wish just one person in Congress seemed willing to stick their neck out for non-Piloted people, Sophie wrote. *If we had someone with power to ask our questions, we wouldn't have to waste so much time on trying to get their attention.*

What about Griffith? Julie wrote, then erased before hitting send. Too risky, especially if her fake persona wasn't American, and anyway, was it even true? Her job was to follow up on constituent issues, but she wasn't sure what he'd say if she came to him with this one, given the district jobs BNL brought.

Instead, she wrote, *It figures that they all finally find common ground on something and it's this. Here in Canada, too.*

Blame Canada, some rando responded. It wasn't a private conversation, but Julie still got annoyed at the interruption. Sophie didn't get the movie reference, and went off on how it wasn't Canada's fault the US was exporting bad ideas, and the conversation moved on without her.

On the third night, Julie got irredeemably, irrefutably hammered, finishing an entire bottle of sauvignon blanc on her own, to Val's single IPA. She tended not to sleep on nights that Sophie was out, and the more nights Sophie strung together, the more strung out Julie became. The drinks had been Val's idea, and Julie approved all through the pleasant stages, the exuberance and the expansiveness and the warmth. She went to bed before her body discovered her betrayal.

The next morning, said body informed her it was fully aware, and what's more, it did not appreciate her effort. Her head pounded to a beat that pulsed behind her right eyeball. Her Pilot was a megaphone pointed her way, sound and light churning her organs. She put her pillow over her face to block the sun.

"Oh Lord, Mom, are you hungover?" The words were dipped in an elegant combination of teenage indignation and disgust. Julie lifted one corner of her pillow to make sure she wasn't dreaming. Sophie stood over the bed, hands on her hips. She was so damn pointy, from her elbows to her words, but she was home. Julie struggled to a seated position, swinging her legs out of bed. Mistake. Her stomach took a moment to catch up with the movement and protested having been left behind. Sophie would never forgive her if Julie puked on her shoes.

"I can't believe *you* lecture *me* on responsibility."

Julie groaned and staggered to the bathroom. She closed the door and found her voice. "It's not irresponsible for an adult to get drunk in her own home. Regrettable, but not irresponsible."

She practically heard the eye roll through the door. *Don't leave again*, she prayed. *I'm not lecturing. You started it.* She opened the toilet and vomited.

Once she'd brushed her teeth and washed her face and tried to make peace with the world, Julie stepped back out into the bedroom. Sophie had disappeared—who would want to hang around listening to her mother puke?—but the door hadn't slammed, and she was hopeful.

She located her daughter in the kitchen scrambling eggs, and resisted offering to help; Sophie would accuse her of being controlling. Instead, she poured coffee from the pot Val had started before her run, then pulled three whole-grain English muffins from the breadbox. If Sophie didn't want one she'd eat them all herself, or Val would eat one or two depending on how far she had run.

She didn't trust herself to say anything, lest Sophie misconstrue it. She was happy to be in the same room with the girl again, even if she'd never seen anybody scramble eggs with so much attitude, and the odor was making her queasy. Six broken eggshells lay strewn across the counter beside the range. Funny the signals Sophie sent: *I am home, I am making breakfast for everyone of my own volition, but I refuse to enjoy it. You will see no remorse except for my effort.* At least that was Julie's best guess, and who knew if it was anywhere close to accurate.

The front door opened and closed. "Cooking again?" Val called from the front hall.

"Sophie!" She crossed the kitchen and threw her arms around the girl at the stove, who didn't have time to ward off the hug. Julie wished she had done something similar: unabashed joy was one thing Sophie couldn't defend against. If only she could rewind twenty minutes.

Granted, it wasn't her fault they had started off yet another morning on the wrong foot. Sophie had gone after her, not the other way around. Still, jealousy; no, turn it off. Be grateful she still allowed Val to hug her. Enjoy it vicariously. Eat eggs and toast with her as if nothing were broken, as if none of this had ever been any way else. Don't let her catch you missing any other iteration of her. They were all difficult. You might as well sit with this one while she allows herself to be present.

Julie arranged the toasted muffins on a plate on the kitchen table. She opened the cabinet to take out three plates, then got knives and forks from the drawer. Every movement was careful, both for her throbbing head and the fear that any word or action on her part might send Sophie running again. Sophie couldn't object to cutlery. Sophie turned from the stove with her pan and shoveled eggs onto each plate. They all sat.

"Thanks for breakfast, Soph," Julie tried tentatively. Sophie, mouth full, nodded at her; that was positive acknowledgement, at least.

Val spread peanut butter on her toast. "How did your meeting go?"

"Meetings," Sophie said, emphasizing the plural. "There's so much going on right now we've been having them every night. It's the only way to keep on top of everything."

"What's going on right now?" Julie tried to keep the question light and innocent, as if she hadn't spent two nights online trolling action after action.

Sophie gave her a withering look, but deigned to answer. "Congress is working with BNL to subsidize Pilots for all ninth graders below the poverty level. That's practically making them mandatory! Can you imagine the pressure on those kids? How can anyone refuse?"

It startled Julie to hear Sophie refer to those five years her junior as kids. She was still a kid herself, as far as Julie was concerned, though she knew better than to say as much.

Val frowned. "I see how that would have your group concerned, Soph. What are you doing about it?"

As always, Julie was impressed with Val's ability to ask questions that came across as genuine interest. Or maybe it was that Sophie assumed Val's interest to be genuine and Julie's suspect. Or maybe it was all in Julie's head. Or maybe this was guilt for having snooped so much online that nothing she asked could truly be an innocent question; she knew the answers already.

"For that one we're teaching students how to do organized walkouts. We've got an education campaign going aimed at the kids—that one's going all the time, but we're ramping it up—to let them know the risks, and let them know they can refuse. Another for teachers and administrators, and another for parents."

"Who is 'we,' Soph?" Julie asked, though she knew the answer. "Is that just locally?"

"Not just local. Local chapters are handling the on-the-ground stuff, but it's a national campaign." She paused, then added, "I wrote one of the handouts myself, though," with more than a touch of pride.

"Which one?" Julie asked, then panicked. Had she implied she was familiar with the materials?

"It's aimed at students. 'Sometimes a Free Update Isn't Free.' Ads on all the social networks, and we have somebody who hacks into school computer systems to distribute mass e-mails through a fake student account. Then paper copies at the schools and in the neighborhoods."

A quick frown passed over Julie's face. She tried to disguise it, but it was too late.

Sophie glared at her. "What's the matter? Oh. You didn't like the hacking bit? Too illegal for you? You don't have to worry, Mother. I did not personally hack anything. I don't know how to do that. You can go another night without having to worry about bailing me out of federal prison and save your concern for Central Booking downtown. I'm not doing anything Fed-worthy."

That had been exactly Julie's concern. She hadn't read anything about systems hacking, and she thought she was privy to most of what went on in the local chapter. There must be other places where the leaders gathered that she wasn't welcome. That made sense; at least they were smart enough not to broadcast the illegal parts of their actions.

Sophie was still talking, and Julie's Pilot had allowed her to track both the conversation and her own diverging train of thought. Not that she needed much attention to follow Sophie as she worked up a head of steam on the protection thing again.

". . . I can't believe you're more concerned for my safety than you are for the thousands of kids who are about to get Pilots forced on them before they know the ramifications, or that they have a choice. If their parents and schools won't protect him, it's on us to inform them." Her spiky hair bobbed and weaved as she spoke, like it was fighting its own boxing match.

Julie homed in on something in Sophie's rant. "If their parents won't protect *him*?" she repeated. "Is that a dig at us?"

"I meant them. Parents won't protect *them*." Sophie flushed, then pulled herself back to righteous anger. "But you do know how I feel about David's Pilot: the same as I feel about all of them. Yours is maybe worse, since you saw David struggle, and you decided to do it anyway. You made a fully informed stupid choice."

Julie resisted the urge to send her daughter to her room over "stupid choice." Instead, she threw her plate in the dishwasher and left the room. The food had helped her hangover a bit. She went back to the bedroom and climbed into the unmade bed.

Cool autumn sun filtered through the open blinds. Funny how the quality of sunlight changed from summer to fall. You would think sunlight would be sunlight no matter what, but it wasn't so. The level of intensity, the angle, everything changed. You were more grateful for it in autumn, too. In summer, it burned your skin and heated everything to the point of unbearable. By mid-October you just wished it would play across your face a little longer. She heard Val's chair scrape the kitchen floor, then her steps on the stairs.

Julie knew her apology long before Val entered the bedroom. "Sorry about that. It was her or me, and I thought it was better for everybody if I left."

"I think that's true." Val threw herself on the bed. "I told her I'd go to the meeting with her tonight."

Julie propped herself on an elbow. "She said you could? For real? How did you convince her?"

"I didn't convince her. She asked me."

"I'm guessing I'm not invited?"

"No way," Val said. "You're the enemy, Jules. Sorry about that." She sat on the bedspread and took Julie's hands. "At least I get to see what goes on. Also, I think she'll let me drive her, so that's one night we don't have to worry about her on the bus."

Better than nothing. One night of less worry was definitely a good thing, a night where her worry might still force her to look at the military sites, but not Sophie's. She'd grown up with a sheepdog-crossed mutt, a herding dog. He had tried to gather her and her parents in the same room every night and wasn't satisfied until everybody was watching TV or scrolling phones or reading in the same space. She hadn't realized how much she'd become like Max. At least tonight she'd have tabs on everyone but David, even if she couldn't be there herself. Max hadn't been able to delegate, so she had that on sheepdogs.

CHAPTER THIRTY-FIVE

VAL

Val had been angling for an invitation to Sophie's group for ages. Since before the meetings existed, when Sophie attended her first rally and Val had played the world's worst spy. The rally had spoken to her, and it was only the realization she'd be stepping on Sophie's toes that kept her from going back. Gabe and his father were a team; maybe Sophie would see her that way someday, too. She wouldn't be the one to broach it. If that meant she couldn't be part of the movement, so be it.

She waited. When her school decided not to bring her back from suspension, they scraped by on Julie's paycheck. It took a full year for her to find a job in a public high school on the west side, coaching and teaching non-Piloted geography, which by then was the actual class name. She made sure the students in it knew she thought they were smart and capable, and she took joy in the fact that, Piloted or not, running was still running, and students still needed her advice on body mechanics, on training, on strategy.

She was one of only four teachers at her new school without Pilots, and they all taught the non-Piloted classes. They sometimes chatted about how fast it had all happened, about the way Pilots had so quickly become the default, so that the class choices were geography and non-Piloted geography, or the fact that there were five freshman geography sections, and the non-Piloted one had only twenty students. Same in other subjects as well.

When FreerMind formalized its existence, she cheered quietly. When Gabe and Sophie got the two local jobs, which were supposed to be field organizer and assistant field organizer, but instead insisted on co-running the branch at a ridiculously low wage that split the difference, she cheered them on while defending their decision to Julie.

Val loved the idea of a meeting where you could talk with other non-Piloted folks, but she didn't want to stifle Sophie's participation in her own group; Sophie needed it more than she did. She celebrated proof that they'd managed to raise a competent adult capable of holding a job in an increasingly tricky economy, even if it wasn't the job they'd envisioned, or enough money to live on.

When Sophie and Julie exploded at each other over breakfast, and Sophie asked Val to come with her and "see what we actually do, instead of whatever the two of you concoct in your paranoid brains," and Val played it cool and said sure, she'd be open to attending, she had been hoping for that invitation for years.

Val let Sophie chart a circuitous course to the meeting, amused Sophie thought she could deceive Val, and hurt that she thought she needed to; Val had been driving and running through this city since long before Sophie existed. They skirted the neighborhood that housed the first public school she'd taught in; these were the kinds of neighborhoods she'd grown up in herself. Another parenting failure if she'd never shown Sophie she knew firsthand that love and hope and despair and rage at systemic inequality existed here, too, and needed to be looked at head-on rather than avoided. She decided against questioning the directions.

She waited until they'd parked to say, "I don't want to step on your toes."

"Be yourself. Most people are pretty quiet at their first meeting. Do you want to be introduced as my mother?"

"That's your call."

They stepped into a long, echoing room. The floor was inlaid with chipped square tiles, drab green and drab gray, interspersed in some pattern known only to the person who had placed them. It had worn in distinct paths, showing the foot patterns of several generations of lodge members. An actual moose head overlooked a long bar covered in stacked flyers. The moose was enormous, with antlers that spread like branches, and which someone had festooned with plastic leis, giving him the look of someone who had over-stayed a party. She wondered where you bought moose heads if you were in the market for one, or if you had to kill one yourself. Online auction, maybe? The postage would be obscene.

On the walls hung pictures of the lodge's members through the years, left behind when they moved out. Juxtaposed with those abandoned old men was evidence of the new inhabitants: informa-tional posters, medical posters, pictures of various successful ac-tions. They'd tacked up several Pilot ads, which people had defaced, overwriting the propaganda with the truths their movement held dear.

The building clearly needed TLC, but that was secondary. The thing Val noticed when she entered—after the moose—was the vibe: the warmth of the greetings, the aroma of whatever was cooking, the way not a single person looked like they'd been left to sit alone if they didn't want to. Her first thought was, *No wonder Sophie likes it here.*

Sophie craned her neck and then waved through an open office door at the back, where Gabe sat wolfing a burger at a cluttered desk. He looked out into the room at that moment and returned the wave. He took a final bite, chugged from his water bottle, and came their way.

"Sorry. I get sick of crockpot meals sometimes. Just needed a—whoa! Mama Val! Long time no see!" He threw his arms around Val, a hug she returned.

"Gabe! Good to see you. How's your dad? Does he come to these meetings?"

"He still speaks at actions and rallies, but he's not a meetings guy."

Sophie glanced at the clock. "This is a touching reunion, but we should get started." She herded them toward a circle of chairs, then rang a bell. The others in the room, a dozen maybe, took their seats.

"Welcome to FreerMind! I'm Sophie, co-head of this chapter. I'm glad you all could join us tonight. Thursdays we usually discuss media strategies, which is not the most glamorous topic. First, let's start with everybody introducing themselves and their pronouns. You can say as little or as much as you want."

She started on her left, so the circle would end with Val rather than begin with her. The first person was a youngish Black woman, David's age maybe, with a forearm crutch resting against her chair. Her head was shaved, a small bandage at her temple. Val tried not to stare: she'd never seen a deactivated one before. "Hi, I'm, uh, Tommie. She/her. I had a Pilot for thirteen years, until I had it taken out last week. I wanted to see what these meetings were about."

Thirteen years! That made her one of the earliest adopters; even earlier than David. "Welcome, Tommie" and "Congratulations" and "Freedom!" came from the circle, then they settled back into introductions.

When the circle came round to Val, she introduced herself by her first name and pronouns, adding "never had a Pilot." She liked that better than the other phrase she'd heard, "Pilot-free by choice," since that suggested those who had chosen were somehow better than those who had the choice made for them.

She wanted to say more, but she shut herself up. For all the things she wanted to get off her chest about teaching in a Piloted world, about her paranoias living with a Piloted spouse, about her heart aching for their daughter who had created a life out of a battle she shouldn't have had to fight, she didn't think that was why Sophie had invited her. She suspected she was meant to be there as a witness, not a participant, and that talking about herself would show Sophie she'd misunderstood her place. Here, at last, was something Sophie could shape and control, something that was hers and Gabe's in a way that nothing had been theirs before. If Val spoke, she'd want to speak again, to be a part of this, which would mean Sophie would forever be stuck with her mother hanging out in the place where she had established herself as an adult.

The seizure only reinforced that. When Sophie stopped speaking midsentence, her hand clutching for something out of reach, Val knew exactly what was happening. She had barely shifted in her chair when Gabe glanced at his phone and smoothly took over the sentence, directing everyone who wanted to work on public response over to the bar. Val stuffed her hands into her armpits and forced herself to stay seated for a long minute, until Sophie came back to herself.

"I'm okay," she said. "I'm okay."

Gabe glanced down at his phone again, then nodded at Val, who returned a tight smile. Her daughter had people who knew what to do and looked out for her.

"Why?" Sophie asked her in the car on the way home. "Thank you, first, then why?"

Val smiled. "If you're saying thank you, that's why. It was your meeting. I didn't want to step in if everything was under control."

"Was it? Under control?"

"Gabe started talking as if it had been planned that way, and he kept an eye on how long it lasted. I don't think anybody thought it was all that strange. If anything, they thought he missed a cue, not that you dropped out."

"Good. That's what he's supposed to do. A few others know, too."

Val put a hand on her knee. Sophie let it stay there. "Was it hard for you, Ma?"

"Not stepping in? A little. A lot, maybe."

"Thank you, again. What did you think of the meeting?"

"It was really interesting, Soph. You know what you're talking about. You're a good leader. I've got to say I'm impressed by what you've got going."

"But?"

"I think you're in a safe place once you get there, but I don't think I'm any less worried about the getting-there part. Have you been keeping track of your seizures?"

"Yeah. Two this week. One definitely got triggered by heat, or maybe heat and stress. This one, I don't know. No reason. Are you going to tell Mom?"

"I'll tell her what I just said: you're in a safe place, and you have people looking out for you, and you're a good leader. I didn't realize how much you were in charge of." The light turned red and she met Sophie's eyes. "I'm proud of you, Soph. You're doing an amazing thing."

Sophie smiled and sank back into her seat.

Back at the house, Sophie disappeared into her bedroom, though her footsteps were soft, and the door closed rather than slammed. Julie lounged on the couch, television on, maybe dozing, but she opened her eyes when Val walked in.

"How did it go?" Julie shifted her feet to let Val sit, then let them drop again into her wife's lap.

Val kneaded the ball of Julie's right foot, eliciting a groan. "She's really good at the thing she's doing. Organized, inspiring, well-spoken."

"And?"

"I think she's safe there. I'd prefer she crash there than go back and forth, honestly. I don't think we should be setting a curfew. She's an adult."

Julie frowned.

"It's good people there. Not just Gabe. They've got her back."

"What about you? Are you going to go again?"

Val shook her head and switched feet. "I don't think it's for me."

CHAPTER THIRTY-SIX

DAVID

At the airport the civilian airport almost home people crowds laughter announcements beeping carts instrumental versions of songs from movies music means you can't hear what you need to hear tune it out tune it out David tried to tune it out. He kept his back to the wall even here however many miles from where he needed to keep his back to the wall he didn't know the miles he'd never needed to know the miles there was an ocean between a desert between the miles didn't matter keep your attentions elsewhere, soldier. It didn't feel like less of a need here it didn't feel any less urgent the space was so vast there were so many people so many corners so many angles. He scanned the crowd like he'd been taught like he had practiced a thousand times in a thousand rooms on a thousand streets. It didn't matter that this place was supposed to be safer. Supposed to be home whatever that meant anymore.

Some homecomings got military jets to the base, families on the tarmac. Big publicity stuff. Not David's. He'd arrived home commercial. He preferred it this way. He wasn't much for open spaces these days. He stayed close to the wall.

Beyond the security checkpoint, some volunteer greeters stood ready to welcome, and families waited for their soldiers to step out. Dolenz pulled a woman into her arms; Tuvim was quickly surrounded by children with balloons. David's eyes did their customary sweeps, his Pilot boosting and processing the signal so he could check the rafters the windows the doorways the alcoves in a quick glance. A yellow balloon bounced against the skylight high above, and a sparrow cut panicked arcs around it. Plain black bag unattended near a potted plant whose bag nobody's bag where was security a woman next to the garbage can tossing a coffee cup returned to the bag nothing to see here. The other soldiers looked relaxed. David was more like the sparrow.

He walked past the happy reunions, overwhelmed by guilt. His moms would have loved to be here. Would have been here in a second, if David had told them to come. It wasn't their fault David had been unable to visualize the reunion scene, unable to imagine hugs or kisses or any fuss made over him. He didn't want to draw anyone out into the open. Didn't want it to be his fault if anything happened.

He fumbled with his stateside phone, hoping it had kept its charge. Twenty percent. Enough to message both moms. On my way home—surprise! I'll be at your door tomorrow.

He tucked the phone back into his pocket and made his way down the corridor, his pack over one shoulder slightly obscuring his peripheral vision on the right, so he kept to that wall to compensate. He dug for his wallet as he walked. He should have done that on the plane, so he wouldn't have to do it here in the open. Already he'd slipped.

He took a deep breath and stepped away from the wall, then out the door onto the train platform. The machines to buy rail tickets were still the same one broken one working no line there was also an app these days but he didn't have it. He negotiated the menu while his other attentions examined the people on the platform. Mostly airport workers finishing their shifts: tired, routine, IDs still around their necks, some with safety vests, fingerless gloves, dirty fingers, some in polos, varied as jockey silks based on their airlines. An acned white teen in a purple jacket slumped on a bench, the only one who seemed out of place. No bags, so he wasn't a traveler. No airport or police badge, unless he had it under his jacket. David jammed his ticket in his pocket and reframed himself so the boy was the center focus, everything else peripheral.

The train arrived and new passengers negotiated the geometric dance that put them all at the farthest points from each other. David took the first rear-facing seat in the first car, so the only person behind him would be the driver. The teen chose some car down the line. Not David's problem anymore.

He could have ridden straight to the bus station then home but instead he got off downtown, just past the tourist-sanitized areas. Was it odd that he felt more relaxed in a place where he was supposed to keep his guard up? He knew how to do this. He marched two blocks and booked into the first cheap motel he came across. The desk clerk attended him from behind bulletproof glass and overcharged him for a bottle of brandy from under the counter. The seal was broken but he took it anyway.

His room had a busted and patched door, like somebody had punched out the lock. A piece of plywood over the hole, and a new doorknob slightly below where a doorknob should be. His key worked, so he didn't care. He locked the dead bolt and the chain, then dumped his bags behind the door for added security.

The bed passed his cursory bedbug check, and he collapsed onto it, boots and all. The brandy tasted watered down, but there was still some alcohol in there so he wasn't complaining. His buddies would log into their Pilot apps at this point and change back to this time zone, maybe add a cycle-down period, something they all removed during deployment. He didn't bother since he couldn't tell the difference. He drank until he felt his own version of cycle-down, the slight diminishment of attention the difference of attention. Being drunk helped somewhat. No, being drunk helped a lot.

He missed his unit. Alone was okay, but he wasn't used to it anymore. He tried to think of whom he could phone. He tried Milo, but disconnected after one ring when he realized the time. Milo had come back a couple of months before him, was back with Karina. No point in disturbing him.

The phone rang a minute later.

"Are you stateside?" Milo asked. "Why'd you hang up?"

"Wasn't sure if it was a good time."

"You know you can call whenever you need."

"I just thought it might be late."

"It is. Whatever. You okay? You home?"

"Okay enough. In some fleabag motel for the night. I wasn't ready to go home yet."

"Are you sure you're okay? Do you want me to meet you somewhere?"

"Nah. I'm wasted already. Just wanted to say hey."

David closed his eyes and listened to sirens voices noise in the pipes TV from next door until sleep took him with his boots on. Woke once bolt upright to someone trying the door, then a knock. Held his breath, waited, calculated his options. The knock moved on to other doors. Someone looking for drugs or a friend or a room number forgotten.

He woke the next morning with a head full of fuzz and no clue where he was. That only lasted a moment, but a moment in which he thought he might have died or been captured the sunlight was wrong the room was wrong everything was off from where it should be. He tried desperately to cut through the fog as his Pilot created more fog, processing the sounds from the other rooms and from outside. A stinkbug careened off the walls and the ceiling. Water in the pipes. Car alarm outside.

"Take it in threes": that was the advice from his first activation and calibration tests. Dr. Abrams he remembered in particular, a blond woman with no Pilot who was reduced to bony angles and painted-on eyebrows in his mind. "I can't keep up with everything you can pay attention to with your implant. List them in threes for me. It'll help you process and show me how fast you're adjusting."

He told her he saw blue-seven-F on the multikeyed charts. He told her he saw doctor-intern-notepad, even when he saw and felt and heard all those things and more at once, doctor-intern-notepad-coldass table-intern's missing button-antiseptic smell-doctor's leaking pen-dot of something maybe blood on an otherwise clean floor-sky out the window-person watering flowers on the adjacent roof-voices down the hall-blue-seven-fucking F. It was hard to put words to full, nonprioritized attention. He remembered panicking at that stage. Even as he got used to it, it was already overwhelming. Take it in threes.

After the threes came prioritization. They got the basics early on, rudimentary methods of tuning out nonessential stimuli. It wasn't until the Army that he understood the need for prioritization. Person on the adjacent roof comes first, then voices in the hall. The rest, even the doctor, is noise. The Army taught him that, except they thought there was an end to noise a finiteness a finity was *finity* a word. In high school in the Army everywhere everybody talked about the Pilot in different terms than the ones he used. Like it had a beginning and an end. Their noise had a different quality than his. He didn't know why. He took the tests he passed the tests he did everything he was supposed to do. They all just coped with it better maybe. Maybe he had no cope he was weak somehow defective.

He climbed the hill from the bus stop. Scanned the parked cars for movement the treetops the rooftops you're home, soldier, stand down, but he couldn't. He walked the familiar street the street he'd grown up on the street where he knew he should feel safe. He did feel safe safe-ish anyway but that didn't mean he knew how to stop to turn off to quiet the instinct to cover every angle.

He and Julie saw each other at the same time. Julie stood on the front stoop in a striped dress, reading something on her tablet. She stood like she'd just stepped out but he could tell she'd been waiting awhile from the sweat on her upper lip. It was okay he was sweaty too, soaked really, from the effort of watching out without anyone else to watch out with him. He pulled her into a bear hug he was facing the doorway he couldn't see enough what was behind his back he didn't know and if her eyes were closed she wasn't watching the street. He swung her in his arms he'd never done that before but she was lighter than he expected and he needed to see the street the cars the neighbors four houses down watching and smiling. She smelled like her shampoo, like mint and something else, a flower, the kind of thing you wouldn't remember, like this is what my mom smells like, until you smelled it, and then you relaxed a little, just for a second. The scent gave him the smallest permission to lower his guard, the smallest implication someone else was still watching his back, in a different way than he was used to, a way he remembered but had forgotten.

She found her footing, ran a hand through her hair, drawing his attention to her own Pilot by her ear. "What are you doing here? Why didn't you tell me they were sending you home? I thought you had another month!"

"They kept talking about extending the tour and I didn't want to tell you one thing and then find out another."

"How long have you known?"

"Only a couple days," he lied. She wouldn't know; he'd had a couple of deployments now where they hadn't been able to communicate at all, and he hadn't always had advance notice himself. She seemed to buy it, in any case.

She pulled him in close again. "I'm not complaining. Just surprised. Like, I would have taken time off to spend time with you or something. I would have cleaned. Your ma was so upset not to be here when you got home, too, but it's a school day, and Sophie is off somewhere . . ."

"Since when do you need to clean for me?"

"I don't. I haven't touched anything in your room, beyond vacuuming. I just . . . I have to go to work and I want to be here and hear how you are and I've been standing here hoping you'd arrive before I had to leave but now you're here and . . . it's so good to see you."

He smiled. "Good to see you, too. Go to work. I'll be fine."

"I hate leaving, but I guess you can use some time for yourself after all those flights and whatever else?"

"Definitely."

"Can I bring dinner back? What would you like? Thai? Szechuan?"

He gave a groan of delight. "Oh God, yes. You don't even know."

"Sweet. The spare key is on the peg if you don't have yours handy. Help yourself to anything in the house if you're hungry. Why am I saying that like you're a guest? It's your house. Eat. Drink. I love you. I'll be back soon."

She pushed him through the door and headed off. So she'd been waiting for him to make sure he could get in. He felt guilty he hadn't come the night before, but he'd needed the night to transition.

He walked through the house his house home. It smelled right, familiar, he couldn't even say what the right scent was but this was it. The cool old clock in the living room his grandmother's grandmother clock did its tick-tick-ticking thing as he walked through the rooms and a loud bird did its loud-bird thing somewhere out some window a window must be open somewhere for it to be so loud but he didn't see an open window.

His room looked exactly as it should. She'd said she hadn't touched anything and it didn't look like she had. Another noise downstairs the icemaker in the fridge doing its icemaker thing. He dropped his bags and went to the kitchen and opened the fridge and found Val's beer and chugged one he didn't even like IPA downed two there were eight he left six. Crushed the cans and hid them under the other recycling since it was still morning and he was an adult he was a soldier he could drink if he wanted but his parents would judge even if they said they wouldn't.

He sat in the chair he and Sophie used to fight over, the armchair that reclined violently when you swung the lever. He swung the lever and his feet elevated. It was too comfortable too soft, so soft he could sleep, really, and it didn't feel right to sleep. He stood, paced the room, finally situated himself on the couch arm. When they were kids they got yelled at for sitting on the arms for climbing on the back for swinging the armchair lever too hard, but he wasn't going to do any harm sitting on the arm. It was a good place. Not comfortable not soft. From there he got the full view from the bay window, five six seven eight houses' worth of across the street, neighbors coming and going, the mail carrier in shorts and a broad-brimmed hat and earbuds making her slow way along the street singing to herself.

Even here even here home his family's house home even here David kept watch. He had some memory that his head had been quieter here had some hope that when he returned he would be quiet again but it was false a false memory a memory of before the Pilot sped him up turned him on filled his head with constant input vigilance noise protective noise. He watched he watched he listened he watched he watched.

CHAPTER THIRTY-SEVEN

SOPHIE

The figure sitting stiffly on the couch arm in the front room was familiar even in shadow. He wore his Army Combat Uniform, which didn't do much to camouflage him against the leather couch. He'd abandoned his hat on the end table, and his head was shorn of curls. He had no expression on his face.

David leapt from the couch the instant she entered, breaking into a wide grin. He crossed the space between them in three long strides to pull her into a bear hug, lifting her from her feet.

"Softserve!"

"Davey Not-So-Wavy!" She ran a hand over the soft fuzz on his head. "You can put me down now."

"Yes, sir." He lowered her, but didn't let go. She held on, too, for a long minute. He felt wiry beneath the thick uniform, all muscle. When he finally relaxed his grip on her, she shut the door and kicked her bag to the side, then collapsed on the reclining chair catty-corner from the couch. He crossed to the door as well, to bolt it, then returned to settle into the couch this time, though Sophie got the impression it was a deliberate attempt to look at ease, not actual comfort. She bent to unlace her own combat boots, ashamed for a moment of the trappings of war—the boots, David's old jacket—she had adopted. She wasn't sure he'd ever seen her in them before, and she felt as if she were playacting.

"What's with the boots, soldier?" he asked, as if reading her mind.

She hoped the dim light obscured the flood of color to her face. "Nothing. They're comfortable. You wear them all day, too, right?" He nodded and she relaxed. She put her boots behind the chair, out of view, and tucked her feet under her.

"Where are they?" she asked, deliberately changing the subject.

"Ma is still at work, and Mom went to get takeout in my honor. You have no idea how much I've missed Chinese food."

"I don't think we've had it the whole time you were gone. At least not any night I've been here, I don't think."

"Civilian sacrifice for the sake of the soldiers. I love it." As he said it, his body tensed and his eyes darted to the window. Sophie squinted and spotted their neighbor Mr. Winters, walking his old bloodhound past their house.

"Is it weird to be home?" she asked, trying to bring David's attention back inside. His eyes returned to her, but she could tell his attention was split. Piloted people always thought they were being subtle when they chose to expand their focus, but they often let their jaws go slightly slack, and the muscles around their mouths. She didn't know if anyone else noticed.

"Weird but good," he said. "I think it'll take a while to get used to being here. To not being there."

"I keep wanting to poke you to see if you're real."

"I'll thank you to not poke me. Did you even know I was coming back today? When Mom went to get food I offered to go with her but she said I should wait here for you."

Sophie shook her head. "I asked them not to tell me. I figured I'd see you when you got here and I would get a nice surprise out of it."

"That makes sense, I guess. It's weird, but so are you."

She stuck her tongue out. How quickly they reverted to their childhood relationship. They didn't have an adult one, not yet; he'd been gone for too long. In any case, she was glad she'd stuck with the surprise story. She didn't think it would benefit him to hear she'd chosen not to be told when he was coming home not because she liked surprise, but because she didn't like anticipation. She didn't like counting days, or the queasy feeling of almost-here. On the rare occasions when she felt auras before her seizures, that was what they felt like: an imminent arrival. The pairing of the two feelings made her uncomfortable. She felt like she might bring him bad luck if she hoped too hard for his return.

He glanced at the door and seconds later Sophie heard the dead bolt slide. Having Combat David around was like having a dog in the house. Every movement outside was a cause for concern, or at least curiosity; thankfully he didn't bark. He was on his feet and moving toward the door before it had swung open, and had Val in a hug before she was fully into the house. From where she sat, Sophie saw pure joy on Val's face. Val dropped her messenger bag next to where Sophie had left hers and hugged David, who was not only taller than her, but twice as broad through the shoulders. Sophie didn't know how it was possible for him to take up so much space when he was so skinny. Maybe it was the uniform.

"Why are you two sitting in the dark?" Val asked, turning on a lamp. She'd stopped hugging David, but kept her hand on his sleeve.

"Hadn't bothered turning on the light," answered Sophie, though she didn't actually know David's reason. They hadn't really gotten beyond superficial greetings yet. Dancing around a relationship that had been put on hiatus for ages. They had messaged each other a little bit during his deployments, but those interactions had been superficial, too.

Julie arrived with a plastic bag in each hand, a smiley face emblazoned on each. The smiley scales of justice, weighing her down equally on both sides with rice and dumplings and spring rolls and chicken. Sophie watched from her easy chair, not removing herself from the family, but observing briefly from the outside, as she had often done.

Theirs was a strange family. Four people, but only one blood bond. She didn't feel any less their child, any more than she doubted for a second that Val, who had still not stopped holding on to David, was his mother in every sense even if she hadn't given birth to him. Even with his new adult face, he looked more like Val than Julie, held himself more like Val than Julie.

She knew she didn't look like any of them, but it didn't matter. They were bonded by nineteen years in the same house together, the rest of them longer. Family was all of those things: blood, but also common experience. Whatever had happened to David while he was away, he had changed. His edges were different. He made all the motions of home without looking like he was fully with them. She could certainly relate.

The dinner conversation avoided every interesting topic. Sophie wanted to hear about David's experiences, the real ones, and what had made him so jumpy, so attuned to his surroundings. She could only imagine. She'd never written to him about the movement, so she wasn't surprised he didn't bring it up, but she still wanted to tell him more about it, wanted his opinion on the subject, touchy as it might be.

Instead, their mothers steered the conversation as if they were navigating a ship through rocky waters. She didn't blame them for trying to make his first meal at home a joyous one, though it did feel forced. Save the contentious issues for later, or let David raise them when he was ready. They asked him about plane travel, the places he'd gone, as if he were some jet-set playboy, rather than a soldier. They spoke about their jobs and the neighborhood. He let them guide the topics at hand, and Sophie stayed mostly silent.

After the meal, Julie went into the kitchen and returned with a round cake, the words WELCOME HOME! scrolled on the frosting in script, and DAVID in block letters. How long had they known today was the day? They'd certainly managed to keep it from Sophie. She knew she'd asked them to, but she was surprised they'd been able to pull it off.

"So," she asked finally, her mouth full of ice cream cake, "what are you doing next?" That had been the other question she was surprised nobody else was asking. She realized too late that there might be a reason. "I mean, if you want to talk about it."

He maintained a steady rhythm of cake to mouth for another few bites, then turned to look at her. "I'm leaving the military."

Sophie's mouth dropped open, genuine shock she then papered over with a smile, in case the moms already knew and she'd been left out of the knowing; she would never have expected him to say that particular sentence in a million years. Both mothers exchanged a glance, so he must not have written about this decision. The surprise was on everyone this time.

"Leaving?" Hopefulness tried to bust through concern on Val's face.

"Yeah, my commitment is over, and I could re-up, but the timing is right to make a jump to private-sector work." He tipped his plate and let the last of the ice cream swirl from one side to the other. As a kid he would have licked it, but now he watched it run.

"Will that cause any problems with your military benefits?" Leave it to Julie to quiz him on a practical detail instead of celebrating the news.

"If nobody else is going to say it, I will," Sophie said before David could answer their mother. "David, I have never been so relieved at anything in my whole life. I'm proud of what you've done for the country and all that, but I am ten thousand times happier to have my big brother back."

David grinned at her, though the smile didn't reach his eyes. Still, he looked relieved. "There's a whole separation process. I already found a job, so there won't be a gap in my benefits. And I'm not being discharged involuntarily, in case any of you were thinking that."

"Why would we think that?" asked Julie.

David shrugged. "I don't know. People get weird ideas into their heads. I wanted to make sure you know this is my choice."

"I don't care whose—" Val picked up the melting cake and left the room midsentence. Sophie heard the freezer open and shut, then Val returned. "I don't care whose choice it was. I'm happy you made it out in one piece. That's one worry off my worry list forever."

"Now you just have to worry about car crashes and random shootings and killer viruses like the civilian families do." Sophie thought it was funny, but the others gave her looks of various degrees of disgust. Everyone was a critic. She should know better than to bring up other things to worry about in any case, since those lists invariably included her.

"So, what's the new job?" she asked in hopes of getting the conversation back on track.

David smiled and tapped the light above his ear. "It should be really interesting work. Balkenhol Neural Labs."

Sophie was on her feet so quickly she knocked her plate to the floor. "Balkenhol? BNL? You're not serious." She clenched her hands into fists, then dropped them to her sides. He had to be joking.

The smile had vanished from David's face, replaced by confusion. "It's a good job. Pilot ambassador. It pays well. I'll get to travel to interesting places without people shooting at me."

"Somebody please tell me he's joking." Sophie wiped a tear from her cheek and fought the others back. She would not cry. She was a soldier. She turned on her heel and headed straight for the front door.

Once outside, she realized she'd probably been rash to leave with no ID, no cash, no phone, no backpack. She couldn't go downtown. Still, she had to go somewhere, now that she'd left.

She walked to her old primary school's playground, five blocks away. She crossed the shredded rubber and chose a swing. The evening was cooler than the previous ones had been, and only a couple of people were out walking their dogs, their blue Pilot lights bobbing and blinking like fireflies as they navigated the darkness. One light got closer. He stepped under the streetlamp, and she saw it was David.

"Can we talk?"

"It's a free country. You're welcome to talk."

Sophie pushed off with her legs and started to swing. She pumped hard, aiming for the sky, full of billions of twinkling Pilots. After a minute, she noticed David was beside her and swinging too, catching her, passing her. She tried to gain a few inches, pulled even, but then he managed a big swing that took him nearly vertical. She stopped trying and slowed until she was again scuffing the ground with her boots. David kept going. She contemplated walking away while he was still swinging, but she knew he would notice. He'd probably jump off in midarc and land on his feet. He could probably fly.

"I'm sorry," he said a short time later, earthbound again.

"You should be."

"They told me. I didn't know it was a thing for you."

"A thing for me? How could you not know? Oh yeah, because you've been gone for six years."

"You never said anything about it. Not on the phone or in messages."

"I didn't want to bother you. You had enough to worry about."

"But then how can you blame me for not knowing?"

"Because you should have just known. Even if I never said a word. You know how hard school was for me without a Pilot. You remember how tense things were when Mom started talking about getting hers." That had been only two years after he had gotten his, before he left. "You've never even liked it all that much, yourself. You've said so. So why sell it for them? They don't need help."

He put his face in his hands. His Pilot gleamed above his ear.

"Soph, I'm sorry. It's . . . I've been thinking of getting out for over a year, but I couldn't figure out what I wanted to do. Then Balkenhol called me out of the blue looking for spokespeople who had used their Pilots to achieve excellence in their fields, and I was already on their list from that ad the Army had me do. How could I say no?"

Sophie put a hand on his back. "You would have found a job eventually. You could have said no."

"Or I could have cost more people their lives like—you don't understand how done I was with being there." He looked her full on for the first time in the conversation. "I have to do this, Soph, but maybe they'll let me talk about how it really is. Maybe they'll let me say it saved me and my unit a hundred times over, but I hate the noise."

Sophie doubted it, but kept her mouth shut.

CHAPTER THIRTY-EIGHT

JULIE

Julie wished there could have been one night without drama. Sophie stood so quickly she knocked her plate to the floor. She didn't stop to pick it up when it broke.

"What was that about?" David asked after the door slammed. "Should I go after her?"

Julie went to grab paper towels for the ice cream and crumbs, leaving Val to answer. "She'll be okay. I don't think she'll go far without her bag. Your sister has become very involved in the anti-Pilot movement. You know there's an anti-Pilot movement, right?"

"Yes, but I don't know anything about it."

Julie listened as she cleaned, curious how Val would characterize Sophie's group. "They think it's been adopted too fast. It's leaving people behind, and they say there's negative data being suppressed, and BNL is lying to the government, and the government is lying to the parents, and the schools are going along for the ride because it helps their numbers."

"That's a lot of lying," David said. "Do you think it's true?"

Val raised her palms. "I think there's probably some lying going on somewhere in there. You know me: I wasn't a fan of the idea to begin with."

"What about you, Mom?" David asked.

Julie stood, plate shards in one hand, dirty towel clutched in the other. "My Pilot has never been anything but helpful, so it's hard to see the downside. Like yours."

David got to his feet. "I'm going to go find Sophie."

After the door had closed on David as well, Julie went into the kitchen to throw the plate shards in the trash. Val came up behind and held her.

"I can't believe he's back for good. He really did say that, right? I'm not dreaming?"

"He said it," Julie confirmed, tossing the rag in the sink and turning into her wife's embrace. "No more checking body counts online. For us, anyway."

"Do you think he's planning on living here?"

"No idea. I would think he's got the money to get a place of his own, but I'm not going to push him if he hasn't thought about it yet. He can stay as long as he needs, as far as I'm concerned."

"Me, too." Val pulled away to load the dishwasher. "But if he still eats the same way, we should probably ask him to chip in for groceries."

Julie laughed. "And we may have to dig some trenches if those two partisans are both under one roof."

"I don't think David's all that partisan, Jules. It sounds like it's just a job for him. Hopefully he can get on his feet and then move on to something that'll cause less family friction."

Val disappeared into the bathroom and Julie walked through the house, turning off lights. She left the door unlocked in case neither kid had taken keys. Half an hour later, already in bed, she heard the door creak and two whispering voices and footsteps and two closing bedroom doors, and all was right in the world, if only for a night. She closed her eyes and waited for her Pilot to cycle down to sleep.

Even in a morning mall, populated only by strolling seniors and Piloted guards, Julie noticed the changes in David. He walked with a tension that went beyond military bearing, like a drawn bow. He stayed close to the wall on one side. She followed the movement of his head and eyes from the corner of her own eye; Pilot watching Pilot. His eyes darted to the rooftops, to each passing shopper, to the storefronts, to the kiosks and planters and garbage cans. He clenched and unclenched his fists, touching his sides occasionally.

"You okay, Davey?"

"Fine," he said. The hairs on the back of his neck began to curl with sweat.

"What are you looking at?"

He shook his head. "You don't want to know."

"Try me."

He stopped, so she did, too. He looked her full in the eyes. Adult to adult. Then he turned and began to point. "Before Pilots, there was a specific order. First soldier would check the rooftops, second had the next floor of windows down from the roof, next person the floor below that. There was still a risk you were missing something in the building on the other side of the street. We still technically do that, but Pilots let us take it all in, over and over: left, right, forward, up, back. It's hard to turn off. I can't stop checking."

"I'm sorry, Davey. I didn't realize. We shouldn't have come here."

"I asked. I need clothes, and there's no point hiding in the house. Might as well learn to deal with this sooner than later."

"Are you, uh, will the Army pay for counseling? Not that you're not doing okay, but maybe it would help?"

"We're supposed to attend these sessions on fitting back into civilian life. I wasn't going to go, but maybe it's not a bad idea."

"Not a bad idea at all," she agreed. "Now, let's find you some clothes."

They resumed walking. He didn't look any less tense or less vigilant. They passed a guard, who stared at David with the same cool assessment David used to eye everyone else. If security was trained to watch for people who might crack, David's demeanor certainly would ring some alarm bells. She wanted to take his hand, to unclench it for him, but it wasn't her place, and she didn't want to embarrass him or make it worse.

CHAPTER THIRTY-NINE

SOPHIE

The second the front door closed behind Julie and David, Sophie dived for her phone. She didn't trust anything this important to even their most secure message boards, let alone a call or a text. Her message to Gabe the night before had read simply, Coffee. Tomorrow ten a.m. Hugs.

Hugs meant "urgent." *Urgent coffee* meant to meet at the anarchist coffee shop; they'd move on from there. She kept her phone muted so her moms wouldn't hear it, but checked it repeatedly until she fell asleep. He hadn't responded, but now she saw a message had come an hour before. Hugs. See ya.

She glanced at the time: nine thirty. Great. Yesterday's clothes back on, and she didn't have time to spike her hair, so she made do with gelling it straight back into a narrow ponytail. She ran out the door, then realized she'd forgotten to take her pills. Back to the kitchen to slam the meds, but it threw her timing off; her bus sped past the intersection as she sprinted toward the corner.

"Dammit," she said, slowing to a walk. No sense in rushing now; the next bus would be twenty minutes. She had used the code for "urgent" and she was going to be late to her own damn meeting. She stood in the empty bus shelter and fumbled for her phone to text an apology. She didn't think her lateness inconvenienced

Gabe too much, but she didn't want him to think she didn't take things seriously.

A car honked, and the passenger window lowered. "You're from the meeting, right? The other night?"

She stooped to peer into the open window. It was the kid from a few nights ago. She had guessed he was fifteen, but he must be sixteen at least to be driving. Still a kid. What was his name? She tried to come up with it but drew a blank.

"Dominic," he said, rescuing her. "And you were Sophie, right?"

"I still am."

"Do you need a ride somewhere?" The door unlocked.

She hesitated for only a second. "Yeah. I'm late to meet somebody, actually. You heading downtown?"

That was a stupid question, since his car was already pointed in that direction, but he nodded. She slipped into the front seat, squashing her backpack on top of her feet. A zipper dug into her shin and she smoothed it, then buckled herself in. "Thanks. I'm supposed to be at Stomping Grounds in twenty minutes and I missed my bus."

"No problem. That's where I was headed, too."

Sophie didn't know cars, but this was a pretty luxurious one. The seats were leather, and the interior was roomier than her parents' electric cars. The dashboard looked like a spaceship's. She held her head away from the seat back in case her hair stuff stained it. Her clothes felt grubby all of a sudden, and she hoped she didn't smell.

"Do you live around here?" she asked.

"A couple of neighborhoods north. In the county." He waved a hand in the direction he'd come from and made a face. "As soon as I graduate I'm moving to the city."

"Graduate? Are you a senior? I thought you were way younger." She shouldn't have said that; people took her for younger all the time because she was short.

He made another face. "Sophomore, but I'm seventeen. I got held back for not having a Pilot."

"What's your story?" Sophie asked. "Why no Pilot?"

"Paranoid grandparents," he said. "They were the ones who suggested I go to the meeting—but don't get me wrong; I think they're probably right to be paranoid. I just haven't decided yet."

"That's reasonable. Too bad more parents don't let their kids decide for themselves."

"Yeah. That mandatory thing you were talking about at the meeting was pretty crazy, but I feel like things are headed that way. I mean, driving tests are all geared for people who are Piloted now. I barely got my license. They expected me to know what was in front of me and behind me at the same time."

He didn't have trouble driving, despite the complaint. The car weaved smoothly in and out of lanes, avoiding a squirrel and then a woman with a baby carriage. A few raindrops spattered the windshield, making her grateful she'd accepted the ride.

"So what did you think?" she asked. "Of the meeting?"

He flashed her a smile. "It was pretty interesting. I mean, there's so much going on. I don't know if I'm ready to be an activist—I haven't made up my mind if maybe I should go with the crowd on this after all—but you definitely gave me a lot to think about."

"Good. All we want is to show you there's an option not to have one. It doesn't matter if you want to be an activist. Though we'd love to have you . . ." She blushed and was momentarily glad he didn't have a Pilot and wouldn't see the color in her cheeks. He was older than she'd thought, but still too young for her.

The coffee shop was on the corner of a main street and a block of boarded-up rowhouses. The busy street was parked up, so Dominic turned onto the abandoned one, which had several empty spots. He parallel parked pretty well for a county kid, if Sophie was any judge, though the fancy car gave him guidance, some of which he listened to and some of which he ignored. He got it right the second time.

She got out, then waited for him in the rain as he set a gear lock on the wheel.

"My grandparents insist," he said.

"You're lucky," she said. "I bet most grandparents wouldn't let you park a car that nice within a mile of this place."

He scratched his head and beeped the car a second time, as if he wasn't sure if he'd done it already. "Yeah, um, they don't exactly know I'm here. I meant they insist when I drive anywhere."

"Gotcha," Sophie said.

Stomping Grounds was the type of coffee shop that attracted only the truly dedicated: dedicated to caffeine, dedicated to revolution, dedicated to spending long hours hunched over a computer. It made no concessions to attracting commuters. There were no fancy coffee drinks, no flavor shots, no blenders. Nobody would have etched art in your foam, even if you had foam. They had the basics: coffee, assorted loose-leaf teas, scones, and muffins catering to a range of tastes and intolerances.

The music, when there was music, was dealer's choice, usually a barista's band, or the barista's friends. Two public computer terminals sat in one corner, tribute to the old world order; the manager who maintained them was an expert on Net privacy. An actual working phone booth occupied another corner, with a landline phone. This was less for countercultural purposes than for the few old-school radicals who had refused cell phones. A sign taped above it read WE DON'T THINK THIS PHONE IS TAPPED, BUT LIKE ANY TECHNOLOGY, USE AT YOUR OWN RISK. Below that, someone had added, EDUCATE YOURSELF, and below that, someone else had written WHY DO YOU THINK I'M HERE? Subsequent graffiti digressed into metaphysical issues.

It took Sophie a moment to adjust to the dim interior, though the day outside wasn't particularly bright. She brushed the rain from her eyes and searched the room. Several barstools were occupied, as were most seats at the communal tables. She recognized some occupants from various meetings; others looked like homeless guys trying to escape the rain. On closer inspection, one of the homeless guys was actually Gabe with his locs tucked under a stained cap. He waved, and she waved back, holding up her index finger to tell him to wait a second.

"Hi. Herbal tea to go," she said to the barista, digging her travel mug out of her backpack. The barista motioned toward the teas, and Sophie spooned some Lemon Mint into her mug's infuser. The barista filled it with hot water, and she headed for the door.

"Mind if I tag along?" asked Dominic, grabbing a disposable cup. Sophie had forgotten he was behind her. "I was supposed to meet a friend, but I don't see him here."

She looked at Gabe, who shrugged. "Your news, your decision."

She debated for a second. How secret was her news? Anybody could find it out if they wanted to. She motioned him to follow.

The rain had slowed, thankfully. The Grounds was a pretty safe place to talk, but you never knew who was listening; better to walk around. This was one of those spitting rains that would soak them slowly, in increments, like boiling a frog. She was glad for the heavy canvas of her Army jacket and her boots. They were comfortable and reminded her of her brother, but best of all they were practical.

Sophie took a sip from her mug as they walked, burning her tongue. She took another sip anyway, then a deep breath. Gabe was waiting. He didn't like drama, and she wasn't trying to be dramatic. Just careful.

"You know my brother?" she began. All in.

"The soldier. We never met."

"Yeah, exactly. He came home last night. He said he was leaving the military. And get this? He got a job at Balkenhol."

Gabe stopped walking and stared at her. Dominic, a pace behind in what seemed like a misguided attempt to be unobtrusive, collided with Gabe's back, sloshing his drink on himself. Gabe ignored him.

"You're kidding, right?"

"No. For real." Sophie knew she'd done the right thing in telling Gabe. This wasn't drama. This was important.

"Think of the access," Gabe said, walking again, faster now. Sophie jogged to keep up.

"Not that it'll be easy," she warned. "It's not like he'll leave his passwords around."

"No, but I'm sure you'll hear things. Maybe you can ask for a *take little sister to work* day."

"I am *not* playing a kid card," she said sharply.

He slowed. "Yeah. Sorry. Getting ahead of myself. We'll figure something out. This is definitely useful intel. I apologize. Just thinking how to get you into the building."

"I guess I could say I'm interested in an internship or something," she conceded, now that the sting was gone. "I can play a role if we need me to."

"Nah. He knows you're not interested, right? He'd get suspicious if you suddenly wanted a tour. And I don't know if Balkenhol would consider someone for an internship who didn't have a Pilot. We'll use this in another way."

"They don't," said Dominic, speaking for the first time on the walk. "Balkenhol doesn't take interns without Pilots. Why would they? We're inefficient."

Gabe eyed him. "How do you know that?"

"My grandfather worked for a defense contractor before he retired last year. He tried to get me in for an internship and they said no. We went through his whole list of contacts, but nobody would hire me. He said it's the last legal line of discrimination."

"Your grandfather is right," Gabe said. "How do they get away with it? 'Most qualified applicant' my eye."

Once he got onto this topic, there was no stopping him. Sophie was usually right there with him. This time she let him rant on his own. She hadn't thought far enough ahead to have a useful suggestion ready. How could she capitalize on David's position? She'd have to think about it. This was not an opportunity to be squandered.

They'd never gotten this close to Balkenhol before. Imagine what they could learn, given the right access; she'd have to start with making amends with David. Maybe she could lull him into forgetting she had a cause? Fat chance. At least maybe he'd be too preoccupied with the new job to notice her fishing for information. It was worth a shot, in any case. She ran her burnt tongue over her teeth, thinking.

On David's first day of work, Sophie made sure to be waiting in the front room for him when he got home. She had a tablet in front of her, open to the anti-Pilot boards. It was work that needed to be done, whether or not she was setting a trap for her brother; meetings needed advertising, and the letter-writing campaign still needed more letters. She answered some messages, posted a template, hooked it to the local captains to spread.

When the door opened at six thirty, it took her by surprise. So much for her trap.

"Hey," he said without looking in Sophie's direction.

The old David would have kicked his shoes into the corner behind the door, but this one sat on the bottom stair to unlace his shoes and remove them. He placed them neatly beside the coatrack, in line to the millimeter, then headed for the kitchen.

Sophie locked her tablet and tossed it on the couch. She closed her eyes and listened. The fridge opened and closed, followed by the snap and hiss of a beer can. She counted a full minute before joining him.

When she came around the corner, David was already looking in her direction. Sometimes that was eerie. She remembered trying to sneak up on him when he'd first gotten his Pilot. It hadn't worked then, and it certainly wouldn't work now that he was so well trained.

"Do you want one?" he asked, indicating the beer.

"I'm nineteen, dummy," she said.

"So?"

"So, my seizures are mostly under control these days, and I like to keep them that way. It's not like I've never had a drink. I just don't want one."

He looked chastened, as if he'd forgotten about her seizures entirely. Good. One point for her. She pulled out the chair opposite his and reversed it so she could lean over the back.

David tipped his head and drained the entire beer. He tossed the can, and it made a perfect arc into the recycling bin. A few drops sprayed out as it went, but he acted like he didn't notice. Sophie knew that was an act; he noticed everything. He opened the fridge, grabbed another can, and turned his chair to mimic hers.

"How was your day?" she asked.

He shrugged. "First day. All paperwork, then more paperwork."

"As much as the Army?"

That one got a smile. "You remember me saying that, huh? Yeah, I guess today could give Army bureaucracy a run for its money. At least I think it's temporary in this case."

"Did they give you a badge? Are you official BNL?"

David reached in his shirt pocket and flashed an ID card at Sophie. "Official. Now people won't stop me every two seconds to figure out if I belong there. That was a pain all morning 'til they hooked me up."

Sophie mentally filed that information. She tried to get a look at the badge and whether it had a bar code or a chip alongside David's face, but it was back in his pocket before she could gather any further details.

CHAPTER FORTY

SOPHIE

In the end, Sophie couldn't believe how easy it was to get hold of David's ID badge. Saturday morning, she brought her dirty clothes to the basement, and there it was, clipped to a shirt at the top of his laundry basket. Saturday was her laundry day, but it used to be his, so she could understand why he hadn't started the load yet. He thought he had all day.

"David?" she called.

Julie's voice carried down the stairs. "He just left for a run."

Maybe that was another reason he hadn't bothered to start the laundry yet. He'd have more dirty stuff when he returned. Before she could lose her nerve, she slipped the badge into her hoodie's pouch. Then she checked the directions on his shirt collar, emptied his basket into the washer, and moved the dials to cold wash. She didn't want him any madder than he already would be.

She left her own basket beside the machine and pulled her phone from her pocket. She needed someone to take her to the meeting space quickly enough that she'd have a chance of being back before David. Dominic.

He seemed happy enough to hear from her, and happier when she explained she needed a favor. "Yeah! No problem! Where should I meet you?"

"Same place as last time?"

"Will do."

Sophie shouted, "Back in a few minutes" as she slammed the door behind her, not giving the chance for either mom to question where she was going or when she'd be back.

Dominic was as fast as he'd said he would be, gliding that fancy ride into the bus stop. She ducked into the car, then stole a look back. That would be her luck, for David to spot her. No. Even if he did, he wouldn't guess what she was doing; today was nothing but good luck.

The bus would have taken an hour, but Dominic got her downtown in fifteen minutes. She jumped out while he was still parking. His car clanged in protest.

"You're not supposed to open the door while the car is in motion," Dominic said.

"Sorry! Tight deadline!" She had the keys out already. Her fingers shook as she fumbled with the lock. *Stay calm*, she told herself. *Stay cool. No seizures. No panic. A quick errand.*

The door jangled when she shoved it open. Normally she'd pull it shut behind her, but she left that for Dominic. She flipped the light switch to identify where the sleeping bodies were, then turned it off again when somebody groaned from the back.

She made it to the office without stepping on anyone. Gabe raised his head from his sleeping bag on the couch. "Sophie, man. What brings you in this early?"

She flashed the ID at him in the same way David had flashed it at her. Gabe was on his feet in an instant. He wore flannel pajamas; he was the only person who stayed there who actually brought pajamas as opposed to crashing in his clothes. It made a certain amount of sense, given how often he slept there. His dad didn't give him any grief at all.

"Is that your brother's ID? You work fast!"

Even after all these years of friendship, Sophie still loved it when she managed to impress Gabe. "Opportunity presented itself."

"What's the plan?"

"First we copy it." She tossed it on the copier's scanning bed.

The machine always took forever to warm up, but this morning forever felt extra long. The copy, when it finally came through, looked decent. No glare from the glossy finish. So far, so good. Her brother's serious face stared back at her.

"Then we laminate." Gabe did that part. He was better with the laminating machine than she was. He put it through three times to get the right thickness, then carefully trimmed it to size. She removed the clip from the original and affixed it to the new badge.

She hadn't realized Dominic had come in until he spoke. "What if it has a chip? I think those things have a chip."

Sophie smiled. "Now we destroy it."

The kitchen was next to the office. She pulled one of the smaller soup pots off the rack—they came in medium, large, and giant—and filled it with water. She held the new badge under, swirling it.

Gabe frowned. "If I had known this part, I wouldn't have bothered with three layers of laminate."

"It still had to be the right thickness. What else would happen to it in a washing machine?"

They took turns beating the new card until it looked like it had been through a few rinse cycles.

"Do you want to call National?" Gabe asked. "They're going to give you a raise for this."

Sophie glanced at her phone for the time. "You can do it. I'd better get back. I'll leave the original with you, in case anyone snoops around my room."

She made it back to the house an hour after she'd left. The shower was going, and David's running shoes stood neatly by the front door. Nobody in the front room. Perfect timing. Down the basement stairs, toss the new badge into the washing machine to soak against his clothes a little longer, and then back upstairs to play the innocent.

"What's got you out of breath?" Julie asked. She was sitting at the dining room table drinking coffee.

"Checking if David switched his laundry over. I started it for him and everything."

"He just got back from a run, so probably not yet."

"I noticed. No worries, except someone should tell him Saturday is my day now."

"Why don't you tell him?"

"Maybe I will." Sophie poured herself a glass of water. Julie was right. She was more than breathless; her heart beat out of her chest. *Relax*, she told herself again. *You did it.* She headed to her room to wait for David's explosion.

"Who messed with my laundry?" he shouted a few minutes later.

Sophie yelled back through her closed door in calculated indignation. "I didn't mess with it! I started it for you. I checked the labels and everything. Try saying *thank you* instead."

There was a pause, then a faint "Thank you" floated up the stairs.

She waited some more for the next part, which turned out to be a long string of curse words. "My work ID was in there! It's ruined!"

Julie's voice joined the conversation. "I'm sure they'll give you a new one."

"After one week? That's an awful first impression."

"Hopefully you've already made a good first impression and they'll chalk this up to nerves or something. At least they'll know you practice good hygiene. I've met guys who only wash their work shirts once a month."

The conversation continued on without Sophie. She relaxed; he was annoyed, but he didn't sound suspicious.

The feeling of having gotten away with something exhilarated her. She never got away with anything. She wasn't even supposed to lock her bedroom door, and she'd been sixteen when she finally convinced her parents she would move out if they kept peeking in on her at night. But this? It had practically been a spy mission.

Straight out of the movies, complete with subterfuge and counterfeits and a switcheroo made in the nick of time.

It wasn't until evening that her excitement was replaced by guilt. She walked into the kitchen to find David sitting at the table with a bottle of IPA in one hand, the ruined ID badge in the other. She panicked briefly, afraid he suspected something, then noticed the glum look on his face.

"I'm sorry. I didn't mean to get you in trouble." That was true. She'd figured it would be easy enough for him to get a new ID. "Maybe it won't be a problem."

He flashed a thin-lipped smile in her direction. "Maybe. Maybe I'm worrying for nothing."

"You're good at worrying. You were, I mean. I don't know if you're still like that."

"I think that's a hard one to grow out of. I'd probably worry I wasn't worrying enough."

Sophie grabbed the ID card from his hand and sat opposite him. She used the opportunity to examine it and make sure it still looked right. Yep. It still looked like a waterlogged picture of David. One corner had separated and she fought the urge to peel it. She waved the card at him instead.

"I bet you've had way worse things to worry about than this." It was meant to be a lighthearted remark, but she regretted it the moment she'd said it. His face passed from morose to unreadable.

She tried to change the subject. "Are you going to see any of your old friends now that you're home?"

He shrugged and took a swig of beer. "I don't know who's around."

"There's a guy from your class who comes to our meetings, but I don't think you were friends." She felt a thrill mentioning the meetings while holding his forged ID.

"Who?" David asked, his face still neutral.

"I probably shouldn't say—well, except he goes to protests, so you'd see him on the news if you were looking, so it's not really a secret. Will Yuen."

"Will-You-Answer-Already?" He smiled. "That dude was weird. Always took ages to answer a teacher's question, like his voice was beaming in from light years away, before and after his Pilot—wait. I thought your meetings were for people who didn't have Pilots."

"People who don't have them, including people who never got one and people who had theirs deactivated."

"You can have it turned off?" The life came back into his face. He sounded genuinely interested.

Sophie tried to figure out if he was messing with her. "Of course you can. You didn't know that?"

"I mean, I guess I did. I know they disable it if a soldier is having trouble after a head injury. I didn't know people did it on purpose."

"Don't you remember Ma asking you to turn yours off, back when you were complaining about it that first year?"

He scratched his head, then nodded. "I guess I never considered it a serious option. I would never have done it then. I knew how much they'd spent, and how hard I'd begged. I would never have admitted it was a mistake."

"Was it? A mistake?" She tried not to sound too eager or look too expectant when he took a minute to answer. He looked out the window, though she could tell his attention was on her as well.

"No. It's helped me, even though it can be irritating. It's saved my life."

She hadn't expected him to say otherwise, but for a moment it had seemed possible. She would have loved to have him back on her side of the great divide.

CHAPTER FORTY-ONE

VAL

The sun had begun to set over the outfield, painting the sky in purples and pinks as the family picked their way through the full stands to the nosebleed seats. A baseball game had seemed like a good idea for an outing, with lots of distractions to keep everyone occupied.

Unfortunately, the change of venue hadn't made much difference. The first problem was that David and Sophie had wound up seated next to each other. Val wouldn't have thought that would be an issue with two adult children, but they acted determined to regress now that they were living under the same roof again. She didn't hear the conversation start, or a change in tone, just a seamless continuation of the same unbearable low-grade sniping that had been going in the house for weeks.

"Enough." Val looked from David to Sophie and back. "How old are you two? Do you really have to fight like that?"

"He started it." Sophie crossed her arms, mimicking Val.

David frowned and ran both hands through nonexistent curls. "All I said was I couldn't take you to work with me. Jesus, Soph, I'm still new there. Let me gain some traction before I start trying to pull strings. I already got off on the wrong foot when I laundered my badge."

"But I thought you were doing presentations at schools and stuff. I want to watch you present. Is that so wrong?"

"That's not wrong, just weird. Why would you want to watch that? I thought you were anti-Pilot."

"I am. I'm curious about the arguments you use to convince people."

Val silently agreed with David: Sophie's position was strange. Still, it was the bickering that was getting to her, not the content. "I don't care who's right and who's wrong. Find a way to deal with this that doesn't give me a headache. You're both adults."

Val hoped that was the end of the arguments as Sophie and David both reoriented away from each other. She was starting to feel she was the only one in the family actually there for the game. Julie had her tablet and her phone out, scrolling the former while thumb-typing something on the latter; she might as well not be with them, though if quizzed she'd probably know the score.

Sophie watched the players below and flagged down every vendor. She'd always loved ballpark food: hot dogs, pretzels, nachos, Cracker Jacks, ice cream. As a kid, this had been the one place where they'd allowed her that junk, and she still made the same indulgences. In between snacks, she pulled out her phone and typed, her fingers lightning fast.

David watched the crowd more than the game. He had no stillness in him. David and Julie both had twelve-dollar beers in plastic cups. Every once in a while he would exhale, then tilt his beer back. Val noticed that even while he drank he kept his eyes open to his surroundings.

Fine. Val would pay attention for all of them. The runner on first inched out to steal. The pitcher whipped the ball to second, but the runner had seen the pitcher turn and was already safe back at first.

"Why do they let the players get Pilots?" asked Julie.

Val glanced over to see how her wife had read her mind. Really, it wasn't mind reading. Julie had always been able to follow her thoughts. She didn't think she was that predictable, but there it was.

"It doesn't add anything positive to the game. I get it for umpires, but why players? It's just another enhancement, and everyone has to get them now or they'll never play. Why would—" Val tore her eyes away from the jumbotron and glanced at Julie, who had a wicked grin on her face. The kids were watching them and snickering. "Are you messing with me?"

"Maybe."

Val sighed and rubbed her neck. She didn't want to give them the satisfaction of seeing they'd gotten to her, but really, they knew that already. The least she could do was be gracious in defeat. She gave Julie a wry smile. "How do you know exactly which buttons to push to start me ranting?"

"Long years of practice, love."

"It's not like your rant button is hard to find," said David. "It's labeled 'RANT' in all caps."

Julie grinned. "And it's the size of a barn."

"You're right about all of it, Ma." At least Sophie had some loyalty. "But they wouldn't tease you if you weren't so easy to tease."

"*Et tu?*" Val asked. "I thought you'd have my back, at least."

"I do, Ma! I wish the players didn't have Pilots. You're right that it's lousy for the game, but what are they supposed to do, get them turned off? The younger players get them before they ever know they'll make it to pro levels. The older ones get them so they're not benched. You've given that speech at every ball game we've been to for years."

"And all the games on television, too. Every sport."

"And at meets you've coached."

"And at end-of-year sports banquets."

She looked from one face to another, from Julie to both kids, both laughing, their argument seemingly forgotten. If mocking her brought them together, she wouldn't stand in the way.

"Fine," she muttered. She sat back to watch the game again,

but they'd reached the seventh-inning stretch. The jumbotron showed the usual distractions: the food race, with the animated hot dog dancing as it crossed the finish line first; guess the crowd size; dance contest. When they did the cartoon shell game, Julie and David both muttered "two," though Val had long since lost track.

The shell game disappeared, replaced by David's face. Val glanced around, looking for the camera, hoping it wasn't a kiss cam since he was sitting beside his little sister. Except it wasn't this David, who wore shorts and a T-shirt; Screen David wore a crisp collared shirt with the Balkenhol logo. He sat more formally, too, his military bearing on full display.

"My Pilot saved my life and my troop's lives more times than I can count," Screen David said. Real David slumped low in his seat. Sophie was at full attention, and even Julie had set aside her devices. Stock footage of Piloted soldiers replaced David, and Julie closed her eyes and covered her ears. For all the body-count sites she'd frequented in their son's absence, she had never been able to stomach the videos; too easy to imagine him there.

This particular video was clearly designed to showcase their Pilots. Soldiers started to move, then paused. The doorway they would have stepped into exploded, but they'd already taken shelter, their Pilots presumably having delivered them some crucial information. The soldiers gave way to an operating room, then a classroom, then a plane's cockpit. "Pilots are paving the way for a better tomorrow. They save lives in other ways as well. Pilots improve the attention of surgeons, of drivers, of pedestrians. They increase productivity and make our world safer."

Back to the image of David, handsome and alert, staring right into the screen. "My Pilot makes me the best me I can be." David dissolved into the Balkenhol logo.

The guy behind David nudged him. "Hey, buddy, was that you?"

David nodded, sitting straighter, as if remembering he was supposed to be a role model.

"Thanks for your service. It really saved your life?"

David nodded. "Yes, sir."

Val turned to look at the guy. Thick-bodied and leather-skinned, late fifties or early sixties, maybe, or someone slightly younger who had done a lot of outdoor work.

"Like on the screen?"

"Something like that, sir." He held his bearing, but his beer shook in his hand.

"Did you lose any—"

Julie interrupted. "I don't think my son wants to go into detail."

The guy glanced at her. He didn't have a Pilot, Val noticed. He was the customer Balkenhol wanted. "I'm just trying to tell him I'm glad he got back okay, all right?"

"You said that already. Now you're pushing him to talk about things he doesn't want to talk about."

"Jules," Val whispered. "He can take care of himself."

David had taken the moment to compose himself again. "Thank you. I'm going to get back to watching the game with my family. Have a good day, sir."

The man sat back, mollified by one or the other or both responses. Val glanced over her shoulder and saw the whole section watching them. Julie and David had probably known that the whole time. Had it changed how either had conducted themselves? David had to know an ad like that made him a face for the company, and anything he did would reflect on them.

"David," Val said, her tone low enough that the man behind hopefully wouldn't hear. "Did you know about that ad?"

He shook his head, then shrugged. "I mean, I knew they were filming me, and I knew it was for an ad. I didn't know I'd be the only one speaking in it and I didn't know they were going to show it here, or I wouldn't have come. It's weird seeing myself on a screen. I wouldn't have minded getting used to it phone-sized and maybe working up to the jumbotron."

Sophie eyed him. "If you'd had a zit it would have been the size of a car."

"Thanks for that."

"It's true, but you looked good."

"Thanks?"

He was right to be wary of a compliment from Sophie. "You looked good for a giant sellout."

"I'm not a sellout. None of that was a lie. It saved our lives. Just because I don't want to talk about it doesn't make it untrue."

"I know that part is true, and I don't need you to talk about it, but 'My Pilot makes me the best me I can be.' Do you actually believe that?"

He paused, then shrugged again. "That's their new slogan, that's all."

"If you say so." Her voice carried a note of triumph.

By the eighth inning's end, everyone except Val looked bored and ready to leave.

"Time to go?"

They were all on their feet before her; they'd been waiting for her to call it. Behind the stands, others were streaming from the stadium as well, as happened in a lopsided game. Several people stopped David to shake his hand, though nobody was as rude as the guy who had sat behind them. A few asked if they could pose for pictures with him, and one young woman asked if he would give her his card so she could figure out whether or not she wanted a Pilot.

"I don't have a card yet. I just started at the company."

"How about your phone number, then?" Her friends all giggled, and he blushed.

They were clearly all going to have to adjust to living with a celebrity.

CHAPTER FORTY-TWO

DAVID

Being home was like being home was like being home was like being on a movie set dressed to look like home. The house still the same cozy familiar mostly still the same. The moms still the same cozy familiar if maybe a little different something changed in them or maybe in him David could never tell whether something else was different and he was the different in the sameness.

He knew he was different yes of course how could he not be the things he couldn't unsee were part of him. He knew he couldn't talk about those things with anyone here couldn't help the way he tensed the way he sweated the way he didn't notice his teeth clenching until his jaw ached afterward and he noticed in the unclenching. He could describe the location of every fly on every wall in a room full of flies but he didn't notice his body's reactions until he counterreacted to them.

Milo was the only person who understood. He felt bad bothering Milo when Milo and Karina were still getting reacquainted, but when he texted Milo always answered, and he wouldn't admit to anyone how deeply he appreciated that fact.

After the baseball game, after he realized Balkenhol was plastering his face everywhere—billboards, TV, Internet ads, seriously, he didn't even know why, it wasn't like they were hurting, it seemed like everyone had a Pilot now—it got even harder for him to walk out the door. He knew he got looks, that his own suspicion marked him as suspicious, and he mostly confined himself to his commute.

The exception was when Milo asked him to get a drink, because it was one thing to text him, another to ask him to hang out, that was maybe too much, and then Milo would know he wasn't handling himself that well, that he needed something he wasn't finding, that despite the ads, the posters, the smiling, confident persona, he was falling apart. When Milo finally said want to grab a drink, he said yes, name the place, I'll be there, wherever there is, is right now good, yes, cool, see you then.

Milo arrived in a tiny electric coupe just as David reached the bar.

"Karina's," he said, waving at the car. He wore a button-down shirt and suit pants, but no jacket, and he had let his hair grow a few inches. He'd been home four months longer than David.

They sat at a table by the bar's far end, near the kitchen. In threes: the scent of fry-grease, the sizzle of the grill, the cooks' quick Spanish. Its own triplet: the bartender's rhythm of hand-washed glasses scrubbed, sterilized, flipped to air-dry. David noticed he and Milo both rotated their chairs out from the table, so they had their backs to the wall. They turned their heads to talk to each other, cradled ice-cold bottles, their eyes moving to the doors, to the glass blocks that let in light instead of windows, to the two other customers. The floor was carpeted in thin dirty maroon-worn-to-black except an eight-by-eight square laminated dance floor and a DJ booth. Behind the DJ booth, an emergency exit they could duck out if danger came through the front door. A window air conditioner made a valiant and vocal attempt to cool the space. Even with that, compared to most places, it was practically a sensory-deprivation scenario. He wondered if Milo had chosen it for that reason, if Milo, too, craved the relative quiet, the confined spaces.

"I was hoping you would say it gets easier," David said.

Milo cocked his head. "What gets easier?"

"This. All of it."

"You were hoping you'd stop casing the exits? You've only been home a few weeks. Give it time."

David swigged his lager. "You've been here six months and you're still doing it."

Milo shrugged. Laughter from the bartender, news on one television and baseball on the other, the scrape of a chair. Milo understood David better than anybody did. Even when he thought he'd had enough of the noise, he wondered if he'd feel worse if he was no longer able to notice everything.

That was the problem with multiple attentions; he could never put anything fully away. There was an unspoken fourth and fifth and sixth and twentieth thing in every three he listed: the way the words on the bartender's black shirt stretched and distorted over her breasts, the guy tapping his foot on the brass rail, the soda gun's hiss, the boy who blew up in front of him, the IED he never would have seen, not with a thousand Pilots firing full bore, all focusing on everything they were supposed to focus on, and all the other things he had to consciously, constantly unremember.

They ordered a second round, then a third, and talked about mutual friends, from the Army and from high school. David would have been happy enough to keep going, but Milo begged off. "I promised I'd be home to make dinner for Karina."

David stayed, ordering a burger and another drink. Better to eat here and drink a little more and then get sober than show up to dinner at home drunk.

CHAPTER FORTY-THREE

SOPHIE

Sophie momentarily couldn't figure out why the meeting space was so packed, but then she realized it was first Monday: the general meeting. The risk in running an ongoing rolling meeting space—she'd lost track. First Mondays were the lure for new folks: free coffee, free chili. Music. The hope was that even if they didn't become regulars, they'd show up again for big actions.

Normally, Sophie celebrated gathering so many anti-Pilot people. Tonight, though, she'd hoped to talk with Gabe about the ID caper. That likely wouldn't happen; they'd have their hands full managing the crowd.

A tall Black woman approached her. She carried a chipped chili bowl and a coffee mug against her body, using a forearm crutch as she navigated the room.

"Can I get that for you?" Sophie reached for the chili, and the woman let her put it on the bar. Sophie tried to gather a name, but the woman settling herself on a stool looked only vaguely familiar. She pulled out her notebook and flipped back to the night she'd brought Val. She'd had a seizure that night, so anybody she met then might be a stranger today.

There were a few descriptions that didn't match this woman, then "Tommie—shaved head—Pilot kill after thirteen! years." A glance at the woman's fresh scar said she'd recently had her Pilot removed. A likely candidate. Sophie tucked her notebook away.

"I don't know if you remember me," the woman said. "My name is Tommie."

"Thirteen years, right?" Sophie asked, to show she remembered. Tommie didn't need to know the notebook had jogged her memory.

The woman nodded, touching her head. "I still can't believe it's gone."

"You must have been one of the very first. My brother was the first one I knew, but even he hasn't had his for as long as you."

"I was part of the trials. I was twenty and failing school and I needed the money."

"Did you? Finish school?"

"Yep! Even made honor roll my last semester."

"I guess that's how it works sometimes," Sophie said. "I never figured school out. Do you mind if I ask why you had your Pilot removed? I usually see them deactivated, not removed."

"That's what I wanted to talk to you about," Tommie said. She sipped her coffee. "I wasn't sure if y'all knew about the new studies."

Sophie didn't like to be out of the loop. Fake it 'til you get the gist. "I've heard some stuff. Which new studies?"

"BNL is contacting people from those early trials. They're asking us to do different things. Some are just having tests done. You know, to see if their batteries are still going strong, to see if the implants are still as effective as they were at the beginning."

"And?" Sophie leaned into the bar.

"We're not supposed to tell people, so you didn't hear this from me, but they paid me fifty thousand bucks to have mine taken out entirely."

Sophie was glad she was leaning. She probably would have fallen over in surprise. "Why?"

"Why the money, or why did they ask, or why did I do it?"

"All the above." She didn't try to hide her interest or her ignorance anymore.

"I wasn't sure at first. I might not have done it, except, well, that's a lot of money. I figured I could always have it put back later."

Sophie frowned. "Have it put back later" was not exactly a catchphrase for the anti-Pilot movement. "So, you said yes."

"If I invested some of that money I wouldn't need a Pilot. I wouldn't have to work."

For a few years, thought Sophie, and you'd still be Pilot-less in a Piloted world.

Tommie continued. "They made me do some tests, then had me return the next week. They removed it, and they asked me to come back a week later. They ran a bunch more tests. I think the same tests they were running on the people who hadn't had their Pilots removed."

Across the room, Gabe tried to catch her eye. He made an *is everything cool?* gesture, and she gave him a quick nod. "What kind of tests?"

"The same old stuff. Verbal questions and physical puzzles to do simultaneously, timed. Math problems while counting flashing lights."

"Okay?"

"And I tested the same."

"The same?"

"The same as before."

"The same as before you had the Pilot, or the same as when you had the Pilot?"

"As when I had the Pilot. All the multitasking stuff."

Sophie ran a hand across her hair. "So you're saying you never needed it?"

"No." Tommie was clearly frustrated with her. "I'm saying they took out my Pilot but my brain still thinks I have one."

"I don't understand," Sophie said, her cheeks flushing.

"Have you heard of neuroplasticity? Brains rewiring themselves around a problem?"

Sophie nodded. You don't read about seizures without reading about hemispherectomies and laser ablation and brain functions regained.

"My brain is still firing the way the Pilot trained it to fire, without the Pilot."

"I don't get why you're here," Sophie said. "You're not anti-Pilot."

"I'm not, but I'm not sure this is a good thing."

Sophie had to get over the fact that not everyone chose sides. The fact that Tommie was here was enough. "Okay," she said. "Thanks for telling me. That's definitely a concern. I'm going to tell Gabe about it."

She strode across the room, leaving Tommie to her chili. Something was bothering her about the rewiring, but she couldn't figure out what. Maybe Gabe would figure it out, except Gabe was busy talking down some semiregulars who wanted to paint the school board building Pilot-blue.

"Not a good idea," he said. "Destructive without demonstrating anything new."

"But it would look cool," protested a guy whose name Sophie couldn't recall.

"Looking cool is not part of our mission. Only actions that further the cause."

After them came a hippie white girl who was either on speed or one too many cups of coffee.

"Flagpole sitting," she said. "It was a fad in the 1920s. Good publicity stunt. People did hunger strikes on top of flagpoles, like, for days at a time. I've been practicing. I could totally do it."

Gabe cocked his head. "Believe it or not, I'm not entirely opposed to the idea. Nobody gets hurt and it'd be so weird you'd probably get coverage. Have you been through our media training?"

The girl shook her head.

"Chat with Lucinda over there"—he pointed to Lucinda Scott, their media guru, doling out bowls of chili—"and tell her you want in on the next training. If you're trained, if you show us you can speak eloquently on topic and stick to the talking points, I think we could support it."

The girl smiled and walked off in the direction he had pointed. He turned back to the other group, still gathered nearby. "Did you hear her? That's how we get things done."

They variously nodded and shrugged. Sophie hoped they weren't one of those subgroups so hopped up on the idea of action that they went ahead with their silly plan. They'd get arrested for vandalism and give the cause a bad name.

The crowd finally dwindled around eleven, though a few people lingered. Lucinda was on her computer, Dominic swept, and others were variously washing dishes or wiping counters or playing some handheld game all in a circle.

"We're going to need to figure out a plan for the ID soon," she said to Gabe, glad to finally have a chance to chat.

"Didn't they tell you?" He frowned, clearly surprised. "The plan's in action already."

The surprise was mutual. "Didn't who tell me?"

"Lana Robinson."

Lana Robinson was their contact at national headquarters. "Why the hell would Lana Robinson tell you something she didn't tell me? Co-leaders."

"Co-leaders, yeah, but she called and I was here and you weren't, and she said she'd try to reach you, too. I would have told you if she hadn't said she was going to."

Sophie fought back angry tears. "Tell me what?"

"She sent someone by to get your brother's ID."

"What? What are they doing with it? I need to be involved. He's my brother."

"It doesn't have anything to do with your brother anymore, I don't think."

"It does. What if they botch it and he gets blamed?"

"They won't botch it. We'd mess up, not them. We're not spies; we're community activists. We do legal stuff and civil disobedience."

"But I thought—" She stopped.

"You thought you'd get to play James Bond?"

"Well, yeah, that it'd be us. BNL headquarters are right here. I thought we'd be the ones to take them down, not National."

"How far do you think your brother's ID gets us? He's not exactly high-ranking. They have some bigger plan, probably. Your brother's ID will be part of it, but it's not the whole plan. We couldn't have done this, Soph."

He put a hand on her arm, and she told herself he was her friend and the gesture wasn't meant to be condescending. She forced her face into a smile. "You're right."

CHAPTER FORTY-FOUR

DAVID

No, David did not want to go to a party. He couldn't think of anything he wanted less than to go to a party. It was a terrible idea.

Sure, he said in the return text. When and where?

And then he was at Karina and Milo's apartment, standing on the landing outside their third-floor walk-up, standing on the edge of the city, standing outside a door that was the only barrier between him and more noise more noise it was already spilling out under the door and through the windows. Noise to add to his noise noise on noise on noise. If it was locked and nobody heard him knock he could walk away and say he'd tried to come and maybe Milo wouldn't point out that he could've texted to say he was there and open the goddamn door.

A car door slammed, voices on the stairs below him, a couple arriving at the landing where he still stood outside the door, both white-appearing and tan in an outdoorsy way, not a tanning bed way, the girl with freckles under light makeup and a scab down one shin, the guy with a slight sunburn on his nose, and maybe they did those tough mud races together or played beach volleyball on a fake beach in some pickup league and that was how they'd met. Karina did those races and had been trying to get Milo to do them, but he said he'd had enough obstacle courses already for his life, thank you very much. The girl looked more like she might be Karina's friend than the guy looked like he might be Milo's, which stood to reason since Karina had way more friends than Milo did. The guy carried two cases of cheap beer, one in each hand. The girl carried two bags of ice. One bag had leaked a trail of water up the stairs behind them.

The guy nodded at the door. "Locked?"

David shook his head and made an ineffectual gesture with his empty hands that nobody in the history of humanity had ever made, seriously, how would it even translate, making that gesture at a guy with two cases of beer in his hands, when clearly the unspoken question was *Can you take care of this problem?*

David turned the handle again and the noise got louder. Pushed the door wide so the guy and girl could walk past him into the apartment. He needed another minute or two.

"David! You came!" Milo threw his arms around David like he'd been stalking the door waiting for David to arrive, and David returned the hug.

"You think I'd miss this?"

"Actually, yeah. I didn't think you'd come. Here, let me introduce you to people."

It was mostly Karina's friends, as he'd guessed it would be, her party, her birthday, et cetera, or anyway, the first few people Milo introduced him to were introduced with their connection to her, a work friend, a high school friend, someone from her obstacle race training group. They seemed nice enough and he memorized their names their faces took in their clothes their drink choices the way they positioned themselves like they didn't even care that their backs were to the windows their backs were to the doors they were shouting to be heard over other people shouting to be heard over a song he'd hated in high school. They leaned in and shook his hand or nodded or clinked their beer bottles to his and said nice to meet you how do you know Milo and he said they'd been friends forever no lie but didn't say they'd served together nobody needed to know that except almost every one of them then said oh, wait! you're that guy from the ad! "The best me I can be" and then some sang an old razor ad and some sang an old Army recruitment jingle and some asked if he and Milo served together and no matter how he phrased it they knew they knew they always knew they asked stuff he didn't want to answer he smiled and drained his drink and said he needed another and made his escape and all the time his eyes were on the door the window the patterns of the crowd the songs the slight rattle in the bass notes from the speaker by the kitchen where he shoved his hands into the ice in the red cooler looking for another beer but also looking for the numbing cold for a moment numbing cold to numb his brain, too.

Someone came into the kitchen while he had both arms elbow-deep in the ice and he knew it looked weird nobody looked for beer with two arms in the cooler and the person said you look familiar and it was possible he knew her from high school but he didn't want to be there while she figured it out and recited his commercial back at him, so he pulled a bottle out with each hand like he was going to bring one to someone in another room and raised them over his head like twin victories and icy water ran down his arms and into the arms of his shirt and over his chest and it did not feel bad at all but now it looked like it was sweat and maybe some of it was because there were so many people in this tiny apartment and it was legit hot outside even before you factored that in. The woman looked at him oddly and he popped both caps and made his exit.

There were more people in the narrow hallway with the picture frames on the walls showing Milo and Karina and Milo and a beagle and Karina and a cat and Milo's family members whom David recognized even if he hadn't seen Milo's brother in how many years and Karina with her family that David didn't know. The hallway bathroom door was locked, but there was another off the bedroom, he was pretty sure. He didn't even need to piss he needed two minutes alone.

He expected the bedroom to be as loud as every other room. The door was closed, and he debated knocking wondered if he'd open it to find it in use like a high school party some couple taking advantage of a bedroom away from parents the way most adults of their age didn't need to do now unless maybe they had just hooked up at the party but he pushed the door open anyway and was surprised to discover an oasis.

Two people sitting on the bed, sandals and wedges kicked off haphazardly, three others on the floor, two with backs against the dressers one against the one bare wall. Four looked relaxed, the fifth, on the floor with back to the wall, looked more alert, like she was taking in everything, fingers tapping on thighs. Floor-to-ceiling windows, no, a sliding door, there was a narrow balcony beyond, he hadn't ever been in their bedroom before. It looked less than cozy, generic edge-of-city, beige-carpeted generic apartment, but maybe they'd cleaned it for guests, hidden everything that made it homey. Air conditioner pumping out through a vent in the wall working on only this room far more successfully than in the rest of the apartment because of the door he closed the door behind him the closed door blessed cool blessed quiet nobody here was shouting and the music was far away.

"Join us?" One of the two people on the bed held out a small candy bowl. Two colors, yellow and teal, same size and shape, the yellow unmarked and the teal with a stylized lowercase q on them. Not candy. Pills. Pills had never been his scene he'd never really had a scene but pills wasn't it.

"Nah, I'm okay," he said.

"If you're in here, you've got to play," said someone from the floor. "It's a good game."

"What's the game?" David asked, out of curiosity. He didn't buy "If you're in here, you've got to play." In his experience, people offered drugs and you took or you didn't and nobody cared either way sort of a *suit yourself more for me* attitude and anyway if they held the line they couldn't force him and he could walk out again into the noise but it was so much nicer in here.

The person holding the bowl smiled it was a friendly smile. They were cute.

A floor sitter said, "One pill makes you larger . . ." but the cute one shook their head and dug a hand into the bowl, coming out with a yellow pill. "This is Superman. It enhances the effects of your Pilot."

Hand back into the bowl for the teal pill, a perfect teal caplet against a smooth white palm. Too smooth to be the hands of one of Karina's tough-mudder race buddies. "And this is the Fortress of Solitude."

"Fortress of Solitude?" He repeated it when they didn't explain further, though he thought he understood.

"It dampens the effect of your Pilot. Tamps it down. Mild euphoria."

The floor sitter said something again about one pill making you larger, like it was a reference to something, oh yeah, *Alice in Wonderland*. Calm, smiling. Fortress of Solitude.

He wasn't a drug person never had a chance he had gotten his Pilot so early and everything he tried had just made it louder louder who would have thought even weed would make it louder but it had so there had never been a point he got paranoid and he was still on guard and he got stoned and he was still aware and he had tried one thing after another just once just to see before he stopped bothering because it was always the same so aware amped hyped noise everywhere same as always. If he was smart he'd take a minute and look these up see what they really were if he was responsible and not five beers in and having a lousy night even though he'd barely been there how long maybe an hour.

He opened his hand, palm up.

"That's not how it works," said the cute one.

He waited again, and this time they explained without his prompting. "You close your eyes and reach in. It chooses you, not the other way around. You swallow it without looking. Ride whichever wave hits you."

"That's why it's a game," said someone from the floor.

There was a crash from the living room, then quiet, then a smattering of applause.

David crossed to the bed. Closed his eyes just for a second he hated closing his eyes around strangers in a strange place hated closing his eyes ever really when there was nobody on watch but he closed his eyes he heard everyone breathing he heard the murmurs that were noise when the door was open he closed his eyes and put his hand in the bowl and took a pill. Put it on his tongue and stuck his tongue out so they saw what he got even if he didn't. It had a sweet coating. He swallowed.

When he opened his eyes, the others in the room nodded approvingly. He put his beers on the nightstand and lowered himself to the floor next to the bed, not the worst place in the room to be situated, he faced the door if anyone came through it anything that came through the window at least the bed would be in the way. For whatever reason nobody in this room asked his name or said they recognized him and he took that as a part of the experience whatever the experience would be.

He waited. Now that the novelty of his appearance had worn off there were two conversations going in the room, the two on the bed chatting about a show he had never heard of and the people against the dressers chatting about a mutual friend he didn't know. Only the alert person against the wall was silent, and she was closest to him.

"How long does it take?" He thought that was the way to go, stay on the topic at hand.

She shrugged, eyes wide. "Fifteen minutes to start feeling it, usually. Half an hour for full effect."

"How far behind you am I?"

"We're all at half an hour."

He looked around. It wasn't that different from a room full of stoned people when you were the sober one.

"You got Superman," he said. "And they all got the other."

She nodded. He tried to imagine an amped-up version of the Pilot an even more aware awareness molecules moving through space dust through the air. He couldn't picture it.

"Friend of Milo or friend of Karina?" David asked.

"Karina's big sister," she said. "Alyssa."

"Oh, cool," he said. "I didn't know she had a sister. I've been friends with Milo forever."

"Are you David?"

"Yeah." He waited for the inevitable questions about the war or the commercial.

"Karina thinks you're great."

He was completely surprised by that. "Really? I always figured I'm the guy making Milo drink too much and dragging him away from her to sort out my problems."

"Nah. The way she sees it you're a practical influence with a good job also you have amazing curls." Her sentence ran on but he had no problem following.

"Thanks." He ran a hand through his hair, still short but already ignoring orders. "I've always had a love-hate relationship with the curls. This is the first time in ages I've let it get this long."

She looked like she was maybe going to reach out a hand to touch his hair, and she was cute and he would let her if she did, but he turned and straightened the two haphazard pairs of shoes that had been kicked off by the people on the bed, to interrupt any move she might have made before it had a chance to happen. Karina's big sister. Cute but a bad idea unless he checked with Karina and Milo first. If Karina actually liked him he wanted to keep it that way, since he needed Milo. Milo was the closest thing to a person who understood him, who believed him about the noise.

"Do you want to step out on the balcony? I want to go outside."

The balcony, in full view of the people in the room, seemed like a better plan than this intimate corner of the floor. Alyssa sprang to her feet like someone who thought she was moving like a cat. David followed, watching the others watch them go.

The balcony was two feet wide, not big enough for furniture, just a couple of potted plants, one flowering one green, neither of which he recognized. What was the point of a balcony this narrow? You couldn't sit, and the Plexiglas barrier was too high for anyone not as tall as him to lean on. It was comfortable enough for him, but wouldn't you want a balcony where you could have a meal or sit and watch the sunset, but this was south facing he was pretty sure so no sunset anyway.

Outside, the music and conversation spilled from the apartment but the sound was baffled buffered diffused except for somebody shouting something a joke an anecdote something endless above it all. There were sirens far off but they didn't get closer. He had a feeling an inevitability in his stomach a knowledge this was a party where the cops were going to get called. Mixed-race mixed-class city-suburb neighborhood same for the party probably the kind where the police knock politely and say everyone has to leave not the kind where people end up arrested but it could go either way any night always depending on who came and what mood they were in and the response when they opened the door and what the neighbors had said and of course all of this was hypothetical. The air smelled like the flower he didn't recognize, drippy white and yellow blooms.

"What are you feeling?" He asked because he was curious and she was clearly altered and he still didn't know which way he was going and this was all a terrible idea but information would be good at this point.

"It's pretty cool." The barrier he leaned on at chest height was at her shoulders, so she lifted her forearms onto it and put her chin on her hands. "Actually, describing it would be cool. I'll try. It's like even more input. Like, that honeysuckle is overwhelming, heady, sweet, and I've never seen somebody pot honeysuckle before, but it looks healthy so I guess it's working, and I wonder if it could grow big enough to sort of flow over the balcony's edge and if that's allowed here—Karina says there are rules against everything in this complex. And I keep counting the cars in the parking lot and I know exactly where everyone is in that bedroom and they're all watching us and Justin—the guy in the corner—keeps picking between his toes which is disgusting in company but he clearly doesn't care or doesn't think anyone is noticing and Alex on the bed is looking at you like you're a snack and they're trying to decide if I'm hitting on you or not and I can pick out at least six different voices of people I know in the living room and I can almost kind of follow all their conversations at once but it's a little confusing and there's a black cat slinking at the edge of the parking lot and it's a rush like a rush of information a rush of stimulation it's like I can follow all of it at once and it would be overwhelming if I didn't also have this feeling of competence, like I can keep up, this is just me. Why are you staring at me?"

David knew he was staring, the same as he knew the heady sweet scent and now he knew it was called honeysuckle and he heard the conversations even if he didn't know the people behind the voices, and the cat had already twice pounced at prey in the dark—mice or voles or something else small and fast and elusive, the cat did not succeed either time, but was already hunting again, and this was him, this was always him.

This was a chance to ask without sounding stupid, for once. He chose his words carefully. "How much more, um, information is it than you're used to?"

She cocked her head. "A lot? I think it would be exhausting for any length of time."

"But, like, what's it like normally?"

"Normal."

She gave him a look like he was asking weird questions, like people always did. As far as they were concerned, a Pilot felt like a Pilot and there was no point in trying to describe that to others, particularly others who also had one.

He tried again. "I'm trying to get a sense of how different it is."

"Okay, you know how normally you—no, I can't put it into words. It's like there's that and then there's this and this is so much more than that. Hey, the cat caught something."

They both watched the triumphant black shadow move against the black trees.

Oh, how he wished she had said something else. He wished she'd put words to normal the way nobody ever did. Even now it rose in him, agitation desperation anger at everyone who said his Pilot was normal managed to make him feel like he was somehow abnormal without being willing to say as much, yes, abnormal for his questions, but they couldn't fathom that his Pilot might be different that he might be different, no, they assumed he couldn't handle it, that the thing falling down the thing failing was his cope his competence not the implant in his head surely nothing was wrong with that. Sometimes he wondered if other people had this problem. He'd wondered it so many times but he didn't know where to find them or how to find them without calling more attention to himself.

His sister said he worked for the devil and he told her he needed to—was that a betrayal? Did she know what it was like in his head? How could he explain why he was working for them anyway, how he was sure it was him that was wrong and not the Pilots in general nobody ever said they felt like this this mounting surmounting mountain of stimuli God if Alyssa had said "noise" he would have dropped to one knee and asked her to marry him just for the sheer relief of hearing someone else say it. As it was, disappointment settled over him like a wool blanket, another itch, another shred of his attention fragmented off to scratch that itch, to resent, to mourn a moment where he could have shared this with another person.

Except it wasn't how she felt not how she normally felt the thing she was describing was the thing he felt every day but it was a high for her momentary fleeting he had forgotten to ask how long this drug lasted. And—his stomach dropped at the thought—what if he had chosen the Superman pill instead and what a name, was the thing he normally felt a Superman feeling? Would it have amped his brain up even more? He tried to imagine it tried to imagine what it would be like to have even more stimulation he would go crazy he would be the person who clawed his own eyes out who ran his head into a wall unless it was like the way stimulants worked with ADHD he'd seen brain diagrams they somehow worked with the overcharged brain instead of making it explode.

He checked the time and it had been only fifteen minutes he

still didn't know which pill he'd taken but his heart was racing like he knew he knew he knew he had made a mistake he was going to die this was how he would die not an IED not like the little boy not a sniper just his own brain exploding because he took a pill at a party. Kids, don't do drugs. What had he even been thinking. He watched Alyssa watch the world through his normal everyday hyper-aware hypervigilant eyes. Fun for a little while, maybe.

He didn't remember it being fun ever. If she panicked he could tell her all of his coping mechanisms, the things that worked on patrol to control it the things that worked in a mall with his mother as much as they worked at all he was still a work in progress. Running. Fighting. Playing with language like it was a puzzle a toy a Rubik's cube. He could tell her all those things if she asked. If she needed.

She didn't look like she needed. She looked like she was enjoying herself, and this wasn't a comparison he would use out loud, he wasn't that dense, but she looked like a dog on a car ride with her head out the window. Eyes alert and darting everywhere, body tense. He watched her watching the world, watched with her, considered how rarely he could count something as a shared experience. He didn't seem to be ramping up.

And then it happened. An un-thing. An unclenching. Not a blanket he had to fight out from under, but a blanket wrapped around him, arms wrapped around him. The feeling behind the feeling of being told everything was going to be okay and believing it. Punctuation on a sentence that had been running so long in his head he didn't even remember where it had started. Quiet.

CHAPTER FORTY-FIVE

SOPHIE

Sophie ignored the first knock on her door. And the second. They had no reason to assume she was awake at eight a.m. Then her phone beeped, which was unusual, since the rule was the moms had to knock three times. Before she could reach for it, her door opened.

She was about to open her mouth to say they had a deal, three times, but Val threw up her hands like a surrender. Sophie expected a lecture on how the rule wasn't license to ignore them; the look on Val's face quieted her.

"What's up?" Sophie asked.

"Turn on the news."

Sophie reached for her tablet. She didn't need to go to a news site because it had already come to her. Three of her keyword alerts had brought hits during the night, and they were all queued and waiting.

Break-in at Balkenhol was the headline. An unnamed intruder had been arrested. It didn't say how they'd gotten in, but a shiver ran along her spine. Three alerts for the same article. The "Balkenhol" keyword was the obvious one, right there in the headline. The second was "Pilot," as in "The company is best known as the manufacturers of the ubiquitous Pilot implants." She was afraid to look at the third, afraid to see if the phrase that had triggered the third alert was "David Geller-Bradley," which would mean her brother's stolen ID had gotten him in trouble.

The third alert was "anti-Pilot," as in "believed to be an anti-Pilot activist," which was obviously why Val had told her, and which in itself was bad, bad, bad, but at least she saw no mention of her brother or his ID.

Val still stood in the doorway. Watching her reaction? Waiting to see if she was surprised?

"Thank you," Sophie said.

"Of course." She shut the door behind her.

Sophie texted Gabe first. How goes it?

She dressed, waiting for him to respond, but nothing came. She wasn't supposed to contact Lana Robinson from her personal phone, but really, someone should be telling her something. It wasn't fair that they would leave her in the dark, especially if this involved her brother's ID.

Her phone chimed. It goes, wrote Gabe. Hugs.

So it was urgent, but there was no hint of where to find him. Given no mention of coffee, the default had to be the meeting space.

The lights were off when she arrived, the windowless space giving the impression the sun hadn't yet risen. She stepped carefully over the occupied sleeping bags scattered across the floor.

There was a Gabe-shaped dent in the office couch, but he sat at the desk talking on the phone. He nodded at her as she walked in.

"Yeah, you can print that we have no idea who that is, and we did not send him. Gabriel Clary. Yeah. Uh, you can say 'a spokesperson for the local group.' Yeah. You, too. Yeah." He disconnected and turned to her. "That's like the twenty-seventh call. It's been ringing since six. They've all asked the same things over and over except one reporter who actually seemed interested in knowing something about our meetings and what we do"—he waved a scrap of paper, then stuck it in the top drawer—"Eduardo Toledo. I wrote his name down in case we want to talk to him when things aren't crazy." As if on cue, the phone buzzed. He glanced at the caller ID, then ignored it. "They can leave a message."

"What do we know?"

"Exactly what I said on the phone. We don't know who it is, and we didn't send them. Which is totally true." She waited for him to say more, but he shook his head. "I don't know anything else, I swear."

The phone rang again, and as Gabe and Sophie both reached for it, a woman walked into the office. She wore a Pilot-blue dress and matching blue lipstick like she was reclaiming the color.

"Knock fir—Lana?" Sophie said, letting Gabe answer the phone. "What are you doing here?"

Lana ignored the question. "Who are all the people I just stepped over to find you? You're supposed to be running a field office, not a hotel."

"It's sanctioned by the landlord and field office operations." Sophie closed the door. "They need a safe place to crash, and they repay us with endless volunteer hours. It works."

Lana eyed the couch like she was debating sitting on it, then decided against it. "No reporters have stopped in this morning?"

"There've been a bunch of calls, but nobody has come here." Sophie looked to Gabe, still talking quietly on the phone, and he nodded in confirmation.

"And that phone stays locked up, right? Neither of you put any apps on it that access the microphone?"

Sophie bristled at the suggestion she might be that amateurish. "Only Gabe and I have keys to this office. Also, it's a landline. No unapproved apps."

Lana rubbed her neck, and Sophie realized that up close, under her makeup, she looked exhausted. "Hmm. Okay. It must have leaked someplace else."

"Must have." *Especially since we were never told anything*, Sophie didn't say.

"It's not like you had any information to share," Lana said.

"Exactly." Sophie was getting annoyed. "I pretty much have

no idea what you're talking about or what happened, but feel free to leave it that way if you want."

Lana sighed. "I'm sure you saw the news. Someone got into Balkenhol and then got arrested. Everyone assumes it was an anti-Pilot thing, so we're getting calls from the media and the cops. If they haven't called you yet, they will. We had nothing to do with it, of course."

"Of course," Sophie repeated. Though if that was the case, why did Lana happen to be in the city?

"I'm going to make the rounds of your local news broadcasts to put our best spin on it before they start poking their heads in here. This isn't the image we want to project." She eyed the couch again. "Just keep doing what you're doing, both of you."

She swept back out of the room, and Sophie looked over to see Gabe watching her with curiosity. "What did she say? I missed some of it."

"What you said, more or less, and that the police may stop in to chat."

"Oh, they did already. Before dawn. My first wake-up."

"You didn't say that! Why?"

"Why do you think? They wanted to know who was in charge, and if we had planned a break-in, and who hung out here. I said we didn't keep a roster, and we didn't do break-ins, which is true. And they asked if we had ever been to BNL, which I said yes, outside, to protest. I probably shouldn't have said anything, but I thought those answers would get rid of them faster than refusing to talk to them."

He didn't point out that it was good Sophie hadn't been around, that if this did in fact have anything to do with her brother's ID, it was better their shared surnames hadn't been invoked. Or that it was good the whole thing had been taken off their hands.

Sophie knew not to raise any of that out loud. Lana had said something about a leak, the only important detail in the conversation. She probably wouldn't have come in if she thought either of them was the culprit, unless she wanted to look them in the eye while she asked.

All of which left Sophie with almost as little as she'd learned on the news. Someone had been arrested and charged in conjunction with gaining access to BNL. If it was someone from National, something had gone wrong. She still had no clue if this was the operation with David's ID or not, which was something she very much wanted to know.

CHAPTER FORTY-SIX

DAVID

The party at Milo's only confirmed what David had known for years: he was broken. If he wasn't broken, dysfunctional, a little off, what could explain that there was a drug that took other people to exactly where he lived his life? They were playing games, literal games, with something that had bothered him since he'd gotten his Pilot. When he realized it, he'd wanted to shake that woman Alyssa, to shake everyone in the room.

Instead, in the dawning, blissful quiet the Fortress of Solitude brought him, he asked, "What if you got stuck in that state of awareness?"

"Stuck?" Her eyes still darted around; he'd long ago trained himself to focus so he didn't go out of his head.

"Yeah. What if you didn't come down?"

She laughed. "It's physiologically impossible. It's just a drug. The effects wear off."

"But what if? What if it somehow broke your brain? Could you train yourself to work with it?"

"I don't think I could live at this level of sensory overload. I love chocolate cake but I couldn't eat it for every meal. This is like everything is too rich, too saturated, too intense. Fun for a while. Speaking of fun . . ." She turned and walked into the bedroom, where everyone else still sat enjoying the pill David had taken, the one that was wearing his edges off, wrapping him in blankets like something delicate in need of protection. His questions had driven her away, he was pretty sure, but he didn't need to care. He leaned against the railing and watched nothing in particular, listened to nothing in particular, let nothing in particular catch his attention. It was glorious.

He slept until three the next afternoon. He woke as he usually did, head smashing into consciousness, too much consciousness, alive awake alert enthusiastic, as the song Julie used to sing to him went, minus the enthusiasm. Except even more alive more awake more alert than usual, maybe, or maybe that was just the result of having experienced a moment of less awake less alert with which to compare. If the drug had any hangover associated, or any gradual return, he'd slept through it. His brain was back along with the loud bird outside his window the icemaker in the fridge his heartbeat in his chest. He squeezed his eyes shut and tried to recapture the quiet but quiet was gone, gone, loud bird gone.

By Monday, he was completely back to his own normal. Back to a job he didn't want but was afraid to give up. Back to the noise nobody else believed, noise that people played at during parties even while saying it's a nice place but we wouldn't want to live there. He hated everyone.

He tried to remember what the quiet felt like. His own personal Fortress of Solitude. He tried to get himself back to that state, but it had never been a thing he could do. Meditation, yoga, alcohol: he'd tried it all a hundred times. Nothing had ever worked, until that pill at that party, and how long had it worked? Hours. He'd left his car there and walked all the way home, four miles, eyes open for stranger danger but awareness gloriously dulled. Anyone could have snuck up on him or stepped out of the shadows, and he'd have missed it entirely, laughed at the novelty even while handing over his wallet.

His day consisted of two health fairs, morning at a high school and afternoon at the downtown jail, the latter for the employees at both the jail and the nearby federal prison. He'd never been to a jail before, and he'd been curious, but the health fair was situated in the outermost vestibule and he didn't actually get to see anything. About half the staff already had Pilots, and his job was to convince the other half to get them. This wasn't the worst gig he'd had. It was probably true that in their line of work a Pilot would make them safer. If he worked in a jail he'd want heightened awareness, the same way he'd appreciated it on deployment.

The trickier thing was answering questions about Piloted inmates. What would it mean to have a prison full of Pilots? All the more important for the guards and inmates to be evenly matched. Was there a way to turn their inmates' Pilots off? No. Well, there was a way, but it involved surgery; not something they'd be doing for people who were with them for the short haul, and an invasion of rights for even those on the longer ride.

He almost mentioned the pill he'd taken. Wouldn't that be their solution? Something temporary to mute the effect for the people they didn't want heightened? But that involved explaining the party, and possibly getting his friends in trouble, and he hadn't yet even researched whether it was an off-label use of a legal drug or something over-the-counter and legit or a controlled substance that could get him fired.

Better not to know, so he could claim ignorance. It would be nice to find out it was a legal option, but if it wasn't, he'd feel obligated to leave it alone. He was already itching to take it again, to reclaim that blessed quiet that had been his, however briefly. He hadn't wanted anything that much for years. He didn't want definitive answers that would force him to decide.

Instead, after he'd packed his display, he drove to the Installation Center. Not the VA, not the clinic in the building where he worked, but the civilian place where he'd first gotten his Pilot installed. He hadn't been in it since that appointment he'd made on his own in high school, and he wouldn't have noticed much at that time, but now he took it in: the slick and modern design, silently speaking *we are the future* to the prospective patients; the baking cookies scent, designed to put them at ease; below it all, not waiting-room Muzak, but a low hum at a frequency that seemed to want to settle him, even if it couldn't.

The clinician, a Dr. Nguyen, didn't hide her surprise at seeing him. "Don't you have your own doctors at BNL or the VA?"

"I do, but I'm allowed to come here, right?"

"Of course. Is there a problem?"

There has always been a problem, he didn't say. He'd said it so many times, but nobody had listened. "I was wondering if there's a way to . . . dampen the effect sometimes? To quiet my head."

"You should be able to cycle down with the app."

"Yes, but what if I can't?"

"I can check if you're working with the most up-to-date app." She reached for her tablet.

"It's current. What if the cycle-down isn't enough?"

"I'm sorry. I have no idea what you're talking about."

They never did. He took a deep breath. "Can you turn it off?"

"I'm sorry?"

"Can. You. Turn. Off. My. Pilot." He repeated himself slowly.

The doctor frowned. "Why would you want that? Is there a problem with it?"

"I told you. It's too loud. It never cycles down. You can look in my file; I came in about this years ago."

"Are you sure you don't just need to practice the exercises again to regain your focus?"

How many times did he have to say it? "This is not about exercises. I shouldn't have to beg. It's my head."

"Yeah, but . . ." The doctor trailed off. "You're literally the poster child for the implant. Your face is on our billboards. Won't you be out of a job if you do that? Maybe you should think about it."

David tried to control his mounting frustration. "It's my head. Haven't you turned them off for other people?"

"Only for medical reasons. If someone develops a tumor or seizures or that kind of thing. Look, I'm going to call in the counselor . . ."

"I don't need a counselor, for fuck's sake. I need my head to be quiet. Why can't anyone ever understand that?"

He didn't see her press a panic button, but she must have, because there was a knock on the door and then a burly white male nurse stepped into the room without waiting for a response. When the door opened, David caught a glimpse of a security guard standing in the hallway. He knew what it looked like: he was a tall, fit ex-soldier, yelling at a much smaller woman.

"I'm sorry. I didn't mean to yell. I just don't understand why I can't have my Pilot turned off if I want it turned off. It's obviously possible, since you said you do it for people who medically need it removed."

The nurse nodded like he understood. "It's something we can do, but we usually encourage people to talk to a counselor first, to make sure you actually want to do this, since you spent all that money to have one put in. And to decide whether you want it turned off, or removed entirely, which we discourage because of the risks of scar tissue and brain damage . . . In either case, you'd need to schedule an appointment."

"That's ridiculous. I made this appointment. I'm here."

"You made this appointment as a consultation, not a procedure."

"Fine. I'm leaving." He wasn't getting anywhere. They had no reason to placate him; he had to deal with them if he wanted this done, and they obviously weren't going to let him do anything while they thought he was threatening them. The security guard followed him out.

Fine, so what was next? He had tasted quiet; he was done with loud. He pulled out his phone and used the app to cycle his Pilot down. It was supposed to slow the rate at which the Pilot fired, like downshifting a car, but as usual, it had no effect.

A few days later, Milo messaged David to meet at a club near his apartment. It was a tacky suburban tiki bar franchise, tropical vibe thousands of miles displaced from the tropics.

"What do you think?" Milo asked.

"It's a bar?"

"I'm working here. Weekends. Bouncer, when the DJ's spinning."

"Seriously? Congrats."

"Thanks. It's not much compared to you, Poster Boy."

"I'm happy to recommend you anytime you want."

"They won't have me."

"Of course they will. You might not be pretty enough for posters, but you can still do the presentations. And you like yours more than I like mine."

"A, fuck you, and B, fuck you and your fucking noise."

That was how it always went. David never knew if it was his term for the thing he was feeling that was off. Like nobody was speaking the same language as he was. At least Milo didn't humor him.

He remembered the other night, and Alyssa, who had said that her sister thought David was a good influence. Thinking about her made him remember the quiet he'd felt on the balcony that night. "Hey, Milo? I don't suppose you'd give me Karina's sister's number?"

Milo eyed him suspiciously.

"Not to hook up with her, I swear. My intentions are pure. I want to follow up on something we talked about at the party."

"Let me ask Karina if she's okay with that. I'm already in trouble with her over this job. She says I can do better."

David didn't want to push, so he dropped it. Later that night, Milo sent the number, along with a note saying he loved David, he trusted him, and if he did anything to hurt Alyssa, Milo would be contractually obligated to hunt him down and kill him. David agreed to the terms.

The harder part would be asking his question without sounding too eager, without implying interest he didn't have, or interest he kind of had, but was secondary to his primary question. Life was complicated. He still wasn't exactly sure how to phrase the greeting so he didn't come off badly, like he was trying to use her, the exact thing Milo was warning him off doing. *Hi, this is David from the party?* Or *Hi, this is Milo's friend David? Remember that guy you got high with the other night?* He didn't send any of them.

CHAPTER FORTY-SEVEN

DAVID

David Geller-Bradley, please dial extension 1412.

David grabbed his report on prisons and Pilots off the printer and headed back to his desk, thumbing through the pages as he walked. Really, he should have armed himself with this information before the health fair the week before; he resolved to do better about that in the future. If he was presenting at a place with specific needs, it was important to research them in advance.

There was an e-mail for his supervisor stuck to the bottom of his report. Nina printed and filed all her e-mails. David thought it was odd and wasteful, not to mention she was constantly forgetting to grab them off the printer, so that they'd all gotten used to making extra deliveries. He knocked on her open door and handed it to her.

David Geller-Bradley, please dial extension 1412.

She pointed at the phone quizzically.

"On my way back to my desk," he said. "I'll get it there."

He'd heard them the first time, of course he had. They hadn't given him two seconds to reply. He didn't know which department 1412 was in. There were so many departments. The funny thing was that everyone knew him, the poster boy, but he didn't know everyone. Need a speaker at an event? Call David. Need a ribbon cutter? Someone to talk on the radio? David's your guy.

David Geller-Bradley, please dial extension 1412.

He dialed extension 1412. "This is David?"

"Hi, David. This is Dr. Morton. Can you come see me in Health Services?"

"Sure thing." He was supposed to say yes. Say yes, hear what any department wanted from him, decide if it fell within his purview. If he thought it was outside the bounds of what he was supposed to do, he went to his supervisor.

Tash Johnson peeked over their shared wall. "New poster, poster boy?"

"Maybe. New ask, I'm guessing. Maybe another health fair? They just like me best because I'm famous."

Tash grinned; they were one of the three others in Recruitment, though David was the only one whose face had been in the first big ad campaign, so nobody else had the street recognition he had. The others didn't seem to mind.

It wasn't until he pushed open the Health Center door that he realized if they had wanted him to go to another fair they'd e-mail the date and say "be there." No time-consuming visits necessary.

When he said he was there for Dr. Morton, the receptionist waved him through without making him sign in. "Third door on the right," she said.

The first two doors were open medical examination rooms, but the third was a well-appointed office, the kind with diplomas on one wall, leather-bound medical journals in built-in shelves on another, and an enormous wooden desk at the focus. It had large windows, though they faced the parking lot. A brass clock ticked away on a shelf at eye level, and someone was running photocopies somewhere nearby.

"Dr. Morton?" David knocked on the open door.

"Shut the door and have a seat, David."

Cold washed over David, even though this was not his supervisor or Human Resources or anyone in any position to give him bad news. There was something about this room, this desk, the clean-shaven white doctor with the yellow-gray comb-over that started just above his Pilot, that suggested a principal's office, a sergeant's rebuke, a telling-off. He shut the door and chose the right-hand chair of the two identical chairs on the desk's near side, the one two feet farther away from the ticking clock, like that would do any good.

"David, as I'm sure you know, BNL runs Pilot clinics all over the country."

"Yes, sir." He tried to think of a reason BNL would send him to one of their own clinics. Maybe the doctor was going to ask him to do a recruitment video specifically to play on waiting-room televisions.

The doctor continued. "What I think maybe you don't know, or haven't considered, is that those clinics are the same entity as the corporation we work for. All one system."

David was already sitting straight in his chair, but he sat even straighter. His back broke out in sweat.

"So, David, to spell it out, when an employee goes to a BNL clinic, it's the same as if they came to see us here at Health Services. All the same system, you understand."

David noticed that the paper file on the doctor's desk had his name on it. He kept silent.

"So when an employee goes to a BNL clinic and asks to have their Pilot deactivated, that gets reported here. If the employee went into the clinic in an agitated state, that gets reported here as well. We obviously don't share this information with Human Resources or your supervisor or anything like that—"

"Obviously."

The doctor continued as if David hadn't spoken "—but it is of concern to the company nonetheless. So it falls on me to ask you a few questions. Do you mind?"

David knew this wasn't optional unless he planned on walking off the job today. "Go ahead."

"Why did you visit the clinic instead of coming here or going to the VA?"

"I was under the illusion the clinic would be more private. I was wrong."

"And why did you ask them to turn off your Pilot?"

"That wasn't what I asked first. First, I asked if they knew any way I could dampen it a bit. Quiet it."

"They said you were combative and aggressive."

"I was frustrated, but I didn't threaten or anything. Maybe I shouted a little, but only because I wasn't being heard."

"Is your Pilot malfunctioning?"

"I've said so a dozen times, but every time you all test it you say it's working exactly as it's supposed to. Eventually I stopped asking that question, since it makes me feel like *I'm* malfunctioning."

"Have you considered you might just need to practice better focus?"

David didn't answer, but instead scanned the diplomas on the wall. Chester Morton, doctor of psychology. Great.

"Have you considered the ramifications that decision might have on your career here? Your entire position hinges upon you being a brand ambassador, so to speak. How could anyone trust that you believed in the product if you weren't using it yourself?"

David stayed silent.

"David, would you mind answering? Or telling me what you're thinking?"

"I'm thinking it's bullshit, sir, no offense, and an intrusion of privacy, that you would be talking to me about my job when your office is supposed to be here to talk about my health."

"This is your health, David. Mental health is health, too, and you are clearly dealing with something I'd like to help you deal with before you jeopardize your job. Why didn't you answer the question about focus exercises?"

"Everyone assumes user error when I say my Pilot is too loud, like all I have to do is practice and I'll be fine. You have no idea how hard I've practiced. I'm a focus machine. How do you think I survived? Translate the inputs, integrate the inputs, do it all in a millisecond or you're dead. I know it saved my life. I know the benefit of having all this information. But. It. Never. Stops. It never stops."

"I hear you. Have you considered longer down-cycles?"

David fought the urge to slam his head into the desk. Longer down-cycles. Next the doctor would ask if his app was current. Nobody ever got it. He gave up. "I'll try that."

The doctor beamed. "Great. Why don't you check back with me in two weeks and tell me how that's going for you? I'll put it on your schedule as a consultation so your supervisor doesn't ask any questions."

"Great idea, sir." David forced a smile onto his face. If this doctor was good at reading people, he'd see right through it, but Morton looked like he'd just negotiated world peace. This was how it always went.

And what kind of bullshit was it that allowed the clinic to share his information over here? It hardly seemed legal, but if they were all the same system he guessed it made sense. He should have known he didn't have any privacy. He was a public figure, the poster boy. They had invested in him. They wouldn't let him go this easily.

Tash didn't stand when David came back, but their voice carried over the half wall. "What was that about?"

"Consultation," said David. "They have some dumb idea about the clinics."

"Ugh. Have fun."

David sat at his desk and listened to every finger every keystroke on every keyboard every voice on every phone work calls personal calls all the calls somebody's headphones bleeding smooth jazz into the room every fluorescent light overhead with its own hum one bulb flickering three cubicles over Mackenzie Vogel eating her afternoon popcorn the smell of said popcorn slightly burnt someone else's coffee someone else's tea the microwave going with someone else's late lunch and what jerk heated fish in an office microwave the printer in the corner and above it all his own thoughts incessant no app could fix this he had tried he had tried he had tried he had tried he had tried.

CHAPTER FORTY-EIGHT

SOPHIE

Sophie could think of approximately ten million things more likely than what David knocked on her door to ask. He might have walked in, sat in her desk chair, and said, *Let's get a pet chinchilla*, maybe, or *What are the ranks aboard a gravy boat?*

She absolutely did not expect him to ask her if she knew where to get a Pilot deactivated.

"Why?" She let all her suspicions drip into her voice. "Is your company going to do a sting?"

He surprised her again by bursting into tears. She had no idea what to do. She racked her brain for any time ever that he'd cried in front of her, but if he'd cried as a kid, it was before she was old enough to remember. And that would have been kid tears, the sort elicited by unfairness or pain or fear of pain or the unfairness of pain, because weren't those the same thing in some ways? If she cried at unfairness she'd never stop.

If someone cried in the circle, which happened sometimes, someone else grabbed the tissue box from the bar and offered them. She didn't have tissues in her room and didn't want to walk away right at this moment, so she opened her top drawer and pulled out one of the unmatched socks that floated between the balled pairs. It had pandas on it, and she kept hoping she'd find its mate again, but in the meantime, snot wouldn't ruin it.

At least it made David laugh when she offered it. He wiped his eyes on his sleeve, then blew his nose in the panda sock.

"Thanks," he said. "Sorry. I didn't mean to do that. I'm just stressed."

She gave him a hug. He sat in her desk chair, swiveling side to side, and she was standing, so it was a shoulder hug, hard and brief. She tried to think of what to say to sound supportive instead of accusatory. "What are you stressed about?"

He smashed the snotty sock into the side of his head. "I'm done. I want it turned off, taken out, whatever they can do to make it stop."

She hadn't expected that, either. "You? The poster boy?"

"I wish people would stop calling me that! I'm sick of it, Soph. It was one thing when it was supposed to save my life, but now it's making me miserable. I know there's something wrong with it, even if they tell me there isn't. There has to be. I need it out of my head. Please."

The "please" convinced her. It was a broken please, a child's please, a please she hadn't heard from him for years and couldn't remember when she'd ever heard it. Not the night he'd asked for his Pilot. She still remembered that one; it was an *everybody's doing it* please, the whine of someone willing to do anything to keep up with his friends, slightly desperate, but not out of options. This sounded different, like he needed real help.

She hesitated, weighing what to tell him. "There's a place. It's not like the BNL clinics. They do body mod stuff."

"Body mod stuff? Not the same."

"You don't get to be suspicious if you're asking for off-the-books surgery. I've gone there with people. They're fully licensed for all kinds of things, and they do stuff most doctors won't, including Pilot stuff, though most doctors would say it's proprietary and they don't want to get near it." She didn't say she'd gone with someone from the group who had gotten this weird new anti-facial-recognition thing put under her skin. She'd seen Pilot disconnection on the list of things they did, and had wondered at the time who would go there instead of to BNL. Answer: her brother, maybe.

"Would you go with me?"

He kept surprising her. "Davey, are you sure you're doing the right thing? I'm the last person to talk someone out of this, but why not do it through the BNL clinic, where they know you and know their product?"

He shook his head. "I don't want to go back to that clinic. Will you come with me or not?"

Sophie examined her brother's face. His gaze was steady, his expression hopeful. For all that he'd been through, his emotions still showed so clearly. She wasn't sure she'd ever been in a position to do him any favor before, or at least no favor bigger than unloading the dishwasher on a night he wanted to go out, or grabbing him a Popsicle when she grabbed one for herself.

She nodded. "Yeah. I'll go with you."

"It doesn't smell like cookies," David said.

"Is it supposed to?" They sat in a small waiting room in a ramshackle two-story house turned body-mod parlor. They'd taken two buses to get there. It smelled like antiseptic, like hospital, scents Sophie tolerated only because her brother had asked her to do this thing with him. She hated hospitals, but at least this visit wasn't for her, and it wasn't a hospital, not exactly.

"The BNL clinics always smell like fresh-baked cookies. I think it's supposed to make you relax? I always found it forced. Like, hand me a cookie if there are cookies, or don't make me think about them."

"Maybe it works better on people whose parents bake? Hmm . . . now I'm thinking about cookies, so thanks a lot."

They both went back to examining the room and presumably thinking about cookies. David browsed the articles and licenses on the walls. He'd been surprised to find this wasn't some clandestine operation. Maybe even disappointed? She couldn't tell. If she were in his shoes, she would want to know that the person working in her head had every available certificate, diploma, license, and credential. The law that had allowed BNL to open minor brain surgery clinics outside the traditional hospital setting had paved the way for places like this to legitimize as well.

"David?" A pink-wigged, blue-scrubbed woman with a *Star Trek*–style series of bumps embedded in her forehead stood in the doorway to the back room. "You missed a question on the intake form. Do you want the light deactivated as well as the implant?"

Sophie shot the nurse a narrow look; she wished the woman didn't have a Pilot. "Wait—you can turn off a Pilot without turning off the light?"

The nurse nodded. "A lot of people like that option. The light is superfluous. Branding. Leaving it on gives the impression they still have Pilots, so they don't face the pressure and questions. We don't take them out here in either case—that's a far more invasive surgery than just snipping the leads, with way higher risks."

A strangled noise died in Sophie's throat. She looked at David, daring him to keep it. He had already taken advantage of every benefit the stupid implants had to offer; it would be just like him to keep the social cachet that came with the Pilot while deactivating the Pilot itself.

He sat silent for a long minute. Sophie could tell he'd made his decision when his chin lifted right before he spoke. "Turn it off. I don't need it anymore."

The nurse made a notation on the form, then held it out to David to initial. "Do you want your friend to come with you?"

"My sister." He stood, looked at Sophie, gave a shaky smile. "Nah. I'm okay knowing she's out here. Let's do this."

Sophie gave him a thumbs-up, but he'd already turned to follow the nurse, so she grabbed a scrapbook off a corner table and started paging through different mods Dr. Pessoa and her staff had performed, ranging from the subtle to the freaky. She wondered what her moms would think if she came home with a septum piercing or a unicorn horn. She was old enough that it was her choice, and she'd always had a high tolerance for pain, but none of that felt like her thing. Maybe a tattoo someday; that reminded her of the art she used to hide under her bed. She went through the book categorizing mods into "maybe," "no," "hell no," and "whoa." Some categories overlapped.

She'd never have imagined she would be in a place like this with David. David was the most by-the-book person she knew: a follower of orders, a follower of order in general. She didn't know if he'd changed and she hadn't noticed, or if this circumstance was extreme. It felt like the latter.

David returned in less time than she'd expected, a baseball cap pulled low over his eyes. She studied his face. "How do you feel?"

He shrugged. "Massive headache. It was just a local anesthetic, so I'm not too out of it."

She didn't push him to say more. He was quiet on the ride home, too, and followed her as they switched buses, like he was trusting her rather than paying attention for himself. He took out his phone and stared at his Pilot app a couple of times. At one point, he reached out and squeezed her hand, and she squeezed back. She tried to imagine what it would be like to have a brother who wasn't the poster boy for the company she spent her life fighting. Would they be friends? Neither of her moms had siblings, and neither did Gabe, so she didn't have any models for it other than books and television and movies.

On the second bus, she looked up to see a picture of him in his uniform staring back at them. Real David had his cap pulled low, but at least one person was pretty sure it was him, was poking her friend and whispering. How fast would BNL pick a new spokes-shill? Sophie tried to catch David's eye, but he had his shut tight.

David sagged into the couch the second they walked in the door. No military bearing; a heap on the couch, hands over his face. His cap fell off his head, and he didn't bother to retrieve it. He had an adhesive bandage over his shaved temple, but a blue light still shone through it.

Sophie yelped. "You didn't do it. Why did you make me think you did?"

He dropped his hands to his cheeks and opened one eye. "I did it. This headache tells me so. Look, if you don't believe me, I can show you the app." He unlocked his phone and showed her a screen reading: ERROR—MAKE AN APPOINTMENT AT YOUR LOCAL INSTALLATION CENTER IMMEDIATELY.

"You told the nurse to turn the light off. I heard you."

"I changed my mind when I got inside. It makes sense for my job to leave it on. I like my job."

Rage coursed through her. "What kind of chicken human being hides something like this? If you don't need it, stand behind that decision. And you're keeping that job? You got it taken out because you hate it, because it breaks something in your head, but you're still going to sell it to other people? Do I have that right?"

"I've told you before. I don't hate it. I think it's good for other people, but it's not good for me. If turning it off makes my head better, it's a health thing, right? Why should I lose a good job over that?"

"Never mind. If you don't get it, I don't think I can explain it to you."

She didn't bother to pull her boots off. She tried not to stomp back to her room. People always accused her of walking off in a huff when all she wanted was to get away from whatever or whoever was frustrating her. Put stairs and a door in between and she could exorcise it without losing her cool completely.

Maybe she'd been hasty in envisioning him joining her cause, coming to meetings, making them a family affair, or near enough, but it truly baffled her how he was still willing to work for them. Even if she accepted his premise that his implant was bad, that the experience was worse for him than for other people, she still didn't understand how he could make the distinction. He was a mystery to her. Not an enemy, still not a friend. She'd been silly to think otherwise.

Also, she really, really wanted a chocolate chip cookie, but she was not going back downstairs to forage in the kitchen if it meant passing the traitor on the couch.

CHAPTER FORTY-NINE

DAVID

I t was just as well he'd left the false blue light on; the headache went away, but the noise didn't. David ran through the exercises, telling himself he felt a little less focused, a little quieter, a little less able to process. He wanted so badly to believe it had worked that he was willing to deceive himself. For a while.

A week passed, two. He woke every morning and immediately assessed the situation. Loud bird? Check. Loud head? No need to ask.

"Most people who want this go to BNL, so I don't have statistics to report," Dr. Pessoa had said. "From what we've seen, it could take an hour or a day or a week."

The thing was, he hadn't noticed any change at all. He found himself irritated with everyone. Tash had asked what was wrong and he'd snapped, and now Tash was avoiding him. He wouldn't have minded telling them, telling someone, but he knew better than to say anything about this at work. It was his stupid secret.

He went to his "consultation" with Dr. Morton in a stranger predicament than he'd been in at their first meeting.

"David, good to see you," the shrink said. "Have you tried the things we talked about at the last meeting? Longer down-cycles? Meditation?"

All crap that had never worked for him. He chose the one

truth he had to tell. "I've been doing the exercises like I did when I first got it."

"Good, good, good. And has there been any improvement with the, ah, issue?"

That was trickier. If he said no, if he convinced them to believe him, they might send him for tests and discover his Pilot had been deactivated. If he said yes, it would be a flat-out lie and a betrayal of anyone else who might be in the same position as he was. There had to be other people like him. He chose his words carefully.

"I'm working on it." A vague, useless statement. A doctor who actually cared would call him out on the nonanswer.

This guy was so focused on the result he wanted to achieve, he didn't notice. "That's great, David! Glad to have you back on board with the program."

David lied through the rest of the appointment and then went back to his desk to stew. On some level, he was embarrassed. What if Dr. Pessoa was a quack who had taken his money and claimed to deactivate his Pilot without actually doing anything? She'd offered a persuasive reason not to bother turning off the light, but what if that was something she did to everyone who came to her?

In the end, feeling stupid, he knocked on his sister's door again.

"What do you want?" She hadn't spoken to him since she'd seen his light was still on.

"I need to talk to you. Please."

"Anything you have to say, you can say through the door."

"I can't. I need your help, Soph." He didn't call her Softserve. He hoped she noticed.

"Fine."

He opened the door. As usual, she sat on her bed, doing whatever it was she did that involved online organizing. He'd never asked.

"You've got two minutes." She fixed him with a withering gaze. "Don't bother sitting."

He closed the door and leaned against it. "Soph, how well do you know that doctor we went to?"

"I told you. I went there once with a friend, but she has a good reputation."

"I know, but . . . do you know anyone who got their Pilot de-activated there?"

"One person came to our group once, I think? Most people get theirs done at BNL." She narrowed her eyes. "Why?"

He looked at his feet. He had a mosquito bite on top of the right one that he hadn't noticed, but now that he saw it, it itched. He felt suddenly ashamed to tell Sophie, like this was a personal failing, like the stupid psychologist was right and he was doing something wrong and that was why he was like this.

"Why, David?"

He shrugged, still looking anywhere but at her. "It's not work-ing. I mean, it's still working. It doesn't feel like it was turned off."

"Did Dr. Pessoa tell you how long it would take?"

"She didn't know exactly, but I got the impression this isn't normal. If it's not on anymore, it shouldn't act like it is, right?"

"Hmm."

"And I can't tell anyone. Like, I can't tell BNL I got it turned off, and I feel funny going back to a doctor who made me sign a form saying I understood she hadn't done many of these proce-dures. I thought maybe she lied and didn't turn it off, but she came across as ethical. I don't think she lied. I don't know what to do."

"Wow," his sister said. "It's still exactly the same?"

"Exactly."

Sophie tossed her tablet facedown on her bed and studied his face. He looked back at her, daring her to make fun of him. When had she gotten old enough that her opinion mattered to him? He hadn't caught up with the times; in his absence, she'd become a whole person instead of an annoying kid sister. He remembered occasionally treating her like an adult, but mostly at times when he'd been dispensing the wisdom of his years, not listening to her. Now he found himself wanting her advice more than anyone else's.

"I don't know if this is relevant, but a woman came to our meeting recently who'd been in the original trial—she had her

Pilot even longer than you've had yours. And they're—BNL—they're contacting some of the original people with some new questions. They paid her a bunch of money to get hers out entirely, not just off like yours, but, um, when she had it out, she said her brain still thought she had it. She said—what was the word she used?—*neuroplasticity.* She said her brain had learned to fire like that on its own. That the younger you were when you got it, apparently, the more likely it was to teach your brain to do the work itself."

He slid down the door to the floor. Sophie didn't tell him to stand. "Did she say anything about noise?"

"No. She said she'd liked hers, but they gave her enough money to consider it."

"And nothing changed when she got it out?"

Sophie shook her head, and David groaned and covered his face in his hands.

He thought of something else. "You said this was a few weeks ago? Before I had mine turned off?"

"Yeah."

"Why didn't you tell me?"

"It was a few weeks before that, and I forgot until you said that just now." She cocked her head, thinking. "She got hers out entirely, not turned off, and it was your company that did it, and hers wasn't a problem for her like yours, so I guess it slipped my mind. I'm sorry."

He sighed. "Not your fault. Like you said, it didn't seem related."

They sat in silence. David's noisy brain spun up all the hits at once. He'd trapped himself. If he'd gone through with having BNL deactivate his Pilot, they'd be on the hook for whatever was happening to him. Now if he went to them, it wouldn't look like coincidence that it was off, if it even was. On top of that, he had no idea if there was any sign marking Dr. Pessoa's intrusion, or if the reversal was reversible. He'd probably voided his own warranty.

He had so many questions. Why was BNL asking people to remove their Pilots, and what was wrong with his head, and did anybody else feel like him or was he a weak link, and he had no-body to blame but himself, he had chosen this, what if this was as turned off as it would ever be, and this was him forever, his on-going status, a permanent deployment, noise forever and ever amen.

He struggled to convince himself to stand, but couldn't do it. Sophie didn't make him go anywhere, just lifted her tablet and re-focused on whatever she'd been working on when he interrupted, and the room got dark around them until the only light was the tablet bathing her face in a glow, and, in the closet door mirror, the blue pinprick meant to mark him as part of the Piloted masses.

He extricated his phone from his pocket and scrolled back through his message history with Milo until he found Alyssa's number. Hi, this is Milo's friend David from Karina's birthday party. Sorry if I asked weird questions. I wasn't in a great space that night, but it doesn't excuse being rude. Hopefully that struck the right note of genuine apology and urgency. He hadn't meant to be so intense with his questions. Sometimes he forgot the body he in-habited, the space he inhabited, the way he came across. He'd say that, too, given the chance. He left the actual question he wanted to ask for a follow-up conversation.

Alyssa didn't write him back for two days, two days in which David had jumped every time his phone buzzed. Her message was cau-tious. She remembered him, thank you for the apology. He tried to calibrate the tone of his response, continued to hold back his ask. He wanted it to come up naturally.

At work, he tried to hold himself together. Worked on his trainings, tried to avoid anything that would get him sent back to Dr. Morton's office, like a teenager trying to avoid the principal. Since he was on an apology kick, he apologized to Tash for snap-ping at them, and they accepted the apology, at least superficially, though he got fewer visits over their shared wall than he had previ-ously.

He tried to get information on the early-adopter trials Sophie had mentioned, but either he wasn't a good investigator or there was no information to be found. BNL was a huge corporation. The Research and Development Department was siloed from his department and was siloed from the subsidiary that ran the clinics, though they apparently had the right to pass his medical records along like he was livestock trading hands. There was no internal path from where he was to anyplace else. He tried the shared server, the company intranet, the printer folders that people in his department sometimes forgot to clear. The others were more fastidious. Dead ends all, passworded and firewalled and it was impossible to look for something when you didn't know what you were looking for.

He started to doubt any of it existed. Maybe Sophie had made it up, or the person who had mentioned it to her had. Maybe it was speculation, without any research behind it. After a week of searching, he decided that had to be the case. Which was why he was shocked to find the very thing he'd been looking for.

He had brought a handout over to the copier/printer outside his supervisor's office to photocopy. People were always forgetting their originals in the feeder, walking away with the copies but not the original, or else printing something to one machine thinking they'd printed to another, and then sending the job again when it didn't turn up instead of searching the other machines. David had done it himself. He'd found all kinds of things that way: a pay statement showing him how much more his boss made than he did, flight confirmation numbers, receipts for items that were definitely not company purchases.

He glanced at the name on top: Nina Flaherty, his supervisor. Normally if he came across something abandoned in the printer, he'd bring it to the person whose name was on top, or leave it where it was, or toss it in the shredder, under the assumption that whoever had left it, likely Nina, would print it again if it was needed. She printed everything; everyone complained behind her back how wasteful it was. He would have done what he usually did this time, if the e-mail's subject hadn't read "Can we spin this?" He didn't try to read the rest while standing there out in the open. He made his copies, then casually gathered the printed e-mail beneath his own original, put both at the bottom of his copy stack, and carried everything back to his desk.

His own copies were of a handout he was supposed to bring to a hospital the next day. Students mostly used their phones to access the info and play his quizzes, but there were still older nurses at the hospitals who preferred the paper version. They were the ones he was there to recruit, and this small concession pleased them. The next day's training was early enough that he had planned to leave with all his materials, rather than come in early the next morning. That made it easy to walk out with the e-mail buried in his box.

He often waited until everyone was gone for the day to head home, to avoid the five p.m. lobby scrum and the anxiety it instilled, but this time he thought it made sense to walk out at the same time as others.

"Not staying late?" Tash asked when they and David stood from their desks at the same time. "People will think you're slacking off, Poster Boy."

"Nah. Early training tomorrow." David tossed a few more random brochures into the box, to further bury the e-mail.

"Can I carry something for you?"

"No! I mean, I've got it. You can hit the elevator buttons."

The elevator was already packed, and Tash held the door while David attempted to maneuver in without hitting anyone with his box or messenger bag.

As he turned, someone said "Hold for me?" Tash stuck a foot in the closing door, and Nina squeezed herself into the remaining space. "Thanks!" Then "David! You're leaving on time for once!"

Tash said, "He'll be back to overachieving tomorrow, I'm sure."

David forced a smile. "I had no idea people cared when I left."

"Nah, I'm glad to see it," said Nina. "Work-life balance is important. You've been looking stressed lately."

David tried to exude unstressed. It felt like everyone in the elevator was looking into the open box he carried. Surely his boss had already spotted her name on the e-mail buried deep in his stack.

He tolerated being squeezed in, but he wished the elevator weren't stopping on every single floor. The box got heavier. He was the tallest person in the elevator, a good vantage. Someone smelled like coconut deodorant covering sweat, and somebody sniffled like they were holding back a sneeze, and someone had earbuds in that spilled snippets of a self-improvement podcast into the compartment. This was why he didn't leave with everyone else.

They finally reached the ground floor. The guards had no reason to give him a second look; he left with boxes several times a week. Even if they stopped him, he could always say he'd grabbed it by accident. Still, he felt a terrified thrill walking it out under their noses.

Why risk this? He didn't know for sure that it would prove to be anything, but that title had intrigued him. How funny if this was how he found something; total dumb luck after all his attempts at subterfuge had uncovered nothing.

Ordinarily he'd leave the next day's materials in the car under the assumption that nobody wanted to steal flyers, but this time he hauled the box into his room. He gave himself a paper cut digging the e-mail out from under the other papers.

He tried not to hope. Didn't know what to hope for in any case, aside from answers to a question everyone seemed determined to avoid. "Can we spin this?" It could be anything.

The e-mail was to all the department heads, including his supervisor. "Can we spin this?" was followed in the first line by "or bury it?" The attachment line referenced a document he didn't have, titled *Neuroplasticity in Early Adopters*.

Before he could change his mind, he slipped it under his sister's door.

CHAPTER FIFTY

SOPHIE

The first thing Sophie noticed about the paper under her door was the single smudged blood-brown fingerprint. She stepped over it, closed the door, then lifted it by the corner, in case it had more blood on it than she could see. She wasn't squeamish about her own blood, but she didn't think it was sanitary to touch somebody else's, even if it was her brother's blood—her assumption when she unfolded the page to find an internal BNL e-mail. She considered knocking on his door, but if he'd wanted to talk about it, he would have handed it to her in person.

The title was "Can we spin this?" She wished she had the attachment mentioned, *Neuroplasticity in Early Adopters*; the brief e-mail thread that followed repeated six variations on "bury it." If her brother had given this to her by hand, she would have hugged him. As it was, she sent him silent thanks, took a quick shower, restocked her bag with meds, and headed back to the meeting space, too excited to wait until morning.

She'd taken the night's last northbound bus to get home, and the last southbound would've passed ages ago. She usually avoided transit apps because she didn't like being tracked, but it was the only option short of flagging a hack, which would give her moms heart palpitations and made her kind of nervous herself at this time of night. App it was.

"Are you sure that's your destination?" the driver asked.

"I'm sure," Sophie said firmly. "Do you ask everyone that question?"

The woman turned and drove. Sophie knew she'd been curt, but it was nobody's business where she was headed. Just because she was small and young-looking didn't mean she didn't have places to go.

The meeting space was dark, but light spilled from under the office door, allowing Sophie to navigate past the sleeping bodies, stepping on only a few. She thought she recognized Dominic's muffled "ow" just outside the office.

Gabe frowned when she pushed the door open. "I thought you went home?"

"I did. Then I came back. Check this out." She pulled the folded paper from her backpack and passed it to him.

"Whoa."

"Right?"

"Your brother?"

Sophie nodded.

He read it again. "Are you going to turn it in to National?"

"I didn't like what they did with the ID—no offense!" As she said it, she remembered Gabe's part in that. "I just thought they squandered the opportunity, and as far as we know nothing came of it. I think we should handle this ourselves."

"What are you thinking?"

"Wasn't there that one reporter who called after the break-in who seemed trustworthy to you? I think we should give this to a reporter. National would tell us to wait, and I don't want to wait."

"That makes sense. Hmm. There was that one who asked different questions than the others, like he had a different angle. Maybe him? I kept his name somewhere."

"Cool."

Gabe poked around the cluttered desk, and a minute later, pulled a scrap of paper from under some other scraps of paper. "Eduardo Toledo. I remembered it because he had a cool name, and when I looked him up he'd done a bunch of investigative stuff. He asked the same questions about whether we knew about the break-in, but then he also asked about the meetings themselves, and the demographics of the attendees, and if they differed from donor demographics. He wanted to know if it was only people who'd never had Pilots, so maybe he has some related angle?"

"Sounds good. Do you want to reach out, or you want me to?"

"How about I'll message him but tell him to talk to both of us?"

That made Sophie happy. Not because it had to be only her, but because she wanted to be part of it.

CHAPTER FIFTY-ONE

DAVID

The call from Nina's office came at nine thirty a.m. They'd had a meeting scheduled for ten a.m. to discuss his idea for a new outreach project to help people like Milo who struggled after leaving the military, and he was still gathering his thoughts, which was why he was surprised to be paged half an hour early. He entered to find her table ringed with Nina, a security officer, the head of Communications, and a fourth stranger, who introduced herself as Ms. Ritter, HR.

This office always irritated David because Nina kept music on low volume, this weird staccato electronic stuff where he couldn't quite find the beat, and if he found the beat he could file it away, but the beat kept changing and bringing itself to the forefront of his attention. She had clacker balls on her desk, too, and a couple of other toys he never saw her touch, all of which caught the sun and tossed it around the room at odd angles. The security officer stood and resituated himself behind David, near the door, leaning against the wall like he'd meant to leave but hey, he might as well hang out, though the casual lean was betrayed by a nervous foot that he tapped in a nonrhythm entirely unlike the music's nonrhythm. David's head hurt.

A tissue box had been placed at the table's center, so David knew he was being fired. He didn't know why he knew that; he'd never been fired before. Something about the combination of these things: his supervisor's office, HR, security. He'd gotten that feeling when he walked in, but the tissues solidified it. He debated leading with that, but decided to make them work for it.

"David," the HR person began. "First of all, we want to thank you for all the hard work you've done for our company since you started here. The Pilots for Prison Guards initiative was a success because of you."

Nina and Communications both nodded their heads in agreement. There was a pause where he thought maybe he was supposed to nod his head as well, maybe agree, or say how much fun it had been to work on the campaign. He kept his mouth shut.

"But, well, we think we've got a new direction for marketing, and we're afraid we're going to have to part ways with you."

"And the others?" He couldn't resist. "Do the others still have jobs?"

Ms. Ritter smiled; he preferred the serious expression. "Who is and isn't staying isn't your concern, David. We're going to have to ask you to clean out your desk and leave."

"That quickly?" He tried to remember his terms of hire and whether he was owed two weeks or more explanation. He supposed it made sense for a company with this many secrets to force people out quickly, without a chance to take anything with them that they might offer to a competitor.

"You'll be paid for two weeks, and one additional week for the year you've been with us, but today will be your last day of employment. Your e-mail address is being suspended as we speak, so no need to send any company-wide good-byes."

"Wait—am I being fired or let go?" He turned to Nina. "Will you give me a reference?"

Ms. Ritter spoke first. "As a policy, we don't give references, but if anyone calls us we'll verify your dates of employment."

"But nothing else? Not even that I was in good standing when I left, or that I wasn't fired?" He dared them to say it.

"Nothing else."

"I don't understand. My performance reviews have been stellar. You could move me to another team. Unless there's something else?"

Ms. Ritter sighed. "David, someone carrying your ID card was caught trespassing in the building."

That had not been what he expected her to say. "I don't know what you're talking about. Wait—you mean that break-in on the news a few months ago? Why wouldn't you tell me then? Or fire me then, if you thought I had anything to do with it? I didn't."

"I believe you, David," said Nina. "But security policies are zero tolerance."

"Zero tolerance on things I didn't do, that happened months ago? With no chance to defend myself?"

"This is the best I could do. You're being let go on good terms, despite this, because I said you've done great work for us. Sign the papers."

He didn't cry. He opened his mouth to thank them, then shut it again. What was he thanking them for? An uncomfortable fame, Dr. Morton's medical intrusion, an unjust separation, an accusation with no chance to defend himself? He signed the papers they put in front of him, which basically said he wouldn't use any information he had gained here in any other position, and he wouldn't talk to the media about parting ways with the company.

One clause brought him pause. "It says here if I initial and accept the three weeks' pay I'm not entitled to see my personnel files. Does that include whatever medical reports Dr. Morton has downstairs? Is that personnel, or something else?"

Nina and the HR woman exchanged looks, then Ms. Ritter spoke. "That isn't technically part of your personnel file. You can put in a written request to see the contents."

"Have *you* seen the contents? Any of you?"

"No," Nina said. The others shook their heads.

He signed. It was only after the security officer followed him from the room that he realized he'd asked the wrong question. He should have asked whether they knew the contents of his medical file, not whether they'd seen it.

People on television always left work with a box, but he didn't keep much personal stuff at his desk: a mug his moms had given him, with a dragon tail for a handle; his headphones; a few snacks he'd stashed in a drawer. The guard leaned against the wall and watched him. David made his motions slow and deliberate, so the guard saw he was putting candy in his mug, not, say, USB drives.

When he finished, he leaned over the shared wall with Tash's cubicle. "Hey, it's been fun working with you."

"You, too, David." They had the grace to look surprised, though they had to have noticed the guard.

In the meeting, HR had said not to talk to the media, but hadn't said he couldn't talk to Tash. He lowered his voice anyway, so the guard couldn't hear. "I was going through a lousy time. I still am. I'm having problems with my Pilot and now I'm getting let go and I don't know why but it might have something to do with that? Anyway, go team. Carry on."

Tash looked like they had a thousand questions. "Shit, David. Good luck?"

David pulled a watermelon-flavored lollipop from his mug and held it out to them. They took it and nodded at him.

The guard followed him to his car. He held his mug out in a silent toast, then put it in the passenger seat. He wanted to sit for a minute, but the guy kept staring at him and clearly wasn't going to stop until he left. He drove off the property and three blocks more, then pulled into a residential cul-de-sac and turned off the car.

The ID thing had to be bullshit; if they'd really thought he was connected with that, they'd have fired him back then. Nobody could have noticed the e-mail he'd grabbed; he was sure of it. Too much prying into other departments? If they'd found out about that, they would have said so, he was pretty sure, and besides, everything he'd searched for could have been explained as answers to questions people had asked him at trainings and recruitment sessions. As far as they knew, he hadn't turned his Pilot off. He hadn't disparaged it in public. He had passed the medical assessment with Dr. Morton, or so he'd been told. Nobody could possibly know he'd taken that one printed e-mail or that he'd had his Pilot turned off. He had no idea what he'd done wrong.

CHAPTER FIFTY-TWO

JULIE

Julie had a theory. She believed that one should never for a moment let into her head that she was as happy as she could possibly be. Every time she had ever allowed that thought to nuzzle at her, every time she'd extended her open palm to it, it had bitten her.

Once, eight months pregnant with David, lying on her back in bed, thinking, *I am so happy already. How could having this child be better than preparing for him?* Later that night the pain had started, and the problems that had nearly caused the loss of her own life and David's.

She had allowed the same thought in the night she held Sophie for the first time. She'd wanted a second child badly, had wanted David to have the sibling neither she nor Val had. When the doctors had said she couldn't have another, adoption was an easy second choice, not second choice at all. Val had been for adoption all along, even if the process took far longer than they'd anticipated. She remembered when Sophie's seizures had started, the first ones a terrifying absence, moving on to other, even more terrifying variations.

And she'd been stupid enough to let that thought into her head when David came home from his last deployment and said he'd left the military. *Finally,* she thought. *Finally I can stop worrying.* Stupid. She was a numbers person, a facts person. She allowed herself one superstition, but she couldn't even get that right. It was a statistical fact: every time she had that thought, something went wrong.

Or maybe she took the wrong conclusion from the numbers. Maybe perfect happiness was impossible, and all good was temporary, all good came with a chaser of bad, because otherwise how would you differentiate?

David was hiding something. He went to work every day as he had since he'd returned stateside. He came home different. Before, at dinner, he'd talk about interesting trainings, or at least he did when Sophie was out. He'd talk about what it was like filming promos, or, if pushed, the surreality of being recognized.

No stories now, no matter how she and Val pried. The funny thing was, he didn't look like he was avoiding her questions. She couldn't get anything out of him. How was your day? Fine.

She knew what a bad patch at work felt like, when everyone was on her about something or an election loomed close. He didn't look stressed, though. Muted; like he'd run out of things to say, but he didn't mind. On the nights he ate dinner with them, he closed his eyes while he chewed, didn't volunteer anything, didn't ask any questions. Other nights, he came home late and went to his room and shut the door.

He was an adult. She resisted the urge to pry: Is something wrong at BNL? Is it Milo you're hanging out with or someone else? None of it was her business, even if he was living under their roof. He'd always been an open kid; he would talk when he was ready.

That was what she figured, until the day she followed him by accident. She had finished a project early and couldn't start on her next until she got one additional document that hadn't yet arrived. A good excuse to head home, except when she left the office, the day she ran into was so perfect she felt like it would be a disservice to the planet not to acknowledge it in some way. Perfect days were a rarity.

She shouldn't have followed him. Wouldn't have if she hadn't pulled up behind his car sitting at a four-way stop as if it were a red light. She waved, but she couldn't catch his eye in his mirror, so she put on her flashers and waited as other cars stopped at the intersection, eyed him, then proceeded. When someone honked at both of them, she waved them around.

Just when she was going to get out and ask if he was having car trouble, he started moving again. She followed. Not to spy; spies had discretion. She tailed him from right behind, so he could easily have seen her if he'd looked. That made it okay.

He crawled through several intersections, nearly causing accidents at each, and she followed him, a strange entourage. A parade of two.

He drove past four schools, a hospital, and two business parks, and each time she assumed he would pull in, step out with a display-in-a-box, but he kept going until he reached the waterfront park's lot. She pulled in a few spots away.

Again, she hoped he'd lace his running shoes or, really, do anything to indicate purpose. He walked into the park with what seemed like no intent whatsoever. The funny thing was, this had been exactly where she'd been considering going; they hadn't been to this park since before David had deployed, though it had been a favorite when the kids were younger.

The playground had been updated, the splash pad, too, and the long corridor of weeping cherry trees that ran along the seawall was still stunning. The trees were older and fuller than she remembered. People sat on the benches that punctuated the trees: a couple of women with matching haircuts and a wire-haired mutt twining around their feet; two older men engaged in some handheld game battle; a little girl trying to drag the woman she was with toward the splash pad. Parent? Sibling? Nanny? Julie was no good at telling ages anymore; Val had always been better at that, since she worked with teenagers.

The next two benches were empty, and if her afternoon in the park hadn't turned into a David hunt, she'd have considered sitting to watch the water. No, more likely, she would have pulled out her phone or her tablet. She wasn't good at doing nothing. Not in the same way as Val, who craved motion; hers was something else. She often thought their compatibility came partly from how she and Val both lacked an essential stillness; it meant they each understood the other's activities, even if they didn't share them.

She kept walking. The mutt she'd passed went flying by, trailing a leash. She reached to grab it but missed, then stepped aside as one of the women ran past, yelling "Radish!"—presumably the dog's name, not an enticement. They made it past the next bench before the mutt spotted a Weimaraner and made a beeline for the leashed dog, whose walker immediately started shouting, while trying to keep his dog and leash from getting tangled with the loose dog, now growling. The pursuer tackled her dog and dragged the wayward Radish away, the two still snapping and lunging at each other.

Julie took all of that in while also taking in the person sitting on the next bench. The curly hair, the ramrod spine. She was one hundred percent certain it was David, except David would have grabbed for the loose dog; the guy on the bench didn't turn his head toward the commotion. It was David, obviously David, but something was off. She remembered the way he'd scanned the area on their first trip to the mall after his return, and his tension at baseball games all summer, trying to keep track of everyone around him.

"Hey, Davey," she said, walking closer to the railing so he'd see her.

He startled. "Oh, hi, Mom."

He smiled at her, then returned his gaze to the water. She sat on the bench beside him and looked to see what had his attention: ducks. She watched for a minute before impatience overtook her.

"What are you doing out here? I would've thought you'd be at work."

He turned to face her. Something in his expression unnerved her. It was an absence of expression, really: an unexpression, an unalertness, his eyes unsparked. Everything about it was un-David.

He didn't answer her question, and after a minute she won-

274 | Sarah Pinsker

dered if she'd asked out loud. They watched the stupid ducks for another minute or ten; she couldn't tell how long because they were watching ducks.

When he finally spoke again, she almost didn't recognize it as the answer to her question, there had been so much separation between the two. "I'm not working at BNL anymore. I'm looking for a new job."

She opened her mouth to say the first thing that came to her: *What are you talking about?* Just as quickly, she imagined how Sophie would respond if she asked something like that, the defensive turn the conversation would take. *Proceed with caution, calm, nonchalance. Channel Val.* "Oh. I didn't know. You can tell me more if you'd like."

He shrugged. "They said they were going in a new direction."

"Oh." She matched his placid tone again. "Was this today?"

"Nah."

He wore his BNL work polo and slacks, so either he was wearing them to job interviews—odd given the tech no doubt woven into the logo—or he was wearing it to fool his family when he left each morning. In which case who knew how long he'd been doing it. She wanted to ask *when*. She didn't.

"I'm sorry, kiddo." The funny thing was, he didn't seem particularly upset. He didn't seem anything at all; he looked peaceful. "I feel like I'm disturbing you. Do you want to talk about it? Or do you want me to go?"

When he didn't answer, Julie stood. "See you at dinner?"

Another delayed response. "I've got plans. I'll see you later, though."

She kissed the top of his head and left him to his ducks. She had to let him decide when to come to them for help.

That night, neither kid appeared at dinnertime. Val had made some variation on green curry, bright and spicy. Both kids would've liked it, even with the brown rice.

"I know they're adults," Julie said, "but they should still tell us when they aren't coming to dinner, as long as they're both still living here."

Val shrugged. "Does it matter?"

"It's rude. You've gone to the effort of cooking for them."

"They'll eat it as leftovers. I was going to cook this much either way so we'd have lunches. What's the difference? It's not like it'll go to waste."

"Still."

"You said 'they're adults' a second ago. You know they'll get irritated if they think we're trying to limit them. I don't want to do anything to make them think we're keeping tabs."

"I'm not talking about a curfew. Just common courtesy."

She had no reason to be irritated over Val's nonchalance, but she was. Val was always better at these things. Better at letting them loose, better at understanding where they were coming from.

Julie had a piece of information her wife didn't have, about the odd conversation with David at the park. Would that change Val's tune, if she knew David pretended to go to work? He hadn't asked her to keep it secret, and she didn't intend to, but she decided not to mention it now. Not for any reason, but because if Val shrugged that away, too, she'd go from irritated to upset. It was worth being upset about. He was lying to them. Was lying to them part of being an adult? Val would say he was free to make his own mistakes, that given the chance he would sort it out. Which was probably true.

Julie cleaned up after dinner, then joined Val in the living room, settling in the reclining chair. It wasn't as bad as when David had been deployed, but her habit of scanning for news about them was a hard one to break. She checked the local police and emergency feeds. When she didn't see anything, she logged into the anti-Pilot action site's chat in her GNM persona, looking for Sophie.

GNM!

Hi Grandma!

A few regulars greeted her, then went back to the conversation they'd been having before she arrived. She scrolled back and saw they were chatting about an upcoming neurologists' convention they were planning on interrupting. Sophie had been part of the conversation a minute before and chimed in again a minute later, suggesting a tweak to the plan. It was a good tweak, but better yet, it meant she was safe wherever she was. When GNM responded enthusiastically to the idea, it was as much for that as the idea itself.

Sophie wrote: *Learned something that I've been thinking about a lot. Did you know it's possible to turn a Pilot off but leave the light on? Is there any way we can use that information?*

Julie read the post, then read it again, then a third time. Other posts piled onto that one, musing on the possibilities. Maybe this was a turning point. If the Pilot no longer implied a better worker to employers, maybe it would no longer be a source of job discrimination.

Was it really possible? She looked on BNL's Pilot FAQ, the one for people considering getting their first Pilot, but she didn't see it mentioned. *Q: Can the Pilot be turned off? A: Yes, if you need to, you can have it turned off, though the number of people who have done this is less than one in ten thousand.* There was no mention of keeping the light on.

Julie had wanted her Pilot, but it hadn't hurt that it demonstrated she was committed to improving herself in the name of improving her work.

GNM wrote: *I wonder if that would lead to employers doing working interviews that tested function instead of assuming based on the blue light. They still have to maintain the illusion they're not discriminating.*

She hoped she wasn't explaining something Sophie had already thought of. If she'd said it as herself, Sophie would roll her eyes, say, *Isn't that what I said?*

Sophie wrote, *Good point, GNM! Yeah . . . maybe we sit on this until we see whether it's useful info.*

The door opened.

"Hey, Davey," she called.

Val glanced at her, surprised, and she realized she shouldn't have known which kid was at the door from her position faced away from it. She knew because she was conversing online with Sophie, and Sophie didn't tend to use her devices in transit, so she was either at home (which she wasn't) or at her meeting space. Julie shrugged as if that was an explanation.

"Hey, David," Val said, but he still didn't respond. Then, as he headed upstairs, louder, she deepened her voice to mimic his. *"Good night, Moms?"*

"Oh, hi," he said. "Good night."

Val raised an eyebrow at Julie. This would be the time to tell her about the weirdness at the park, but she didn't mention it. If Val thought their kids were adults allowed to come and go as they pleased, then she shouldn't care if they didn't say a proper good-night, either. She'd tell her once Val acknowledged she was right. They were adults, but there were rules of engagement. There was courtesy. Family had different rules.

CHAPTER FIFTY-THREE

SOPHIE

I t had been three weeks since she and Gabe sent a copy of David's stolen e-mail to Eduardo Toledo, and Sophie assumed he'd passed on the story. She hadn't sent it to anyone else because she didn't know what else to do with it. If the journalist who had been most interested in working on their issues didn't bite, who would? National would know, but she still didn't want to involve them.

Another three weeks later, when he texted Sorry for the delay— I had to research the claim—do you still want to talk? she was taken completely by surprise. Finally. Hopefully. Maybe.

She met him at Stomping Grounds. The fact that he knew it was a point in his favor, as was the fact he didn't have a Pilot. When she arrived, he was already there waiting for her, his own travel mug indicating he knew the drill. Normally she'd suggest walking out to prevent eavesdropping; when he didn't suggest it, she didn't, either, for fear it might sound paranoid. She was paranoid, and for good reason, but this probably wasn't the person to let see that side of her.

"So," Toledo said without preamble. "This is legit. Nobody else knows about it?"

"I haven't told anyone else."

"And your source hasn't given it to anyone else?"

The "your source" part felt like a spy movie to Sophie. She didn't know for sure, but it seemed unlikely. "No."

"Can you tell me your source's name?"

She shook her head.

The journalist sighed. "I understand. I was able to verify that the study referenced exists, and that both the sender and the receiver of this e-mail work at BNL, so the source isn't as important, but it would still be great to talk to them. Would they be willing to talk to me as an anonymous source?"

"I don't think so. They didn't give it to me directly—just slipped it under the door." That was all true, even if it suggested the door in question was the meeting space, not her bedroom.

"Okay. Is there anyone else who could speak to the human interest side of this? Someone in your group, maybe?"

She thought of Tommie, the woman who'd been paid to have her Pilot removed, though she'd probably signed something saying she couldn't disclose. "I'll ask."

"Thanks. Now, I'll be calling your national office for a quote—"

"Don't!" said Sophie, then, less vehemently, "Please."

He looked surprised. "Why?"

"They'll make it into some national thing."

"It *is* a national thing. The letter came from here because BNL headquarters is here, but the study has national implications."

"I know, but is there any way you can hold off on that?" It was hard to explain that she didn't want to lose control. She was being silly. This was a big deal; it wasn't about her. "Until nearly the end. Do the rest, then call them?"

"I can't make any promises. If I need something they'll know, I'll need to ask them, but the story is mostly about BNL, so I don't think anything they say will change the meat of it. I'll try to wait as long as I can. I get wanting a story to be yours as long as you can hold on to it."

He understood.

CHAPTER FIFTY-FOUR

JULIE

The wrongness in David had grown, magnified; Julie felt a strange electric charge whenever she saw him. He had lost weight, and there were dark circles under his eyes, even worse than when he'd first come home from his deployment and struggled to sleep. Those were nights she'd stayed up with him, and they'd drunk coffee despite the late hour and talked about nothing in particular while she'd waited for him to bring up the things that actually kept him awake.

She was pretty sure he'd told the truth when he said he wasn't at BNL anymore, but he still hadn't said it to her again after that one mention in the park that he seemed to have forgotten. She couldn't tell if he knew that she knew. Why did he bother with the deception of wearing the BNL shirt if it wasn't to fool them?

It took her longer than it should have to realize Sophie must have been talking about David when she posted her discovery that Pilots could be turned off with the lights still on. Not until she caught him at breakfast one morning, still in his BNL uniform but looking like he must have slept in it. He sat in the kitchen chair he usually hated, the one with its back to the room instead of the wall, drinking coffee with his eyes closed.

"Good morning," Julie said, and David startled so badly his

coffee left his mug, like a cartoon, hovered above it for a second, then spilled over his hand, his lap, the table.

"Why would you sneak up on me?" He sounded petulant; he'd never been a petulant kid.

"I didn't. I walked into the room and said hi. It's a normal thing to do. Are you hurt?"

"No, but now I have to change."

"It's not like you're going to work," she said. "Put something else on."

He stared at her. "How do you know?"

"What do you mean, *how do I know*? I ran into you in the park a few weeks ago, remember? You said you weren't working at BNL anymore, so I don't know why you're still wearing their uniform."

His expression was laced with doubt, but she didn't know which part he doubted. After a minute, he went upstairs. She wiped the table and chair and poured her own cup. He returned wearing jeans and a button-down shirt.

She searched for a question to ask him that wouldn't sound like parental nudging. In the end she settled on apology in the name of clarity. "Sorry if I surprised you. You're usually aware I'm coming into the room before I even know I'm coming in."

He shrugged. "It's okay. I was distracted, I guess."

"I hope it wasn't too much of an inconvenience to change."

She waited for him to say no, no inconvenience, he didn't need to be wearing those clothes anymore, this was his plan for the day, any or all of the above. He just shrugged again, got up, and left.

She thought about it all day at work. Got back to find Val making her usual giant dinner.

"Hey, love," she said, putting her hands on Val's waist and kissing her neck, careful not to get in the way as her wife stirred whatever was in the pot. It smelled good, like onions and butter. "Can I do something to help?"

"Nah. I'm almost done, but thanks."

"Is either kid here?"

"I don't think so."

Julie took a deep breath. "Have you noticed anything strange about David recently?"

"Strange, like what?"

"Have you noticed he's distracted? Like that thing the other night where he didn't hear us say hi when he came in? I think . . . I think his Pilot is off."

"Like it's broken?"

"Like the light is on, but I think the Pilot isn't."

Val turned and frowned. "Is that possible? I've never heard of that."

"I saw it mentioned somewhere."

"Huh. I guess he'll tell us when he's ready, if that's the case . . . crap." Val turned back to the stovetop, where the onions had started to burn. Julie waited for her to say more, but she busied herself with salvaging the meal. It figured she wasn't as concerned as Julie about this.

The front door creaked open and then shut again. "What's burning?" called Sophie.

Val smiled at Julie to share her happiness that one of the kids had joined them for dinner. Julie changed the subject to ask how Val's day had been, so they were on safer topics than Pilots and the lack thereof when Sophie entered the room.

CHAPTER FIFTY-FIVE

VAL

Val was good at ignoring the outside world. She'd never seen the point of social media, so she'd never felt the temptation to check for updates during her school day. She kept her phone on "do not disturb," with emergency overrides for her family.

The day after Julie said she thought David had deactivated his Pilot, she found herself itching to go online, for the first time in ages. It had come to her after lunch: the memory of the BNL Pilot parent forum that she had looked at only once, the morning of David's activation. At the time, she'd been surprised to find that every post was positive. She desperately wanted to know whether that was still the case. She waited through her afternoon's classes, then track, trying to keep her head in the game, to give her focus to her students, as they deserved. What did David deserve? Something better than noise.

While her last students finished their cooldowns, and the neighborhood joggers and walkers replaced them on the track, she sat on the bleachers and pulled out her phone. She navigated to BNL's website, but couldn't find the forum. Was she misremembering? Had it been on some other site? No. She distinctly recalled wondering if the fact that it was owned by BNL meant they would censor negative comments. Maybe they'd deleted it entirely.

She tried a web search for "Pilot parent forum" with no results, then "Pilot forum," also nothing, then "Pilot group." *Did you mean to search for "Pilot Survivor Group"?* She hadn't, but now she most definitely did. It was on a site she boycotted, but the privacy restrictions were set so she could browse it without an account.

The pinned post began *They tried to shut us down but we're back.* Below that, one story after another, all of which she read in David's voice.

I tried to tell them it wasn't working like it was supposed to . . .

It's hard to find the language to explain the way the Pilot makes my head feel. I got it checked but they said it was working fine.

The FDA said the company hadn't reported any complaints.

They told me it might take a while to get used to it, and I should do the exercises and wait out the static. I waited. It's still here.

That last one sounded exactly like David, if you substituted "noise" for "static."

She read on. She waited for somebody to mention FreerMind, for her children's worlds to intersect, but the more she read, the more she realized these people weren't looking for political action or support groups; they were struggling to survive their own heads. Like David.

What she wanted, suddenly and more than anything, was a friend who wasn't her wife. When was the last time she'd had one? Angie at her old school, years ago; she'd been too embarrassed about the way she'd left to keep in touch. She was friendly with the other non-Piloted teachers here, but they all treated each other like they'd been thrown together by circumstance, not choice; alliances more than friendships, all afraid to seem cohesive lest the whole group get yoked together. She wanted a friend to sit in a coffee shop with, not that she ever did that, or go to a bar with, not that she ever did that anymore, either. Someone to chat about her family with who was outside of her family.

That had never been a thing she needed before. She'd had three modes forever, family, school, and solitary, with no time for anyone else. Where did you find new friends, especially if you narrowed it down to people without Pilots? Online communities weren't her thing, and she didn't want to invade Sophie's space. She wanted to talk with someone who would understand when she said she looked at those lights on the heads of people she loved and she felt like she'd been balancing on top of a fence for too long, and any moment she would fall to one side at the expense of whoever was on the other.

When she looked up, the sun had dropped behind the trees and the joggers had gone. Some fraction of her family was probably waiting for her to come home and make dinner.

CHAPTER FIFTY-SIX

DAVID

When he'd left the military, David waited until he had a plan to tell his family; that seemed the right way to go for this as well. Go in with an announcement, not a question. If he arrived at family dinner and said he'd been let go, they'd have asked a million questions about why and how, alongside the *how dare they?* editorials. Then they'd suggest places for him to apply, and offer to look at his résumé, and before you knew it, the whole thing would have been a family project.

He didn't want a collaborative process. He wasn't sure what he was qualified for, or what he wanted to do, for that matter. He didn't have a college degree, but he had plenty of life skills. He'd learned a lot from the military and the job with BNL.

He left the house every day in his BNL polo to stave off questions. He spent the mornings applying for jobs, and in the afternoons he went to the park and took one of the pills Alyssa had given him. They'd been introduced as Fortress of Solitude, but he had started thinking of them simply as Quiet.

The park was his own dare, a chaotic environment of joggers and ducks and ships and strollers and dogs and children and waves and sky that evened itself out as the pill kicked in, smoothing the sounds, the colors, the movement in his peripheral vision. He was exposed there on his bench, a target in the open. Sitting there, in the Quiet, he proved to himself over and over that not everyone was out to get him.

He'd told Alyssa he wanted the pills for a party game like hers, and she had given him a dozen in a breath-mint tin; he ran out in a week. He didn't want her to know how many he was taking, in case she told Karina who then told Milo, but one day at the park he noticed someone else sitting the way he did, and he struck up a conversation, and that guy gave him a name and number, and before he knew it, he had a guy who was happy to sell him as many as he needed, no questions asked.

Alyssa hadn't told him to space the pills out. She hadn't said anything about them at all, and he went out of his way not to seek any information. He didn't want anything to disrupt the Quiet. He wouldn't have minded taking a second one as the first wore off, to sit in the Quiet forever. His self-restraint in taking only one every afternoon was his way of showing himself it wasn't a problem.

Okay, sometimes he took a second in the evening, but that was a reward for the progress he was making on being out in public without panicking, just as the first was a reward for a morning spent sending out his résumé, going on interviews, concocting new and creative ways to explain parting ways with BNL. If he took one in the morning occasionally, that was to relax before interviews, to concentrate on what mattered and filter out the noise so he didn't spend the whole time tracking every hand movement, every rattling air vent, every flickering fluorescent, every intern in every busy hallway.

He'd been on twenty-seven first interviews and one second interview without a single offer. The first one had been a shock, but none since had surprised him. He'd be depressed if he weren't so elated over the Quiet. What he needed at this moment was to work on himself, to better himself, to fix everything that had broken. That was what mattered.

If his Pilot had trained his brain into the noise, had done it so successfully that even deactivating the Pilot couldn't stop it, then he needed to try to train his brain back into its natural state. He approached it with the same dedication that had allowed him to get past the noise and finish high school and survive his deployments. Retraining his brain was his job now. Put on your oxygen mask before you help others. He didn't research whether retraining was possible; it had to be.

Sometimes he ate dinner with Milo and Karina, but he was conscious of the intrusion on their lives. More rarely, with them and Alyssa, though he'd been careful to tell her he was working on himself and needed to take things slow. Sometimes he hung at the club where Milo worked, until Milo said his boss had called David a distraction, so if he went out at all he just drank until Milo got off work. He still hadn't told Milo about the Quiet.

Mostly he sat in the park and watched the ducks and then the dusk and then the darkness, and let the one move through the other gradually, a progression, a natural linearity his brain had never allowed him to witness before. Quiet.

Sometimes he sat there all night, slept on the bench until a cop roused him, and then he apologized and said he must have dozed off, and yes he had a car in the lot and a place to go home to, and he allowed his ironed shirt and his famous face to grant him the privilege of a dignified exit. He drove home, slipped upstairs and into his bed to get enough sleep to repeat it all the next day. It was a strange routine, but he was learning, he was growing, he was forcing his brain to change, maybe, hopefully.

After a while, David had to admit to himself that his attempts at brain training were making no difference. If anything, it had gotten worse. Quiet worked, but now there was a comedown he hadn't remembered before, the ocean of noise ebbing then returning in a tidal wave, so that the gaps between the pills felt worse than anything he'd previously experienced.

He called the BNL clinic. Since he didn't work for them anymore, he didn't care what they knew.

"I need my Pilot looked at," he said when he reached an actual human.

"Is there a problem?"

"Yes. I had the implant deactivated, but I haven't noticed any difference. My head is still full of noise."

He heard the frown through the phone. "What was your name again?"

He repeated his name and implant ID, as he had to the machine at the beginning of the call, which had promised to route him to the right department.

"Mr. Geller-Bradley, our records don't show that you had your implant deactivated."

"I had it done elsewhere. Your doctors wouldn't do it for me." *You kicked me out*, he didn't say. If he was lucky, that note wasn't in his file, but he couldn't imagine it wasn't.

"I'm afraid if you had your implant deactivated at a non-BNL facility, unless it was a documented emergency procedure at an accredited hospital, you voided the warranty on your implant."

"I'll pay for the appointment. I don't care about the warranty."

"No, I'm afraid it's not a matter of payment. If someone else altered your Pilot, we can't do any further work on it. It's not an insurance matter; it's about liability."

This time he said it. "I went to you to do it, but you kicked me out."

He could have waited for whatever the operator said next, but instead he channeled his inner Sophie and hung up without niceties. He had missed this fine print, but it wasn't like he hadn't tried to go to them first. It made him feel lousy about ever having worked for them, that they would leave him high and dry like this. Maybe his sister was right.

She couldn't be right. For her to be right meant he had to be wrong, that he'd bought into a bad system and worked to propagate it. He'd let them use his face on billboards in service of a bad system. That was too much to acknowledge.

He closed his eyes, searching for a solution beneath his eyelids. He dialed the doctor who had deactivated his Pilot and made an appointment to get the light turned off, too. Dr. Pessoa's schedule had gotten busy, so he scheduled a month out. Still time to change his mind.

He imagined Julie giving him a hard time about how limited his job options would be once the light was off. Val would be supportive, and that might be even worse; he'd pushed so hard for his Pilot, and he couldn't shake his concern that the problem lay with him, not the Pilot. Even now he wasn't ready to disavow the utility of the Pilot—it had still saved his life—but he didn't need to be a walking advertisement anymore.

CHAPTER FIFTY-SEVEN

JULIE

Julie led the noon staff meeting, suddenly conscious of the blue lights on every head in the room. She wondered if anyone was faking it, like David. If anyone else had gotten theirs taken out but still pretended to have it so that nobody could question their focus and commitment.

She checked off everything on her day's to-do list and started on the next day's list. On her way home she drove past the park: David's car was there again.

Neither kid came home for dinner. Julie and Val watched two episodes of *Co-Pilots*, the mystery series where a young Piloted priest and a skeptical old-guard reporter investigated their town's stratospheric body count. When Val announced she was going to bed, Julie said she wanted to stay up a little longer. She puttered for a while doing her usual paranoid searches. Sophie was online, just as Julie liked it. If she was online, she wasn't off getting arrested or seizing somewhere.

David didn't come home until after two a.m. Julie had sat on the couch with the view out the window, and from there she watched him glide the car to the curb, then sit another minute, two minutes, five. It was light in the room and dark outside, and her eyes followed the blue pinprick from the car to the door.

He turned his key quietly, closed the door quietly, paused to remove his shoes. The opposite of the Sophie whirlwind.

"Hey, Davey," she said.

"Oh, hi! I didn't think anyone would be awake."

"I couldn't sleep." A little lie. The kind that didn't matter. "Sit with me a sec?"

He came into the room and settled in the high-backed chair. She studied his face. He didn't look stressed or aggrieved or anything other than tired.

"How was your day?" A carefully calibrated question. Not prying.

"It was okay."

She tried another. "Do anything interesting?"

"Not much."

She had to ask her real questions if she wanted real answers. "Did you notice my car behind yours the other day?"

"Huh? No. Where?"

She named the intersection.

"Oh. I didn't see you. Guess I was distracted."

"You were more than distracted, honey. Cars were pulling around you because you sat there for so long."

"Huh."

He looked uncomfortable. She knew it would be smarter to stop, but she couldn't. "What's going on with you, Davey? Talk to me. No judgment."

"Nothing. I'm tired. It's two in the morning."

"It wasn't two when I sat behind your car, and it wasn't two when I saw you sitting in the park. What's going on? For real."

"Are you following me?" He frowned and rubbed his head. "None of this is any of your business."

"It is, sweetie. You're living in our house, and technically that's our car you're driving." Wrong tack. She knew it. No good ever came of that kind of conversation, and she'd always tried hard to be a chill parent, at least to their faces. She tried to walk it back. "I don't care about any of that, though. I just want to help. You were so distracted in the park, and the other day when you spilled your coffee . . . Is it your Pilot? Are you having problems since you had it turned off?"

David groaned. "You don't know anything about my Pilot. You never have."

Julie opened her mouth, but David kept talking. "And you know what? I don't need you telling me that I'm living in your house and driving your car. I don't need your car or your help."

"Davey—don't you, though? You're not working."

"I'll be fine. I haven't been trying. I can get a job tomorrow, or else I can reenlist."

She froze. Not that; she'd never be able to go through that again. If she didn't weigh what she said next, that would be the first thing he did in the morning, given how this conversation was going. What could she say that wouldn't influence the outcome? "You're right, David. I only want you to do what's best for you. I'm sorry for prying. Let's go to sleep and talk about this in the morning. It's too late to argue. I just wanted to help."

"Help. Huh. How could any of this help?" He was still upset, but she couldn't tell which way the upset was directed. "Telling me I'm leeching off you? Telling me something is wrong with me, as if I don't know that already?"

"I didn't say you were leeching. I just want to help fix whatever's bothering you."

"Tell me how your Pilot feels."

"What?" That wasn't what she'd expected him to say.

"Tell me what your Pilot feels like."

"I don't know. I'm so used to it. That's like asking me the mechanics of breathing, or reading." She saw his frustration and fished for something more. "It's—I don't know. It doesn't feel like a particular thing. If I think about what it's like when it's cycled down, or if I try to remember what it was like before? It's exactly the same, just, like, the opposite of morning before I've had coffee, or the opposite of hungover or that thing where you have the flu and everything is underwater? It's the opposite of that. That's all."

"No noise?"

The noise again. How many times had he said that, and they'd dismissed it? She'd assumed it had gotten better, because he hadn't mentioned it in so long. He'd gone to work for BNL and talked about how it had saved him; she thought he'd learned to live with it.

"No noise, Davey, I'm sorry. Is that what this is about?"

"That's what everything is always about. Nobody ever believes me, and nothing helps, so I don't know how you expect to help."

"I can try. I want to help, you have to believe that. I just don't know what to do. We'll talk to BNL again."

"I don't want to talk with them ever again."

That was new. "How are you going to get this fixed if you can't talk to the people who caused it? The VA?"

"No."

"Okay, then. How about we start over with getting you a new job, then. And maybe someone else can address the noise? A psychologist?"

"Mom. Did you honestly just tell me I need my head checked? You said you want to help, that you want me to talk to you, then you suggest I'm imagining it?"

His face flushed. He was angry, and she didn't want to be angry back, but she couldn't help herself. It was late, and she was tired, and he misinterpreted everything she said. "I didn't say you were imagining it, just that if it's not the implant it must be something else. In the meantime, you need to deal with it, the same as you always have. Get a job. Maybe staying here has you thinking it's not a priority? Pull yourself together, so you're not scaring me by sitting at stop signs, and you're not sitting in the park all day like some old man without better things to do."

He fished in his pocket, then tossed his key chain on the floor. It had a small flashlight on the end, which switched on when it hit the ground. "I don't need your car. I don't need you to help me get a job. I don't need a shrink. I need some quiet, and I can't get it here."

He was out of the house before she could say another word.

Unlike Sophie, he didn't slam the door; he left it open, so she could see him walk away, shoulders soldier-square, never looking back.

She watched him go, replaying the conversation in her head. Had she really said anything that bad? Was he already on edge and she'd hit a sore spot without realizing it? She shouldn't have given him a hard time for living in the house or using the car they'd been about to junk in any case. Had she kicked him out? She'd told him to get a job. Had she told him to leave? She didn't think so. She'd only been trying to help.

Val would be furious. All either of them wanted was to know the kids were safe, and now she'd driven Davey out in the middle of the night. Hopefully he'd go to Milo's, or else he'd walk it off. Maybe she'd even said something he needed to hear, and catalyzed change. That was the optimistic view, anyway. She waited a few minutes to see if he'd come back, then left the door unlocked so he'd be able to return if he wanted to.

She slipped into bed beside Val, who stirred and shifted over. "Everything okay?"

She should tell, Julie thought. Instead, she spooned herself around her wife. "I love you. Go back to sleep."

She'd tell in the morning. She'd find a way to frame it so she hadn't driven their son out into the night, or she'd find the thing to say to bring him back before she had to tell. They always came back; they usually did. She played the argument over in her head again and again until the sun rose.

"Did the kids come home last night?" Val asked as she got out of bed.

"I don't think so," Julie lied. She realized why Val had lied that time years ago when she'd had her narwhal meltdown, and why sometimes lies embedded themselves before you could tell the truth. Some truths were too painful to look in the eye.

CHAPTER FIFTY-EIGHT

DAVID

Milo and Karina said David could stay while he found a place, and he added an apartment hunt to his job hunt. He should have moved out of his parents' house while things were good; nobody would rent to him now that he was unemployed. He should have canceled the appointment with Dr. Pessoa, too, held off making his prospects worse by turning off the light, but the day came, and he committed. For one moment that night, peeling back the bandage, he imagined his Pilot had finally been silenced, but the fantasy didn't last any longer than the thought.

In the first weeks after leaving BNL, he'd applied for the kinds of job he thought that position had prepared him for: communications, outreach. Whether because he didn't have a college degree or because he couldn't explain why he'd left BNL, nobody bit. He needed a different approach.

The first place he applied after getting his light turned off was the prison where he'd promoted Pilots not long before. He could be a compassionate guard; his parents would flip at the danger, but it was one option. He applied for jobs at the VA, security guard positions, a few others where his military experience might be valued.

When he came across a listing for a safety officer at his high school, he threw an application that way. The interview request came two days later: his first in weeks, with radio silence on all the others.

He arrived for the high school interview twenty minutes early, which put him squarely in Lunch Period One. He hadn't taken a pill that morning, though he craved it. He waited in the car as long as he could, knowing the school would be all noise at this hour, from the second he exited the car, and his mission through the entire interview would be to hide that it bothered him; he'd forgotten how much it had bothered him as a student. He'd learned coping mechanisms that came back to him now, though none had been as effective as Quiet: count the tiles as you walk, or the bricks, or the lockers. Focus on that and only that. Tune out the voices, the chaotic movement, the knots of students everywhere. Sweat pooled in the small of his back, and he was glad his moms had insisted that if he owned only one suit it should be a dark one.

The interview was in the vice principals' office. He didn't recognize their names and didn't remember whether any of them were the same as when he'd attended. It hadn't been that long, even if it felt like a lifetime; they probably still had access to his student records. Would that affect his chance at the job, if they saw he'd been a mediocre student whose teachers always wrote that he was strangely distracted for someone with a Pilot?

The receptionist looked at him like she was trying to place his face.

He smiled, to confuse her, since he never smiled in the commercials. "I'm here for an interview with Mr. Redding."

"The chemistry teacher position?"

He shook his head. "Safety officer."

"Ah. Great. Fill this out, please, and he'll be with you shortly."

The application she handed him basically asked for all the same information that had been on his résumé and the online application he'd already filled out. He had copies of both those documents with him, and would have liked to just hand them over instead, but he supposed this was part of the process. He balanced the clipboard on his knees to transfer the information from one page to the other in his best handwriting.

By the time he handed the clipboard back, it was five minutes past the interview's scheduled time. The woman nodded and buzzed the intercom.

A tall Black man with a shaved head emerged from the office behind her. He looked young, maybe a few years older than David. A Pilot gleamed on his temple. "You're David, of course—I've never had a celebrity in my office before. It's an honor. Come in! Let's chat."

David shook Mr. Redding's hand. "Nice to meet you, sir."

They entered an office that breathed private endowment. The furniture was modern, all metal and glass and sharp angles, in contrast with the ivied outer walls. Redding gestured toward one of three orange chairs on the near side of the desk, then surprised David by sitting beside him, instead of behind his own desk. He had David's clipboard in front of him and a tablet that displayed his résumé.

"So, David, is it strange to be back here?"

"A little," David admitted. "I had to remind myself—" He was going to say *that I was older than the students*, but that sounded terrible in an interview. He finished with "—that it's been a few years," which sounded silly, but at least didn't imply he couldn't separate himself from the students he'd be protecting.

"I know the feeling," said Redding. "I graduated a few years before you got here. They make it pretty easy to want to come back, I guess. I wasn't famous like you, though. What piqued your interest in this position?"

"I wanted a new challenge."

Redding raised an eyebrow.

David tried again. "I wanted a new challenge that didn't involve selling something I'm not as enthusiastic about as I once was."

"You were at BNL, I see. I wasn't sure if you worked for them or just did their commercials."

"Yeah. My position involved convincing people to get Pilots.

They sent me everywhere: schools, hospitals, health fairs, prisons. I adapt well to new situations and meeting new people. I like being a friendly face." He'd practiced ways to tie the two positions together. "And before that, I was in the military, so I'm comfortable in stressful and dangerous situations. I keep my head."

There was a shout outside, and David turned toward the window.

"So what would you do in a situation where you found a—I'm sorry, I should have offered you something to drink. Do you need some water?"

David nodded, and the man crossed in front of him and left the room, returning a minute later with two mugs. The one for David had #1 TEACHER written on it and a cartoon cat. "Sorry for the mug; this is a coffee town. So, I was going to ask whether you have current CPR and first aid certification?"

"No, but I've taken them before and I can get them again. This weekend, if you want." That hadn't been the question he had started asking before he left the room, David was pretty sure.

"And why did you leave BNL?"

"I wanted to do something better reflecting my skill set. I'm not a salesperson."

"What do you consider to be your skill set?"

"I'm a quick thinker. I'm good at being aware of my surroundings, and what should and shouldn't be there. I'm good on a team. People trust me."

"The familiar face probably helps with that."

"Well, yes, sir, I guess, but even before that. Part of what I learned as a soldier was how to put people at ease, since my presence was by nature an intrusion in many situations."

"And this is where your career has led you?" Something had changed around the time Redding had gone for water, but David couldn't tell what it was. David thought he was still making a good case for the position, but Redding looked done.

"It was great to have you in, David. We'll be in touch. Wait until I tell my wife you were here."

It had been a bizarre interview. The one hypothetical question had been cut off midsentence, and after that, Redding hadn't asked anything that felt applicable. What had caused him to go from enthusiastic to awkwardly uncomfortable?

It took a few days for David to realize. A few days, and three more interviews, all of which seemed oddly curt. It was his Pilot, or the lack thereof. Redding had been on the other side of him when he entered the office, and hadn't seen that David didn't have a Pilot until the noise outside had made him turn his head the other way. Then he'd gone for water to get a look at that side of David's head and confirm it.

It was illegal to discriminate in a job interview because somebody didn't have a Pilot, but how could you prove that was happening? They'd just say there was a more qualified candidate. The proof was right there on the side of your head, saying you were not as fast as you said you were, couldn't possibly be, and even if you were, maybe something was wrong with you that you couldn't have one.

It didn't matter that his Pilot was still going strong, that his brain had adapted, that things were as chaotic as ever in his head. He had no light, so they didn't think that was the case. They didn't have to say it, or say anything; they simply wouldn't call back. Not even at his alma mater, for a stupid security job he was overqualified for. He was screwed, and he'd brought it on himself.

CHAPTER FIFTY-NINE

SOPHIE

It took Sophie longer than she cared to admit to realize her brother wasn't living in the house anymore. She wasn't unobservant, but it was easy to assume they were keeping different hours and missing each other; that had happened often enough. She didn't exactly go out of her way to see him, and vice versa, except when he'd come to her for help with his Pilot. There had been a moment where it had felt like that might bring them closer, but then he went and wrecked it again, leaving the light on, keeping the status his Pilot conferred. Making clear that he wasn't interested in real change, just changing his own situation.

So if she didn't encounter him at breakfast or dinner for a few weeks, that didn't seem overly strange. It wasn't like she was there for most meals, either, and they'd gone stretches before without running into each other. He'd been using the basement bathroom for several months, saying it wasn't fair to make her share when she'd had theirs to herself for so long, so there hadn't ever been any beard hairs in the sink for her to notice an absence.

No, the thing she noticed was the laundry. His basket had sat downstairs, unfolded, uncollected, for a month now, the same coffee-stained BNL shirt still on top. He'd have to have run out of work shirts or underwear or something, but nothing had moved, and everyone else had gone on doing laundry around it. She checked every day, not because she had to, but because she was curious. Where was he, and why was nobody talking about his absence?

She tried raising the subject at dinner one night, but the reactions were odd.

"He's away," Julie said. "He said he'll be back soon."

The way she said it reminded Sophie of when they'd evaded her questions during David's early deployments, except this time Val looked at Julie like she was also interested in more information, and found that to be oddly short on details.

"Is it a work thing?" Sophie asked.

"I think so. He doesn't need to tell us everything he's doing."

That answer won another look from Val. The whole thing was highly suspicious. Either they were lying to her, or Julie was lying to them both. Sophie wouldn't be particularly surprised by either of those scenarios, but she was curious what would bring about the latter.

Curious enough that when she overheard them through the air vent between their bathrooms later that evening, she kept quiet and listened.

"I still don't understand where he went that he wouldn't be able to talk with us," Val said.

Sophie heard water running, spit, rinse, Julie's voice. "He said we could call, but he might not respond."

"You know that's weird, right? We've always been able to talk, other than the secret deployments."

"I know. I don't understand, either . . ."

Sophie waited until they left their bathroom to brush her own teeth. They'd never realized about the vent, and as long as she didn't make any noise when they were in their bathroom, her secret was safe. And now she had new information.

She almost missed it. If she hadn't been on the message board at the exact moment the comment came through, then vanished, she would have gone on oblivious.

After listening to her mothers argue through the air vent, she'd thought about David. Thought about the fact that he'd turned his Pilot off but left the light, which nagged at her in a way she still couldn't understand, so she asked again if anyone else had experience with that.

Sixteen other people were active on the chat at that moment, according to the icon in the corner. The bottom of the screen said *Greggg is typing*, then *Greggg, Gabe, and GNM are typing* appeared. First, an annoying person who went by Greggg, who always had to be first to comment, but rarely had anything useful to say. He meant well, but as usual, his comment wasn't worth reading. Then Gabe, who said something typically Gabe-smart and insightful. Only *GNM is typing* still, which meant either it was a long comment or she'd gotten distracted and walked away without completing the comment.

GNM usually had interesting takes on whatever subject was at hand. The chats were full of younger people, so sometimes it was nice to hear from someone with more perspective. Sophie waited to see what she had to say.

I've been thinking since the last time you mentioned it, GNM wrote. *If you can deactivate a Pilot without turning off the light, what does the light mean?*

That was Sophie's question, too.

Another pause, then:

It means the brand is winning. Why would you turn it off if you had the option to leave it? I mean, I don't believe in the things, but if it's working fine there's no reason to go and have surgery again a third time, I would think. Why wouldn't you do it the second time while you were in there already, unless you wanted to keep the benefits but lose the noise?

Sophie froze.

The last sentence blinked from existence, then returned without the last four words.

But lose the noise. Was there anyone who talked about noise other than their family? And that specific scenario with David's descriptor? Grandma was not who she said she was.

Sophie had moderator access to everyone's profiles. She'd been thinking of her as "Grandma" for so long, as she'd insisted they call her, that she'd forgotten "GNM" actually stood for "Godnotmod." When she'd originally applied for the group, she'd said she was a religious woman who didn't believe in altering the body that God had given. Since then, she'd posted over two thousand times. As a precaution, the group didn't archive posts older than a week, so Sophie couldn't look back to see if she'd said anything similar before, or anything out of character.

The e-mail address didn't give anything away, either. They insisted on real names for application purposes. Sophie couldn't remember whether she'd been the one to approve the application, or someone else had. The name was generic: Deb Harry, from New York. Sophie remembered she'd been the one to approve the application, and that it had been irritating to verify her information, since there was an old singer by the same name. Had she given up trying? She couldn't remember.

If this was one of her family members, it was obvious who. Val wouldn't have bothered hiding, since Sophie had made it clear she was welcome in anti-Pilot spaces. David wouldn't have been able to post during some of the time GNM had been posting, since most sites were restricted from the bases where he'd been deployed.

Which left Julie. Julie, who always had two or three devices open in front of her. Julie, who never had trouble justifying anything she did. Julie, who would have convinced herself it was perfectly reasonable to spy on her daughter in the name of making sure she was safe, or something like that. Julie, who probably thought she was helping.

Julie, who *had* helped. Sophie couldn't deny that Grandma had made hundreds of useful comments. There were a dozen bores like Greggg who liked the sounds of their own voices, liked being first to comment, liked thinking they were useful without ever doing anything remotely useful. Grandma had been in a different category, with the people who weighed their words.

Except she was a spy. No, not a spy, because if Julie was here, she wasn't reporting to anyone. It still didn't mean she had any right to be here, any more than someone without a kid should go to a parent group and pretend they had one, or someone without a medical condition or a connection to it should fake it in a support group. This was a group for people who believed Pilots were bad for society, and no matter how many good ideas Grandma-or-Julie had, she didn't belong.

Sophie contemplated the flaws in their system. If Julie could convince them she was one of them, were there other people who'd snuck through? She thought about what had been said here over the years. They generally treated this as a public space, one where anyone could be listening, where anything could be copied to the public. Anything secret was discussed in person. People—including herself—sometimes said stuff that was maybe too private, might be considered oversharing, but she didn't think there was anything useful for a spy. Just public organizing. Public organizing with at least one traitor in their midst.

The more she considered it, the angrier she got. It was a lie, sure, but more than that, it was a violation. Her finger hovered over the "deactivate account" button, but then she thought better of it. Don't let on that she'd noticed. Hold on to this for the right moment. Gather all her med bottles, not just a few days' worth, and walk out the door, because her home, where she was supposed to trust people and be trusted, was suddenly a place she couldn't stand to be. Better to go back to the meeting space, where she was surrounded by friends and strangers who thought she was smart and capable, not a kid to keep tabs on.

CHAPTER SIXTY

VAL

Val had long since gotten used to one kid or the other not coming home for the night, though she never liked it. She knew sooner or later someone would move out for good, but while they still lived there, she preferred knowing where they were at night.

What she wasn't used to was neither of them coming home, and not knowing where either was, for multiple days in a row. Stranger still, when she asked Julie, when she'd pointed out that Sophie usually took only a few days' worth of her meds with her, but had taken the whole bottles this time, Julie shrugged and said their kids were adults with busy lives, and it wasn't their place to keep tabs. Of course it was, to some degree. She didn't need an exact location for them: she'd settle for a city, a state, a state of being.

In the fifth week of shrugs, the fifth week of no David, the fifth week of no answers to her phone calls, the fourth day of no Sophie, she left school after practice and drove to Sophie's headquarters. She remembered the time Sophie had allowed her to come to a meeting and how carefully the kid had chosen their route, a curated experience. She had found it sweet, the assumption that she didn't know her way around the city, that she wouldn't recognize she was being led on a circuitous route to avoid the worst neighborhoods in between their home and the meeting space. She'd let Sophie have that deception.

Now she drove the most direct route. The neighborhoods in between were poor and besieged with drugs and dealers. Pilots hadn't changed that. The dealers had them, their lookouts had them, the people on the streets had them to keep themselves aware. A system in dire need of change, but the wrong change had arrived. The wrong changes were everywhere.

Val's thought had been to sit through the meeting, but when she opened the door she suddenly felt intrusive. She had every right to go inside, but invading her daughter's space for information, not solidarity, felt wrong.

She closed the door without entering. Instead, she leaned against the Formstone wall and waited. It was a nice evening, neither cold nor hot. The basketball court on the corner was full of laughing teenage girls. Two Black men sat on the stoop of a house directly opposite, each with a can of beer in hand. One raised his and pointed to it, a question in his raised eyebrows. She was about to shake her head no, then reconsidered. If she was waiting out here until people started departing, she might as well have company.

As she crossed, the guy who'd offered stepped into the row house, then returned with a second can, ice-cold. She took it and clinked hers to his, then the other man's.

"They never cause trouble, but a lot of people go in and out of that building night and day," the one who'd brought her the beer said. He was older than the other, but there was a family resemblance. "What've they got going on?"

"It's the headquarters for the local anti-Pilot organization. They've got meetings and stuff."

"No kidding? You should go, Will." The older man, who had a Pilot, nudged the younger.

Will frowned. "I'm not anti-Pilot. I'm anti paying for one. They're only subsidized for teenagers."

Val regretted having said anything; she felt like she'd stumbled into the same private conversation that her own family had argued out so many times. If they kept going, she'd make her excuses and march into the building.

The father turned back to her. "What about you? I notice you didn't walk in there yourself."

"My daughter's in there. I didn't want to intrude."

"Isn't that what parents are for?" Will's tone was teasing.

"Sometimes, I guess." She took another sip. "She's mad about something, and I don't want to give her more reasons to be mad. I don't think I'm on the bad list yet."

"Fair, fair," said the older man. "What about you? Anti-Pilot, anti-paying, or something else?"

"Anti-Pilot." She surprised herself with her lack of hesitation. Had she ever said that out loud before? She usually said she was in solidarity with Sophie or she wanted to wait for more information, but the truth was she already had her own answer. It felt good to say it.

Will looked at her. "Do you work?"

"I'm a teacher."

"And they haven't found some excuse to phase you out yet? Are there a lot of teachers without in your school?"

"Three," she admitted. "They haven't said anything yet about phasing us out."

"Uh-huh."

They drank in silence. When Will went inside for another round, Val declined. She nursed the first beer knowing she'd be driving home soon enough, hopefully with Sophie, not that she would count that particular chick until safely back in the coop.

The door opened across the street, and a single person walked out. A minute later, three more.

"That's my cue," Val said. "Thanks for the beer and the company."

"A pleasure," the father said.

She waited for another few people to exit, then marched herself through the door.

Sophie and her friend Gabe both looked over when Val entered. Gabe raised a hand in greeting. Sophie looked surprised, but not entirely hostile. Whatever had her staying away from home wasn't Val's fault, then. It gave Val the courage to approach, which was hilarious on some deep level, that she was this nervous to approach her own daughter.

"Did she send you?"

Definitely mad about something. Luckily, Val could profess ignorance in complete honesty. "Julie? Why would she send me?"

Sophie sighed, the exact sigh she had always sighed. She would make that sound at eighty, Val was sure.

"Look, Soph, what if I buy you dinner somewhere and you tell me what's wrong? I'm honestly here to listen."

"We've got chili here."

"Okay, then. I skipped dinner to come talk to you, and I'm hungry. Can I eat some chili while you tell me what's wrong?"

Sophie considered, then nodded toward the kitchen. "Go help yourself. I'll be there in a minute."

That wasn't the worst response.

In the back, a mismatched stack of ceramic bowls and an astonishing array of spoons stood next to an enormous slow cooker. When Val lifted the slow cooker's lid, she was hit with the rich scent of beans, tomatoes, onions, garlic, chili, cumin, something else. She ladled a portion into a red bowl and grabbed a spoon with Snoopy etched into the handle.

It looked like the meals she herself was best at making: hearty, healthy, throw everything in a pot and leave it alone, but whatever that extra ingredient was, it tipped it past anything she usually made in the taste department.

She half expected her daughter to head out the door with the crowd and leave her sitting here alone, but Sophie joined her after a couple of minutes.

"Who does the cooking? This is delicious."

Sophie smiled. She had bags under her eyes. "It's pretty good, isn't it? It was my turn tonight."

Val tried to hide her surprise. "You? Really? But—"

"But it's good?"

"I was going to say *But you don't cook*. It's terrific. Since when do you cook?"

"Just because I don't, doesn't mean I can't." Sophie lifted her chin, and Val resisted the urge to throw her arms around the girl.

"Well, like I said, this is delicious. Maybe you can improve the quality of meals we eat at home. There's something special in here. It's more complex than the chili I make."

"Cocoa powder. And red wine vinegar. I don't think you put either of those in your chili, do you? But I'm not going back there. She's a liar."

Val would never in a million years have thought to add cocoa powder to chili. She filed the information away and focused on the more important thing. "What's she lying about?"

"She's been spying on me."

"Spying?" This was the kind of conversation where she'd keep repeating key words and hope they would eventually lead to a place of understanding.

"Online. For ages. She created a whole fake persona and she's been hiding in my groups spying on me and not telling me it was her."

Val thought of all the nights sitting on the couch with Julie watching TV and puttering online at the same time. Sophie was obviously mad about an intrusion, as she had a right to be, but Val also bristled at the idea there had been nights where she wondered where Sophie was, and Julie had known and not said. Nights where she'd said "Whatcha doing?" and Julie had responded "Work" or "Shopping."

Sophie stared at her, clearly waiting for her to defend Julie. If Sophie was right, Julie's actions weren't defensible.

"Oh," she said.

A weak response if ever there was one, and Sophie obviously agreed. "Of course you'll side with her. You probably knew."

"I didn't know. I'm processing. That's a horrible thing to do to you, but I also can't help thinking she must have had a reason."

"Her reason was spying. Infiltrating. She was pretending to be one of us the whole time. And what really sucked is, I liked her. She had good ideas. I thought she was on our side."

"Oh, honey. That's awful. I can't even guess what she was thinking. You're sure about all this?"

"Of course I'm sure."

"Did you confront her about it?"

"She'd just say she was trying to help. She wouldn't have the decency to be sorry."

Val imagined that was true. "She probably does think she's being helpful."

"Don't excuse her, please. It wasn't right to deceive me, no matter what the reason."

Val nodded.

Sophie continued. "I know you love her, and I love her, too, but she's lying about a bunch of stuff, and I'm sick of it. She's a hypocrite. She's hiding other stuff, too."

An icy heat flooded Val's veins. "Hiding what?"

"You should ask her." Sophie looked away. "I'm staying here until it all gets sorted out."

"What else is she hiding, Soph? I don't like being in the dark."

"Tell *her* that."

"I will, but can you give me a hint? Please."

"When was the last time you saw David? Or spoke with him?"

Val had known that was the other thing. It was so obvious. All the times she'd said it was strange he wasn't calling home, where had he been? Of course Julie knew something, or she would have been as concerned as Val. Val was naive, oblivious, had missed something everyone else knew. She felt like a fool.

"Okay," she said. "Stay here and do your thing, because you're obviously good at it, and you don't need anybody checking on you. I love you. I'll only ask you not to shut me out just because you're mad at her. I'll talk to her. I'll figure it out."

She was afraid Sophie would make her choose, and nearly

broke when the girl leaned over and gave her a hug. "Okay, but you really do need to talk to her. For all of us."

Sophie took the empty chili bowl from Val and walked it to the kitchen. When she emerged, she went over to where the remaining people had gathered, without looking back over. Val understood she'd been dismissed.

She drove home numb, angry, sad, angry, confused, working out one thing after another that she wanted to say to Julie, to ask Julie, to demand answers about. They were supposed to be a team.

All the lights were off at the house except in the kitchen. Julie was drinking coffee with her tablet on the table in front of her. "Hey! I was wondering where you were!"

Val didn't need a Pilot to notice that as Julie said hello, she'd blacked her tablet screen. "Whatcha doing?"

"Puttering. Waiting for you. It's late." There was a question in that, which Val recognized but refused to answer. She'd said she was going to be late and wouldn't have time to make dinner. Normally they didn't make each other explain more than that. They trusted each other, or they had.

She sat opposite her wife. Direct or indirect? She'd had enough of indirect. "Where's David?"

"I told you. He said he had to go out of town for BNL."

"Bullshit."

Julie flinched. Val continued. "I call bullshit, and I call you're hiding something, and I call you really, really need to tell me what's going on."

Julie closed her eyes and pinched the bridge of her nose, then nodded. "I . . . I don't know where he is."

"Why would you lie to me about that? What's the point?"

"I was embarrassed."

"About what?"

"I think it's my fault he left."

Julie looked miserable, which almost made Val feel bad about pressing her. Almost. "Your fault how?"

"My fault for pushing him."

"You're making me ask each next question, Jules, and I'm not sure I'm asking the right things. What if you tell me the whole thing and I listen?"

Julie nodded. "There's a lot, though."

How did words hurt so much? "There's a lot" meant she had been hiding things for a while. Lying, obscuring, gathering information or whatever this was and keeping it to herself instead of sharing it the way they'd promised to do. "Though" meant she knew it was a problem.

"He lost his job," Julie began. "I don't know when, and I don't know why, because he wouldn't tell me even after I figured it out. I figured out he had his Pilot shut off, too, even though the light was still on. I ended up driving behind him one day and he stopped at a stop sign and then he just sat there, for ages, and I waited for him to go, but he didn't. And a while later I asked him about it, and told him I knew he didn't have a job, and I knew about his Pilot, and then he left and didn't come back."

David had an even temper. He'd never been one to stomp or storm. Not like Sophie, whose blood ran drama. "That was all you said?"

"Well, no. I—I was mad he'd been lying to us. He said it was none of my business, and I said it was my business while he lived under our roof, and that's when he tossed his keys on the floor and left."

It still didn't seem like enough. Val waited, and Julie corrected herself. "No, I guess that's the version that makes me feel better, like I didn't do anything wrong, but he was trying to tell me something, and I don't think I handled it well. I think I told him it was shortsighted to get his Pilot turned off, and he said that thing about noise again, and I said he should see a shrink about it."

"Oh, Jules. You didn't." They were both fighting back tears.

"I know I shouldn't have. I know whatever that noise he talks about must be real, but he's coped with it before. I was trying to suggest that he figure out how to cope with it again. It came out badly. But he was talking about reenlisting, too, and saying all these things that didn't sound like him, and I tried to say he should get some help dealing with whatever he's going through."

Val had been forming another question about why he'd kept all that stuff from them, and how Julie had figured it out. She generally bent toward forgiveness. She believed Julie was telling the truth now, and that she'd hidden it out of embarrassment and hope that David would come home and she wouldn't have to admit to any of it. Julie had said what she thought she should say, and it had come out wrong.

Still, "reenlistment" jarred Val, as she knew it must have jarred her wife, and if Julie kept pushing his buttons after he said that, had pushed hard enough to drive him out the door and possibly back to that option, except this time they didn't know where he was, when every time before they'd at least known a general spot on the map to focus their worry?

Julie still hadn't said anything about Sophie's issue, either. Yet another lie, or lie of omission, which didn't feel like it even belonged in this conversation and yet was intertwined with it. Since when did they lie to each other like this? All these droplets, these individual forgivable omissions, added up to an unforgiveable ocean. Walking out hadn't been a very David move, but Val felt the reasonableness of it now.

She was tired, she'd had a beer and chili, the sun had long since set, but she went up to the bedroom, changed into running clothes, dug out her headlamp—the battery of which miraculously still held a charge—and headed out into the darkness; she didn't have any other idea what to do to escape the feeling they were failing, they had failed, the mistakes outnumbered the successes. There were no mistakes in running, not if you were careful where you placed your feet.

Her parents had been loud people. Not shouters, just loud, taking out frustrations in their footsteps, in thrown objects, so that any spare money went into replacing the things they had broken. She remembered sitting trapped in her room at twelve, at thirteen, while their possessions crashed into walls, and it was like the door wasn't even closed. Despite their warnings that it wasn't safe to leave at night, she started slipping through the window to run when they fought. She could outrun whatever was bad out there, and whatever it was couldn't be worse than being trapped listening to silence shatter.

She knew she was capable of that same loudness, had it in her bones, her genes, though she hated giving over to it; given the choice, she'd rather run. All of which was why she'd tried to instill in their kids the opposite of the trapped feeling, and why she was glad David had chosen to go, given what Julie had said, and furious that Julie had put him in that position. They'd spent so long trying to create a home as haven, only to ruin it in a few words.

When she returned, the kitchen light was still on. She didn't enter. Instead, she went to the basement and grabbed clean clothes from the load she'd done that morning. She showered in Sophie's shower and then went into Sophie's bedroom and closed the door, knowing the kid wasn't coming home anytime soon. She hadn't even gotten to Sophie's issue. She lay in Sophie's bed and listened until she heard Julie's trudging footsteps on the stairs, their bedroom door opening, Julie's sigh, their bedroom door closing. Two doors between them, two angry children, too many lies.

CHAPTER SIXTY-ONE

DAVID

QUIET
Quiet
quiet

quiet

quiet

quiet

Quiet was everything David had been looking for, the only thing he had ever wanted. For the first time in his adult life, he had a blanket of Quiet that he could pull over himself all day long, even if Karina gave him dirty looks. If he let the Quiet run out he heard them whispering about him.

Karina was on day shifts these days, but usually went to the gym after to push tires or swim in barbed wire or drag ropes or something. She returned sweaty and smiling tightly at him. "How's the job hunt going, David?"

"I had a couple of calls today." That was a stretch. His phone had rung twice from numbers he didn't recognize, and he'd answered. Neither was job related. One was his credit card calling to tell him his payment had bounced, the other a robocall suggesting if he gave them his bank info they'd consolidate his student loans. He didn't have student loans, so the joke was on them.

The only other calls had been from his parents. If it was Julie, he ignored it. If it was Val, he ignored it with a side of guilt. Sometimes he muted the phone entirely, but then he worried he'd miss a call from a nonexistent job offer or interview. So he left the phone on, but took enough Quiet to drown it out; if he didn't hear it, he didn't have to feel bad about not answering.

"How about apartments?"

He shook his head. "I called about one, but they said I needed to show my income was three times the rent, which it isn't."

"Argh. What about a room in someone's house?"

"They're a bit thin on the ground. I don't know if it's the wrong time of year or I scare them off somehow or they're all doing short-term rentals for more money . . ."

She nodded and sighed. Only when she'd walked past into the bedroom had he realized it would have been polite to ask how her day had been. Better yet, if he'd gotten himself off the couch to make dinner an hour ago, so they'd all have a chance to eat together before Milo headed out.

Milo was in the bedroom getting ready for work. Through the thin wall, David heard Karina ask Milo how long David would be on their couch. "I know he's your best friend, but this place is too small for three people. I can't even tell if he's looking."

"Give him time, baby," Milo said. "He's trying. I was here all day today. I'd know if he wasn't putting in the effort."

Karina's shower started, drowning out the rest of their conversation, which David shouldn't be listening to in any case. Milo emerged from the bedroom in his black-polo-and-jeans bouncer-wear. "Do you want to come drink while I work?"

David shook his head. He knew the subtext was *Would you get off our couch so Karina can have some time to herself in the apartment she pays for?* but he didn't have spare money for a drink, and really he was opting out of it all: drinking, the noisy bar, making small talk, or else being one of the weird unsocial guys who clearly didn't have anything better to do. Better to retreat back into the glorious Fortress of Solitude in the semiprivacy of the couch.

"Suit yourself."

Milo left. The shower stopped, and five minutes later, Karina walked into the living room in sweatpants and a T-shirt. She looked disappointed but not surprised he hadn't gone with Milo. Not that he was looking at his best friend's girl, but she'd obviously put a bra back on after a day at work, a workout, and a shower; he was the asshole here for not taking the obvious hint that he was supposed to go with Milo, and for being so predictable that she had already known he wouldn't go. She wanted to watch TV, or play a game, or take off her bra and eat dinner. There was only so far her tolerance for him would stretch.

"I was just finishing something," he said. "Then I'm going out."

Her relief was evident, and he felt like an ass all over again, but at least he felt like an ass who had made the right decision for once.

He hadn't showered in at least three days. He couldn't go to Milo's bar because he had no car and no money for a ride. It didn't matter. He needed to give Karina some space. He grabbed his backpack and phone and headed out to no place in particular.

He paused outside the door. The air was cooler than he expected, and he tried to remember when he'd left the apartment last. He had to find a new situation; he didn't want to lose Milo over this. Quiet would help; he shook a pill from the container and swallowed it.

A woman pulled into the parking lot, but didn't turn off her car. She was talking to herself, maybe talking to someone on speakerphone, but her eyes were on him. He knew what he looked like: a large guy, unshaven, wrinkled clothes. She clearly didn't want to walk to her apartment with him standing there. He walked toward the next building and then down through the parking lot, making it clear he wouldn't get near her car or watch where she went.

He should've walked toward the street, though, since he had no car here. Now he was trapped in the parking lot until he was sure she was inside, all because he didn't want to make a stranger nervous. He walked to the far end and sat on the curb, trying to decide what to do next. He felt eyes on his back, and turned to see the black cat from the night of the party. It met his gaze.

"Here, kitty." He tried to sound warm, but the cat kept its distance. Smart cat. Something caught its attention in the grass, and it slunk away.

The hunting cat reminded him he wasn't sure when he'd last re-upped his Quiet. It was obviously out of his system: he'd heard the whole discussion in the bedroom, and he'd noticed the woman looking at him from her car, and he'd felt the cat watching him.

He shook a pill from the mint tin in his pocket and swallowed it dry. Fifteen minutes to start feeling it, half an hour to full effect. He remembered he'd taken one outside the apartment a few minutes before, and it just hadn't kicked in yet. The action had been automatic. He was a big guy; he'd never taken two at once, but two couldn't hurt.

A police siren wailed in the distance. He glanced toward the apartments and saw the woman from the car standing on a third-floor balcony, a phone to her ear, watching him.

Time to go. He still hadn't done any research on the pills in his pocket, still didn't know what they were, or what the penalties were for holding them, if any. He'd thought ignorance would protect him, give him an excuse to keep taking them as long as he didn't know what they were doing to him, allow him plausible deniability. It occurred to him now that wasn't how the world worked.

He should ditch them, in case the police siren was for him, in case the pills were illegal, but he couldn't afford to buy more. He walked into the woods behind the complex, trying to become as background as the black cat.

The shallow woods weren't much of a hiding place. They backed onto a high chain-link fence keeping people or deer from wandering onto the light-rail tracks. The complex stood halfway between two stations a few miles apart, which made the light rail useless if you didn't have a car or at least a bike. He didn't have either. The sirens had stopped, but blue and red flashing lights bounced off the fence and voices carried across the parking lot.

If the pills were legal, or legally his, he wouldn't be carrying them in a mint tin. He hated the idea of tossing them, but he knew he should. Well, he could keep one if he swallowed it now. With a sigh, he emptied the container into his hand and threw the rest over the fence and onto the track. They were sugarcoated and didn't leave a trace on his hands, but he tossed the tin over too, and then rubbed dirt on his hands.

A flashlight arced across his face.

"Hey, buddy, can you come out? We want to chat for a second."

He debated making a run for it, but that was stupid. He had nothing to hide. He raised his hands to show they were empty.

"Step toward me," the voice said. Her flashlight was too bright, her voice too loud.

When he cleared the trees, he stopped, his hands still raised.

"Do you have ID on you?"

"Yes," David said. "In my pocket. Do you mind if I reach for it, or do you want to?"

"You can do it. Slowly."

He pulled his wallet from his pocket and tossed it at the cop's feet. Her partner picked it up and leafed through. "David Geller-Bradley. That sounds familiar."

David shrugged. "It's a common name."

"Nah . . . wait . . ." He held his flashlight in David's face. "You look awful, but you're the guy from the Pilot ads, aren't you?"

"He can't be. He doesn't have a Pilot."

If ever there was a time to trade on celebrity, this was it. "Yeah, that's me. I had my Pilot deactivated."

"No way. Why would you want to do that?" The flashlight lowered, as did the gun.

"I had a problem with it."

"Is that why you look so rough? We got called out for a sketchy homeless dude lurking in the bushes."

"I'm . . . on vacation. Visiting some friends who live here. You can check with them." He gave the apartment number, hoping Karina would vouch for him and not be pissed off.

"But, uh, why were you back there?"

"I think I scared a woman in the parking lot accidentally, and I wanted to show I wasn't following her, so I walked away."

"Into the woods instead of toward the street?"

David's answer wasn't a total lie. "It was silly. I wasn't thinking. I'd never been back here, so I thought maybe I could cross the tracks and come out by the shopping center. Didn't realize there was a fence."

The cops both looked more relaxed. The woman paused. "Do you mind if I take a picture with you? My girlfriend thinks you're cute."

He didn't object to using his celebrity in this context. If they were taking pictures with him they weren't arresting him. They hadn't even asked him to empty his pockets, so he hadn't had to toss his pills. Except that was stupid; they could just as easily have had him on the ground. They might not have recognized his famous face under his depression beard. Instead, they let him go with a warning to try to look a little less sketchy and go somewhere else.

Now he definitely couldn't go back upstairs. The apartment windows looked out this way, so Karina had probably seen the whole thing. Embarrassing enough without the fact that he'd just thrown away all his pills. He'd taken one, so he'd be good for the next few hours, but he had nothing to stop the noise from creeping in again.

He had never bought Quiet from anyone other than Karina's sister and his buddy in the park, neither of whom he could ask right now. Where to go, then? There was a liquor store down the road a mile or so that had the right look, with a scattering of Piloted white teenagers hanging around in the alley outside. He watched them from afar until he noticed them watching him back, sizing him up. One whispered to another and they scattered. They weren't going to sell to him; they probably thought he was a cop.

He walked over. Let them see him up close; let them smell him, for that matter. They could decide for themselves if he was undercover. He browsed the store shelves until two lookout kids repositioned themselves, then he bought a fifth of cheap whiskey from a cashier behind bulletproof glass.

"Hey," he said as he walked out, before the kids could leave again. "Do you know where I can get some Quiet?"

The first looked at him blankly, and he realized that was his own name for it. "Fortress of Solitude, I mean. I call it Quiet 'cause that's how it feels. It has a lowercase *q* on it. Teal pill. Bluish."

The second guy shook his head. "I've seen those, but that isn't a *q*. It's a *b*. You were reading it upside down."

"What's *b* for?" his friend asked. "Blue?"

The second guy shrugged. "Beats me. Maybe. I don't have 'em either way. Sorry."

At least he'd tried. David opened the whiskey and took a swig. Offered it to the two guys, who declined, exchanging pity glances. He felt a little sorry for himself, too. As he crossed the street, he called Phil from the park, one last effort to avoid the thing he knew he would do if he had to.

"Already?" Phil asked. "I mean, not that it's my business, but I saw you yesterday."

"Went to a party," David said.

"Gotcha. Like I said, not my business. But I'm afraid to say, I can't help you tonight. Empty house."

David was about to disconnect, again picturing blue pills in gravel, when his friend added, "Hmm. I do know one guy who can help you."

He rattled off an address on the other side of town. David didn't have enough cash left to get there and buy from a stranger, who would know that for Phil to have sent him, he must be desperate. Not to mention, even with a referral, he was obviously giving off bad vibes tonight. There was no guarantee they'd trust him, and he'd have gone all the way over there for nothing.

"Thanks, anyway," David said. "But hey, one other question. What's the *b* on the pill stand for?"

"Balkenhol. You know, BNL, like the Pilots."

David hung up, his mind reeling. Why was Balkenhol making pills to dampen their own Pilots? Was that even their purpose? Were they on the market, available if you told the right doctor you had a noisy head? He couldn't stand the thought that the same people who ruined his head and refused to fix it might also have manufactured the only bandage he'd found for the wound they'd created. He was still theirs, just in a different way now. He craved the Quiet, or whatever it was.

His next thought was a terrible one, but in the incipient Quiet, it was the only thing in his head, and he fixated on it. How pathetic was he, to even imagine doing that? In that thought, he recognized the seeds of addiction, of a need that obliterated common sense. In the same moment, he didn't care, because he didn't care how he achieved Quiet, and if this was the way, so be it.

He ducked into the woods a couple of complexes away from Karina and Milo's, so he wouldn't scare their neighbors again. The fence was topped with barbed wire, not razor wire, and it was easy enough to wrap his jacket around it and throw himself over. It took more effort than it should have; he'd fallen out of shape in recent weeks. He landed on his feet, but there was a thin tear in his jeans down the length of his shin, and an even thinner tear in his leg, starting where the barb must have gone in above his ankle, and trailing away to just below his knee. It didn't hurt, at least.

He walked along the fence line, trailing one hand along it, enjoying the sensation. Wrapped in Quiet, he could focus on his fingers and the fence, the metal lattice and the spaces between it, a luxury to be able to experience that without also noticing the footing, the needles, the broken glass, the damp air, the far-off clanging, his position in space. Or noticing, but at a distance, muted, unimportant.

A train passed, moving slower than he would expect this far between stations, and then another in the opposite direction, gathering speed. He was glad again for the Quiet buffering the rattle and the violent displacement of air. He knew it was there, knew how overwhelming it would be without his fortifications. This was a necessary mission. A few minutes later he came to a place where the double track narrowed to single, which explained the slow trains.

When he reached what he thought was the right area, he refocused. He was looking for twelve pills in a gravel sea. Teal, but teal would look gray in this light, and he didn't want to turn on his phone's flashlight in case somebody in the apartments saw it. He looked for smooth and rounded, for shine. He was grateful to be too Quiet for embarrassment. This was necessary.

He found his mint tin before any of the pills, and considered that a victory. How far had he thrown the pills? He remembered them arcing through the air, scattering like stars.

After however many minutes, he found a single pill in a grassy patch beside the tracks. He wiped it off, peered at it. Was it his? He didn't imagine anyone else was wandering around tossing pills. It looked white, but the grass was damp and the color might have bled away. It tasted right, like a slight hint of sugar, like round. It held the right shape on his tongue. He realized after he'd taken it that he'd never taken two in succession before, let alone three, and never taken one while still feeling one, let alone two.

He was having trouble holding thoughts in his head. It was glorious, the Quiet settling heavier and heavier, a welcome weighted blanket. He settled onto his knees in the gravel, picking through handfuls, sifting through then letting them go, watching the stones fall back to earth. He found another pill and put it in the container in his pocket. Found another pill and put it on his tongue. Found another pill and didn't remember what he was supposed to do with it, so he put it in his pocket beside his phone. Why was he doing this in the dark? He turned on his phone's flashlight and found three more pills between the tracks.

There was a noise, far away. A noise from outside his blanket, quiet then loud and loud and louder, and a light, bright and bright and brighter. He remembered he was on a train track, and he should get off it, though surely he would hear a train before it came close. He stepped off the track, to be safe, and in perfect time, too, because a train whipped past inches from him, displacing air, displacing David. It was a great sensation, and in the Quiet it was an all-encompassing everything.

The train passed, and he stepped back onto the track and laughed at how good it had felt, and how much better the Quiet was in its wake. In the back of his mind, he fought to hold on to the thought that the last time a train had passed in one direction, another had passed in the opposite direction a moment later. He was on the track, and that was okay, because this train had just passed, except there was only one track, it was single track here, and as he had that thought, something shifted on the track, pinning his left foot.

He had been pinned once before, in a different place, in a different way, a figurative pinning, they had used the words "pinned down" on the radio, *we're pinned down, we're safe in here for now*. He had spotted the first rooftop sniper, and maybe he would have had time to say something except at the same time as he spotted the barrel, he spotted a tiny blue light, a Pilot light, and even with all his raging attentions he paused, because he had never seen a Pilot on the other end of a gun.

In that same moment, McKay fell, a bullet through his neck, which meant David hadn't been fast enough, he had been distracted, he had failed McKay, and all he could do was put that aside, keep it together, work with the others so they all stayed alive, and David saw the open shop door, and he was shouting, they were all shouting, but he was able to make himself heard, and they spent the next six hours in that cramped, dark haven, waiting for backup, waiting for the bullets to come through the window, watching McKay die even while they tried to save him, McKay's blood drying on his hands, and BNL were the only ones who made Pilots, why were they selling to the other side, a thought for later, and he had failed McKay but not the others, not yet, and for all his attentions this never left his mind, and he worked constantly to keep it tamped down, pinned down, pinned down.

He had all the focus he needed, all the Quiet, too much Quiet to hang on to any thought, the focus so tight he couldn't even see what he was looking at, which was his foot, pinned by the mechanism that siphoned the two tracks to one or the one track to two, he wasn't sure, and it didn't matter and he knew he should move, and told his legs to step, to step, and was it his foot or his shoe that was caught, maybe he had time to get the shoe off, to leave the shoe behind, but untying his shoe was everything, was too much, his focus had narrowed to his shoelace and his phone's flashlight on his shoelace and it was a Gordian knot, a Gaelic complication, a labyrinthian impossibility, and in the Quiet there was a clanging, and in the Quiet he knew this shoe was not coming off, and he stepped back with his other foot, and in the Quiet the train spun him with noise and light, spun him tight in his blanket, and he fell.

CHAPTER SIXTY-TWO

JULIE

Julie had managed to alienate her entire family. Her daughter slept at her weird activist commune headquarters, furious with her. Her son was who knew where, furious with her. Val was camping in their daughter's bedroom, leaving before Julie woke, timing her evenings to avoid Julie, furious with her. Julie tried to accommodate the anger, tried not to enter a room where Val might be; she'd rather not see her wife than watch her stand and walk away.

She had no idea how everything had gone so wrong. Every day was an exercise in wrongness, wrong piled on top of wrong. There had to be something she could say or do to bring them back. Mere apology wasn't doing it; she had tried that. Nobody answered her calls.

The anger couldn't last forever; she didn't think so, anyway. Family; family lasted forever. Good family, anyhow. A part of her thought this was punishment for the way she'd shut her own parents out. That was different; that was survival. That was the family she'd been born into, and this was the family they'd created out of nothing. Created family, bound by love and promises and blood and tears and laughter. Why had it seemed so much stronger? Family was the shelter and the storm, both at once, an impossible thing that didn't seem impossible. You assume your house is sturdy until the roof rips off and leaves you in the rain.

So she carried on. She went to work, she paid the bills, she waited for someone to come through the door and sit with her and tell her she hadn't ruined them. She had the sinking feeling that she was the storm.

Her cooking had, for the first time in her life, begun to improve. Cooking turned out to be yet another thing that wanted attention and practice. She'd always thought of it as a chore like mowing the lawn or cleaning the grout, a thing you did to have it done. In this time when none of her normal coping mechanisms proved adequate, she found comfort in the subskills of food preparation. She watched videos explaining proper knife technique, explaining the chemistry and alchemy of baking and the smoke points of various oils.

Tonight she'd attempted a galette, which was a thing like a savory pie but slightly different, free-form on a cookie tray instead of in a pie dish, which was a thing she knew they had somewhere but had not been able to find. It had thinly sliced yams, yams she'd sliced relatively evenly and only undercooked slightly, and goat cheese, which she'd bought specially, and caramelized onions, which she'd almost had enough patience for. The result was lumpy and misshapen but she'd cooked it right, and it tasted as close to delicious as she'd ever gotten. She wanted desperately for someone to arrive home and try it, to recognize in its flavors that she had always meant well and loved them all unconditionally.

She carved a large piece and left the rest on a trivet by the stove for a family that wouldn't come for it. Sat on the couch—the table was for family, and hers was achingly absent—and turned the television to a rerun of a show she and Val liked to watch. She couldn't bear to watch a new episode; it seemed like a violation of rules that she was the only one left keeping. Except she'd been the one to violate other, bigger rules. This was all her fault, despite her good intentions.

The door to Sophie's room opened, and Julie felt sudden hope that the scents of onions and butter and dough had drawn Val. She wanted to say *There's dinner*, but any invitation could be rebuffed, and that would feel infinitely worse than being ignored.

Val came downstairs, to the actual room Julie was in, and Julie turned, but the expression on Val's face was wrong. "David's in the emergency room. Something about a train."

Julie was on her feet in an instant, her plate on the floor.

They didn't talk. Julie's car was closest, but she passed her keys, because she had too many questions, like which hospital, and what about a train, what did that even mean. Easier to let Val drive than ask those questions and potentially get answers to them.

Val wasn't a speeder, but now she pushed the lights, weaving around cars and gunning through yellows, heading west. Julie wanted to put a hand on her arm, to say *We'll get there, it's okay, slow down*, but she didn't know that any of those things were true without details she was afraid to ask for, or if her touch would be welcome, so she kept her hands in her lap, and tore at her cuticles, and watched the road from the unfamiliar passenger seat of her own car.

Val was in a mode of high competence. Sign in here. Take this badge. Yes, we're both his mothers. It was a weeknight and chilly after weeks of abnormal warmth, and the emergency room was relatively empty. A couple of sniffling children, a person holding an ice pack to their hand. It was easier to focus on them than on the phrase "He's still in surgery."

The television played a home improvement show where people got absurdly excited about other people removing all the personality from their homes, and Julie watched while she ran web searches for "hit by a train" and learned that it mattered what kind of train, how fast it was going, how exactly the person had been hit.

Her Pilot, always reliable, let her watch both screens while also watching the doors for movement, and siphoning off the silent scream she was trying her best not to let out. They sat in uncomfortable plastic seats, and at one point Val's knee touched Julie's and Julie held her breath, waiting for it to be drawn away again, but it stayed, and she narrowed all her focus to that contact, tuning out the television, the other people, the doors, the search results, the scream.

"We should call Sophie," Julie said, then corrected herself. "You should call Sophie. She'll answer your call."

Val shifted in her seat, breaking the knee connection. "No. She doesn't like half states."

"Half states?"

"Do you remember? She didn't want to know when David was coming home until he came home. She didn't want to know the side effects of her medications unless we noticed them. We'll call her as soon as he's out of surgery."

Julie liked the phrase "out of surgery" better than "still in surgery," so that made sense, as long as the one followed the other. "What if he doesn't—"

"Don't say it. Nobody has said that."

"They said 'hit by a train.'"

"But he's alive. He's tough."

Julie risked reaching out and taking Val's hand in hers, and Val squeezed back once, then returned Julie's hand to her lap. The squeeze lifted Julie's heart; maybe everything would be okay. A nurse called them in after what was too long, what was only made better by a moment of a hand in another hand, something Julie had always taken for granted and never would again.

CHAPTER SIXTY-THREE

SOPHIE

It was Sophie's own fault that David had been in the hospital for a full day before she got the news. Val had left two voice messages an hour apart while Sophie was busy, and who listened to voice messages? If the phone had rung three times in a row, she would have answered, maybe. If Val had texted, she'd have read it, but no texts, which was why Sophie didn't even find out from Val. She found out because Gabe held his phone out to her halfway through a meeting and said, "Um, Soph, is this your brother?"

The article was brief, a headline with little more to go on:

LOCAL MAN HIT BY TRAIN

David Geller-Bradley, 25, was struck by a light-rail train when his foot became trapped in the track-switching mechanism. He was taken to Pimlico General, where he is listed in stable condition.

The news story didn't answer any number of questions she had, starting with why he was on a train track, and why he didn't notice a train coming. The important part was "stable condition." She pulled her muted phone from her pocket and discovered two missed calls and two voice mails. They hadn't hidden it from her; they just couldn't reach her.

The whole circle was watching her, and it felt a bit like when she came out of a seizure to find everyone staring.

"I have to go," she said.

Gabe smoothly took over the group, asking a question she forgot as soon as she heard it, clearly meant to redirect everyone. He was a good friend.

She went to the office to get her wallet and make sure she had enough money to get out to the hospital on the opposite side of the city. Not that it was about inconvenience to her. If that was the closest hospital and they had saved him, then it was the best hospital ever. Her stupid brother, *Local Man Hit by Train*.

"Is everything okay?" Dominic stood in the doorway.

"Yeah. No. Uh, my brother is at Pimlico General. I've got to get over there."

"Do you want a ride?"

Relief washed over her. "Please, if you don't mind. I feel like you're always rescuing me."

"My pleasure. Anything for the cause. Or for the leader of the cause."

"I'm not the leader," she said.

"Co-leader, then. You've got to know this group is so good because of your energy. You and Gabe both."

"Sure, I guess."

She followed Dominic out to the street and into a driving, cold rain. For a minute she thought the rain must have somehow confused David, but no, he had been hit the night before, not tonight. Clear skies. *Hit by a train*.

They didn't speak as Dominic programmed the hospital into his GPS and pulled a U-turn in the first intersection. Once he was pointed in the right direction, he broke the silence. "Do you want to talk about it?"

"I don't know anything! Only what was in an article stub Gabe showed me, and a voice mail from my mom. It said my brother was hit by a train, which makes no sense. I mean, sure, he got his Pilot turned off, but it was still working. Even if he was walking on a train track for some stupid reason, he should have known there was a train coming. He should've been aware. I don't get it."

"A train? Holy shit. He's okay?"

"The article said 'stable.' That means okay, right?"

"I think, yeah. Yikes."

"Yikes," echoed Sophie. "Anyway, thanks for taking me. I really appreciate it. I don't often get frustrated that I'm not allowed to drive, but this is one of those times."

Dominic dropped her at the visitor entrance. She hadn't been to this particular hospital, but she was hospital level: expert. She'd never been on this side of things, was all. Never rolled up on an information desk on her own to ask where David Geller-Bradley was, yes, she was immediate family. Never slapped a visitor sticker on her chest instead of an ID bracelet around her wrist.

She rode the elevator to the fourth floor, medical surgical, and followed the room numbers. His was a double room, but the first bed was empty. David was in the second bed, David with an IV and several monitors, but no bandages on his head, David awake and smiling a not-quite-David smile at her.

Val rose from the chair beside the bed and flung her arms around Sophie. "I didn't know if you got my voice mails."

"I just got them. I'm sorry. Have you ever considered text messages? They've been all the rage for my entire life."

David snorted, and Sophie turned on him. "Oh, sure, laugh, train boy. What happened?"

"I'm still trying to work that out," he said. "Everything is fuzzy."

"But you're okay? You look surprisingly okay."

David nodded, then gestured at himself. She followed his hand down the bed. A sheet was draped over his legs, but something was wrong with the shapes.

"Oh," Sophie said, trying to sort it out.

"The foot they had to amputate is the left, but it looks like it's the other way around because the stump is all bandaged. Ma says they did a bunch of scans and brought in a vascular surgeon but they couldn't save it."

"Oh," she said again. He was remarkably blasé for a guy talking about his own emergency foot amputation. "Does it hurt?"

"Probably," he said. "But whatever they've got me on is pretty amazing. It even cuts the noise."

He smiled again, and she realized why his smile looked funny. He didn't look like himself without noise behind his expression. Something about it made her feel like crying, but she didn't want to cry in front of him if he was taking it so well. She swallowed it and smiled back.

Julie's voice arrived in the room before she did. "I brought ice cr—" Her voice trailed off when she saw Sophie. She hesitated in the doorway, her hands full of ice cream bars. "I can leave if you want."

Sophie shook her head. "I'm still mad at you, but not the kind of mad where you have to leave."

"That's what I said, too." David smiled his un-David smile again. "Truce and ice cream."

Julie looked at her hands. "I only have three! I can go get another."

"Sophie can have mine. I don't need one." Val's expression was easy for Sophie to read; she didn't care if she never had ice cream again if her whole family was in one room and talking to one another. It was strange to have everyone talking and laughing, and nobody mentioning the train and the foot and whatever David would have to deal with in the coming months. The weirdest reason for a reunion, or maybe bad reasons were sometimes necessary for family to come together.

Sophie had spent a lot of time proving to her parents that she was an adult, not the kid in the back seat, but now that nobody was making her feel small, there was something comforting about riding in back with her moms in the front. Heading to the house that felt like home, on a night when home was a comfort, too, not an idea she had to push back against. God, she was tired of pushing.

She didn't mean to cry. It started as quiet tears, which she thought she was hiding, until she heard a sniffle from the passenger seat, and then Julie was bawling, and they were all crying, and the crying turned into laughter, because it was all so ridiculous.

"Only David could get hit by a train and only lose a foot," Sophie said. "How does anyone walk through the world with that much luck?"

"Ssh," said Julie. "It's bad luck to talk about luck."

That set them all cry-giggling again, although Sophie was pretty sure Julie was serious.

CHAPTER SIXTY-FOUR

VAL

David had kicked everyone out toward the end of visiting hours. Sophie rode home with them, and didn't ask why Val ducked into her room ahead of her, which Val was grateful for. When Val carried her pajamas and clothes into their own bedroom, Julie gave her a look of such joy she forgot for a moment what had made her so angry she'd moved into their daughter's room.

It meant she had to settle things in her mind quickly, so she didn't confuse Julie. Was she back because she was ready to forgive, or because she missed being comforted by her wife? Her person. She absolutely missed that.

She settled for echoing their children. "I'm still upset, and I think I will be until I'm sure you understand what you did that I found so hurtful, but I miss you, and I need to be with you tonight. Is that okay?"

"You're looking for my permission to come back to our bed? You know you're welcome."

"I just want to make sure you know it isn't done just because I'm here."

Julie sighed. "I understand."

When they got into bed, each of them settled on the far edge, their backs to each other, not touching. After a few minutes, Julie shifted so the bottoms of her feet grazed the back of Val's calves, and her breath got quiet like she was afraid that if she moved, Val might withdraw permission for the contact. She didn't; it was solid, reassuring contact, and she'd happily admit she'd missed it but she didn't want to admit it first.

Val was almost asleep when Julie whispered, "Is it my fault?"

"Is what your fault?"

"All of it. David. His foot."

There were a few possible answers, and Val chose carefully. "Some parts, maybe, but not the foot or the train. He made choices. Maybe we could have helped him deal better with whatever he's dealing with if he'd been here, but I don't think we know that for sure."

"So you don't blame me?"

"Not for this."

She woke before Julie as she always did, but stayed in bed. No run today. Not because she heard rain on the window behind the drapes, but because she'd missed the simple pleasure of lying beside someone she loved and watching her sleep. She had to remind herself she was still angry, but then she wondered why she needed to hold on to that. Julie knew what she needed to fix; maybe that knowing meant Val could let go and see what happened next. She closed her eyes again and put an arm around Julie, and Julie nestled into her.

When she woke again, Julie was gone. It took Val a minute to remember what day of the week it was—Saturday, no alarm—and then everything came back. She heard raised voices from downstairs, and sighed, resigning herself to another round of family drama. They hadn't even been able to maintain a day's truce.

Except as she rounded the corner to the kitchen, she realized they weren't shouting at each other. It was a shared anger.

"What's going on?" Val asked, yawning.

Julie shoved her tablet into Val's hands. "This."

Val rubbed sleep from her eyes and focused. It was a news aggregation site. The clickbait headline was *You'll Never Guess Which Celebrity Jumped in Front of a Train This Week.* She frowned, fully awake. "Do they think he did it on purpose?"

"Some imply that. Also, their definition of 'celebrity' is debatable," said Sophie.

"There are more." Julie took the tablet back and paged through her open tabs. "*BNL Expresses Sympathy for Troubled Ex-Spokesperson. Ex-BNL Spokesperson Hit by Train Shines Light on the Dangers of Pilot Deactivation.*"

Val looked from Sophie to Julie. "I don't understand."

"Yesterday there was a piece on a local news site saying *Local Man Hit by Train,*" Sophie said. "Some gossip outlet might have recognized his name, but it seems unlikely, since most people know him as 'hey, you're the guy from that ad.' It seems really weird they'd make that connection."

"Not to mention they know an awful lot. How did they know he wasn't working there anymore?"

Val considered. "It probably only took one person connecting his name. If they called BNL for a statement thinking he still worked there, BNL would have said he didn't. Maybe it all rolled from there, with others running with the story."

"Okay, fine, but how did they know he didn't have a Pilot anymore? He still had it when he left BNL," said Julie.

"No, he didn't," said Sophie. "He'd had it turned off already, but the light was still on."

Julie frowned. "You knew he'd had it turned off?"

"I went with him to do it. He was chicken and left the light. I'm not sure exactly when he lost his job, but I'm one hundred percent certain it was before he had the light turned off. He left it on to keep that stupid job."

Val slumped into a chair, fighting the urge to walk out. "When did I get this oblivious, and when did we all start hiding things from each other? Pilots on and lights on and Pilots off and lights off and lost jobs and ten million secrets and I am so sick of all of it. You don't need to tell me everything, but at some point somebody needs to tell me something."

"I'm sorry." Sophie put a hand on her shoulder. "I wasn't hiding things on purpose. It wasn't mine to tell."

"I hid things on purpose that I definitely should have told you. It wasn't right. I'm sorry, too." Julie sounded sincere, and the apology was for the right thing. Driving David out was bad, but hiding it had been the part that had hurt Val more. If Julie recognized that, they had some hope.

Val reached for Julie's hand and squeezed it. "Apology accepted."

"Oh, thank God," Julie said, and then they were kissing, and Val put everything else out of her mind.

"This is all very touching, Moms, and kinda gross, but let's get back to the part where your son's in the news. And, um, what's the visitor policy at that hospital? If these rags know his name and what hospital he's at, what's to stop them from going to his room to get an interview while he's loopy?"

Julie looked at her daughter with an expression of both horror and respect. "Oh no. You're right."

"There was a local news van reporting outside the hospital when we got there the other night, but they didn't stop us," said Val. "I didn't even consider they were probably reporting on David. I was so worried I barely registered them."

"I noticed, too, but I figured it was because of the hit-by-a-train part."

"It probably was." Sophie waved her phone. "I'm sure it started that way. They monitor police frequencies, so maybe they started out reporting someone was hit by a train, and then they followed the ambulance and reported from the hospital, and then got his name somehow, but I don't think his name was as known as his face, so I don't know how they got from there to the other stuff about him being a BNL spokesperson and especially not the stuff about him not having a Pilot any—"

Her mouth stayed open but she didn't finish her sentence. She jumped to her feet, calling back over her shoulder, "I have to go. You should go make sure David isn't telling his life story to some reporter while they have him on painkillers."

Sophie disappeared from the room, leaving her mothers staring at each other. Val couldn't remember getting orders from Sophie before. It reminded her of the Sophie she'd seen at the FreerMind meetings: confident, in control, correct in her assessment of the situation. She'd realized something midsentence, but whatever it was, she wasn't hiding it, just acting on it. Val and Julie wordlessly stood to get dressed and do exactly as their daughter said.

CHAPTER SIXTY-FIVE

DAVID

The nurse who changed his dressings told David there were people downstairs waiting to talk with him. Did he want visitors?

"You mean my family?"

"No. That's why I'm asking."

"My friend Milo?" Milo hadn't visited yet, but he'd called. David assumed it'd be a while before he came; he was solid in emergencies, but squeamish in other medical situations.

"No. Sorry—I think they're all reporters."

The nurse reached the bottom layers of bandage and David started counting dots on the ceiling tiles. He had never been squeamish himself, had watched his sister's procedures with avid interest, but he wasn't ready to look yet. "All?"

"There are a bunch of them. I didn't see how many."

"Why?"

"Maybe because Man Versus Train is an exciting story? I don't know. It's been a busy shift. I haven't actually talked to them."

"Ah. Um, I don't think I want to talk to them, either."

"Cool. I'll let the desk know. This wound is looking good, by the way."

"Thank you. Wait, 'thank you' is a weird thing to say. I'm glad it looks good?"

"I took 'thank you' to mean 'thank you for doing such a nice job keeping infection out.'"

"That, too." David laughed. Whatever painkiller they had him on made him giddier than Quiet. It did the same job, so he wasn't complaining. Without either, this place would drive him out of his mind: the machines monitoring him, each with its own cadence; someone else's machines, on the other side of the wall; a smell he couldn't identify, and another smell; the television; the ticking clock behind the television; the nurses' station outside his door, with its laughter and alarms and telephone; the forced air through the vent; the running toilet.

As it was, he catalogued each of those things separately, with great focus, to avoid paying attention to whatever the nurse was doing at the foot of the bed, where he would not look, even if it looked good and uninfected, which he would not think about, even if it would matter soon, because right now it hurt only very far away. It might be smart to ask what they had him on, to take a more active role in his care, to pay attention; he'd do that sometime soon, maybe.

The nurse left, and he watched television for a while, some combination home improvement and paranormal show, where people renovated purportedly haunted mansions during the day and slept in them at night. Everyone on the show had a Pilot, the better to keep an eye out for ghosts while stripping linoleum and exposing the hardwood underneath. The house had good bones, the host said without a trace of irony, or maybe it was irony and David was standing outside of irony right now, unable to recognize it.

He had never cared for television. He'd watched when they had family movie night, but otherwise he preferred games. Games let him be part of the plot, but also occupied more parts of his brain than TV. TV was usually background as far as he was concerned, one of too many inputs. Except this show was funny, whether or not it was meant to be, and without noise he found himself able to enjoy it in a way he hadn't for years.

The renovators found actual bones in the wall, and the show

upped the drama factor by ten. Could this be the earthly remains of the ghost that had kept them from their sleep? Find out after the break. David was pretty sure the bones belonged to a dead squirrel, not a person. The thought of a TV production plagued by a ghost squirrel had him gasping with laughter.

A phone beside the bed rang, surprising him. He hadn't noticed the room had a phone. Who would know where to call him, and why hadn't they called his cell phone, and where was his cell phone? He tried to remember where he'd seen it last. He remembered a flash in the dark, grainy footage, something else, but maybe that was just the television show, and wow they were keeping him really high.

The phone rang again and he answered it. "BNL, this is David Geller-Bradley," he said, though that wasn't quite right.

"Um." He'd confused the voice on the other end. "This is the visitor desk downstairs. Your nurse said not to let in any reporters, but I have someone here who says she works with your sister?"

He looked at the clock. Seven minutes left in *Haunted House Hunters*. "Send her up in eight minutes."

"Fucking celebrities," the voice muttered as he hung up.

David turned his attention back to the television. They were replaying the moments leading to the discovery of the bones.

"Knock knock?" a voice called from the hall.

He turned, annoyed.

"Can I come in? The receptionist said it was okay."

It had been a while since he'd had any use for his Pilot, but David wished he had enough brain to finish his show and talk to whoever was standing in the doorway.

He sighed. "Come in."

The woman who entered wore a navy business suit and a pale blue silk blouse. Her makeup was porcelain-doll pale except for blue lipstick, an intimidating look. He checked for her Pilot automatically, but didn't see it. Oh. His sister's coworker. She looked more put-together than he'd pictured for an activist; maybe he was being narrow in his stereotype.

"My name is Lana Robinson. Has Sophie mentioned me before?"

David tried to look through her head to the television. "No."

"I work for the FreerMind Association, in the national office. Sophie's organization is part of ours."

Not squirrel bones: raccoon. To be continued, except when another episode started a minute later, it wasn't the second part, but a new one with what looked like an exciting setup: the backyard held a decrepit family cemetery.

He clicked off the television before he got drawn in, and turned what little attention he had to the woman in front of him. "Got it. FreerMind. Lana Robinson. How can I help you?"

"How are you doing? We were very worried about you."

An odd thing for a stranger to say, and maybe she realized it, too, because she added, "Sophie's family is family to us, too."

"I'm okay, all things considered."

"We heard you had your Pilot removed. Is that true?"

He turned his head to give her a better look. "Turned off, not removed."

"Good, good. Listen, David, I don't want to waste your time while you're here resting and recovering, but we had a question we wanted to ask you."

He didn't point out she'd asked at least three questions already. Those had been small talk. Whatever came next was the reason she was visiting, not some fake talk about family.

"David, FreerMind has been impressed with you for a long time. BNL must have known they had a good thing in you. Your charisma, and the way you convey seriousness and intelligence, like you put careful consideration into your choice, and everyone would be happy if they made your choice, too. Your ads made it very difficult for us to convince people not to get Pilots."

That still wasn't a question, so David waited politely.

"We wondered if—when you're recovered—we might convince you to run for office."

That wasn't anything he'd expected, and he wasn't sure how to respond. He settled on "What office?"

"There's a contestable House seat in the state. Harry Andress hasn't been polling well recently."

"House like the US House of Representatives?" He'd expected her to say city council or something in state government. This was a whole different order of magnitude.

"Yes. Like I said, Andress has been polling poorly, and we think we can oust him."

"I don't know the laws, but is this something a nonprofit is supposed to do?"

"Not exactly. We wouldn't be involved, beyond arranging a meeting between you and some party officials. They'd take it from there, help you form a team, all that."

"And you're offering this to me because I got hit by a train?"

"We're offering because we heard you'd had your Pilot out—"

"Off."

"—Your Pilot turned off. We're arranging this because it would be a coup for anti-Pilot activism if someone of your stature entered the race. People like you and trust you. If you said you'd gotten your Pilot out—"

"Off."

"—Off because you'd come to realize the problems inherent, you could turn the tide."

"And what if my opponent pointed out I was dumb enough to get hit by a train?"

"A freak accident. Maybe it was the train company's fault, or whoever maintains the tracks. Have you considered suing? Or maybe you were trying to save a kitten. People would eat that up."

"They would," he agreed. He was fading, whether from concentration or this weirdly intense woman or the pain starting to creep along his leg. "Look, I'm getting tired. Can I say I'll think on it?"

She pressed a card into his hand. "Call me when you want to

get the ball rolling. I think you'd have fun with this. All the good parts of your old job, like talking with people about things that matter to them and to you, without the parts where you're convincing them to install a dubious technology in their heads."

"Yes, ma'am." He smiled and waved at her, hoping it was a wave that conveyed good-bye.

He dropped the card beside the telephone and closed his eyes. The funny thing was, he didn't entirely hate the idea. He liked talking with people about things that mattered to them; his favorite part of the BNL job had been figuring out how and why a given person would benefit from the Pilot, in order to sell it to them. Public office would mean he wouldn't have to prove to another interviewer that he was as good as a Piloted worker; he'd just have to convince voters he could get as much done as a Piloted politician.

CHAPTER SIXTY-SIX

SOPHIE

As she ran upstairs, Sophie texted Gabe. **Coffee. Now. Big hugs!** Big hugs, the highest priority in their silly system that had never mattered more, because it meant she could meet Gabe away from the meeting space, away from the office and phone.

Before she'd gotten to the counter, Gabe stood beside her. "Is your brother okay?"

"Yes! I mean, they amputated his foot, which is awful, but he's alive and he didn't mess up his head or anything, which they said is pretty amazing." She realized Gabe must have thought she'd contacted him because of David. "But that's not why I texted you."

She filled her mug and paid. She started talking the second they were out the door. "I've been thinking for a while now that maybe our phone is bugged."

"Yeah," said Gabe. "Or the office. That's why we do this walk-and-talk thing."

"Right. I still don't know who might have done that, but I've also been thinking: somebody is feeding information to BNL." There had been one terrible moment where she'd thought it was Julie, but Julie was spying on Sophie, not on the group. She wasn't passing along what she learned, just using it to keep tabs.

"And?"

No point holding out for the sake of drama. "It's Dominic."

"That kid? Isn't he like fifteen?"

"He says seventeen, but he could be older and look like a kid, like me. He's always hanging around, and I know lots of people do that, but he's like freakishly always around, offering me rides places, all that. I was thinking, we know from my brother that you can get a Pilot turned off but the light left on, so why couldn't you be a spy for BNL who has a Pilot without a light? The light is just branding, to make sure everyone without one knows they're getting left out."

"Oh shit. That actually makes sense. But that could still be anyone, right? Why do you think it's him?"

"Like I said, he's always showing up and offering me rides."

"Are you sure that doesn't mean he likes you?"

Sophie frowned. "Yes, I'm sure. Stay serious."

"I am serious. You're very likable."

She filed that for later. "But here's why I think it's him: the other night—God, was it only last night?—last night he drove me to the hospital to see my brother. And this morning, there were all these articles connecting *David the ex–BNL spokesmodel* and *David the fool on the train tracks*."

"The article I showed you said his name, or I wouldn't have known it was him."

"Yeah, but nobody else knew his name without seeing his face. In the ads he was 'David,' not 'David Geller-Bradley.' But that's not the important part. I don't think BNL ever knew David had gotten his light turned off. He didn't do it at one of their facilities, and his light was still on when they fired him."

"Would they have a way of checking if a Pilot stopped sending information?"

"Huh. I never thought of that, and that's terrifying, since it would mean they could be monitoring people's Pilots, and if they can be that invasive, they can do all kinds of things we've never talked about, like remotely turn up their input without their knowing, or track their location . . ."

She shook her head, trying to shake off the tangent and the

thought that the company could be doing a hundred things more insidious than the ones they'd already assumed. "Anyway, this morning there were all these articles saying it was him on the tracks and getting statements from BNL about why they let him go and speculation about why he might have turned it off, and the dangers of getting it turned off and all this crap, but assuming they aren't Big Brothering my big brother, the easier answer is I remember I told Dominic last night that David had it turned off, and this morning not only did the papers have that information, but BNL had that information and a spin on it and everything."

"That's horrible and it makes sense. Hmm. So what are we going to do?"

Sophie loved Gabe as always for the "we." "I'm trying to think of something."

"I mean, we can either kick him out or we can use him, if we can think of a way to use him. Like, maybe, to funnel bad information back to them somehow? Trip them up?"

"Yeah." Her heart leapt; some part of her had a taste for espionage.

They stopped for a pedestrian signal with a blinking hand. No time to cross. Sophie stared at it. "Hey, Gabe?"

"Uh-huh?"

"I have another thought. There are four permutations, right? No Pilot, no light, like you and me; yes Pilot, yes light, like most people. And theoretically there's no reason why you can't have a Pilot without a light, like Dominic."

"Theoretically, yeah. And your brother had his Pilot turned off, so that's no Pilot, yes light."

"Yes, except that one has two branches. People like my brother, who had a Pilot and had it turned off, but are still signaling that they have one, but also—"

Gabe smacked his forehead. "—Also people who are signaling that they have one, but never had one to begin with. No Pilot, yes light. Like people who—"

"—Sell a product they want everyone to use but know better than to use themselves. BNL executives."

"BNL doctors. Maybe not some who got good Pilots and then went to med school, but some of them, at least."

"BNL researchers."

"BNL-owned politicians."

"All of them. Gabe, we have to find a way to prove it."

The traffic light had changed and changed and changed back again. Sophie looked around the intersection at the people waiting on corners and in cars, the people walking. Most had the telltale blue lights, but now she knew anyone could be anything and if anyone could be anything, no Pilot yes light, yes Pilot no light, yes yes, no no, then the light didn't matter anymore, and maybe the discrimination could come to an end.

They started walking again, throwing ideas at each other and shooting them down, until Sophie's phone rang, surprising them both. She'd turned on the ringer for once, in deference to her brother's situation. The caller ID said it was Julie. She hesitated, then answered.

"Hey, Soph. David asked if you'd come back to the hospital."

"Sure! Is everything okay? Were the reporters there?"

"Yeah, you were right, but it turns out that even though he's dopey, he's not too dopey to realize he shouldn't talk to vultures."

"There were vultures here? Did someone die?" That was David in the background. He followed it with a giggle.

"He says he needs to talk with you. You should get here before his jokes get worse. Charge a ride on my account if you need to."

"Thanks," Sophie said with genuine gratitude. Her wallet was feeling the strain.

She turned to Gabe. She hadn't been looking where they were walking, but they were almost back to the meeting space.

"I'll hold down the fort," he said. "Go."

"No, I—why don't you come with me? We're not done planning yet, and that way we don't have to find each other later to finish."

He nodded.

The visitor desk insisted on calling David's room when they arrived, which turned out to be because a photographer had managed to get in an hour earlier, which the receptionist said in a passive tone, like he hadn't been the one to let the photographer upstairs.

Both their parents were in the room. Julie had moved a chair over near the door, where she'd set herself up as a formidable sentry. Val had taken the armchair in the corner. David sat awake in bed, still with the not-quite-David relaxation on his face.

"You remember Gabe?" Sophie asked.

"Of course," said Julie. "Though you haven't been to the house in ages. How are you?"

"We live in interesting times."

David laughed and gestured toward the second bed. "Make yourselves comfortable. We're out of chairs."

Gabe sat stiffly on the bed's edge, looking like he was afraid to wrinkle the sheets. Sophie flopped onto the pillow and crossed her legs. "You summoned me, Your Highness?"

David laughed at her fake formality, then reconfigured his face in an attempt at serious. "Yeah, I got an interesting visitor this morning."

"They said downstairs—a photographer?"

"Not that. That was just some ass who tried to take my picture while I napped. Anyway, that was nothing, but something else happened, and I wanted to tell you about it if we're out of the secret game." He paused. "Maybe I should talk to you alone?"

Sophie glanced at the others in the room, then shrugged. "Out of the secret game."

"Wait—why don't Julie and I go grab lunch?" Val stood. "Just because you're all Team No More Secrets doesn't mean you don't deserve privacy."

"If you two will promise to guard the door . . ." Julie looked reluctant to leave, but Val led her from the room.

David waited until they were gone to start talking. "Okay. You know a woman named Lana Robinson, right?"

"Yeah." Sophie glanced at Gabe. "She works in our national office, in state priorities."

"She said she was your coworker."

"Yeah, close enough. Wait—are you saying she was here?" She could think of reasons for a BNL exec to show up, or a reporter, or a photographer, but not FreerMind.

"That's what I needed to tell you about. It was the weirdest thing. She came here to ask me to be part of some anti-Pilot platform."

"Wait, what? Are you sure you weren't drugged or something? That makes no sense."

Gabe leaned back on his hands. "Well, it makes a little sense, Soph. High profile, anti-Pilot . . ."

"But he's not anti-Pilot. He's just anti-Pilot for himself. He was like their salesman of the year!"

"I never saw numbers," David said modestly. "And I was more of a recruiter than a salesman—"

Sophie shot him her most withering look. "You make my point either way."

"—But I'm starting to think you're right, at least about some of it. Even if Pilots can be useful, they have problems nobody is talking about."

Sophie dropped back onto the bed. The hypocrisy boggled her mind. First, David had gone to work for BNL as the poster boy for the product even though he didn't love his own Pilot. Then he got it out and kept working for them, selling unsuspecting people on Pilots. Then her own organization came to him and asked him to be a poster boy for them, too. Why? She answered that aloud: "I mean, I get why. What better spokesperson for the anti-Pilot movement than the former face of the whole Pilot program? I suppose she came here the second her keyword alerts showed her an article saying you'd gotten yours deactivated. Maybe she's got a whole list of people she's drooling to get into the fold. What does she want you to do?"

"Run for Congress."

Gabe cough-choked. "Congress? Like US Congress? You?"

"Is it that ridiculous?" David looked offended. "I'm a decorated soldier, and I'm good at public speaking. I've seen both sides of this Pilot thing. Not too many people can say that."

Sophie stood and paced the narrow space between beds, her hands on her head. "It's not that you're ridiculous. You'd probably make a good politician, all things considered. The kind that cares."

"Thank you?"

"It's that FreerMind shouldn't be asking you—I mean, Lana Robinson works for 'state priorities' in any case, and Congress should fall under federal priorities, if they're even allowed to do that. But also, it's not right that they would come to you in the hospital and assume you're on their side and—"

"That's what I said to her. Or what I'm going to say to her. I'm a little hazy on what happened in real life and what happened in my mind."

Sophie stopped pacing. "So you're not going to do it?"

"No way. You're right. She assumed I was anti-Pilot; she never even asked why I got it turned off." He fiddled with the IV in the back of his left hand, then noticed what he was doing and stopped. "And she never asked why I was on the train track. I thought it would have been important for her to know, and she never bothered to ask. She told me how she'd spin it, but she wasn't interested in the truth, just how she'd change public perception. I'm not interested in playing that game anymore."

"Wow," Gabe said. "Why didn't you lead with that?"

Sophie almost laughed. She was relieved David had seen through the offer. Part of her felt bad about it, because if she was really the good soldier in the Pilot war that she'd always said she was, she should've been excited about the prospect of David running for office, not mad. Lana was right that he would be an asset to their side, and they did have a side, and they were supposed to be on it together, national and local and political and grassroots, all working toward the same goal.

"Anyway," David said, smiling, "I've been thinking about it, and why not you? You're young and energetic and passionate about helping people. You can stand on the virtuous ground of never having had a Pilot. You have a huge network of people in this area. Your brother is a sad-sack one-footed former spokesperson for BNL, whose accident you've vowed to avenge."

"I'm not sure 'avenge' flies in polls," Gabe said.

"Not avenge, then. Whose story you'd be running to tell. Along with your own, of course. Mine doesn't supersede the story of people like you who got left behind by a tech fad that took over everything."

Sophie hadn't realized what it would mean to her to have David acknowledge that. "Thanks, Davey. Wow. I appreciate that, but—"

"But what? I'm telling you. You should do it. I'll tell her I'll support you. She said she'd connect me with state party mucky-mucks. Maybe if I pretend I'm interested I can find out who they are and then bait-and-switch them."

"Wait one sec before you go bait-and-switching," Sophie interrupted. "Thank you for your vote, but I'm not old enough. You have to be twenty-five."

David frowned. "How was I supposed to know that?"

"Civics?"

"For what it's worth," Gabe interjected, "I think you'd be great at it someday, Soph. You'd have my vote. I could keep things running back at the meeting space. Maybe look at ways to break us off from National, since their priorities are so backward . . ."

"That's a good idea regardless," Sophie agreed. "But, David?"

"Yeah?"

"You still haven't said what you were doing on a train track."

He shrugged. "It really was an accident. I've been taking something I probably shouldn't have been, to try to stop the noise, and it got out of hand. When I get out of here I'm going to have to find a healthier way to deal with that, starting with figuring out what those pills were."

"Wait—you were taking mystery pills? Who does that? How do you get them? Do you walk up to a drug dealer and say *Surprise me*? I take three different antiseizure meds and two meds to counteract side effects, and I know what every single one of them does alone and in combination."

"Hey, Soph, go easy on your brother. Anyone taking mystery pills is in a pretty fucked-up place. I think he's probably learned that lesson." Gabe pointed to the shapes under David's blanket.

CHAPTER SIXTY-SEVEN

JULIE

"We should rename them 'office hours' instead of 'visiting hours,'" grumbled the reception desk when Julie answered the phone. "The reporter whose name you left is here. Eduardo Toledo. Still okay?"

"Yes, send him up." The receptionist wasn't wrong; they'd kept the paparazzi out, but taken visits from Milo and Karina and Karina's sister, who Julie thought was kind of cute and might possibly like David, as well as a couple of political activists who'd talked to both Sophie and David with keen interest.

Julie turned to Sophie. "You're sure about this guy?"

"I'm sure. His work is always well researched and fair. He still hasn't run the story I gave him, but I think that's because he's trying to build a bigger story."

Toledo, carrying a box of doughnuts, rounded the corner. David gestured to the table beside him, pushing aside the flowers Congressman Griffith had sent. "Food of the gods."

"I figured you'd be getting sick of hospital food."

"You figured right!"

"Hey!" Julie protested. "I brought ice cream."

"That was days ago, Mom. What have you done for me today?" David smiled his most charming *kidding or am I?* smile, and she melted.

David selected a chocolate-on-chocolate doughnut, then let the others pick as well. "Sophie, I like your friend already."

"That's good," said Sophie. "Because we're about to get very, very personal with him."

Toledo settled into the corner chair and pulled a laptop from his messenger bag. They'd dragged another chair in from the nurses' station, so there were seats for both Julie and Val if Sophie sat on the other bed, which she preferred in any case.

"Okay," he said. "Tell me everything."

Sophie started at the beginning, explaining the relationship of each member of their family to the Pilot, as background, then moving on to her work at FreerMind. Then David told David's story. Val walked out for part of that, ostensibly to get a drink, though she didn't return until he was finished; Julie forced herself to listen to all of it.

Then Sophie started into the stuff she'd figured out about BNL, again with David's help. Pride overwhelmed Julie as Sophie connected the corporate spy and the executives with fake Pilots to show confidence in a product they didn't trust in their own heads. The kid was savvy; no, not a kid, she reminded herself.

"So . . . what do you think?" Sophie asked when she got to the end.

Toledo leaned back, took his glasses off, and rested one stem against his lip. "I think this is a hell of a story, but there are still some gaps to fill in. That thing about the execs is explosive—that's probably the most damning part—but you don't have actual proof."

"I'm sure it's out there," said Sophie. "Are there serial numbers or warranties registered in their names? Can we run a metal detector over their heads?"

"Serial numbers maybe, though they could be faked, and I don't think medical devices are currently required to have them; it's going to be tougher to prove someone *doesn't* have one than that someone does. And they'd have to agree to whatever scan that would be, and we'd have to make sure they couldn't fake that, too. We need the public to doubt them, so they have to prove it to win back trust. That might fly, but I can't run your accusation without proof."

"What about the other stuff?" David reached for another doughnut. "The e-mail I took from BNL?"

"That and the study it referred to are great. I can use that, and it's even better if you're on record as a source."

"The nice thing about my current situation is they can't penalize me anymore," said David. "I'm happy to spill the beans. Not that I know much; I didn't even merit an NDA when I left, just a form saying I wouldn't use their information in a new job."

"Um," Val interrupted. "Maybe don't connect your name with the e-mail and the study? That's still probably corporate theft, even if you didn't sign an NDA. How about all the people online in the same boat as David? There's a whole Pilot Survivor thing going on separate from the anti-Pilot activists."

Sophie looked surprised, and Toledo made a note. "I'll check that out."

"Me, too," said David. "I gave up looking for other people since nobody I asked ever sounded like they knew what I was talking about."

"There's got to be something more." Sophie's frustration was rising. She'd clearly expected the journalist to run with everything she'd given him. Julie wanted to point out that he obviously knew his job well and Sophie should have faith, but it felt patronizing; she kept her mouth shut.

"I mean, there's lots," said Toledo. "This isn't nothing. We need to keep adding concrete evidence until we can prove it."

"Maybe there's something we left out." Sophie looked at each person in the room like she was begging for someone to say the thing that would change the journalist's tune from *keep adding* to *I'm taking this to my editor.*

David frowned. "I can't remember. Did I talk about Quiet?"

"You talked about noise," Julie said.

Toledo put his glasses back on and paged through his notes. "Is there something else, David? You talked about noise, and you talked about getting the Pilot turned off but not the light, and the noise continuing, and taking a drug that counteracted the noise, and then overdosing by accident."

Val stood as if to walk out, then sat again. Julie knew she couldn't stand the parts of his story in which his parents had failed to help him.

"It's not your fault, Ma," said David, who also must have noticed. "I hid it from you. But have we talked about the pills themselves?"

Toledo shook his head.

David reached for a third doughnut, but gestured with it instead of taking a bite. "I'd forgotten this for a while, because I learned it just before the, uh, accident. When Alyssa first gave me the pills"— Julie decided Alyssa wasn't such a catch after all—"she called them Fortress of Solitude, but they had a lowercase *q* on them, and I started thinking of them as Quiet, since they were so good at cutting out noise. Whatever they have me on here is okay at it, but makes me loopy, too, and a little queasy. Quiet didn't have any side effects."

"It did, honey." Julie remembered the blank David she'd encountered in the park.

"Okay, well, from my end, it took away the noise without adding nausea or anything. Except just before the accident, someone told me that what I thought was a lowercase *q* was actually a lowercase *b*, for Balkenhol."

Toledo looked up sharply. "Are you sure?"

"No, but that would be easier to check than that other stuff, right? Whether Balkenhol makes a round teal pill with a lowercase *b* on it?"

"It would. Also, I've done a fair bit of research on this for another story, and I can tell you drugs are *way* more regulated than medical devices. There are strict protocols for every step, from research to trials to FDA approval and scheduling. If this is really theirs, even if it's still in a testing phase, there'll be a trail saying what they think it'll be good for, and how they think it works.

That means in theory they've been aware for years of some issue they were trying to counteract. If they knew they would need an antidote to noise, that means they think noise is a problem for more people than David. And it means that rather than pull the Pilot implant from the market while they figured out if it caused problems, they decided to go ahead and cause the problem, then monetize the solution."

Julie was stunned. She thought of herself as a careful person, even if she wasn't in Val's league on that front. How had she bought into this product so easily? It was horrifying, but more than that, embarrassing. She looked over at Val, who graciously avoided the *I told you so*, but instead watched her with something like pity, which was worse. David's expression was placid with an undertone of guilt. She'd chosen to get a Pilot, and let him get one; he had talked who knew how many people into getting them.

Val asked, "Is it possible these pills are already on the market for something else? Maybe they found a second use for a prescription pill they already had."

Everyone turned to Toledo, who had gone silent, images of pills scrolling on his laptop screen and reflecting in his glasses.

"You're right," he said after a long moment. "Baranor, by Balkenhol. It's only approved for one rare form of ADD. I'll research whether they've done trials for any other usages."

"They're still assholes," said Sophie.

"Assholes," David echoed.

"That isn't harsh enough," said Val, which Julie agreed with. She could think of other words, none of which were harsh enough, either.

The journalist tapped his chin. "All right, okay, this is a big piece to the puzzle. This is something I can work with."

"God, I want to find proof of the other stuff, too," said Julie. "I want to nail them. Let me in your organization, Soph. I'm with you."

"I can't, Mom. You have a Pilot."

"I'll have it turned off tomorrow. This company can't have my brain any longer." She hadn't known she was making that decision until she made it, but it felt good.

Sophie's eyes opened wide. "No, I need you to do some stuff first, starting with recording yourself going to the BNL clinic to see if they try to talk you out of deactivating it, and if they'd let you deactivate but leave the light on."

"That would definitely be interesting," said Toledo.

"Yeah," said David. "I'd be curious, since they wouldn't do it for me."

It felt good to be of use to her kids for once. "Makes sense, but someone should do the opposite, too, right? Ask if they'll install a Pilot with no light?"

Everyone looked at Val, who frowned. "I'm not getting a Pilot."

"You only have to ask, not actually get one," said David. "Somebody take these doughnuts away from me?"

Julie took the box to the nurses' station, then returned.

"They'll never say yes to that one," Toledo was saying. She hadn't missed much. "That's got to be top secret, or it would've gotten out by now."

Sophie put her hand over her mouth. "There's one more permutation. It doesn't need to be you, Ma. I can do it myself."

"There's no way you're getting a Pilot," said Val. "I mean, I'm not stopping you, but even if your seizures didn't preclude it, there's no way you'd do it."

"I have something else in mind," Sophie said. "I've just got to talk to the group. And I've got something else I need you to do, too, Mom."

Julie nodded, not saying that in this moment, she would do absolutely anything any of them asked.

CHAPTER SIXTY-EIGHT

JULIE

Julie didn't think she was back in Sophie's confidence yet, nor did she deserve to be. She accepted her orders hoping that maybe this thing, this huge thing, might earn back her daughter's trust. Sophie played the general, her family willing soldiers.

The first instruction wasn't to test the BNL clinic on their removal policies, which was a relief. While her instinct in the hospital room had been knee-jerk—"I'll have it turned off tomorrow"—that reaction had cooled. She'd been an adult when she got hers, and there was no telling if her brain had adapted or not. Her Pilot had only ever helped her; she had to work up to deactivating it.

Instead, she texted Representative Griffith and asked if he'd meet with her the next time he was in the district office. They conducted most business over e-mail—their last texts to each other had been three months before—so the request had its desired effect. He responded immediately, saying he'd visit on his way home for the weekend.

Which was why, the following Friday, he threw himself in a chair in her office and said, "If you're quitting, break it to me quick."

"I'm not quitting." Though he might fire her by the conversation's end. She closed the door.

He made a show of relief, wiping his forehead with a manicured hand. "And how's your son?"

"Doing okay. Thank you for the flowers." He was a good guy, for a politician. She'd never lost any sleep over working for him; time to find out if her trust had been misplaced. "I need to know what you know about BNL."

He frowned. "Evan is the main contact with them. Do you want to call him?"

"No, I want to know your relationship with them first, not his."

"Well, as I'm sure you know, they've been great for our district. Three thousand jobs, infrastructure, schools . . . They helped us fund a transit expansion out to their headquarters, which spurred housing growth, too—but you must know all that. Is that what you're asking?"

"I'm looking beyond what they've done for us or we've done for them." She took a deep breath. "What I want to know is: Is your Pilot real?"

"What do you mean?" He touched the light on his head.

He looked sincere. If he was sincere, maybe it wasn't a government-wide conspiracy, as Sophie thought. Maybe it was just BNL, or BNL and the military. She wasn't sure which questions were the right ones to get the information.

"When did you get your Pilot? Before or after they started supporting district projects?"

"Let's see. I got my Pilot three months after my daughter got hers, maybe six months after Evan. Mine was the first on Capitol Hill, but Janelle's always been an early adopter and she kept talking about how it helped her focus, and it would give me an edge in debates and hearings. It didn't hurt that they'd just set up shop here, so I felt like I was supporting the home team."

"So they were already here?"

"Yes. I remember chatting with Sylvia Keating at a charity dinner about how I was going to get one. She was so attentive. She was concerned about it being too early to stand out like that, and that they might get banned from Congress, but I said we hadn't banned pacemakers or hearing aids or medications, so why would we ban her devices? I thought she was worrying over nothing. I guess after I said that she saw me getting one as a positive rather than a negative. She made sure my appointment was private, so the press wouldn't run with it until I was ready for them, and she hooked me up with the doctor who had personally installed hers."

"Leroy, what does your Pilot feel like?" She flashed on the first time Val had asked her that after she got hers; no, Val's question had been "Do you feel different?" She had, but it was hard to put into words.

He had the same struggle. "You know. Confident, capable, on it."

"I've worked for you for a long time. You've always been confident and capable and on it. So you're saying it intensifies strengths you already had?"

"Yes," he said, with less boundless confidence. "Why ask that? You have one. You know."

She knew. How many times had she dismissed David's noise, thinking he was referring to the same thing she felt, but describing it differently? It would be easy to chalk the congressman's description up to a communication failure, too. She had a new theory of her own now; maybe she was wrong, but she didn't think so. "I'm going to tell you something, and I want you to listen to all of it before you say anything."

He stood, removed his coat, and draped it over the chair's back. "Sounds like I should get comfortable."

She began. She tried to keep it short, mindful of all the constituent meetings that had overrun their allotted time and how she sympathized but wished they had practiced telling their stories concisely. What mattered? Sophie getting left behind. David's noise. David's accident.

"Wow," said the congressman.

"That's just the personal part. Here's where it gets tricky." She told him about the pills, the studies, Sophie's categories, Pilot on, Pilot off, including the one she had come in mistakenly suspecting.

"So that's why you asked me if my Pilot is real? You thought I might be faking it?" He sounded angry and disappointed, but not entirely disbelieving. "You know me well enough to give me the benefit of the doubt."

"I believe you're not faking it. I'm sorry I asked that question. But—" This was it. This was her theory, new, not anyone else's. "—I think there's one more category. I think you think your Pilot is real, but it's not."

"Wait, what?" He looked genuinely surprised. "What do you mean?"

"What you said. The CEO—hers is fake, I'm sure—didn't want to risk her project getting bad press, and didn't think you'd be on board if she told you the risks, so she set you up with her personal doctor. And I'm guessing when you told other legislators about it, you gave them that number, so they'd get the same privacy you had?"

He nodded.

"They'd never have risked the whole project getting shut down if a member of Congress had a bad reaction like my son's. They installed a pretty blue light in your head, and maybe something that fakes the data the rest of us see on the app, and then let the placebo effect do the rest of the work of making already smart, quick-thinking people believe they'd been made quicker. It's not like any two of us describe the feeling in the same way. We don't have the words, which makes comparing impossible."

"What about my daughter? She loves hers; she wasn't lying. And Evan?"

Julie shrugged. "I love mine, too. They aren't all bad, but none of us knows how many people are suffering because it doesn't work for them and nobody believes them. That's all being swept under the rug by BNL. It's a device, not a drug; they don't have to report."

He buried his face in his hands and went silent for a minute, then two, and she waited to see whether her decades of service had earned his trust.

When he met Julie's eyes again, he looked angry. "The worst part is, I think I believe you. Where do we even start?"

"We start with getting the data. The real data. The studies. People's stories. Hearings."

He nodded. "I'll probably lose my seat, you know. You'll lose your job, and so will a lot of innocent BNL employees who don't have anything to do with this. And if there's too much invested in keeping this quiet, our efforts will come to nothing."

Julie knew, but for the first time, keeping her job didn't matter as much as the thing that needed to be done. Her family would be okay, one way or another, hopefully, but this was the only way to bring together their jagged edges. At least they'd see her trying.

CHAPTER SIXTY-NINE

SOPHIE

Sophie's plan had a lot of parts. She started with torturing Dominic. Physical torture would have been more fun, but she settled for letting slip in front of him that National had developed a device to decrypt any individual's Pilot information off their implant if it was in close proximity. False information, but something to send them scrambling, and distract from the fact that both Toledo and Julie's congressman were now digging into the real Pilot story. Dominic didn't return.

Another facet, convincing her brother he really should run for office, was trickier. She didn't want to manipulate him into something he didn't want to do; she needed to convince him he'd genuinely be good at it, which she believed. He was thoughtful and caring and put other people's concerns above his own to a fault, as was evident if you just looked at what he'd done to himself already. She made sure he stayed updated on what Representative Griffith was doing, and all the things she would do if she held public office, and one day, out of the blue, he said, "When I get out of here, maybe I'll give that Lana Robinson a call."

Sophie had hoped he'd try it her way, going around Lana, but she couldn't have everything. "Just watch out for her. Make sure she doesn't turn you into something you aren't."

"A fire truck? A warthog? I'm not necessarily opposed."

She laughed.

"What if I insist you're in the room? Would you help me do this?"

She had plans of her own, so many plans, but this was a worthy diversion. She attended their first meeting, where David came clean about the Quiet issue, and how he'd gotten stuck on the tracks, and the fact that he wouldn't gloss over any of it. If they wanted games, he wasn't playing. She was proud of him. She'd spent so long thinking he was a BNL tool, but he had always tried to do what he thought was right, even if he was absolutely wrong about some of it.

He was already adapting to the loss of his foot, like it was the accepted cost for everything he'd done. The bigger problem was the Quiet. His doctors hadn't wanted to keep him on painkillers when pain wasn't the issue. They'd suggested meditation and yoga and cognitive therapy, in the same way the BNL doctors had always told him to do more exercises, but he seemed pretty sure that nothing worked as well on the noise as retreating to his Fortress of Solitude, which no doctor would actually prescribe to him.

David had been released from the hospital by the time Toledo's first article came out, the one connecting Pilots to off-label use of one of BNL's drugs. It talked about David's noise and everything, and mentioned the others Val had found with the same problem.

Toledo had texted her to say the article was posting, and she shouted everyone down to breakfast to quote her favorite parts. "'Under increasing scrutiny, the company maintains they have done nothing wrong, and they will continue to offer their groundbreaking Pilot'—what's wrong?" She stopped when she saw the concern on David's face.

"If they go under, who's going to help people like me?" he asked. "The more damage we do to BNL, the more risk they won't be able to fix the problems they created."

Sophie lowered her phone. "That's no reason not to try. They shouldn't be allowed to get away with it."

"Others will fill in the gap," Julie said. "The market abhors a vacuum."

"And if they don't?"

Val smiled. "You can always come running with me."

It was clearly a joke, but he treated it as a serious suggestion. "Maybe when I'm ready I can get one of those running blade things. I remember it did used to help a little."

The look on Val's face said that she couldn't imagine anything better, and for one moment, Sophie wished she could be the person to bring that joy; she'd never been able to run more than a lap without overheating and seizing. Anyway, it wasn't necessary; she knew she made her parents proud. They still had to work on trust, but at least they were all starting to understand that was a group project.

CHAPTER SEVENTY

VAL

They were invited to the campaign launch, David's supportive parents, with their own part in the plan. Sophie and David rode separately, Sophie as part of David's team—she was dividing her time between the campaign and community college art classes and the new group she and Gabe had started after splitting from FreerMind. She'd made it clear she'd help as long as their goals aligned; on her own terms, as usual. That left Val and Julie to drive to the rented ballroom where their son would launch his political career.

They circled three times before finding a spot two blocks from the venue. The streets were busy, too, most people headed the same way they were. Julie grabbed Val's hand and Val squeezed back; whatever came of this campaign, it was exciting.

The crowd inside milled, waiting. A few danced to the music playing through the PA system, some song Val forgot the name of though she'd heard it all over school. Television cameras surrounded the stage, along with a few still photographers claiming their own space. More TV cameras scattered near the walls, where Piloted reporters tested their mics. Val and Julie walked past; David had asked them to sit onstage behind him and Sophie.

David greeted them when they reached the top of the ramp. He'd opted for a dynamic response foot over the microprocessor type, saying he'd had enough computer-controlled body parts. His gait was gradually becoming more natural. "You're cutting it close."

"Parking was awful." Julie hugged him, reaching a hand toward his hair before stopping herself.

He frowned. "I hope that doesn't keep people away."

"Are you kidding?" Val gestured at the crowd. "This is already a terrific showing."

"Especially for an unknown political candidate, months before the primary," Julie added. "You've got people excited."

"She's got people excited. Half the crowd is here because she asked them to come."

"They're here for both of us," Sophie said, joining them. "We were not above using my advantages or yours, Poster Boy."

He glanced out at the cameras. A reporter noticed his attention and shouted, "Hey, David, how's your foot? Are you thinking of getting your Pilot reconnected?"

He shook his head, less an answer than an expression of annoyance. Turning back to the family, he said, "I'm a soldier. If this is what you need from me, this is what I'll do."

"You said you wanted this, remember? Nobody's making you." Sophie looked impatient. "Is it time yet? I'm ready to get started. Hey, how do I look?"

She did a twirl like she was showing off a dress, pointing a finger to her temple. The honest answer was that seeing Sophie with a Pilot light, even a fake one, even knowing Sophie would never have gotten one for real, felt like a knife in Val's heart.

"Like a sheep," Val said, a joke and a truth wrapped in one. "No offense to those who have them."

Sophie took a seat with them at the back of the stage. The lights went off. A spotlight was angled in a way that probably blinded whoever was at the podium, but from the chairs, Val saw into the darkness. Dozens of blue lights dotted the space, like fireflies on long grass. The flickers were an optical illusion, the result of people walking, nodding, talking. It made her remember the first time she'd ever seen a Pilot, back before she'd known what it was, that single pinprick in a darkened auditorium.

David approached the podium to cheers. He bent to speak into the mic so it wouldn't have to be readjusted for Sophie.

In the first-draft speech he'd tried on them, he started with "There weren't any celebrities available, and I've been told I'm the next best thing." Sophie had vetoed it as too self-deprecating.

He used the beginning she'd written instead. "Hi. You know me from a bunch of commercials where I told you to buy a popular product, and you did." He'd wanted to add an apology there, but Sophie had told him to wait.

"I've been told I have a trustworthy face." Some people laughed.

"So I'm here to ask you to trust me on something else this time, and I'll be back to tell you why I'm your candidate in a minute, but first—and I know this is backward—I'm here to introduce you to the smartest, most motivated, most dedicated person I know: my sister." Val was pretty sure Sophie had left the descriptors up to him.

David waited for Sophie to join him, giving her a hug, turning with her to face the cameras. Val thought it was the strangest thing, to watch this movie of her grown kids not only getting along, but supporting each other, raising each other up. David came to sit beside them, and Sophie took his place at the microphone.

"My name is Sophie, and I'm here to tell you my brother should be your candidate. It's going to sound like he's a one-issue candidate for a bit, but that one issue bleeds into everything: education, health, jobs. Everything. I'll talk about that in a minute.

"David got a Pilot early, to fit in and keep up in class, and as you maybe know, it nearly killed him. He's one of the people—we don't know how many yet, but we're going to find out—whose Pilots generate something he calls 'noise,' and the company that makes them calls 'abnormal sensory interference.' And, lucky him, he was one of the *thirty* percent of people who tried to have their Pilots deactivated only to find out his brain had adapted to it.

That's from an actual study—the earlier you get the Pilot, the more likely your brain will adapt. And even though he's still working at his Pilot level, nobody would hire him after he had it turned off because of the perception he didn't have one—no light, no job. Has anyone here experienced that?" The crowd hooted.

"Our mother, Val, is a teacher." Val gave a hesitant wave. "She never got a Pilot, either, but not because she couldn't. She looked at the technology and decided it wasn't something she wanted to do. I admire that about her, her willingness to stand firm when there was pressure everywhere to conform."

Val still remembered the day she'd made that promise to Sophie. It had never been hard for her to keep, but she knew now how much it had mattered.

"This is our other mother, Julie. She got a Pilot because she wanted one. It helped her in her job, and it never gave her one moment of trouble that I know of. I know that's true of a lot of you. Come up here a second?"

Julie had agreed to this part. She walked to Sophie, making sure to keep her Pilot-lit side to the cameras as she hugged her daughter. If Sophie's light was a stab wound, Val didn't know what to call Julie's almost-there. The implant was disconnected, she'd said as much, and Val believed her, but it was hard to divorce the light from the left-behind feeling, even knowing there was nothing behind it, and there were who knew how many people walking around with lights and no Pilots. The Julie who walked back into the waiting room was the same person who had walked out, just as she had been all those years ago. The Julie who reached for her that night, after the deactivation, who recognized that she needed to touch and be touched precisely because of the Pilot and everything it had been in their lives, did not feel any different. That, too, had been trust.

"She always liked it, but she decided to get her Pilot turned off when all the trouble with David happened. You see that light on the side of her head? It means nothing. She got the Pilot deactivated, but left the light on. If I wasn't spilling the secret right now, she could go to work every day like that and her boss would never be the wiser."

That was the first reveal, the reason they wanted to do this while they had cameras interested in David's celebrity. Sophie had promised not to scoop Toledo; his article on the on/off permutations was scheduled to come out simultaneously with the rally.

"So that's our family, but we also have a larger community. Come on up here, everyone." She waited as a group of about thirty people assembled on the stage, Piloted all. Gabe grinned and gave her a thumbs-up. "My other family is the people without Pilots, whether because of religion or health condition or choice, who have been working tirelessly for years to bring attention to the inequities of Pilots. The people who have protested and written letters to Congress and raised their voices.

"Now, you may be wondering how I could be standing here, a Pilot light glowing on my head, talking about being part of the community of people without Pilots, with all these Piloted people standing here with me, but here's the thing—"

At that signal, the spotlight went out, leaving a sea of blue lights in the audience and on the stage, and the steady red eyes of the news cameras, watching.

And then the stage went completely dark. There was a gasp from the back as every blue light extinguished on stage. Practical magic; Val was close enough to see everyone on stage reach up and press their glue-on LEDs, turning them off, and Julie cover hers with her hand. Only a handful of blue lights remained, mostly behind the cameras.

The spotlight came on again. Sophie stood tall, the false light gone. "Those were fake Pilots. The exact same blue light you all have to show your status, but it's a simple LED. Did you know these things could lie? I didn't until recently, but it turns out anyone can put a blue light in their head and pretend they have a Pilot. There's an investigation going public tonight that can show you proof.

"So what does that mean? It means you can have a light without a Pilot, and a Pilot without a light. It means those blue bulbs mean nothing. They're status symbols, nothing more, so maybe we can stop playing games with our brains."

She stepped back, and David returned to the spotlight. "All of which is to say I'm running for this office to be your voice in Congress on all the issues you care about, but first we need to know what they're putting in our heads, so we can decide for ourselves what to do about it. I'm starting with this: accountability from BNL, on everything. My name is David Geller-Bradley, and I'm running to get answers."

The audience roared, and a dozen friends bear-hugged Sophie and David. At the room's fringes, the reporters who had been promised a national-level story talked excitedly into their cameras. The reporters all had Pilots, the better to keep up with the pace of news. Would they even want to hear this? It made them part of the story. Val was still concerned that BNL ad dollars might affect what was said, but the information was loose in the world.

Sophie and David were going to be there for a while, hugging and shaking hands and giving interviews. Julie raised an eyebrow at Val, and Val nodded. They didn't need to stay.

EPILOGUE

Three months after BNL closed the Installation Center where David and Julie had gotten their Pilots, a Tex-Mex chain restaurant opened in its place.

Sophie called from her new apartment to invite them to the grand opening. "No is not an option. Everyone will be there. It's a tangible victory."

It was late January. The sun hadn't shown itself all day, and they walked across the parking lot under a dusk sky wiped gray from edge to edge. A snow sky, they'd called it when the kids were little, taking bets on when the first flakes would fall, Julie complaining she was the only one who wouldn't benefit from a snow day.

"Wait, why does it still smell like cookies?" Val asked, holding the door for Julie.

Julie smiled. "It's a mystery for the ages."

The place was crowded and bright, a riot of color compared to outside. A mariachi band played in the far corner.

"Over here, guys!" called Sophie from the center of the room, where she and David sat surrounded by people. Several tables had been pulled close together. Val recognized a few faces from the meeting space, as well as Milo and Karina and Karina's sister, and Gabe, and Gabe's father, who walked over to greet them.

"Tony!" Julie said in delight. "It's been ages."

He smiled. "It's hard to support them and also give them space, isn't it?"

"We're still figuring it out," Julie said. "I'm glad the three of them are living together."

Val nodded. That solution had delighted them both, as hard as it was to let Sophie go; not that they had any say in it. If she was going to move out, an apartment with Gabe and David was the best solution they could have hoped for. She knew how to look after herself, and they understood how to help her in the moments when she couldn't.

They all looked over at the central tables. A few people from outside their group had recognized David and gathered around him, and he was taking selfies with them beside a nacho platter half as tall as he was, while Sophie and Gabe stole chips off the side for their friends' waiting plates. When David finished posing, he turned back to a diminished appetizer.

"You work for us now, Congressman," Sophie said. "Your nachos are our nachos."

"Hey!" he said in a tragic voice, and the others cracked up. On his current dose of Quiet—they still called it that, even knowing the real name—his noise was dampened enough that this chaotic, loud, crowded restaurant wasn't stressing him out, nor was the fact that he hadn't noticed his sister's prank. Progress.

More people arrived: volunteers from the campaign, anti-Pilot activists.

"There isn't room to sit with them," said Julie.

"That's okay," Val replied. "They wanted us here. That's something."

They sat edge-of-center with Tony Clary, close enough to be considered part of the celebration. Julie ordered a fishbowl-sized margarita, and they all ordered tacos, and their conversation, which started on the kids and their projects, drifted in other directions. That was a form of progress, too, Val supposed.

The party was still going when Julie paid the bill and they put on their coats. Sophie and David came over for quick hugs, then returned to their friends.

Val and Julie had to push through a crowd to reach the door, and on the other side was winter. The snow sky had given over to snow, and a thin layer had already begun to accumulate on the sidewalk. Julie paused to pull on a hat, then threaded a gloved hand through Val's arm.

The flakes were big and heavy, catching in their eyelashes and hair. Val looked up at the sky, enjoying the deeper view, the kaleidoscopic swirl; then back at the restaurant, where another group of diners exited the building and startled at the sight. They put on hats and scarves and started walking in whatever direction would bring them home. Bundled against the falling snow, all blue lights vanished, and it was impossible to tell anyone apart.

ACKNOWLEDGMENTS

I would first like to acknowledge that I'm lousy at acknowledgments. For three albums and three books now, I've been given the opportunity to say thank you to everyone who had a part in the project, and each time I remember that I should have been keeping a list, but by then it is too late, and I'm forced to rely on my memory, knowing I will inevitably leave people out. How could I possibly fit everyone, in any case? You should all have your names in here.

Then, too, given that I'm writing this in the midst of a lockdown that I can only hope will be over by the time the book comes out, this feels particularly like a step out of time. Thank you, past and future readers, reading this book by past me, and this note by present me, who will be past me by the time you read it. Thank you also to everyone who helped keep other people alive, in any way you did that, whether staying home or protesting or doing work deemed essential.

On to the specific acknowledgments:

Zu first, always, because I don't think I'm very easy to live with while I'm drafting a book, and she is always supportive despite my obvious shortcomings, and I love and appreciate her more than I'm capable of showing.

Kim-Mei Kirtland, my agent, exactly the teammate I want for a weird sport where everyone plays by different rules. Also Gabrielle, and Megan, and everyone else at HMLA.

My editor, Jen Monroe, and everyone at Berkley, including Alexis Nixon, Tara O'Connor, Jessica Plummer, and Megan Elmore, along with copy editor Randie Lipkin. Katie Anderson in-house and Tim Green of Faceout Studio for the supercool cover that I have only just seen.

The Future Embodied, Fierce Family, and *Accessing the Future* anthologies, which provided the prompts that got me thinking about this idea years ago.

Sherri and Rep and the Sparkleponies for reading my outline and chapters. My sisters and my mother, the best beta readers. My father and Esther for celebrations and sustenance.

Stephanie Simon-Dack, professor of psychological science, for suggesting the rTPJ back in 2012 or 2013 when I came up with the first story that led to this novel and was trying to figure out where the implant needed to go. Ben Kinney for beta reading with brain stuff in mind. Laura McElwain Colquhoun for answering my questions about the inner workings of a congressional district office. David Vincelli for answering computer-related questions (within the book! I did not ask my brother-in-law for IT help). Karen for helping me with the military stuff. Mary Wontrop at Epilepsy Foundation Maryland, and everyone I had the good fortune to get to know at EFMD and AN/EFCR. Seizure first aid is simple to learn and can save lives. If you're interested in more information or getting certified, go to epilepsy.com.

Kellan Szpara for being my best writer buddy. Karen Osborne for the terrific pictures and occasional company back when we were still allowed to write in the company of others. Randee Dawn and Judith Tumin and everyone else who let me crash at their homes while writing. The Red Canoe for letting me work in the corner all day back when it was safe to do such things. My occasional video chat coworking buddies. My Goucher students from this very bizarre spring, and everyone at the Kratz Center for Creative Writing. The Ivy, Bird in Hand, Atomic Books, and Greedy Reads for making Baltimore such a great place to be a writer, as well as all the other booksellers and festivals that hosted me, virtually or in person, and do the same for their cities. The Baltimore SFF community and the larger SFF community all around the world. The readers and reviewers and podcasters. All of the editors who teach me how to be a better writer with their comments and questions.

I read Jeanne Lenzer's *The Danger Within Us* after I'd finished my second draft, and it helped tremendously with David's journey. If this work of fiction made you interested in more information on the real-life gray areas and moral ambiguities in which some medical devices exist, I suggest checking out that eye-opening work of nonfiction.

And finally, everyone on my morning calls, which have gotten me to my computer to start work even on days when work seemed impossible in this year of weirdness. Thank you.

ABOUT THE AUTHOR

Sarah Pinsker's *A Song for a New Day*
won the 2019 Nebula Award for Best Novel,
and her collection *Sooner or Later Everything Falls into
the Sea* won the Philip K. Dick Award. Her short
fiction has appeared in *Asimov's*, *F&SF*,
and numerous other magazines, anthologies,
and translation markets. She is also a singer-
songwriter who has toured behind three albums
on various independent labels. She lives
with her wife and a very energetic terrier
in Baltimore, Maryland.

She can be found online at
sarahpinsker.com and twitter.com/sarahpinsker.